PICKING UP

Jo Patterson is one of nature's rut dwellers, according to her husband. So? Ruts are cosy and he's an idiot. It's his fault she's marooned in the Yorkshire wilds. The staid suburbanite finds herself tramping the moors as a beater on the castle shoot.

Never mind the sweat, swamps and not knowing the grouse from a canary, she needs the cash! Soon she's hauling drunken spies from wrecked cars, fending off lecherous rock stars – and contemplating adultery. Whatever happened to the respectable housewife and mother? Jo's inclined to blame the dog.

PICKING UP

PICKING UP

by

Kate Fenton

Magna Large Print Books
Long Preston, North Yorkshire,
BD23 4ND, England.

British Library Cataloguing in Publication Data.

Fenton, Kate
    Picking up.

A catalogue record of this book is
available from the British Library

ISBN   0-7505-2021-3

First published in Great Britain in 2002 by Hodder & Stoughton
A division of Hodder Headline

Cover illustration © John Hancock by arrangement with
P.W.A. International Ltd.

Published in Large Print 2003 by arrangement with
Hodder & Stoughton Ltd.

Magna Large Print is an imprint of Library Magna Books Ltd.

Printed and bound in Great Britain by
T.J. (International) Ltd., Cornwall, PL28 8RW

For Ian, with my love as ever,
and for his (and thereby our) dazzling
great grandchildren: Henrietta, Tilly and Ned

ACKNOWLEDGEMENTS

For their expertise, tolerance, and clever ideas while I was knitting this plot, I owe a great deal to my friends Gerald Gradwell, Martin Leeburn, Jenny Beechey, Robert Smith, Ian Ready, Richard Lennox, Martin Vander Weyer, Stephen Wood and Chris Stuart.

For helping me unpick the tangles in the result, I am profoundly grateful – as always – to my editor, Richenda Todd.

And I can't thank enough the keepers and beaters of Danby Moor for the most glorious fun – and £23 a day.

The End

OK, the happily-ever-after goes like this.

You're on the doorstep, lit by the kindly gold of the afternoon sun. For some reason, which you'll come up with in the fullness of time, you have reacquainted yourself with the contents of your make-up bag. Your eyebrows are plucked, your legs waxed, and you have even paid a recent visit to the hairdresser. You're wearing some floaty white number, or maybe a cuddly sweater, depending on the weather. White, either way. We're talking domestic goddess here, the kind of female who could advertise face cream for the mature skin. Get the picture?

Anyway, the old familiar car is trundling down the hill – look, there's the dent in the right wing where you fell foul of a supermarket trolley. That was in your other life, to be sure, where there were such luxuries as decent-sized supermarkets. In Plan A, the car would wind down through hosts of nodding daffodils, with clouds gambolling like lambs across the pale spring sky. This was necessarily amended to B, in which it meandered between the blossomy, blowsy summer hedge-rows. Soon it will be nosing past coppery tangles of brambles and berries. Whatever – *whenever* – that vehicle will halt with the squeal of an outraged cat, because there's no way, in your absence, that the dodgy brake-pad will have been seen to.

13

He almost falls out of the driver's door – yes, he does. Staggers towards you as though he's disembarking from a ship come into harbour after a long and particularly stormy passage. Which, metaphorically speaking, he is. He looks – older. There's more grey round the temples, new lines etched on that handsome brow, shadows round those famously bright blue eyes.

'My darling,' he gasps. 'What can I say? I've made the most godawful mistake. Can you ever forgive me?'

The domestic goddess smiles her wise, womanly smile.

'Only after I've strung you up on piano wire,' she breathes – no, she doesn't. Of course she doesn't because, unlike this pillock, she knows what love is. And it isn't a pulse-jittering, wit-shattering fever you catch like the measles. That, as all we grown-ups realize, is mere infatuation. Which is instant, intoxicating, infectious and that much more injurious the later in life it's contracted. Also, by and large, involuntary. Whereas love, real *love*, takes sweat, sacrifice and a healthy dose of common sense, as she bloody well intends to tell Casanova here. But perhaps not immediately.

For now, with saintly forbearance, she just stretches out her loving, compassionate hands (NB, maybe include a manicure along with the leg wax) to embrace this errant lamb, this father of her innocent children, and her face is as tenderly forgiving as that of any Madonna.

'Welcome back to the rut,' she crows – sorry, *croons*.

14

Cue music, applause, curtains.

So much for the ending. What about the story so far?

Well, we can skip over twenty-one years of marriage; they've passed in a flash, anyway. One minute you're scribbling your finals papers with, OK, an unrevised-for bulge under your waistband, the next you're packing that bulge and its little brother off to universities of their own, and you and their dad are rattling round the family home like two peas in an unnaturally tidy drum. But that's fine. Now's the time to become a couple again, to relax, hang loose and enjoy the rewards of your frantic, twenty-one-year obstacle race. What's more, you have the means to do so, because not only is the business thriving at last, but, in the first well-timed act of her existence, your mother-in-law has popped her poisoned clogs, leaving you (or rather him) a quarter of a million smackers. Net. In the Halifax. You can almost find it in your heart to forgive her for presenting you last Christmas with a bottle of Woolworth's bubble bath. Again.

To be sure, her only and best-beloved son (who received, that same Christmas, a fridge-sized hamper of Dior for men, not that you're counting) might have some barmy notions about what to do with this delicious lump of lolly, but that's only to be expected. Forty-eight is a dangerous age for males, even when they haven't suddenly found themselves orphaned. The half-century is looming, the hairline receding, the waist expanding, and they start asking why God

15

put them on this earth instead of where you've put their clean underpants. Goes without saying, according to them, that dear old mum would want them to use her bequest to realize, at last, their long-suppressed life's ambition. In your average husband, this might mean buying a yacht to circumnavigate the globe for a year or so – or at least the local reservoir of a Sunday afternoon in a natty peaked cap. If, however, like me, you were dumb enough to hitch your star to an Andrew Lloyd Webber manqué, then your man will see this legacy as his chance to finance for himself a staging of one of the musical master-pieces he has been dutifully shelving through all the long child-rearing, nest-feathering years. Perhaps it isn't kind of you to remind him tartly that, far from shelving such masterpieces, he has been composing them at regular intervals ever since you've known him, and hawking them round the offices of anyone in the business of musical theatre. It certainly isn't kind of you to add that the resounding lack of enthusiasm shown by these gents over the years might be justified – adding, for good measure, that if you fancied gambling a quarter of a million quid, you'd rather back racehorses than a musical. At least you'd have fun, get to wear a pretty hat, and there might be a gnat's chance of a return. He soon sees sense.

Well, not *soon* exactly. But he comes round eventually.

In fact, you gotta hand it to the boy. He comes round big time.

PART ONE

'When men make promises of eternal constancy they are always deceivers. Alas! We love without heeding reason, and cease to love in the same manner.'

Giacomo Casanova, *History of My Life*

1

'All right, lover,' said Mike, jerking up the shrieking handbrake. 'You can open your eyes now.'

I didn't, though, not at once. Tell the truth, I hadn't been keeping them tight shut. Nor would you, if you'd been clenched in the passenger seat of a car driven by my lunatic husband down what felt like a lumpy roller-coaster track with water splash at the bottom. No, honestly. We'd hit that water with such a smash my feet had nearly gone through the floor, stamping on imaginary brake and clutch. Bet your life my eyes flipped open then. Once I'd clocked that we were ploughing across a ford rather than into a brick wall, though, and caught a sideways glimpse of a dinky rustic footbridge, I'd obediently blocked out the world again, and resumed my prayers. I wasn't asking for my life to be spared, actually, just that this great 'surprise' wouldn't be too – surprising. After last night's disrupted slumbers, I was afraid I might not be up to manufacturing the appropriate effusions of gratitude, and I didn't want to hurt Mike's feelings. The poor sap had been seething with excitement ever since he'd loaded me and our overnight bags into the car yesterday afternoon, and headed for the A1.

'Well?' he said now.

So I squinted up one eyelid, then the other –

and I rather think my heart stopped. Just for an instant. It was a blindingly silver-bright November morning. We were parked in the crook of a valley banked by rusty crags of moorland, with a stream twirling below, and a trio of handsome old trees stretching coppery branches up to a sky as blue as a swimming pool. Beside us stood a cottage. Not just any old cottage, but the definitively perfect country cottage, right down to the fat, frost-nipped roses nodding over a white-painted porch as it snoozed in a sunny fold of the hillside – the sort of haven you dream about in stinking tube trains, or horn-honking traffic jams of a Monday morning. And the whole glorious higgledy-piggledy patchwork of lichened stone, blistered woodwork and curly russet tiles was tied round, like a gigantic box of chocs, with metre-wide shiny red ribbon, puffed into a bow the size of a sofa across the front door, and bearing a suitably outsize gift tag.

For my love, with all my love.

That's what the tag said, in print as bold and black as a newspaper hoarding. Even so, I could hardly make out the words, through a fog of tears.

'Hey-hey-hey, Jo, this isn't like you,' said Mike, as I flung my arms round his neck.

'Not like – not like you, either,' I wailed, and I was still snivelling into a fistful of tissues as I stumbled after him up the mossy path.

'Strewth,' he muttered as he shunted the hardboard gift tag to one side and prodded the girdling of ribbon. 'The boys certainly went to town on the gift-wrap. I warned 'em to make it weatherproof, but...' Heaving up the bow, he grinned over his shoulder. 'I slipped the stand-fitters a few quid to drop by on the way back from a fancy goods fair at Newcastle.' As I joined him at the door, I saw this was no flimsy satin ribbon. More like the heavy-duty vinyl you might use to upholster the benches in a burger joint. Mike gave the bow an experimental tug. A bird rocketed out of the roses with a squawk, but the sash didn't budge. 'Shit,' he muttered, grabbing it with both hands now, bracing himself, and heaving for all he was worth. To no visible effect. I felt a wicked tremor of laughter, and had to blow my nose loudly. Eventually, after a couple more grunting assaults, looking this way and that as if expecting a handy machete to materialize in the undergrowth, my hero turned back to me. 'You, um, haven't by any chance got a penknife or something, have you, honey?' Just so might Romeo have looked if he'd had to apply to Juliet for a rope-ladder. 'Only this stuff's as tough as chainmail, and the dickheads seem to have stapled it right across the door...'

'Men, eh?' said the woman, smiling.

'He was so crestfallen, poor baby,' I sighed, shivering and clapping my arms to my sides. 'He'd have taken a tyre jack to it, only I said I'd sooner he didn't demolish the place before I'd set foot inside. Still, I could forgive him anything just now.'

'You're sure there's nothing I can do? There may be tools in my car.'

'Don't worry. He's only whipped over the hill to

21

the pub where we stayed last night, to borrow some kit. He should be back before I lose any toes to frostbite. That's assuming the bar hasn't opened yet, of course.'

She laughed. 'Oh, but of course.'

I'd opted to wait here because, like a kid on Christmas morning, I couldn't be separated from my present. 'Beck Holme', I'd learned my new domain was called, from a splintered sign beside the gate. Having wandered round to the back, I'd looked up from my rapt inspection of a water-trough – a weather-battered, moss-dripping, granite monster any Home Counties gardener would kill for – and found I wasn't alone. A spaniel, pretty as the ornament off a fireplace, was gazing at me and, behind it, stood an equally pretty woman, a doll-like creature nearly lost under a big dark-green coat and fluffy fur hat.

'Gosh, I *am* sorry,' she'd cried, thrusting out a tiny gloved hand to steady me, because I'd nearly toppled into the through. 'Did we startle you?'

There was a charmingly musical timbre to her voice, and not a trace of Yorkshire. This was a voice you could imagine reading poetry. She looked poetic, too. The flowing skirts of her coat were nipped into a tiny waist, and the tawny halo of fox fur framing a pale, heart-shaped face put me in mind of the heroines of doomy Russian novels – Lara, Anna Karenina, that sort of female – although there was a merry and not at all doomed twinkle in her eye as she watched me wrap my skimpy mac more closely round my ribs against a wind blasting direct from the North Pole. They don't manufacture winds like this on

Wimbledon Common.

'You *are* the new owner of Beck Holme, aren't you?' she'd begun, with a shy smile. 'Only, when I couldn't see a car, I began to wonder whether you were perhaps just a passing hiker, taking a look round.'

'In these heels?' And my explanation for Mike's absence had inevitably led to our sharing sisterly jokes about the loopiness of the male of the species as we strolled back to the front garden to escape the gale.

'So sweet, though,' she said, smiling down at the gift tag. 'Even if it does make my mission seem hopeless.'

'Mission?' A hefty four-wheel-drive vehicle, richly mud-splattered, was pulled up by the gate. Her car, like her clothes, was eminently more suited to these parts than mine.

She shook her head and laughed. 'Oh – oh, it doesn't matter.'

'Go on,' I urged. I'd taken a fancy to this woman. We were much of an age, I guessed – which was to say forty-one in my case – and of similar height, because I'm also on the short side, although I felt a clumpy dwarf beside this wispy fairy.

'To be honest' – she pulled a face – 'I came to make you an offer for your house.'

That startled me. 'You want to *buy* it?'

'Not me,' she said instantly, 'a friend, or rather a family member. Peter's my husband's cousin, and he's wanted a place of his own up here for a while. He would've snapped up Beck Holme the first time, back in spring, if only – well, if only

23

we'd known it was on the market. Rather an absurd situation, actually, because–'

I interrupted. 'The house has already changed hands once this year?' My enchantment was momentarily spiked with apprehension. Not that I don't trust my husband, but... 'Pity's sake, don't tell me it's falling down, or they're building a nuclear power station next door?'

'Heavens, no. I don't know exactly why the chap's selling on again so quickly.' An impish smile tilted one corner of her mouth. 'Although the word locally is that his wife's behind it. However ...' She hesitated, and then continued all in a rush: 'The fact is, Peter inherited some money – rather a lot of money.' She blushed rosily. 'I mention it only because we would – that is to say, *he* would – be prepared to offer you, say, twenty thousand more than you've paid?'

'Sorry?'

'Twenty-five?' But she must have read my face, because she bit her lip. 'Never mind, I had to ask. I do hope I haven't embarrassed you.'

'Don't be daft.' I gestured round, shrugged. 'But I'm afraid there's no way I'm parting with this place. It's my every dream come true, if that isn't too corny for words.'

Her smile was warm, if wistful. 'Sounds heavenly to me. I hope you'll be very happy. Gosh, here's your man roaring down the hill to the rescue, and my car's blocking the lane. Floss? Here, darling.'

And with a wave and a wag of the tail, they were gone.

'Twenty-five thousand quid, though,' I breathed, as I stroked the pitted, blackened beam above the fireplace of what was going to be my sitting room. Chintz curtains, I'd already decided. Big, fat, crumpling-on-the-floor curtains, and to hell with trendy minimalism. 'Just like that, clear profit.' Not that I was remotely tempted, but it wouldn't have been me if I hadn't felt obliged to spare at least a thought for our bank balance.

'No bloody way,' retorted my husband, who's never felt obliged to give much thought to bank balances. Nor to insurance policies, pension plans or anything else that comes in windowed envelopes. Money in the bank, in his view, is money going to waste. He regularly marvelled – most recently that very morning – at how he'd managed to stay married for twenty years to a tight-fisted old killjoy like me. I marvelled, too – didn't I just. And now that we'd finally dropped anchor in the safe havens of financial solvency, he would probably never appreciate just how much skilful navigation and sweated baling-out had been required to deliver us here. Anyway, just because my first words on opening a bleary eye today had been that the landlord of the Stowham Arms should bloody well knock half off our bill, that does not mean I am, by nature, either tight-fisted or a killjoy.

Look, we'd been kept awake until nearly dawn by the carousing downstairs which had culmin-ated – I kid you not – in gunfire, interspersed with the shattering of glass. Pillow over my head, I'd braced myself for the wail of police sirens, but that's what living in London does to you. Here in rurally remote North Yorkshire, it had ended only in a bout of angry shouting, predominant in which I recognized mine host's voice. No, he'd told us this morning with a weary half-smile as he dished up our bacon and eggs, his dining room wasn't actually strewn with bloodied corpses. The revellers had been a shooting party from the castle, regulars who should know better at their age, silly buggers, but a card game had gone on too late, and they'd taken to firing at empty bottles. Only an air pistol, he'd added.

'Only?' I'd squeaked, but the poor bloke looked so bog-eyed as well as shame-faced that, far from demanding refunds, I'd found myself adding a hefty tip.

'Stop fretting about money,' said Mike now, tweaking my fringe.

'Wasn't actually.' I measured the gap between window and wall with my outstretched hands and wondered if my old pine corner cupboard would fit. 'Although I can't believe I'm turning down all that dosh without a blink.'

'Didn't you always say you wanted a place in the country?'

'Yes, but–'

'We can afford it. *However*' – with a flourish he produced a sheaf of papers from his inside pocket – 'you wanna sell, I can't stop you. Because this joint's all yours, Mrs Patterson. See? The deeds are in your name only.'

'Oh, Mike, you fool.'

'Bought outright for cash, I might add, before you mention mortgage repayments.'

'Four bedrooms, all that land...?' I stared at

26

him. 'But it must've cost a *fortune*.'

'Strike you as a bargain at two hundred and fifty K? Good old Mum.'

'You've used your legacy?' My eyes were filling up again. 'You've spent *everything* your mother left you, to buy me this? Oh God, and I was such a cow about you wanting to mount your musical, and now you've given up on it, just to–'

'Given up on it?' He grabbed me into a bear hug. 'Course I haven't given up on it. There's more ways than one to get a show on the road, as Gaynor keeps telling me.'

'But–'

'Mind, the way she's ripping the book apart, I'm beginning to wonder if we'll ever finish the rewrite. Memorize this face, sweetheart. You may not be seeing much of it.'

It was his stoicism that cracked me up. Under the brave grin, the sturdy protestations that I deserved every penny, he must have known he'd kissed goodbye to his last chance of seeing one of his shows staged. No one had ever offered to put fifty quid into a Patterson masterpiece, let alone a quarter of a million. But without a murmur about the monumental sacrifice he'd made, he was asking – asking anxiously – whether he'd done the right thing in buying me this cottage instead: 'You do like it, don't you?'

'Like it?' I howled. '*Like it?*'

2

To say Beck Holme was the best present Mike had ever given me doesn't come near. At a quarter of a million quid, how could it be otherwise? But the money didn't mean nearly so much to me as the fact that, for once, my husband had taken soundings in my soul and come up with something I truly, passionately wanted.

Oh, he'd always been one for the big romantic gesture – Valentine cards the size of barn doors, sheaves of out-of-season roses in a red to match the even thicker sheaf of unpaid bills on the mantelpiece. Most memorably, four weeks after I'd given birth to Ben and had breasts like angry watermelons and thighs the size of telegraph poles, my devoted spouse presented me with a wispy, peek-a-boo bra and suspender set. In magenta pink and size ten – and to add insult to injury, he'd absent-mindedly charged them to my own store card. I rather think that was when I told him if he ever wanted to see me wearing this ensemble, he'd better consult a surgeon about a vasectomy, pronto.

Yes, yes, I'm an ungrateful old bag with no sense of romance – as I've been told a million times. But someone has to be sensible – as I'd retorted a million times. Beck Holme, however, was an acquisition as practical as it was beautiful, and not just because property is always a sound investment. I never for a moment saw it as belonging to me, incidentally, whatever sweet nonsense Mike had put on the deeds. This was a weekend cottage for the whole family, and with our daughter in her second year at Leeds and Ben just starting at York, what could be more useful? Moreover, unlike the island-hopping Caribbean yacht Mike had chartered at mind-boggling cost supposedly to mark the fortieth birthday of a wife allergic to sun, sailing and nightclubs, I couldn't suspect self-interest here. My husband might have been happy to gyrate his conker-tanned body round plunging decks and throbbing dance-floors for three interminable weeks, but he'd always regarded the English countryside as so many gaps on the map to be motorwayed past as speedily as possible. No, he really had been thinking of me when he bought Beck Holme.

So I could hardly resent his being too busy to join me at our new cottage. Well, I was too bogged down in the pre-festive scrum myself to manage more than one swift foray before Christmas. Once I'd dished up the roast turkey, cold turkey and turkey curry, though, I began heading up the A1 at every chance, to scrub, strip and paint. Mike, bless him, was very tolerant about microwaving himself frozen lasagne for days on end, quite uncharacteristically so. In return, I didn't complain about finding myself home alone at Wimbledon, because he was round at his lyricist's again, bashing away at the poor bloody musical. I knew the score would join its dusty band of brothers up in the attic soon enough.

Lover, this one was called. At least, that was the working title being discussed over the Christmas pud for this rocking romp through the adventures of Casanova. *Giacamo Superstud* had been my daughter Sarah's witty alternative, although Mike didn't seem to find this as funny as the rest of us did. It's hard to be a genius in your own family. I had a hunch crisis point would come earlier than usual on this oeuvre, not least because he had opted, halfway through, to rope in a collaborator on the words side. Since Mike's compositions are only marginally less precious to him than his children, and his new lyricist was a strong-minded female who was already working with him all day at the company, I'd queried the wisdom of this at the time. Now, though, in the interests of maintaining our new-found harmony, I kept quiet. Mike and I hadn't co-existed in such serene accord for – well, ever. Nice when a marriage finally grows up and settles down, isn't it? That's what I said to myself, as I roared back up North to get on with my decorating. There was so much to do.

The cottage might have struck me as heaven on wheels at the outset, but you know how it is. Soon as you start thinking about a tweak here, spot of paint there, one thing leads to another. Besides, it had its eccentricities. Most of the decor was inoffensive enough, but the biggest bedroom sported tiger-skin wallpaper, if you can believe it, while a downstairs chamber had purple mock-suede walls, with white shag-pile carpet crawling up the skirting board. The Seventies revival may the height of ironic chic, but not if you're old enough to remember platform boots the first time round. Still, Eden wouldn't be Eden without the odd worm, and the banishing of such monstrosities gave me profound satisfaction, although the purple suede was a pig to strip. I ended up hiring a steamer.

It wasn't until the beginning of March, however, that I discovered a less remediable drawback to my toy. The isolated situation had hardly troubled me, although I occasionally found myself wishing that the likeable woman who'd so wanted to buy the place might drop by to say hello. She never did, however, and I had my radio and too much work in hand to worry about a lack of neighbours. I didn't even mind driving three miles for a loaf, and much further for custom-mixed emulsion. But there came a rainy morning when, realizing I'd run out of milk, I flung myself into the car, zoomed down the lane – and nearly came to grief. In fact, if I hadn't happened to slow as I neared the ford to check that my purse was indeed buried in my cluttered handbag, I don't like to think what might have happened.

I suppose I'd noticed that the stream – that twinkling, friendly beck to which my house owed its name – was looking murky, and even that its steeply shelved, shaggy banks seemed curiously to have shrunk overnight, but I was absolutely not prepared for the roaring, gravy-coloured torrent which confronted me at the ford. A fallen branch, itself the size of an infant tree, was being whisked past on the current like so much dried grass, and the wonky, white-painted measuring pole, which normally stood well clear of the water, was not only in the stream now, it seemed to be telling me it was submerged to a depth of – *three and a half feet?* I hit the brake just in time, and stared round-mouthed. This isn't the kind of traffic hazard you encounter on the South Circular. It took a moment or two for the implications to sink in, for me to work out that, yes, there was indeed only one route to my house and, yes, that route truly did now lie waist-deep under water. As, with inching caution, I reversed away, I began to appreciate that the dinky footbridge arching to my right might be more than a picturesque piece of rustic set dressing.

'Oh, aye,' confirmed the nice lady at the Stowham shop-cum-post office, which was the only place I could think of to telephone for guidance, 'always best to leave your car this side in bad weather, and walk over the bridge.'

'I'm *marooned*,' I wailed to Mike, 'and it's still pelting down. We're supposed to be at the Burchills' silver wedding, I've got the plumber coming in on Monday...'

My husband, with a stoicism I would once scarcely have believed, told me not to worry. He would handle plumbers, friends, everything, no prob. He'd be fine on his own, course he would. And if I was going to miss the party anyway, wouldn't I sooner stop in Yorkshire until next weekend? Finish the bedroom or whatever?

'Bathroom,' I said dazedly. 'I'm on the bathroom now. Well, if you're sure...'

This led, amongst other things, to my first real encounter with the natives. Until now, an odd nod in the post office, or a wave of thanks when squeezing past a backed-up vehicle in a lane, had been the sum of social intercourse locally. Three days after discovering I was cut off even from this minimal contact with the world, however – by which time I was heartily sick of milkless coffee, frozen pizza and my own company – I realized, with a quickening sense of shock, I could hear car engines. The slamming of doors, too, along with a faint echo of shouting. I was up a ladder at the time, pondering whether this blue wasn't a touch too intense, but like Robinson Crusoe sighting a sail on the horizon, I scuttled down ladder and stairs and bolted through the front door without so much as casting aside my brush.

Even so, I emerged into the blustery morning only in time to see a scatter of figures heading off towards the top of the valley, too far away for me to tell whether they were male or female, never mind what they were up to, although I could discern sticks, hats and some frisky dogs. There was an engine still revving throatily by the ford, though, so I marched onwards. But then the noise died, and I mean *died*. You know that heart-sinking sputter? This was followed by a lusty curse and the most terrific splash, at which I upped my pace and rounded the bend to find a silver estate car with its backside thrust deep into the water on the far side. A lithe young man, presumably the driver, had just thrashed out of the shallows and now took off for the fields at a fast canter.

'Hello, there?' I called politely. 'Anything I can do to help?'

In that wind, of course he didn't hear. And by the time I'd upped my voice from cocktail-party cooee to rugby-field bellow, I was too late. I was just reflecting that it wasn't surprising he'd got into difficulties over there, given the tangle of mud-splattered vehicles squashed into hedge and ditch, when a movement caught my eye, and I turned back to stare at the stranded car. At first, I thought I'd imagined it, but then the entire rear end of the vehicle lifted again – gently, oh so very gently – skewed a few inches towards me, and settled once more. In the same instant, I saw the car was occupied. There was someone in the passenger seat, a man, judging by his height and the breadth of his shoulders.

I cupped my hands to my mouth. 'Hey! You OK?'

My words scattered on the gale like so many dried leaves. I pounded up the narrow steps of the footbridge and across to the middle. The beck was churning below in a fairish impersonation of the Amazon in spate, rocking the car as though it were a rubber dinghy.

'You're *moving*,' I shrieked. Still no response. Was he asleep? Or too wimpish to get his feet wet? One more surge of that current, though, and it'd be a lot more than his feet getting damp. I looked round. Up by the wood, figures were converging on the driver, but they were a long way off. I still had the big paintbrush in my hand. What else could I do? After a swift shake to rid it of at least the worst of the Cerulean Blue, I hurled it down on to the roof of the car. Bingo! The dark head jerked forward, and at last he must have clocked what was going on, because he groped for the handle and flung his shoulder against the door. But that side of the car was facing the current, with the water already lapping almost to window level.

'You'll never get it open,' I bellowed. 'Climb over to the driver's side.'

He heard. I know he heard because he peered upwards. I glimpsed a pale, gaunt face scowling at me through the rain-spattered windscreen. But then, to my bewilderment, he just slumped back into his seat again. Made not the least attempt to scramble free, even though his car was bobbing like a cork. Was he mad? Sure, the idea of a grown man drowning in a tuppenny-ha'penny stream in broad daylight seemed far-fetched to me, too, but...

'Here, Dad,' yelled a voice from beyond the hedge. The lane filled with green-clad, flat-capped people, variously shouting, whistling for their dogs or laughing. No one looked up my way. A rope appeared, and one of the Land-Rovers revved away from the hedge in foul blue gusts of exhaust. The young driver now waded back into the water to hitch up his vehicle, amid a chorus of jovial mockery from the bank.

'Practising our three-point turns, were we, young Miles?'

'I thought he'd passed his test?'

'Driving test, maybe. Must be trying for his bloody seaman's ticket now.'

'You don't think he backed into that beck by

accident, do you?' A sturdy old gent, with bowed legs and a bedraggled spaniel at his heel, cupped craggy hands round a roll-up cigarette as he touched a match to the tip. 'Ask me, he were after polishing off his dad and getting his hands on his inheritance.'

With a final tug to test the soggy rope, the lad turned, grinning. 'Fat lot of good my inheritance'll do me, Aidan.' Unlike the Yorkshire brogues of his friends on the bank, his accent was very public school.

'Nay, nay, bonny lad,' sighed the other. 'Never tell me you hadn't the wit to tek some decent insurance out on your dad before you tried a-drowning him?'

'You think I'd get anyone to insure a maniac like him?'

It had already struck me, observing the scene from on high like a cherub in a fresco, that this repartee was being swapped less to entertain the crowd than to jolly up the silent man in the car, when the window slid down and he poked his head out.

'Your mother managed it years back,' he roared. 'Go ahead, cut the bloody rope and bugger off. Should see you OK for a few quid.'

Dad, it seemed, was not in the mood for jokes, and he certainly put a damper on the merry mood of the crowd. Even after the boy, scarlet-faced, had folded himself into the driving seat, and the sodden vehicle was being hauled up the hill with water spurting from every orifice, there were uneasy glances exchanged, and some shuffling of boots.

'Don't look too rosy, Mr Jack, does he?' grunted one.

'Early days, yet,' observed another philosophically. 'Early days.'

'Gosh, *yes*,' burst out a tubby man behind them, 'when you think what the poor chap's been through.' This speaker was distinguished not only by vowels even posher than the boy's, but also by his headgear. In place of the ubiquitous flat cap, he sported a tweedy, beribboned deerstalker. I'd thought the only creature in the world ever to own such a titfer was Sherlock Holmes. 'Perhaps I shouldn't have dragged him out with us, but I thought...' Here, though, he broke off and raised a hand to his eyes, squinting up the hill at the departing vehicle. 'Odd,' he said. 'Am I imaginin' things, or is there some blue mess on top of Jack's motor?'

This was my cue, and I cleared my throat. I can't imagine anyone heard, but as if by magic all the flat caps, one by one, turned up to stare at me. And I suppose I could understand why the collective gaze reflected a certain bemusement. Here shivered I, in the blustery March gale, in shocking pink leggings, interestingly holed and laddered, under a baggy old sweatshirt of Mike's, much paint-spattered. My hair was bundled into a polka-dot scarf to stop unscheduled flashes of blue being added to the blonde streaks already planted there at great expense by my hairdresser, and this dashing ensemble was completed by lime-green pumps, lavishly sequined. One of those sales bargains that seem irresistibly witty after a bottle of Chardonnay with your girlfriends.

'I'm afraid it's paint,' I faltered. 'The man in the car didn't seem to hear when I shouted. I threw my brush to try and alert him, you know?'

They looked at one another; they looked back at me. Ever been out-stared by a field of cows?

'He was just sitting there. I was afraid he might get carried away.' I could have been talking Chinese. Possibly they were just too polite to tell me what a twerp I was to have imagined, even momentarily, there'd been any danger. 'It's only emulsion,' I added feebly. 'Should wash off.'

The roly-poly man in the deerstalker came to life first. 'Lord, yes,' he said. 'Not to worry, not to worry. Good of you to try. Snag is, the poor fellow can't actually shift himself about these days, had a fall, don't you know, pins all kaput. Nothing he could do.'

'He tried to open his door–' I began doubtfully.

'Sure he appreciated your efforts, though,' the man swept on, unhearing, 'and all's well that end's well, eh, what?' Yes, he did truly say that: *eh, what?* Whereupon, touching a hand to the brim of his absurd hat, he turned aside. 'Where now, Aidan? Try catching up at Fettles Wood, or back in the cars?'

They were all moving, gathering up sticks, whistling their dogs. I scampered down the splintery steps on their side of the bridge. 'But what are you doing?'

'Beg pardon?' Deerstalker blinked. His was a kindly, if not over-intelligent face, remarkably like that of the puffing, chubby Labrador at his heel – no Sherlock Holmes this, but a dead ringer for Dr Watson. 'Huntin',' he said. 'Well, followin', you know.' It must have been obvious that I didn't, because he added: 'Beagles?'

Which wasn't over-enlightening, but there were more pressing questions I needed answering. 'Just tell me, the river – beck – does it often flood like this? Only my car's been stranded over there since Friday.'

'Dear me, you must be at Beck Holme?' He thrust out a plump hand. 'Hugh Hough-Hartley, delighted to meet you, and I'm sure my friend in the car, Jack Bidcombe, would wish me to pass on his thanks, best wishes from the castle, new neighbours and so forth. The beck, well, hard to say really...'

'Not above two or three times a year,' contributed the bandy-legged old geezer, lurching up behind us, twig-thin roll-up still clamped in one corner of his mouth – Aidan, had the boy called him? Your Yorkshire yokel straight from central casting, anyway, with a waxed jacket which looked as if it might recently have been used to patch the roof of a pigsty, and a face cobbled together like a dry-stone wall. Only stonier. 'Proper floods, I'm talking about,' he continued, deadpan, 'when t'watter's high for a week or more. Not tiddly runs like this.'

'*Tiddly?*' I gulped. 'How long will it last, then?'

He put his head on one side, as though giving the matter profound consideration. 'Well, I do remember the time that house were cut off thick end of a month...'

'Oh, Aidan, *honestly*,' protested Hugh Hough-Hartley.

He didn't relent. Although the fag might have

39

twitched a millimetre. 'Aye, well. Happen t'bugger generally goes down quick as it comes oop.'

3

Fortunately, he proved to be right. Second thoughts, maybe that should be unfortunately.

Whichever, by lunchtime the next day, I'd about had enough. I couldn't finish the bathroom because I'd chucked my big brush into the river, and I was damned if I was going to paint acres of wall with a piffling three-incher. Anyway, the blue *was* too bright and I was sick of the stink of paint. I'd just begun wondering whether I could summon a taxi to meet me over the footbridge, when a tractor so rustily antique it looked like an escapee from a heritage museum chugged up to my gate. Behind the wheel sat none other than the stony-faced joker, roll-up still glued to his mouth. He didn't squander words. By the time I emerged from the kitchen, he'd already hitched a chain to my little hatchback.

'Like as not you'd mek it any road,' he grunted, as he swung back into his cab, 'because t'beck's down a good two foot, but I reckoned you'd sooner be safe than sorry.'

I'd barely flung myself into the driving seat before we were moving, and he wouldn't hang around for me to thank him, either, once we'd surged across.

'Happen you'll know next time,' was his only comment before chugging off up the hill again.

'*Rescued*,' I yelled happily into the phone. 'Tell Mike I've – oh, never mind, Gaynor, I'll tell him myself. Just let him know I'll be home about sevenish, OK?'

And it was at exactly two minutes past seven, with the rum-te-tum of *The Archers* just beginning, that I turned into Milton Chase, SW19. I remember flipping off the radio, feeling I'd had my fill of rural life for now. With satisfaction, I saw my husband's car in the drive. I was ready for company, a warm house and a cold glass of wine or six.

'Home,' I called as I flung open the front door and dumped my bags. I can't say the mess in the hall surprised me. Mike has always believed clothes have a supernatural ability to climb back on to hangers unaided – launder and iron themselves too, come to that. Mothers have a lot to answer for, especially his. But I only clucked indulgently when I tripped over his new loafers, and automatically bundled up his jeans which, for some reason, were sprawled across the telephone table. I discerned music upstairs. Not real music, just the usual bellow of my best beloved singing in his bath. One of his own compositions, too, because I recognized the tune. Sounded different, though.

Surely this black jumper wasn't his? No, of course not, this was a woman's pully. Was Sarah home too, then? My spirits rose higher still. Mad, isn't it? For twenty kid-infested years you dream of peace, quiet and dinner *à deux*, and the minute

41

you've got 'em, you're bereft. Looked like she was, yes, because that skirt wasn't mine, either. And even when I spotted the black bra dangling over the banister at the half-landing – believe this if you will – I only wondered from where it had been unearthed, because I hadn't worn black bras for yonks. Smiling wryly at myself (middle age is surely here when you worry more about what your neighbours see through your T-shirt than what your husband sees in the boudoir) I did nevertheless wonder what was going on. Someone having a turn-out for Oxfam? With each step I climbed, whisking up a sock here, underpants there, the singing grew louder – borne towards me, I might add, on a sweet and all-too-familiar waft of my own Rose Geranium bath elixir. I suppose it was the knee-high, spike-heeled, crocodile boots capsized by my bed – *our* bed – which at last slowed my cheery housewife's progress. I'd been about to yell that if Pavarotti through there in the en suite had been nicking my best bath oil all week, he could bloody well buy me another bottle. Instead, I halted. And gazed at the boots. Then, very slowly, I turned to survey the rest of the room. Seven o'clock in the evening and the bed was – wrecked. Well, no great surprise. The bed-making fairy had been in Yorkshire. But there was a champagne bottle on the bedside table, nearly empty, along with a trendy croissant-shaped handbag. While on the bed, beside the pillow – my pillow – there nestled a black, silky, frilly … *thong?*

'"Fidelity's no deal for me,"' bawls that well-known voice from behind the bathroom door with, I may say, the lusty gusto of Tom Jones and Sid James combined.

'For while one girl may be heaven,
Who wouldn't rather shag eleven?'

For an instant – for a tumbling eternity – I'm frozen where I stand. The raucous ditty pounds in my ears, but I'm a robot and someone has punched the 'off' switch.

'And even when too much slap and tickle
Gives you clap, you know your prick'll
Rise to fight another day – TWO! THREE!
    FOUR!
Rise to fight an-oth-er...'

The power snaps back on. I can feel it surging through my every vein and sinew. Kicking those tarty crocodile boots not just out of my way but clean through to the landing, I stomp across the bedroom carpet – my bedroom, my carpet – hurl open the bathroom door, and...

PART TWO

'All things are linked together, and we are the instigators of events in which we are not actors. Hence, anything important which happens to us in this world is only what is bound to happen to us. We are but thinking atoms, which move where the wind drives them...'

Giacomo Casanova, *History of My Life*

4

And six months later, here I am, eavesdropping on a bizarre conversation behind a grouse butt on Stowham High Moor.

Oh, come on. You don't need me to tell you how I ended up living full time in the wilds of Yorkshire. *Temporarily* full time. I mean, what do you suppose happened when I flung open that bathroom door and found two heads and four knees emerging from the sweet-scented foam of my Rose Geranium bath elixir? No prizes for guessing that the other head belonged to the colleague who had failed to relay my phone message. Yup, this was Mike's right-hand woman by day and theatrical collaborator by night, Ms Gaynor Steele. Looking back, I can't believe the idea had never so much as crossed my mind that she and my husband might have abandoned composing duff musicals in favour of making sweet, sweet music. Gaynor obviously couldn't believe how dim I was either. So she'd set me up to stumble upon them in such fragrantly delicious *flagrante delicto*. And while Tolstoy might claim unhappy families are unhappy in their own way, it strikes me deceived wives and cheating husbands all spout the same soap opera clichés.

Self: How could you do this to me?

Him: *It isn't what you think...*

It's me or her – *I never meant it to happen* – She goes or I go – *You don't understand* – You've got a simple choice – *It's more complicated than that...* And so on and so forth for, oh, I forget how many tearful days and nights, punctuated with the recurrent refrain of my pea-brained, pig-headed husband wailing that he loved me, couldn't imagine a life without me, hated himself for what he was doing to me, *but...*

Quite. The inevitable 'but'. I believe he might even have said something about this thing being bigger than both of us – and by 'us' he didn't mean *us*. At length, then, in a towering fury and a dangerously overloaded car, I withdrew to my stronghold in the North. Where I was going to stay, I said, until Casa-bloody-nova came to his senses. He knew where to find me, and he needn't bother phoning because even if he crawled up to Yorkshire on his hands and knees, I wasn't speaking to him again until That Woman was gone. Gone, banished, sacked from the firm and otherwise expunged from his life completely and totally and permanently, was that understood? And yes I bloody well was taking the brass reading lamp, it'd been a present from my aunt not his. Which was possibly the only original line uttered throughout. The rest you can fill in ad lib.

As to how, six months later, I came to be crawling round a grouse butt, with my own butt thrust inelegantly skywards – well, that's more complicated. It was the dog's fault. In fact, most of the merry mayhem that followed can be put down to the dog.

Note the way I still say 'the' dog, as though this capricious brown and white mud-magnet has nothing to do with me. Dora, she's called. That was already her name when she was foisted on to me by the kids. My strong-minded daughter, Sarah, seemed to think a three-year-old spaniel would plug the gap in my bed so rudely vacated by her dad. She was, at the time, toying with some notion of specializing in psychiatry. One can only be glad for the sake of her future patients she's shifted her sights back to coronary surgery, because I think she'll be better at plumbing the leaky pipework of the human heart than its manifold mysteries. As for Ben, before he floated off to worryingly non-specific destinations in the US of A for the whole of his summer vac, my son actually had the nerve to suggest Dora would protect me in his absence. It should have been apparent even to an airhead like him that, short of licking them to death, this animal was unlikely to deter passing psychopaths.

Moreover, I was dispirited by the implication that my offspring saw me withering into lonely old-ladyhood with only a pooch to cheer my twilight years. As I sternly reminded them, their father and I would soon be reconciled. This cottage was solid, stones-and-mortar proof of his real feelings when not in the grip of menopausal madness. Anyway, we all knew the old fool couldn't survive without me for long.

'Give her a month's trial,' Sarah had declared, deaf to my protests. She'd commandeered the beast from some hapless consultant whose broken hip apparently prevented him giving dear little Dora enough exercise. 'You won't have any problems, because Mr Masterson said they spent a fortune getting her trained.'

What my semi-vegetarian, right-thinking, bloodsport-banning daughter had failed to ascertain was the nature of Dora's expensive training. I myself found out only by chance. Never having owned a dog, I was as surprised as I was relieved to find that, when let off her lead, Dora responded to a summons with the speedy reliability of a boomerang. Would that errant husbands were so easily retrieved, I'd reflected, not to mention so unfailingly affectionate. And although I was certainly not succumbing to the charms of my uninvited canine cohabitee, our month's trial somehow slipped into a second, my newly exercised calves developed a pleasing curvature, and I heard myself mumbling to Sarah that, as dogs went, this one wasn't much trouble. Until, that is, the afternoon we stumbled upon a shoot.

I'd no idea what was going on, of course. This is the woman who'd once complained to a waiter in a very smart restaurant about the ball-bearings lodged in her breast of wild duck. As Dora and I meandered along a creek of a lane, sunk like a tunnel through the moor, with banks of purple heather massing way over head height, I was again scripting the big reconciliation scene – and squinting down at my hands. I'd spent the morning digging over a flowerbed, and seemed to have carried half of it away with me. Well, to hell with fripperies like manicures because, when Mike drove down that hill, it wouldn't be for my pearly fingernails, would it?

'And he *will* be coming, course he will,' I told Dora, who took a womanly interest in my woes. 'I mean, even someone as dippy as him doesn't squander a quarter of a million smackers giving his wife her heart's desire if he wants out of the marriage, does he? Stands to reason.'

I suppose I was aware of shouting up in the sunshine, but if your customary beat is South London, you're well used to ignoring noises off. Even a few muffled bangs barely registered on me. They did on Dora, though. She stiffened, nose outstretched, as though an electric charge had passed through her body. Assuming the poor mutt was scared, I called her name. To my astonishment, she cut me dead. Then there came a particularly loud bang and – *woomph* – she hurled herself up the heathery precipice and disappeared.

I called, whistled, shouted myself dizzy – but to no effect. That, incidentally, was the moment I realized Dora was staying with me on neither trial nor sufferance. Give my precious baby back to Mr whatever-he-was-called? I would as soon chop off my arm. In breathless panic, I flung myself up the bank after her, slithering, sliding and grabbing knotted roots until, red-faced, wild-eyed and bracken-bestrewn, I heaved myself aloft on to the sunlit moor. And found I was staring at the rear view of a stumpy gent in a flat cap, whose battered tweed jacket and baggy breeches looked as if they might originally have been worn by Piltdown Man. One calloused hand was locked round a horn-topped stick, the other, incongruously, held a scarlet flag. Even as I clocked that he was not alone, that the moor was studded with his tweed-capped, flag-carrying clones, and a-bounce with tail-flapping spaniels, I spotted my own. She saw me too, thank the Lord, and began snaking through the heather in my direction with the purposeful ease of a guided missile. And then I observed that there was something dangling from her jaws. A feathered and bloodied something, fully twice the size of her pretty little head.

'*Dora?*' I gasped.

Did she have the sense to drop her incriminating cargo? To scurry up and hide at my feet before anyone saw her? Not on your nelly. In mid-career towards me, she had a better idea, shifted course, and trotted straight to the tweedy figure with the stick and the flag, before whose gaitered legs she deposited the corpse. Then she sat, fluffed out her bosom and beamed saucily up at him.

I think I knew, even before he turned. A memory had stirred as I'd registered the bandy curve of those legs, the thread of smoke winding up from the cap. His face, as it swivelled inexorably my way, was even stonier than I recalled.

'OmyGod,' I whimpered, for I had visions of my baby's summary execution. 'Aidan, isn't it? Look, I am so, *so*, sorry...' He was already bending over to grab the evidence and, as I thought, my murdering pet by the scruff of unrepentant neck.

'It wor a runner an' all,' he growled. But to my

bewilderment he seemed to be – fondling her ears? 'Good lass, good lass. Through that bog like a dose of salts, and beat 'em all to it, didn't you?' His eyes met mine, and the hewn-from-granite features were cracking into something which, yes, could plausibly be construed as a smile. The screw of cigarette paper, at any rate, was tilting up to heaven. 'Knows her job, does this little madam,' he grunted. 'Happen you should fetch her out with us.'

I recount all this only to explain how, weeks later, an unreconstructed suburban housewife like me came to be overhearing a conversation between grouse-shooters at all, let alone a conversation which was, one way and another, to send her life skidding off on such a crazy course.

We'd become regulars on the field, Dora and I, in spite of my assuring Granite-chops, otherwise known as Aidan Brighouse and no less a personage than Head Keeper to Lord Bidcombe of Stowham Castle, that I wouldn't know a grouse from a canary.

'Tha dog does,' he'd retorted, and the fag twitched in a way I came to realize signified mirth. 'Watch her, and happen tha'll learn.'

Novel reversal: dog trains owner. I soon gathered, from grumblings about mix-ups in the estate office nowadays, that we'd been recruited only because a failure to co-ordinate dates with neighbouring shoots meant they were desperately short of beaters. Still, Dora and I were being offered twenty-three quid a day and free beer amid a jovial crowd only too willing to advise this townie how to earn it. After months of solitary brooding, I was chary, but soon began to find the company even more welcome than the cash. It helped that no one asked why I was marooned up here in North Yorkshire. Not all beaters are blokes, but beating is undoubtedly a blokeish pursuit, so there was no girly hearts-and-lives-sharing in the wagon. The talk revolved round dogs, weather, dogs, idiocies of shooters, dogs and, well, dogs, amid a lively crossfire of banter. No new hat, slip of the tongue or fancy sandwich passed unmocked, and my ignorance about all matters rural was a gift to the jokers. Even if I didn't quite need informing that milk came from cows, I was grateful to be shown how to remove a tick from my sidekick's silky ear. And tried not to faint as this blood-gorged baked-bean with legs squirmed in the palm of my hand. I may have felt like an under-dressed, under-rehearsed extra in a costume drama of rustic England but Dora was palpably in her element.

As for the beating itself, well, if you've never tried it, I can only say wading through thigh-high heather, springy as a mattress and pitted with concealed swamp-holes, reaches muscles your poncey Knightsbridge aerobics teacher never dreamed of. At least when you fall over, which I did – frequently – the shrubbery cushions your landing. Simultaneously, you're thwacking the air with a flag and bellowing like a football hooligan to drive the birds up, an activity remarkably akin to the kind of New Age anger-release therapy you'd pay a fortune for in town. In fact, they should prescribe grouse-beating for wives in my situation. I remember reflecting this on the day in question, when it crossed my mind I'd passed a whole morning without once fretting about my husband and the floozy.

Mind, it was one of those golden September days when it's surely impossible to brood. The early, feathery skeins of mist had dissolved into sunshine, and the sky was a vast silken pavilion of blue. As we closed in towards the butts on the last drive before lunch, I was marvelling afresh – and with a dreamy rapture which would have provoked hoots in the beaters' wagon – at the glorious tapestry under my boots. The heather itself, in every shade from delicate spring lilac to rich ecclesiastical purple, was appliquéd with startling tufts of acid-green lichen, drifts of candy-pink bilberry, soaring clumps of blond reeds... And when the whistle blew and the shooting ceased, instead of concentrating on the job and my dog, I was regretfully musing that you could never hope to reproduce such richness of colour and texture in a fabric.

Dora, meanwhile, snaking around industriously, nose to ground, had located her bird. Lifting it in her mouth, she twirled towards me – and discerned I was slacking. I had long since learned that my canine colleague, if I take my eye off her, is both a flirt and a snob. Not only does she prefer to award her trophies on the field to a man – Aidan often being the lucky recipient – but, given a choice, she will unerringly select the classiest pair of masculine boots available. On this occasion she excelled herself. Ignoring the nearest butt, beside which a couple of unprepossessing middle-aged gents were smoking cigars and swapping a hip-flask, she pranced on towards the next, hesitated briefly before a pair of wellingtons of expensive brand name and notably shapely silhouette only to reject them (her instinct for *nouveau richesse* is infallible), and instead trotted on to deposit her bird at the venerable brogues of Lord Bidcombe himself.

I knew who he was, of course, this bumbling, antique aristo straight from the pages of Wodehouse, although I sincerely hoped he didn't know me. I'd recently learned it was none other than his lordship's son and heir who'd been the glum-faced passenger in that long-ago accident at the flooded ford, and thus one of the estate's vehicles I'd so tastefully decorated with Cerulean Blue. Dented the bodywork summat terrible, too, according to Aidan. So I was glad he hadn't perceived Dora, sitting at his toes with her proudly offered bird. He was talking animatedly to a tubby, sandy-haired man whose pink face seemed obscurely familiar, but it wasn't until I spotted a deerstalker hat discarded on the butt that, with a jolt, I recognized this as the kindly Dr Watson-lookalike from the same incident. Hugh something? The sooner I could grab grouse and dog and make myself scarce the better, but Mr Shapely Wellingtons was wandering up behind me, humming to himself *sotto voce*. I dropped to my knees and called softly. Dora pretended to be deaf. This was not the first time she'd made plain I was something of an embarrassment to her on the field. My combat trousers, filched from Ben, and a checked shirt bought for fifty pence in a charity shop clearly failed to measure up to her standards of correct shooting apparel. Judging by the doe-eyed gaze she was directing up at his lordship's tall and lanky frame, his ensemble – voluminous tweed three-piece, ponderous gold watch chain, tattered maroon garters – suited her notions entirely.

'Bloody good question,' he was harrumphing. 'Frankly, I'm losing patience with the pair of 'em. I agreed to give it a year, and, dammit, that year's as good as up now.'

'Surely not?' ventured Hugh thingy. 'Only seems yesterday that...' He cleared his throat. 'Lord, yes, I suppose November will be upon us any day. Point is though, Bernard, any chance we might be seein' Paddy up here before too long? Not that I, ah, want to start a hare, not at all, *not at all*, but they were always so thick, he and Jack, until...' The man blushed even pinker. 'Long and the short is, I'd welcome, you know, a quiet word in his shell-like.'

'What's that?' bellowed his lordship.

'Absolutely don't want to chase the chap, just if he happened to be about–'

'Speak up, Huffers, speak up. You need a spook?'

5

A *what?* On hands and knees, sneaking up on my spaniel, I was startled into a snort of laughter. Fortunately, Hugh Hough-Hartley, whose name I remembered at that moment, broke out coughing, spluttering indignantly that he needed nothing of the kind, so neither noticed me. I was reaching for dog and bird, however, when the *sotto voce* humming behind me ceased, and as though a hole were being burned in the back of my head, I sensed I was under observation. I squinted over my shoulder.

Mr Shapely Wellingtons was indeed looking down at me, his gaze lingering on my up-thrust bum. He actually let out a soft wolf whistle. I was so amazed I nearly laughed again. Offended? Are you *joking?* At forty-two I regard a wolf whistle as an act of compassion – or a sign someone's left his contact lenses at home. Besides, though no chicken, he wasn't at all bad looking. There might be deep lines carved in his tanned face, and the bushy black sideburns curling from under his cap were a sad style error to my eyes, but that ruggedly cleft chin made up for a lot. I found myself wondering whether there wasn't something teasingly familiar about him, too, but the ubiquitous swamp-green gear of the shooting fraternity makes it hard to tell one from t'other. I did notice, though, that his breeches were by no means of the standard baggy cut. His fitted with unusual, nay, indecent intimacy. And this wasn't my hormones having a pre-menopausal flutter: I am a respectable married woman. I couldn't but remark the snugness of his tailoring because my nose was level with his bulging wedding tackle, and he was making no attempt to move away.

Lord Bidcombe, meanwhile, was breezily assuring his companion he should not be at all bashful, in these immoral days, about needing the services of a spook – I had not misheard, he said *spook* – and surely Hughie had Paddy's number at the agency? The Wolf-in-Wellies raised his eyebrows at me.

'Rent-a-ghost?' I hissed, rather wittily I thought. 'Enhance your stately pile with a custom-designed phantom?'

He grinned so appreciatively I felt the blood rushing to my cheeks. Maybe my hormones were having a flutter after all. He shot me a wink, and stepped forward. 'Hey, you guys, what's with the spook business?'

Forget he had an American accent phonier than a nine-cent piece, I should have recognized him from that voice alone, which did indeed, as a popular culture pundit once put it, trickle like warm molasses from a spoon. But I was gathering up the grouse and glaring at Dora.

Lord Bidcombe and Hugh Hough-Hartley both spoke at once.

'*Nothing*,' wailed the latter, who had at least heard the question.

'Paddy'll sort you out in a trice,' continued his lordship, who had not. I'd long since been warned our noble employer was deaf as a dead sheep. Fifty years of shooting your own game without namby-pamby toys like ear protectors extracts its price. He nodded towards the Wolf. 'You met my nephew, Paddy, at all? Most ferociously brainy fellow. Brought the old firm on in leaps and bounds since he took over from Jack. So what's the trouble, Hughie? One of your partners been dipping into the till?'

'*No!*' he yelped, comically horrified. 'Nothing of the sort.'

Lord B. blinked. 'Then why'd you want a quiet word with Paddy?'

From the anguish in his face, you'd think Hughie had been asked why he wanted a Soho massage parlour, but he was rescued by the Wolf, who drawled: 'Oh, spook as in private dick, yeah? Sure, I should've guessed.'

So should not have I. Frankly, I could more easily have believed his lordship was acquainted with twenty of the headless and haunting variety of spook than one of the trench coat and trilby breed.

'Security consultant,' he corrected grandly. 'Strictly big business. Mark you, some of the barefaced villainy he's rooted out in the bluest of blue-chip boardrooms would make your hair stand on end. Had a chap up here the other week, actually, who was lauding Paddy to the skies. I forget the ins and outs, some big conglomerate trying to take over his firm, my friend didn't want to play ball, and the next thing you know he's losing money hand over fist. Well, Paddy starts poking through the books, and blow me down if he doesn't discover–' But at last he noticed me. 'Oh, hello. Having trouble, m'dear?'

I scrambled to my feet. The Wolf-in-Wellies thrust out a hand, and even detained me to brush a twig of heather off my knee, as his lordship began to describe a bugging device this Paddy character had planted in the boardroom of the beleaguered firm, which could, he swore, detect a flea's fart at fifty paces. Sadly, I didn't get to hear the end of the tale because a puce-faced Hugh Hough-Hartley bellowed into his ear that they were being summoned to lunch. Whereupon the Wolf – wait for this – kissed the tips of my muddy fingers before releasing my hand with a squeeze. 'See y'around, Gorgeous. I hope.'

OK, OK, so he was a twenty-two-carat smoothy, and I happened to be the only female within flirting range, but so what? It was a very long time since anyone had called me Gorgeous. I strode back to the encampment of cars and trailers with a swagger.

Shame Sarah wasn't here, I was thinking, because it would have cheered her heart, too. Predictably horrified to learn of Dora's bloody profession, my daughter had been unmoved by my argument that factory chickens had a lousy life compared to grouse, winging wild and free over their expensively conserved habitat. I'd added that a game bird's end was at least swift, although I may have been pushing my luck when I ventured to speculate that it might be preferable to exit the world with a bang than a whimper. Her expression made me feel like Herod discussing child welfare. However, after a little thought, she did concede that my gory pursuit would at least dig me out of the house.

'And you might meet people,' she had continued pensively.

For 'people' read 'men'. Sarah, of course, agreed with me that her father was bound to repent, but had recently and rather worryingly begun encouraging me to cover my bets. Had even hinted I might be better off without him. I soon set her straight. I had not, I said tartly, spent twenty-one years learning to put up with her dad's funny little ways just in order to start all over again now.

'Wouldn't do him any harm to have a taste of his own medicine, though,' she darkly opined, 'and shooting's very much a *boys*' game, isn't it?'

It certainly was. To date, I'd only spotted one gun-toting female, but if my daughter hoped I was mingling with the moneyed shooting classes she would be disappointed. Between those who are paid twenty-three pounds a day to drive grouse up into the air, and those who pay well in excess of a thousand pounds per man, per diem – no, honestly – to blast them down again, there is a gulf such as my egalitarian child never dreamed of. It's very much 'them' and 'us' out on the moor. That brief encounter with the Wolf just now was far and away the longest conversation I'd ever exchanged with a gun. And as I collected the carrier bag containing my lunch from the wagon, I sneaked a glance at the stone-built shooting hut, outside which the guns were about to consume theirs. Corks were popping from champagne bottles, ice was clinking in gin and tonics, and on a white-clothed table, flanked by several dusty bottles of claret and a decanter of port, were arrayed lobster, cold fillet of beef, raised pies, a cornucopia of breads and salads, and a Stilton so stinky I could smell it from here. To cap it all, this picnic in the grandest of grand English traditions was benignly presided over by a butler. No kidding: a walking, talking butler. You can see why I felt this was costume drama, as opposed to the real life I'd left behind in Wimbledon.

I trudged on fifty yards to the patch of hillside where we lesser mortals were lunching, twenty-odd of us, all ages, shapes and sizes, in a clutter of dogs, flags, beer cans, Tupperware boxes, greaseproof paper and vacuum flasks.

'Oh, so she's condescended to join us, has she?' called Aidan, leaning on his stick to one side of the encampment. It was clear some joke was brewing at my expense, but I tossed down my box of bacon butties and affected not to notice. Jimmy would enlighten me, if no one else. I fear this new friend, waiting with my lager, wasn't quite the sort of man Sarah had in mind for me. Barely topping my shoulder, with pebble specs, a brace on his teeth and a beefy black Labrador pup called Tyson, he was Aidan's eleven-year-old grandson, and had recently been nicknamed Harry Potter, in a surprising flash of literary erudition from the Wykesea contingent of beaters. This trio of shaven-headed, ear- and brow-studded youths, who were also sprawling nearby, came out from town in a rusty Mini van, ran a brisk trade in cut-price fags and were themselves generally known as the three musketeers. Today, they were sitting with Leonard, a widowed lay preacher and lifelong teetotaller, who was nevertheless chuckling merrily at a quite unrepeatable story about a sheep, a rabbi and a Scotsman.

'No decorum, they haven't,' declared my friend Jimmy sagely, his pride in this new word in no way diminished by the whistles it provoked.

'That the model they replaced the Fiesta with?' called one of the musketeers.

We beaters were a motley cocktail, for sure, and I'd soon realized that the division between the guns and us workers by no means ran along simple class lines. No one, after all, could mistake the Wolf-in-Wellies quaffing gin down there at the hut for a toff. Equally, a fellow beater, now circulating a cake tin, was a retired admiral of the fleet, looked very like King George V and had an accent even plummier than his wife's fruit loaf.

'Booze those chaps are putting away suggests the birds can rest easy this afternoon,' he remarked, following the direction of my gaze. 'Rather makes one wish for a tin helmet, though, advancing on butts of drunken Bunburies.'

I might have thought Bunbury was a make of waterproof jacket had I not been told today's guns were a syndicate of old friends operating under that soubriquet. Apparently they were regular customers, and notorious for getting up to all manner of juvenile japes during their shoots, in spite of their mature years. Since they mostly put up at the Stowham Arms, it had already occurred to me that these gents were very probably the selfsame blithe spirits who had once kept me awake half the night. Perhaps I should have been thankful they'd only been shooting at bottles, however, because the Admiral now recalled with a reminiscent grimace that they'd peppered a loader and two flankers after a particularly lavish lunch a couple of seasons back.

'Never hit a dog, though,' he conceded, as though this excused a great deal.

'People get *shot?*' Oddly, such a risk had never crossed my mind.

'Not again, they don't,' growled the Head Keeper, looming up behind us. 'Or them Bunburies'll be off this moor, no matter what.' He paused. 'And it won't do them no good kissing *my* hand.' So that was the joke. I might have guessed my encounter with the Wolf had been observed. 'Interesting chat down at his lordship's butt, Mrs P.?'

I was wise to Aidan now. 'Fascinating,' I said instantly. 'He was talking about some friend who's a private detective. Spook's the word he used, can you credit it?'

To my chagrin, this didn't surprise Aidan or anyone else.

'His nephew, you mean, Major McGinty? He's all right, is Paddy.' Since most people were lucky to rate a dyspeptic grunt, this was high praise. I might have asked whether the unfortunate McGinty had indeed been christened Patrick, if the Admiral had not leaned forward to enquire, in a discreetly lowered voice, whether any hope remained now of Paddy rescuing the estate. Aidan either didn't hear or – as it seemed to me

65

– chose to ignore the question.

'Come on then, lass,' he said. 'What'd tha make of our Alf?'

I set my chin nonchalantly. 'Alf?' Funny name for a wolf, I thought.

'"What's it all about, Alf-eee?"' carolled one musketeer, while one of his cronies, shading his eyes from the sun as he squinted down the hill at the lunch party, sniggered that he was amazed the old goat could sit down in them yellow crotch-crunchers.

'Give over,' commanded a booming contralto voice. 'And that goes for you too, Aidan Brighouse.' The redoubtable Mrs Eileen Muxworthy had long since appointed herself my protector in the beaters' encampment. A farmer's wife and farmer's daughter, she ruled her husband, widowed father-in-law and five married sons with the certainty, inbuilt in a certain breed of Yorkshire matriarch, that, while men have their place in this world, it is not in the driving seat.

'If t'Almighty'd planned on fellahs being in charge,' she had recently advised me, 'He'd not've planted their brains in their trousers.'

As a picker-up, she also ran three (male) Labradors with the efficiency of a regimental sergeant major. I wasn't surprised the earringed youths quailed when she aimed her majestic bosom towards them. 'I'll tell you summat for nowt, bonny lads. If you look half as canny as our Alf forty year on, you'll be doing well.'

'By, you're as daft as your sister about that man,' said Aidan, whose sister-in-law Eileen was – but then everyone here seemed to be second-cousin-by-marriage to everyone else. He looked at me, and affected a mournful sigh. 'I tell you, the wife used to come over all coy just driving past the lane to your cottage. And she were that grieved when t'bugger sold it on again, he damn near spoiled Christmas for the lot of us.'

'*My* cottage–?' I began.

'Oh, my own good lady was just as bad,' chipped in the Admiral. 'Got umpteen of the chap's recordings tucked away, too. And she's already served notice I'm cooking my own dinner on November the whatever. You're organizing the charabanc, aren't you, Eileen?'

'I am, and you needn't any of you bother asking for tickets. Well, except you, Jo love, if you fancy an outing to Wakeford.' She scowled round. 'Hen night, ladies only.'

I was all at sea. 'Records?' I said. 'Tickets for what?'

'Nay, never say you didn't know,' cried Aidan, fag bouncing. 'Our local celebrity is Ricky. Only claim to fame we've ever had is Ricky Marvell being born up Stowham Edge.'

The penny dropped at last. 'Bloody hell,' I squawked, *'Ricky Marvell.'*

The tan, the accent, the treacly drawl and the come-hither grin... I couldn't believe I hadn't recognized him at a glance, but then you don't expect to find Yorkshire's pelvis-wiggling, ballad-belting, knicker-twanging answer to Tom Jones in a flat cap and breeches out on a grouse moor. In white flares, black shirt and gold medallion flashing on his hairy chest, it'd have been a different matter altogether. 'You mean to say he

67

lives round *here?*'

'Spain, for many a year,' responded Eileen with a little sigh. 'But he always comes back to shoot with them Bunburies. By, his dad must be laughing down St Hilda's graveyard, his Alf tekking a gun out with the nobs, because old man Mardell were the biggest poacher this side of Pickering. That's what he were called when he were at school with us: Alfie Mardell. His wife were in t'class below, and all. Now, is one of you useless lumps going to find me another can of lager or what?'

He winked at me again as the guns clambered into the waiting Range Rovers at the end of the day. I fear I may have simpered. Even so, the frisson of pleasure at being given the glad eye by this celebrated sex symbol (must ring Mum) was dampened by a reflection that middle age was kicking in with a vengeance if my sad little ego could be bolstered by the likes of Ricky Marvell. Not just had he been strutting round *Top of the Pops* when I was still in knee socks, but his hardcore fans had always belonged more to the blue rinse than the blue nail polish generation. I'd been trying to remember, while bashing through the heather, the last time I'd seen him on the box – years ago, surely? – when I had recollected, with a bittersweet pang, that my husband had actually exhumed this ancient raver to sing at a sales convention as recently as last year. And by all accounts, his still lusty rendition of '*Wild Card*' (God, remember the fringed white leather cat-suit?) had galvanized a sedate gathering of lady cosmetics reps into a platform-mobbing, knicker-chucking riot. Mike had been full of it at the time. But he'd surely never breathed a word to me about...

'Ricky Marvell owning *my* cottage?' I said, as I scrambled into the wagon for the homeward journey to Stowham Castle. The guns may be chauffeured around in leather-upholstered, air-conditioned four-wheel drives; we have a canvas-roofed, wooden-benched trailer hitched to a tractor which is driven at bum-numbing speed over hill and dale by the under-keeper. I wasn't surprised the Head Keeper travelled in his own Land-Rover. I had to repeat myself, not simply because of the tractor's roar, but because my colleagues were animatedly discussing rumours that an offer had been made for the estate. I was far more interested in another property sale closer to home. 'Did I get the wrong end of the stick with Aidan,' I persisted, 'or did my husband – I mean, *we* – buy Beck Holme off Ricky?'

Apparently we did. Well, it certainly explained the tiger-skin and purple suede, but I simply couldn't imagine my showbiz-crazy spouse failing to pass on such a juicy titbit of the house's history. Didn't Mike know? Perhaps if he'd dealt only with an estate agent – or if Ricky had owned it under his real name?

'Beck Holme were his shooting lodge,' Eileen stated, ignoring jeers from the three musketeers' corner. 'That's why he bought it off Mr Jack.'

'That's what he told his wife, more like.'

She turned her shoulder on them, explaining to me that she was talking about his lordship's son.

'You'll not have run across him, because he doesn't get about much nowadays. In a wheelchair, poor lad.'

I gulped, but she was too busy defending both Ricky Marvell and Mr Jack to notice. Clearly she had the soft spot for a rogue, like many a strong-minded female, because this doubty scourge of the male gender was loudly claiming that boys will be boys, although she did concede that both these high-spirited lads had done well to marry sensible Yorkshire lasses, Ricky in particular. For while it was a national disgrace you didn't see him on the telly any more, there was no denying his career wasn't what it used to be, and he might be hard pressed these days to go shooting ducks in a fairground, never mind grouse, if he hadn't had Mavis salting away his money over the years in a nice steady hotel business, instead of letting him fritter it on daft stuff like shooting lodges.

'Oh, come on, Eileen,' cried the head musketeer. 'That place were Ricky's shagging shed.'

'What's a shagging shed?' piped up Jimmy, and Eileen glared at the youth who didn't miss a beat.

'Place for rearing rare breeds of sheep, Harry Potter,' he said, and shot a crooked grin at me. 'That's why he had to get shut of your place. He'd spun the wife this tale about being stranded with his car wrong side of the beck one weekend when it were hosing down, only Mavis come sneaking over the footbridge and finds a little Polo alongside his Jag, and the owner alongside him, upstairs.'

'I'd heard he got two in the bed,' objected his sidekick.

The third of the trio mimed puking. 'How's he pull women at his age?'

'I'm warning you...' growled Eileen.

But they were irrepressible. 'Well, you know what they say about Ricky.' The first lad thrust up his groin and sketched a mighty protuberance before bethinking himself of Jimmy, and winking. 'Grows champion marrows, he does, along with keeping his fancy sheep.'

Even Eileen had to laugh, and everyone else was hooting – everyone except me. I just stared into space, open-mouthed. Forget the rattling wagon, I was back in a dimly lit wine bar in Battersea, with a damson-lipsticked, letterbox-wide smile flashing at me from the other side of the table.

'Hung like a *donkey*, darling, believe me.' That was what she'd said. With a confiding giggle as she divided the remains of the bottle between our glasses. 'Ricky is the original answer to a maiden's prayer. Because let's be honest, it's only bloody men who say size doesn't matter, isn't it?'

And *now* I knew why my husband had failed to fill me in on previous owners of Beck Holme. Knew that, and was dazedly working out a whole lot more besides.

'Jo?' said my friend Jimmy. 'You cross or summat?'

6

The wagon had barely jolted to a halt in the stable-yard before I leaped down. Miraculously, my mobile was in the car. More miraculously still, in these parts, there was a signal and the battery wasn't flat. For six long months I had refused to speak to my husband, communicating by letter if I had to. Just now, though, I would have scorched holes in the paper. Cross? I was incandescent.

Sorry, I'm not explaining myself. She in the wine bar, she of the letterbox smile and the what you might call hands-on experience of Ricky Marvell's assets, was none other than Gaynor Steele, last sighted amid the scented suds in Wimbledon. Time was, you see, when I'd been quite friendly with the woman. She was Mike's number two in a company which was mine as much as his, technically, so when I dropped into the office we girls would occasionally share a bottle over the road. On that particular day, I recalled nodding wisely as she held forth on comparative sizes of the male member, too wimpish to quip that it was twenty years since I'd done any market research. I'd liked her, yes, but smart, sassy Gaynor could always make me feel a frump, a fool and – let's be honest – a bit of a failure. Not least when she gushed the kind of patronizing twaddle sophisticated working women do gush about admiring your happy family, lovely home, adorable kids. You know, like, who needs a glittering career, a sports car, a flat in Notting Hill and a backlist of lovers bearing more than a passing resemblance to the *Sunday Times* Rich List, when you could be baking apple pies? Given the number and calibre of her exes, it was hardly surprising I hadn't instantly remembered the connection between her and Ricky.

'Mike Patterson,' I snapped, when a voice I didn't even know carolled 'Big Event, can I help you-oo?' And then: 'One moment, please. Who shall I say is calling?'

'His wife. And I want to speak to him this minute.'

But I was making all the connections now. *Mike* hadn't dreamed up the bright notion of booking the wrinkled rocker for that sales convention, *she* had. This wasn't even guesswork. At the time, he'd handsomely awarded all credit for the success of the event to his talented sidekick. So let us suppose she had thereby learned that this former lover of hers had a property to offload in usefully remote North Yorkshire...

'Jo? Christ, is that really you?'

Do you see why I was mad? My bloody husband hadn't taken soundings in my soul and discerned my heart's desire for a country cottage. No, he'd simply listened to his floozy's smart scheme for shovelling the wife 250 miles out of their adulterous way. And if I didn't stay good and angry, I might just collapse and sob my heart out.

'Ricky Marvell,' I snarled.

Aidan was approaching with my pay packet, and his roll-up tumbled to the cobbles, he was so startled. I managed a smile, snatched my money and hustled off to a quieter corner of the yard. Still more sickening possibilities were crowding in. She'd already polluted my home in Wimbledon, and if Ricky used to ship his girlfriends up here... 'Oh God,' I burst out, 'don't tell me she's been to Beck Holme, too?'

'What? Actually, love, I've been meaning to ring you. No, listen, this is really important–'

'You're telling me this is important. I met Ricky Marvell on the moor today.'

His voice jumped half an octave. 'You've been talking to Ricky?'

'*Exactly*,' I said. 'I mean, it was obviously her who put you on to buying his – his shagging shed. Oh, get down, Dora.' My dog was very clear on the responsibilities of owners, and Rule One in the manual for the handling of gun dogs is that their welfare must be the owner's overriding priority on returning from a hard day in the field. Warmth, rest and refreshment are to be provided before you so much as pull your boots off.

'Are you talking about Gaynor?'

'No, the Queen of bloody Sheba.' Rule One in the manual for the handling of aberrant husbands is to maintain your cool and your dignity at all costs. Looked like I was failing all round. 'And don't try telling me she didn't have an affair with the guy, because she told me about it herself.'

'Ricky and Gaynor had a brief fling, and it happened a bloody long time ago,' said Mike stiffly. Given what Gaynor had confided about the marvels of Mr Marvell, I could understand him sounding touchy. 'Look, honey–'

'Don't honey me. Of all the holiday cottages in all the counties of England, you just happen to stumble on the one belonging to your floozy's ex-lover? A likely–'

The miracles ran out here. My mobile might be present, charged and receiving, but it was a long time since I'd bought a phonecard and my credit had expired.

I was still twitching as I bundled the dog into the car and set off for home. The phone started chirping as we pulled out of the castle gates, but I ignored it. I wasn't going to have a screaming row with my husband while driving along one-track roads infested with kamikaze sheep. In fact, I told myself, clutching the steering wheel tightly, I wasn't going to have a screaming row at all. Still less was I going to weep. I would just express my feelings, calmly, logically, collectedly – and make that bastard wish he'd never been born.

There was a sticky moment when I crested the hill and saw my cottage nestling in the valley, under the warm gold of the sinking sun. All this time, Beck Holme had been my talisman, my rock-solid proof there was hope for my marriage. The idea that this token of love might have been just a toy to keep the old cat out of the mice's playground was unbearable.

'You've got it all wrong,' declared Mike before

I could say a word. He'd rung on the house phone as I clattered food into Dora's bowl. 'Sure, it was Gaynor introduced me to Ricky, when she hired him to do a gig last year. You won't remember, but–'

'I remember. Make-up ladies.'

'Right, yeah. Well, we got talking in the bar afterwards, like you do, and one thing led to another. Snowballed, really.' That breezy insouciance didn't fool me. He was skittery as a cat on a glass roof. 'Great guy, isn't he? We hit it off from the word go.'

Phone wedged between chin and shoulder, I was stomping across to the sink to fill Dora's water dish. 'And he just happened to mention, completely out of the blue, he'd got a cottage for sale in Yorkshire?'

There was a telling pause. 'What exactly's Ricky been saying to you?'

That he'd see me around – *Gorgeous?* 'He didn't have to say anything,' I snapped, weary thigh muscles screaming as I squatted to give the pooch her drink. I could have done with a drink myself, and I didn't mean water. I began flinging open cupboard doors. 'Once I'd heard he flogged you this place, it wasn't hard to put two and two together and come up with someone last November who had good reason to want me out of the way.'

'Well, you've added up wrong.' Was I imagining things, or did he sound relieved? 'For your information, this time last year there was nothing like that between me and Gaynor. *Nothing*, OK?' He was either telling the truth, or he'd become a much smarter liar in the past six months. 'And for what it's worth,' he continued self-righteously, 'she's never clapped eyes on Beck Holme, let alone stayed there.'

'You reckon?' The sarcasm was reflexive. I didn't disbelieve him, and I suppose I was glad the woman hadn't frolicked in another of my bathtubs, but all at once I didn't want to be talking to Mike. I should never have broken my silence. Angry with myself now, as much as him, I was dog-tired and I bloody well needed that drink. I kicked open yet another cupboard. Half a sodding inch of cherry brandy, and I loathe cherry brandy. It was the old witch's preferred Sunday tipple.

'You were the one walked out on this marriage, you know. I said–'

I cut across ruthlessly. I'd started, so I might as well finish. 'You're telling me Gaynor had *nothing* to do with you buying this cottage?'

'The grief she's given me recently, you'd think she was cursing the day she ever introduced me to Ricky Marvell.' His sudden bitterness startled me so much, I barely noticed he'd dodged the question. 'Anyway that's not why I'm ringing. Look–' But here he stopped dead. So dead, I broke off from my booze hunt to shake the receiver.

'Mike?'

A great sigh gusted into my ear. 'God, darling, where do I start?'

I stiffened, reclamping the phone tight to my ear. 'Sorry?'

'It's just... I don't even know if I can tell you.'

'Tell me what?' Excitement was tightening my throat. Was this it? Right out of nowhere, just when I'm thinking all is lost, he's springing the big repentance scene?

'Oh, Jo, everything's gone wrong these past few months. Badly, horribly wrong.'

This *is* it. Bloody hell. Have I got time to get to a hairdresser before he arrives and sod the leg wax? 'Oh, love, what's happened?' As if I didn't know.

'It's...'

'Yes?'

'It's the company, Jo. We've gone bust.'

There was one consolation. I found wedged at the back of the pan cupboard a dusty bottle of Liebfraumilch bought at the village store in a bleak moment – but not bleak enough, once I got home, actually to drink the stuff. By the time Mike rang off, I'd glugged back two-thirds, which can't have improved my grasp of the financial ins-and-outs. Anyway, he's useless at telling a straight story at the best of times, and particularly now, when he was chiefly concerned with listing the 1001 ways in which he was not personally to blame for the catastrophe. Some things never change.

It seemed our exasperated bankers had pulled the plug after one of our biggest customers folded, owing us a packet. Sounded like other debts had been piling up, too, but I ignored the detail in favour of unravelling the main plot, and began at length to discern that the situation might not be nearly so grim as Mike had at first suggested. Another trait typical of my husband. Works strictly in black and white; shades of grey do not feature on his palette.

'So what you're actually telling me,' I persisted, 'is that we *haven't* gone down the plughole yet? This big firm – what d'you say they're called?'

'Optimax. Optimax Leisure Holdings.'

'They're offering to invest? Rescue us?'

'If you call taking us over, lock, stock and barrel, investing, sure. They'll shoulder the debts, keep the firm in business, that's all.' He snorted. 'But they're giving me nothing up front. Just a lousy forty K a year, provided I sign on their dotted bloody line. I'd as soon tell them to get stuffed and jack it all in, whatever Gaynor says.'

I flinched. 'Can we leave her out?'

He grunted an apology, and made some attempt not to mention her again, but it was transparently plain she was pushing this deal for all she was worth. And what *really* got up my nose was that she'd been trotting out the most unexceptionable common sense about bowing to the inevitable and making the best of a bad situation. Bashing sense into my husband's stupid head was *my* prerogative.

'But I don't want to answer to them – or anyone,' he wailed when, much against my will, I had to agree with Gaynor that forty grand a year and a company still trading was preferable to sweet FA and the Official Receivers. 'Why'd the bank have to put the boot in now – *now* of all times?'

Tempted to enquire, tartly, when might be considered a good time to lose control of one's company, I let it pass. I never got round to establishing Gaynor's role in the buying of my house, either. Still less did I relieve my feelings by blasting this faithless pig off the face of the earth. No, I ended up comforting my poor dejected boy. Old habits die hard.

When, then, did the worm of suspicion begin to wriggle? The suspicion that, within a month, would have me biting my lips, fluffing my fringe, and tugging down a too-short skirt outside a dauntingly grand, pillared and panelled door in Mayfair?

Not that night, certainly. Oh, as I flopped into bed, I half recalled Lord Bidcombe's yarn about his friend's firm, snatched from the corporate giant's jaws by the nephew with the wacky name and wackier job. I saw no parallel though. Partly because, whatever planet his loopy lordship inhabited, I felt it bore little relation to real life as lived by the rest of us. Partly because, at that moment, I didn't give a damn about our company.

My romantic husband would have been proud of me. As I lay in bed with the dregs of the Liebfraumilch curdling my innards, and the dog I'd sworn would never set foot up the stairs snoring into my ear, I was more concerned with auditing my failing marriage than our failed company. Wondering why, after six months of non-communication, Mike seemed to think he could talk to me as if – well, as if nothing had happened. As though he weren't shacked up with his floozy, and I weren't stranded up here with a dog on his side of the bed. Was this a sign our marriage still functioned – or that he thought I'd accepted the split? Please God, not that. He did actually say talking to me had made him feel better. Should we have talked more in the past, as all those bloody patch-up-your-marriage manuals bleat? It was a long time since we'd gone in for the intimate candlelit dinners routine, setting aside the odd birthday, anniversary or power cut, but what d'you expect after twenty-one years of marriage? And even if I'd been Simone de Beauvoir at the table, Delia Smith in the kitchen and Cleopatra upstairs, Ms Steele would have trumped me with her sudden yen to play Hammerstein to his Rodgers. Likely story, huh? If Mike had been into morris dancing, she'd probably have turned up to the office in a flower-strewn boater with bells on her Manolo Blahniks. But of course he fell for it.

'With someone like Gaynor, I can see over the horizon,' he had memorably declared, when we were going the rounds of bloody recriminations. 'Can't you understand, I've got to do something with my life before it's too late? I'll be fifty soon. I have to get out of this rut.'

Rut. Twenty-one years of blood, sweat, tears – of love, labour and laughs, written off in that single, miserable syllable. It had cut me to the quivering quick. I might have yelled that this rut was about to become a wife-free zone, but I'd cursed myself all the same for not having seen the mid-life crisis looming. If nothing else, I should have wondered why, after years of boring me cross-eyed with tricky middle eights and intractable plot knots, Mike had hummed me not a tune, quoted not a line of the masterpiece the pair of them had supposedly been honing night after night.

God's sake, why couldn't he just have fallen for some bimbo baby blonde? At least I'd have understood the boost to his menopausal ego, but Gaynor was thirty-eight. *Thirty-eight.* Nearly as old as me, and not even that attractive. Well, OK, she had long legs (if stringy), improbably voluptuous boobs for such a skinny frame (silicone?), and crow-black hair which was most certainly dyed and swung across her thin, wide-mouthed face in a severely geometric bob. So she had a certain style. Glamour, if you like that kind of thing. Oh, sod it, she looked what she was: a classy, Cambridge-educated careerist with a glitzy c.v. covering everything from PR to magazines to television. Why shouldn't Mike fall for Gaynor Steele? Hundreds of other men had.

'But what the *hell*,' I burst out, unable to contain my misery any longer, 'does Gaynor Steele see in my husband?'

As it happens, I was to discover several answers to that question, and Mike's cute bum wasn't amongst them. But that night, I didn't suspect a thing. Just call me dumb.

7

I suppose I should have smelled a rat when the contracts were delivered by courier's van the next morning, but all I felt was exasperated. These contracts of sale for The Big Event Ltd to Optimax Leisure Holdings were thick as telephone directories, and flanked by a brain-numbing wad of other bumf. No way had this lot been drawn up since I spoke to Mike yesterday. The lawyers must have been at it for weeks, and yet here he was, in two miserable lines scribbled on a compliments slip, saying the screws were being put on him, so could I sign and zap back the relevant bits today, '24 hr delivery, pref'?

'Why didn't he tell me before?' I demanded of Dora, my temper not improved by a hangover from last night's methylated syrup. 'I own half the bloody company. Didn't I have a right to know?'

But this was typical. Mike would always dodge breaking bad news. In the far-off days when I'd worked alongside him in the firm, he hadn't got round to mentioning we were being threatened with eviction until the new tenants' carpet-fitters rolled up.

'Slight cash shortfall,' he'd airily declared. 'Nothing we can't sort.'

I tell you, he's Mr Micawber captaining the *Titanic*. Not only does he live in perpetual sunny faith something will turn up, if that something chances to be an iceberg, he's sublimely confident his ship is unsinkable anyway. And for all I might have spent twenty-one years on lifeboat alert, the truly maddening thing about Mike was how often rescue *did* turn up. We were saved from eviction all those years ago by a forgotten Premium Bond. Now it seemed the good ship Optimax had steamed alongside our struggling craft, offering all hands billets aboard their luxury fleet. Galling though it was, I could see why the floozy had urged him to accept.

That didn't mean, leafing through the various papers, I wasn't riled by the number of times her name seemed to crop up. There were endless references to informal undertakings between HRS (whoever he might be), MP (I knew who he was) and GMS.

'M for Medusa?' I growled, and flung all the explanatory gobbledegook into the cardboard box under the table which served as my filing cabinet. I did cast a conscientious eye over the contracts, however. I might only be signing away my half-share in a few ropey computers and a coffee machine, but it was the least I owed to the company I'd co-founded – the company I'd set up near single-handed, in truth, given my husband's reluctance to 'prostitute his art'. That's what the man had said. At the time, Mike was financing, directing and lute-strumming as Will Scarlet the wand'rin' minstrel in his own pantomime version of *Robin Hood*, at a ramshackle end-of-the-pier theatre where the audience only rarely outnumbered the cast. I

84

recall retorting it was either his art or my body, because something had to be flogged to pay the gas bill.

This was after a bloke from a local tool manufacturer had called by the stage door, asking to hire the auditorium for a sales meeting, and offering us more to rig a few lights and screens for one day than we were taking at the box office in a week. I saw the light. Glory, did I see the light. We were going to do more of this, I announced. Forget theatre on a shoestring for the fickle public, our destiny lay in the fast-growing world of events organizing. We would capitalize on Mike's talents by staging sales conferences, training courses, product launches – all manner of corporate jamborees for fat businessmen with fat corporate wallets. It was probably as well there was no one to tell me this was an industry in which the risks were as heart-stopping as the potential profits, or we might still be pasting up our posters at the end of some godforsaken pier. As it was, in spite of some very narrow shaves over the years, we'd ended up with a company equipped to lay on everything from logo-stamped pencils, cheese rolls and an overhead projector in a hotel room, to the Spice Girls in a laser-lit, dry-ice-swirling arena, with a cast of thousands, buckets of caviare and live elephants.

And I freely acknowledge our success was down to Mike. He was the one who created and staged these shows. Brilliant at it he was, too, endlessly inventive and adored by the clients, even if he did whinge on the quiet about pouring his creative heart and soul into a grand opera starring a new make of lavatory cleaner. He'd consoled himself, when my eye was off him, with the odd foray back into 'real' showbusiness. You know, the kind where the audience actually buys tickets. Or, in his case, doesn't.

Well, there'd be no more of that tomfoolery, I reflected, groping for a working pen, because I didn't doubt that Mike's new bosses would be even stroppier than his wife about stunts like TBE presenting a series of open-air concerts in the wettest summer since Noah built his Ark. Yes, it was a shame our firm was losing its independence, but at least he'd be getting what had been my Holy Grail in the rockier years: a regular, guaranteed income.

'Every cloud...' I murmured, and signed my name bold and clear under Mike's scrawl. Nothing could have been further from my mind than a trip to London – as, a few days later, I was to make very clear to my son.

'On yer bike,' I growled into the phone, before clamping my fingers across the mouthpiece, and leaning towards the open door. 'Take a pew, Eileen, with you in a tic.'

Trust Ben finally to ring just as I'd ushered Eileen Muxworthy into my sitting room, with an armful of curtain material. After weeks of silence during which I'd imagined him variously pasted across a highway, shot, and consumed by grizzly bears or great white sharks – depending on which part of the North American continent he might have reached – he had at last deigned to communicate the unspeakable hour at which his plane was due back into Manchester Airport. Not only was this a week later than agreed, he followed up with a cheery suggestion that his mum could use the spare time to pop down to London and collect a computer his dad was saving for him.

'Drive five hundred miles?' I cried, ignoring his protestations that he needed something to work on when staying with me. Apart from the fact he was flying home with barely a day to spare here before clocking back into university, the words 'Ben' and 'homework' are about as compatible as Margaret Thatcher and lap dancing. Not that I doubted he'd find uses for a computer, but I could do without my telephone bill being escalated into telephone numbers by his gambols round the internet. So I told him the petrol would cost more than that old Commodore in the spare bedroom was worth, and anyway didn't he remember it'd been on the blink ever since his dad knocked a bottle of vodka over the keyboard? But Ben's scornful retort silenced me.

'One of the office machines?' I said. 'How come?'

'Thing is my sister's pricklier than a flaming hedgehog,' Eileen resumed, when I eventually rejoined her in the sitting room. 'So not a word to Megan nor anyone else about me paying you to make these here curtains for her, do you hear?'

I heard, but I wasn't listening. I was thinking about my own flaming husband.

'I'm having to tell her they're just summat my extravagant madam of a daughter-in-law's chucking out, because I tell you, I can't stand the sight of our Meg's front room one minute longer.' Fortunately, she didn't seem to expect a response as she chuntered on about the Brighouses saving every penny, with Megan – who'd always been a worrier – insisting there was no point replacing curtains if they were moving out any day...

This caught my ear only because her words echoed Ben's. I'd just learned from my son – by mere chance – that any day now the company I had until so recently half owned was moving out of our premises in Battersea, and into the Optimax HQ somewhere down Docklands way. Thus this computer – a very smart iMac, barely a year old – was being discarded, along with (by the sound of it) all the rest of TBE's motley gear, as they upgraded in line with their new owners. OK, so I couldn't think offhand of any items I wanted to salvage from the office, but as co-owner I did think I should bloody well have been consulted. 'Are the Brighouses going?' I enquired distractedly. 'I didn't realize.'

'More than like, if his lordship has to sell up. Because even if t'shooting stays with the estate, and the castle isn't turned into some fancy hotel like folks are talking about, our Aidan's past sixty. Besides, he's a cussed old sod.' She was groping for her handbag. 'Stands to reason a fancy new owner'll want a fancy new keeper.'

'I'd no idea Lord Bidcombe was in such dire straits,' I responded, reflecting that going bust must be like getting pregnant. All of a sudden, the whole world seems to be in the same boat as you. But losing our own premises somehow made it all more real. And the sheer speed of the thing unsettled me. The ink was scarcely dry on the contracts.

'Writing's been on the wall for years. But ... but time was, we thought – we all thought – his nephew were going to step in and sort things out ... only now, who knows?'

'You mean his nephew the–?' The spook, I was about to say. But I didn't, because I looked up and, to my utter astonishment, saw that my visitor – bluff, gruff, tough-as-a-tractor Eileen – was quietly sobbing her heart out.

'Was I heckers like,' she growled a few minutes later, stuffing away a hankie as I poured her a mug of tea. 'Bit of a cold coming on, that's all.' But a tell-tale sigh escaped her. 'For all it's enough to wring tears from a statue.'

Of course there's nothing like hearing about other people's troubles to take your mind off your own. Not that I worried about Lord Bidcombe ending up on the streets, butler and all, but I felt truly sorry for the Brighouses. Aidan was a cussed old sod, yes, but you'd have to be an idiot not to discern the butter-soft heart within. Only yesterday I'd found him in my garden patching up a collapsed section of the wall; my fridge door was sagging under the weight of eggs from Megan's hens he'd thrust into my hands before leaving; and I knew I could count on them to look after Dora for me when I went to collect Ben from the airport. Mind, what Aidan had actually said was that he didn't want sheep poisoning themselves on my poncey plants, that he was fast getting egg-bound the rate them bloody hens were laying, and that it would be a pleasure to take Dora off my hands any time, just to stop me spoiling a promising little gun dog rotten. Then slipped her a biscuit from his pocket when he thought I wasn't looking. I could see why Eileen was upset. The Brighouses were country folk, through and through. They'd be wretched as beached dolphins in a terraced house in Wykesea, with a yard out the back and pavement under their front doorstep. But Eileen seemed to think they'd be lucky to afford even that, at today's silly property prices. They'd have a pension, of course, but they'd been counting on his lordship to rent them a retirement cottage locally. At this her voice cracked again, and she had to blow her nose before declaring, perhaps with more hope than conviction, that she for one hadn't totally given up on Major McGinty, not yet.

'For I'll not hear a word against him,' she added defiantly. 'There's none of us knows the full story, but what I've always said is that Mr Jack's done more bloody stupid things in a week than Paddy'll get round to in a lifetime.' She blew her nose again. 'And never mind the money, he's the only one left in that family with owt more than air between his ears.'

Only nosiness prompted me to wonder what particular bloody stupid thing this Paddy McGinty might have done – perhaps because it was obvious from the guarded way others as well Eileen talked that there was some local scandal concerning him and Jack Bidcombe. Never for an instant, though, did I suppose I might find myself needing the professional services of just such a snooper into – how had his uncle phrased it? The bare-faced villainy abounding in blue-chip boardrooms? Quite. Anyway, I got no chance to indulge even this twinge of idle curiosity, because Eileen was already recalling a time their farm's tax had got into a mess – blame for which she apportioned even-handedly between a gin-sodden accountant and a husband who, she declared, was as much use as a rubber cricket bat when it came to bookwork.

I winced. 'Join the club.'

'Aye, but Paddy heard and come round to give us a hand, that's the point,' she said. 'And instead of having to sell a dozen cows, we ended up buying a new bloody tractor. By, he can make figures dance, can that lad.'

It goes without saying I was only joking when I suggested she shove this financial genius my own husband's way, for all it was a bit late now.

'Another woman was it, brought you flitting up here?' asked Eileen, so unexpectedly I nearly dropped my mug. 'Nay, don't colour up, I'll not pry. All the same, men, silly buggers. Most of them see sense in th'end, though, and if yours doesn't, he wasn't worth the trouble in t'first place, was he?' On which brisk piece of philosophy, she hauled herself to her feet, enquired what the curtain-making would cost, and steamrollered over my protest that, with Aidan and Meg in such straits, I hardly felt able to charge.

'This is your bread and butter,' she said sternly.

91

'And don't try telling me you don't need the money, because I wasn't born yesterday.'

I was flushing still brighter now, but I gave in because Eileen was right about this, too. I did need the money.

My penurious state, I should say, had nothing to do with the demise of our company. Life had been hand-to-mouth ever since I decamped to Yorkshire. One of the jibes Mike had flung at me was that I saw him only as a meal ticket, so from the day I left, I'd proudly disdained to touch our joint accounts. I'd show him. Fortunately, for some years, I had been earning a little money of my own. Once both company and kids outgrew me, I'd taken courses in upholstery and soft furnishing – much to my daughter's disgust.

'Good degree, and you want to run up curtains? Honestly, Mother, you're not over the hill yet. Why don't you get out into the world and find a proper career now you've got the chance?'

'Retrain as a nuclear physicist, perhaps? Amateur brain surgeon?'

I wasn't going to admit to my daughter that the world's a daunting prospect for someone who stumbled into motherhood even before graduating. And it gave me a certain satisfaction, once I was up here, to point out that proper careers weren't nearly as portable as sewing machines. I was, I said, placing an ad in the *Wykesea Gazette* forthwith.

'I despair of you,' she'd sighed.

True, I soon discovered the going rates for soft furnishing in North Yorkshire were a joke compared to those in the affluent Home Counties, but my needle had been keeping us in baked beans and dog biscuits. Just about. There wasn't much left in the kitty for unforeseen expenditure, however, such as my son staggering out of the Arrivals Gate at Ringway Airport with his trainers falling apart, his jeans covered in creosote and his only weather-proof jacket somewhere on Staten Island.

In the forty-eight hours Ben stayed with me before returning to college – forty of them comatose on his part – I naturally frogmarched him off to re-equip his wardrobe, and also buy the stack of books he was supposed to have been studying all summer, instead of windsurfing off Long Island. Yeah, yeah, yeah, he mumbled between yawns, he'd had a pretty good time. Oh – just friends of friends. You know.

A mother can take a hint. I stopped probing, telling myself it was a good sign he'd felt able to go away this vac, unlike Easter, when he'd stayed here the whole five weeks, using revision for his first-year exams as an excuse for keeping a beady eye on his newly single parent. He'd actually spent most of the time out and about in my car, using my petrol. Visiting the library? I don't think so. But the thought had been sweet, and the cottage, frankly, more comfortable for his absence. He's at the age and size where he'd make any premises short of the Albert Hall feel cramped. When I packed him off back to York this time, complete with new clothes, books and – yes, I'm a soft touch – a new CD player, my home felt as if a tornado had hurtled through.

Once I'd recovered, though, I drove to the bank in Wykesea to reimburse myself for all the expenditure. I had no qualms about Mike supporting his children, and wrote a hefty cheque to cash on the joint account. It bounced. Or rather, the lady teller, lowering her voice to a hushed whisper suitable for breaking news of death or syphilis in the family, informed me that the household account registered in their Wimbledon branch to Mr and Mrs M. Patterson appeared to be overdrawn.

'Lord, by how much?' I said. Typical Mike, I was thinking, neglecting to keep the current account topped up. That man was incapable of so much as wiping his nose without me there to remind him.

She tapped her little monitor. 'Four thousand, three hundred and seventy-six pounds,' she said. 'And thirteen pence.'

'Four *thousand*...?' I gulped. 'Could you, um, check a couple of other accounts for me?'

8

'Thirty-eight thousand in the red?' I shouted in a Tandoori-perfumed telephone kiosk fifty yards down from the bank. I'd never got round to buying a card for my mobile, so I was feeding coins into the box like sardines to a starving penguin, having tracked my husband down on his. 'You been buying up Asprey's for that woman?'

'Very funny.' Wherever Mike was, all hell and a rock band were letting rip in the background.

'You think I'm joking?' I shrieked, and a little old lady waiting outside the box nearly fell over her shopping trolley. I didn't care. 'Where's it all gone then?'

'Where d'you think?' A sigh gusted down the phone. 'I was trying to prop up the firm because I thought if I could just keep us trading for a bit, something–'

'Something might turn up? Oh my *God*. That's all I needed.'

'OK, OK, so it was dick-brained,' he bellowed back. 'As Gaynor's never stopped telling me, chucking good money after bad. No, listen, Jo. You always said I never admit mistakes, but I am now, right? I screwed up. I should've listened to her and sold out to Optimax months back, but I was desperate to hang on. I wanted to stay my own boss, can't you understand that? I needed freedom to–' He caught himself up, finishing limply: 'You know, freedom to operate.'

'Freedom to bankrupt us, more like.'

'Bullshit. We've plenty of money in property.'

'If you're talking about Beck Holme, Mike, just remember *I* own that cottage.'

'I meant home. House's worth a packet now, and the mortgage is peanuts. We're not... What's that noise?'

'Telephone's rejected my last twenty pence... Oh, *sugar*.'

I waited, seething, in the stinking kiosk with the old lady still eyeing me warily through the glass, for Mike to trace the number and ring back. He

95

didn't. Maybe this stupid machine wouldn't accept incoming calls. Fine, I'd finish the row at home, and let Mrs Shopping Trolley in here. But as I bashed open the door, she took off down the street. Possibly because I'd let out a manic cackle of laughter after noticing the dingy shop front opposite. Dangling over the door, with what struck me as grim appropriateness, was a trio of golden balls. I could hardly wait to tell my feckless spouse I'd located the neighbourhood pawnbroker. See what he said when I told him I might have to flog my jewellery to settle the credit-card bills I'd run up clothing his poor son.

During the drive home, however, I had second thoughts. I wish I could say I'd begun to wonder why Mike had been so desperate to avoid selling out to Optimax, but in truth I wasn't thinking beyond my marriage. I was pondering his glib comment that we still had money in property. Surely – surely, he couldn't already have contemplated selling our home? Because that was the road to the divorce court and Mike had never said anything to me about a divorce. No, he hadn't – truly he had not, whatever Sarah reckoned. And why? Because he didn't want a divorce, that was why. Somewhere, deep down, he knew this affair was an aberration, an infatuation which would blow over, once the novelty wore off. It *would* blow over. Course it would. Except... The upshot was that, by the time I sploshed through the ford, I'd come round to thinking it might be wiser not to press him about money, not right now. I'd arrange for the bank to supply me with duplicate statements, just to keep an eye on the debts, but the last thing I wanted was to prompt Mike into any wild ideas of selling our family home. I wasn't destitute yet, not quite.

And who knows? I might be playing that chicken-hearted, lame-brained waiting game still, had not our old friend Gilbert Rydall turned up and, as he would probably have expressed it, put a rocket up my arse. Not that he intended to do any such thing.

'Long time, no see,' he mumbled as he stood on my doorstep, arms bulging with assorted bits of computer. 'Glad you're still in the land of the living, anyhow.' He glanced back over his shoulder with a stifled shudder. 'Up to a point.'

I admit the place wasn't looking its glorious best that afternoon. But even if the valley hadn't been shrouded in drizzling fog, Gil's no country lover. He'd long ago observed to me that if God had intended man to paddle in mud He wouldn't have invented pavements. Fifty-nine, gay, and bald as an egg with bloodhound eyes and a luxuriant pewter moustache which he chewed when worried – which is to say most of the time – he'd been the perfect company manager for a cock-eyed dreamer like my husband. Mike used to complain the miserable sod's profits forecasts made Nostradamus sound like a stand-up comic. Gil, for his part, marvelled at himself for putting up with an employer who thought end-of-year figures came from eating too much over Christmas. For all his grumbling, though, and regular resignations, I had no doubt Gil would have been holding the firm together still if he hadn't felt duty-bound to take early retirement and look after his barmy old mum in Eastbourne. And while he might swear that coping with a parent who intermittently believed she was the Queen Mother was a cakewalk after playing Sancho Panza to Mike's bloody Quixote all these years, I'd never underestimated the bond between them. Mike used to say we had a three-way marriage, with Gil in the middle.

'You're looking well,' he offered, chomping his moustache furiously as I joined him at the kitchen table, teapot in hand. He didn't add 'considering everything', but that was what he meant.

'Dog keeps me fit,' I responded with a tight smile, stopping just short of quipping 'and the bed warm'. He'd have heard my unspoken words too. Very sharp, Gil.

I suppose it's bound to be a minefield, seeing your husband's best buddy for the first time after a marital split, but there was a further twist here. Gil was also soulmates from way back with the floozy. He it was who'd actually recruited Gaynor into his job when he quit. Do you wonder our small talk over the teacups was stilted?

'So you've brought your mum up to stay with her sister in Harrogate?'

'Balmoral, if you don't mind.'

'Sorry?'

There was a glimmer of the old smile. 'I think we're in Scotland, at any rate. Because when they caught her halfway down the avenue at three o'clock this morning, in her dressing gown and Auntie Connie's wellies, she said she was off to catch a couple of trout for Prince Philip's tea.' He shook his head gloomily. 'No, don't laugh. The policeman was very kind.'

'Oh, Gil,' I exclaimed, 'I have missed you.'

He jumped like a startled hare. I bit my lip, and he glanced away, mumbling something about being here now, anyhow, thanks to Ben. I should say that my unscrupulous son, having failed to persuade me to drive down to town just to collect the computer from his dad, had somehow got wind of Uncle Gil's plan to visit Yorkshire, and hit the phone with the speed of a timeshare salesman. 'Little monster,' I said, and braced myself to name the ghost hovering between us. 'So, how was Mike?'

But in the selfsame instant, Gil asked how our boy genius was taking to the big corporate merry-go-round. At least it made us laugh.

'You first,' I said. 'You collected the machine from him at Optimax, didn't you?'

He didn't reply at once. In fact, as pregnant pauses go, this one seemed to be having twins. 'Mike left it for me at reception, actually,' he said at length. 'Matter of fact, I haven't seen hide nor hair of him since you bust up.' There was another significant silence, as he studied the holes in his digestive biscuit. 'Nor Gaynor.'

'Oh?' I couldn't pretend to be sorry, but I was certainly surprised.

'Probably – probably they think I'm your shoulder for crying on.' Suddenly he burst out: 'And you've cut me dead, because you obviously blame me for the whole frigging mess, but honestly, love, when I brought Gaynor into the

99

firm, I never in a million years dreamed she and Mike would get off together.'

'Course you didn't,' I cried, astonished. 'Strewth, I don't blame you, Gil.'

He did though, because Gil had always blamed himself for everything from the weather upwards. So what with my trying to explain I hadn't phoned him only because I'd been reluctant to strain his conflicting loyalties, and his insisting I'd every right to cross him off my Christmas-card list in perpetuity, we nearly wept on one another's shoulders and enjoyed a good old moan about my bloody husband, just as we'd always done. I was, actually, pretty disgusted at the way Mike and Gaynor had dropped their old friend, obviously as selfishly engrossed in one another as a pair of teenagers. But we delicately avoided mentioning her as we swapped family news, gossip and reminiscences in the old comfortable way, neither of us suspecting the bombshell that was about to detonate.

'Remember the time in Southport the power failed?' sighed Gil. 'And Mike kept three hundred hard-bitten insurance salesmen doing community singing for an hour and a half?'

I remembered – oh, how I remembered. Those were the days when our entire staff had comprised Mike, Gil and a secretary, so I was the company all-purpose odd-jobber. I painted stands, drove limos, rolled out red carpets, mollified fractious clients, rounded up brass-players from the pub – you name it. On the night Gil was talking about, I'd gone hurtling across the town to yank the hall's chief electrician out of his daughter's wedding party, while my husband plonked himself at the piano with a brace of candles. 'And they said it was the best conference they'd ever had,' I said, smiling nostalgically.

'Mike could always make the good times roll,' said Gil, 'whatever and wherever.'

'We used to have fun in those days, didn't we? Before we got big and professional.'

'Bloody chaotic half the time. Mind, even when you wanted to throttle our golden boy, because he'd lost half the running order again, he'd make you laugh – and you knew he'd wing it, one way or another. Talent and charm in equal quantities. I should think Optimax are over the moon, getting him on board.' As he leaned back, grinning, he caught sight of his watch. 'Jeez, is it five o'clock already? I promised Auntie Connie I'd be back by gin time. She's got the vicar round, keeping Ma under surveillance.'

As I held out his coat, he leaned towards me with a shy grin. 'Well, come on then, love. Before I hit the road again, brighten my sad old life and tell me how much.'

I looked back blankly. I half thought he was inviting me to guess how much his admittedly handsome sheepskin had cost.

'Optimax, you pillock,' he said, shouldering himself into it. 'Aren't you going to let me know what you screwed them for?' He must have misunderstood my hesitation, because he continued hastily: 'Sorry, sorry, none of my business these days, but I was the one at the table with the calculator last time we had some of the big hitters sniffing round, remember–'

'*Last* time?'

'You know, couple of years back, the ITI group? My scarf there? Yeah, I reckoned, with the share options and deferred bonuses and the rest, I could have pushed the total package up to three and a half, maybe four mill, if only our beloved boy genius would have played ball, but–' He broke off, leaning forward. 'Jo? Jo, love, are you all right?'

I'd actually choked. 'Four *million?*' I spluttered, when I could get a word out. 'Gil, am I going mad or are you? You surely can't mean someone offered us *four million pounds* for our company?'

He stared back. 'What d'you think I meant? Friggin' jelly beans?'

'My name's Jo Patterson, *Mrs* Patterson,' I said to the black-clad, white-faced supermodel presiding behind the curved slab of granite which passed for a reception desk in the echoing lobby of Optimax Leisure Holdings. You could hangar Concorde in here and still have space for a game of billiards. 'He's expecting me. I'm a bit late, I'm afraid.'

'We need to talk,' I'd stated, with quite wonderful self-restraint, when Mike had finally deigned to answer his mobile phone at something to midnight last night. I'd been ringing ever since Gil left, because his revelation had made a trip to London inevitable, even if the notion of seeking out that discreetly brass-plated door in Mayfair had yet to enter my shell-shocked brain.

'We do?' he'd responded. 'Well, fine. I guess. I'm running round like a blue-arsed on speed just now, but if I can give you a call in the morning, or maybe–'

'In person. Tomorrow. Lunch?' Nothing like striking while the calculator's hot. I'd been busy all evening. The table round me was littered with papers and sums, because Gil had been almost as stupefied as I when I told him we had gone to Optimax for precisely nothing. Oh, he may have backtracked after hearing about the debt problems – in fact, Gil being Gil, he began to blame himself for retiring and abandoning the firm in its hour of need – but that didn't alter the plain facts as far as I was concerned.

'Four million pounds,' I'd breathed, like a record stuck in a groove.

'Fair play, Jo, it wasn't as simple as them handing over a nice fat cheque and waving Mike out of the door. He *is* the firm. They wanted him working for them. Long term.'

'Enough to set the family up for life.'

'Golden handcuffs deal, tying him down every which way. And you know Mike.'

I knew Mike all right. Mike and his precious freedom to operate. When Gil said that, I began to understand why I'd been kept in the dark about that buy-out offer...

'*Tomorrow?*' my husband squawked.

'I'll meet you at work. Don't worry, I'll find the new place.'

'If you'd like to take a seat,' said the super-model now, waving me towards a serpentine sculpture in tubular chrome and scarlet leather. 'He'll be down right away.'

No sooner had I worked out which bit it might

be safe to sit on than I heard the ping of lift doors and suddenly here he was, striding towards me across the glassy marble floor, grinning and holding out his arms: Mike. *Mike*, just as ever was. I hadn't set eyes on my husband in six whole months, and the rush of emotion nearly thumped me back on to the scarlet leather again. To my dismay, given the warpaint I'd pasted on, I felt tears prickle as he clasped my shoulders to kiss me.

'Jo, love...' An inch short of my cheek, he veered aside to call to the receptionist, 'Hey – Carla, isn't it? You know there's an animal loose in here?'

Ah, yes. The animal. When I decided to bolt down to London, I'd taken for granted I could drop Dora off with the Brighouses. Megan was always around the Lodge first thing in the morning, always. Except this morning. What could I do? I was already packaged in heels, tights and the smartest suit I could salvage and sponge down from the back of the wardrobe, and this confrontation with my husband couldn't wait hours, never mind days.

'She's mine,' I faltered, as Dora put her head on one side and surveyed Mike with the air of a country gentlewoman who's suffered five hours in the well of an undersized motor vehicle, has been rudely yanked off flowerbeds in a dusty London park and is finding polished marble chilly under the bum. 'Sorry. That's why I'm late, giving her a run. I meant to leave her in the car, but the only place I could park was in full sun.'

'Noodle,' said Mike, not unaffectionately, and

104

this time he did kiss my cheek. He smelled expensive, exotic – and wrong. In fact, like a blurred picture slowly coming into focus, I realized this wasn't at all my Mike as ever was. His hair was shaved trendily close; he'd acquired one of those droopy suits which look as though they've been tacked together from sacking, and wore a limp charcoal shirt underneath, collarless as well as tieless. All very fashionable, I supposed and, no, I didn't like the new look. Hated it, in fact. Didn't do him any favours, either, because that cropped fuzz showed his hair to be much more grey than blond now, and collarless shirts are not kind to middle-aged necks. Even so, and it pained me immeasurably to admit this, he looked … well. Healthy, vibrant, a-buzz with energy. Dammit, he looked as I hadn't seen him look for years, as though he'd been plugged into an electric light socket. Maybe these sophisticated new premises were suiting him. Better that than his sophisticated new woman.

'Table's booked, but I dunno if they'll let this in,' he said, indicating my pet with one sneaker-clad toe. Sneakers, at his age?

'It's a she, and she's called Dora,' I heard myself saying pettishly, which was all wrong. This was high drama, and I was supposed to be wrathful inquisitress, avenging angel, wronged Madonna – anything but a sad old biddy fussing over her pooch. 'Forget lunch,' I snapped, declaring that I'd come to talk, not eat, and that his office would do fine. Only to falter afresh as, cursing my impetuosity for bundling Dora into the car, I had to enquire in a whisper whether they allowed dogs in here.

'Search me.' Mike glanced, strangely wistfully it seemed to me, towards the big glass doors. 'They issue fatwas on just about everything else. Oh ... I guess we can borrow the conference room.' As he ushered me towards the waiting lift, he shot me a wry grin. 'Typical Jo. Always did pick your bloody moments, didn't you?'

9

'What's that supposed to mean?' I demanded, as the doors whizzed shut behind us. It was a high-speed cube of smoked mirrors, and I looked like a corpse in every direction. My suit was creased, my mascara had dribbled, and my hair resembled nothing so much as the sweepings from a rabbit hutch. Mike's swift hug felt more like sympathy than affection.

'Look, honey, it's great to see you, OK? The stand-off was doing my head in. Just don't tell me, after all this time, you've come storming down to ask for a divorce.'

'*What?*' I yelped, thrown off balance afresh. 'Course not.'

'Thank Christ, because–' The doors flashed apart again, and a female chewing pungently minty gum manoeuvred a computer trolley in.

Because you never wanted a divorce, I was saying rapidly to myself, because you can't imagine a life not married to me, because–

He leaned towards me confidingly, dropping his voice '–because with what I'm juggling right now, that'd definitely be one ball too fucking many.'

We shot up again, leaving my heart somewhere round the fifth floor. At least, in the few seconds before we pinged to a halt at the eighteenth, I realized why he smelled wrong.

'Have you given up the fags?'

'Yup. Kind of. Well – no.' He pulled a crumpled packet out of his pocket, only to stuff it away again. 'No smoking sodding building. This way.'

There was our logo, etched in black on brushed steel across a set of double doors – but even that had changed. Big, bold TBE had become slanting, lower case *tbe*, with a damn silly squiggle underneath. What lay behind the doors, however, in a powerful aroma of paint and new carpet, was even more disconcerting. I could never have believed that this open-plan desert, with its black desks, glass screens, weeping trees and icily bare walls, could be the home of our company. Our offices, and we'd got through a few, had always been a warren of fuggy cubby-holes, with inflatable sharks dangling from the ceiling, obscenely doctored news clippings plastered across the walls, and floor and desks alike submerged under shifting tides of mouldy mugs, lipstick-kissed glasses, staple guns, laddered tights, electric guitars and Lord only knew what else. Music would be thudding and televisions wittering, with no one taking any notice as they yelled into phones or at each other. There was a stifling hush in here. Only two of the eerily blank desks were occupied, and I recognized neither face.

'Lunch exodus,' explained Mike, dodging a glooping watercooler as he hustled me across. 'Company policy to eat your soya bun and bean sprouts in the canteen. Sorry, dining and recreation suite. Fully kitted-up gym too, would you believe. Not that I've been in there, natch. That's me, over in the corner.'

I was looking for a door when, on the wall above a desk perhaps a whisker less barren than its neighbours, I spotted the pink six-legged horse. Sarah's first painting had always hung over Mike's desk. I stared at him. 'You don't even have your own office?'

'Open plan, open minds, open – oh, I forget.'

He shouldered through more swing doors, into a smaller chamber with leather sofas, a low glass table and an entire wall of floor-to-ceiling window. The panorama over the seething metropolis, intersected by one flimsy-looking chrome bar, was like the picture on a Mensa-level jigsaw box. I wasn't surprised Dora snaked under one of the sofas and coiled into a ball. That vertiginous drop made me feel like finding a dark corner, too – or hurling myself over.

Mike kicked the door shut. 'So if you're not after hustling me to the lawyers, what's brought you down?'

Well, I'd never expected him to fall at my feet, had I? Actually, yes, at some unacknowledged level, I probably had. More fool me. I clamped a trembling lip between my teeth and pretended I was mesmerized by the view. Out of the corner of my eye, I saw him digging around in his pocket.

'Sod it.' He shot me a guilty smile as he produced the fag packet. 'If needs be, I'll tell 'em you were a bolshie client who insisted on his democratic right to kill himself.'

I spun round. 'This is *awful*.' I meant the arid building, his miserable desk, the humiliation of having to sneak in here for a smoke like a naughty schoolboy, but he misunderstood.

'I know, I know.' He lowered his lighter, face a-droop with penitence. 'I really hate myself for what I've done to you, done to *us*, but you've got to realize–'

'Not that,' I snapped, which was tactless maybe, but I couldn't face a reprise of his big sackcloth-and-ashes number. 'I'm talking about this place.'

'Oh.' He shrugged and lit his fag. 'Pays the bills. As I'm daily reminded.'

'But they've robbed us blind,' I cried, before remembering where I was. I lowered my voice. 'Look, I saw Gil yesterday.'

'Yeah? I keep meaning to give him a call, only–'

I interrupted without compunction. 'He told me about ITI's offer two years ago.' It wasn't easy to maintain a steady tone. 'Four million quid, Mike?'

At this, he shut his eyes and sighed out a curling plume of smoke. 'So *that's* what it's all about. Did he push them up to four? I forget.' And he might, for all the world, have been querying the price of a bus ticket. I could have shaken him.

'Which you never so much as mentioned to me?'

'Oh, sure. So you could grab the dosh for some lousy pension fund and leave me to rot in harness for the next twenty years earning it?'

'Anything wrong with wanting to secure our family's future?' God, how many times had I yelled this?

'Fuck the future, what about the present?'

'I–' With an effort, I shut my mouth again. I was *not* going to fight the same old battles all over again. That fortune he'd so cavalierly whistled down the wind was history now. It was the penurious present that concerned me.

'I've been going through all the stuff you sent me with the contracts,' I said. 'Carefully, with a calculator. And whichever way I reckoned it, our liabilities didn't add up to more than five hundred grand.' I braced myself for the question that had brought me down to London, the question that was carrying a lot more than sixty-four thousand dollars. 'So tell me, Mike. How come a company worth four million pounds two years ago can be snapped up for debts of less than half a million now?'

I was suddenly aware of the soft sigh of the air conditioning, and a distant – very distant – quaver of a police siren. It felt as if I hadn't heard that familiar urban caterwaul for years.

'Come on, you read about it in the papers every day.' Mike turned away to bury his fag end in a potted fig. 'Dot com outfits worth trillions one minute, can't afford a cheese sandwich the next. Service company like ours is only worth what some mug's willing to pay.' He didn't believe it. I knew my husband, and he was trying to convince himself as much as me. What the hell was going on? He scowled and began rummaging in his pocket again. 'You never had any faith in me, did you, Jo?'

'Can we stick to the point? Which is the value of our company.'

'You think I didn't want this bunch to put cash up front?' His anger, at least, was real enough. 'Blood out of a stone's nothing. Forty grand a year, I ask you.'

'Right now, I'd welcome forty quid,' I snapped back, stung. 'I'm skint, Mike.'

'You're what?' Suddenly, though, he stifled a curse and slung his cigarette packet under a sofa. I heard a soft cough and turned to see in the doorway a slight, grey-suited man with rimless spectacles, choirboy cheeks, and a square jaw with too many teeth. His clean-cut smile and outstretched hand put me in mind of a Mormon doorstep-basher asking if I'd found Jesus in my life yet.

'Mick, so sorry, are you meeting with someone in here?' *Mick?* Since when had anyone called my husband Mick? The newcomer *was* American, East Coast at a guess, and looked young enough to be my son. 'Only I thought I'd had my assistant book the room.'

'My fault, mate,' cried Mike, with the cheesy grin he reserved exclusively for people he couldn't stand. 'Jo, meet my new boss, Henry Rutherford Spiller, God to his friends. Hank, this is–'

'Mike's wife.' I was shaking the man's hand, but

111

my smile froze as I heard Mike say in the same instant: 'My ex-wife.'

God's hand disengaged from mine as though he'd just learned I had bubonic plague. 'Glad to meet you, uh, Mrs Patterson,' he said, and he didn't sound glad. To my ears, he sounded wary, and he no longer wanted to look me in the eye. Instead, he frowned down at his spookily clean fingernails, as Mike burbled apologies for our having presumed to sneak in here, explaining that we'd just wanted a quiet chat about family matters, and that we'd clear out straight away... Honestly, anyone would think he was frightened of this toothy kid.

'I'm glad to meet you, too, Mr Spiller,' I cut across. 'Because, as you must know, I co-founded this company seventeen years ago, and naturally I'm interested to see–'

'Round the building, and I've just been telling her the view from the canteen's a knock-out. Sorry, dining room.' My husband was physically edging me towards the door, exactly as though we were at a party and I – for once – was the one who'd drunk too much. I glared at him. Surely he credited me with tact? Whatever I may have said to him, I wasn't intending to plough in and accuse Hank the Yank outright of robbing us.

'You helped start up TBE, huh?' But he wasn't looking at me. The rimless specs were aimed at Mike. 'Didn't I understand your wife was more a kinda sleeping pardner?'

I fear a rude snigger escaped me, but Hank didn't get it. Didn't so much as smile. 'Unfortunate turn of phrase?' I prompted, glancing at

Mike, but his face was even stonier than his new boss's – and then I realized they both seemed to be staring at my feet. So I looked down too. And saw that my faithful canine friend was sitting there, immaculately upright, with the retrieved packet of Marlborough Lights in her mouth. Satisfied she had my attention, she dropped the fags on my toe and bolted back to her hidey-hole under the sofa, curling her tail over her nose to signify exactly what she thought of this barbaric country and its natives.

I need hardly tell you Hank wasn't amused by this either. He cleared his throat, and felt obliged to warn the ceiling that company policy excluded dogs from the premises, excepting companion animals for the visually impaired, naturally. 'In addition,' he droned, sniffing the air and wrinkling his nose, 'I'm afraid we don't permit–'

'Smoking, I know,' I said, sweeping the packet into my bag, which earned me a grateful wink from my husband, but he resumed his attempts to shove me exitwards nevertheless. I stood my ground. Dammit, I'd travelled 250 miles to find out what had happened to our company, and if this po-faced shrimp was God around here, he was the one I wanted to talk to. Even as I elbowed out of his grasp, however, the door was propelled open again by a swing from a svelte, tight-skirted hip, on which were balanced a briefcase and a stack of files. Not until those had been deposited on the table, and a curtain of black hair shaken behind one diamond-studded ear, did the newcomer turn to face the room. At which she let out a faint gasp and stared at me in a stunned silence to match my own.

'At last,' breathed Hank. Sounding, I'm here to tell you, like a Cherokee-besieged frontiersman when the US Cavalry crests the hill. 'Hi, Gaynor.'

She recovered first. Plunged forward with the familiar letterbox smile.

'*Jo*. God, always a nightmare knowing what to say in situations like this, isn't it?'

'I wouldn't know,' I squeaked. 'I've never been in a situation like this before.'

Which, as wife-to-mistress putdowns go, wasn't bad, but I can't claim it was intentional. A smarter woman would have exited then, in triumph and a puff of Chanel. A smarter woman wouldn't have been in possession of a spaniel wedged under a sofa. There was nothing for it. I dropped to my hands and knees and began groping for her lead.

'Hiya, darling,' I heard Mike murmur, and the casual endearment was like a stiletto in my ribs. 'I thought you were out pitching for that, um, pharmaceuticals job?'

'Petrochemicals. They've accepted our tender.' A pair of crocodile boots I well remembered tip-tapped past my nose. 'You said you were taking her out to lunch.'

'Yeah, well–'

Hank cut in. 'Mrs Patterson here was just telling me about her role in TBE.'

'Correct,' I agreed from under the sofa, but no one took any notice. Gaynor snapped something about ancient history – *oh yeah?* But while I was still struggling to recall my recent contributions to company fortunes – running up new curtains for the ladies' loo? – she swept on to ask Hank, with some impatience, whether their meeting was still on in here. Whereupon he, with a condescension which took my breath away, wondered aloud whether they should ask Mick to sit in since he was around. They wouldn't expect him to contribute, he continued, but it might keep him up to speed. Just whose bloody company was this? I scooped out my unrepentant pet, and sat bolt upright. 'Excuse me–'

Mike leaned over me. '*Please*, Jo. Not now, not here.' And he whispered this with such – well, such desperation, I wavered. Next thing I knew, he'd hauled me to my feet and the door, loudly declaring we'd leave these guys to it.

I wasn't imagining the relief in Hank's face. He even flashed his ninety-two perfect teeth at me for a nanosecond before expressing his sincere hope, intention and belief that The Big Event was well on course to get a whole lot bigger. The past was the past. The future was a bright new tomorrow. Gaynor beamed like a cheerleader at this rah-rah claptrap, although I was glad to see Mike wince. 'Great you've called by to check us out, though, Jo,' Hank concluded, with the warmth of Sweeney Todd waving the Hygiene Inspector out of his kitchen, and glanced at Dora. 'You and – your friend.'

'Yeah, sorry about the hound,' chipped in my pusillanimous spouse. ''Fraid Jo couldn't get anyone to look after it. Worse than kids, eh?'

Whereupon Gaynor shot me a truly filthy scowl, Hank resumed the stocktake of his fingernails, and I plunged out because I didn't trust myself to bid a civil farewell to either of them.

I just about managed to keep my indignation from boiling over until we reached the lifts, then I spun round. 'How can you *stand* it?' I cried. 'That shifty-eyed, jumped-up college kid, graciously inviting you to trot along to his meeting as if – as if you were some office junior. Arrogant, humourless little runt.'

Mike gave a cough of laughter. 'I'm sure he liked you too, love.'

'Why'd you shut me up?'

'No point rocking the boat. We've signed, I'm here, end of story.'

I glanced round to check the corridor was empty. 'But why?' I whispered fiercely. 'You knew what we'd been offered before. You must have known it was a rip-off.'

'Oh, it isn't as bad as it seems. Anyway – anyway, things'll be looking up soon.' Said this latter-day Micawber, with his trendy suit and cropped head. But for once I felt no inclination to jeer at his cheery something-will-turn-up optimism. That brave smile wrung my heart. 'Couple of months and I'll be in a whole different ball game, you wait and see.'

'I don't believe this. You can't tell me you're happy working for this bunch?' He shrugged nonchalantly enough, but he couldn't fool me. '*Mike?*'

'Well, I can hack it short-term, sure. I guess if I thought I'd be clocking in here till bus-pass time...' He hesitated, and for a second the mask slipped. 'Shit, I'd be up to the twenty-eighth and launching myself off the executive fucking roof terrace.'

I don't know where it came from. It certainly wasn't planned, but I suddenly heard myself saying loudly and clearly: 'Then leave.'

He blinked. 'What?'

'Walk out. Quit.' I was talking faster by the minute. 'Tell them to get stuffed. You said you wanted to when they first approached you. So do it now.'

He stared at me. 'Strewth, babe, what about money?'

'Who cares?' demanded the reckless female who seemed to have taken over my mouth. It certainly wasn't the prudent guardian of the Patterson exchequer I'd known all these years, and I wasn't surprised my husband was gaping at me as though I'd sprouted horns. 'We've got plenty of money in property, like you said. If we sold Beck Holme, you'd have the capital to set up in business again on your own–'

'No way.' He grabbed my shoulders. 'You're not even to *think* about selling that cottage, you hear? I bought it for you. It's all yours.'

I remembered him saying exactly that the day he gave me the house, ribbon-wrapped. Tears surged up. 'It's *ours*,' I choked. 'Always was, and we might not even have to sell it, we could just raise a mortgage, but–'

But I couldn't continue, because I hadn't really been suggesting that he set up shop alone, had I? Course I hadn't. I'd meant that *we* should, together, that we could start our partnership – our marriage – all over again. And he knew that as well as I did. Knew it, and was looking for a way to let me down gently, stammering some fatuous excuse about the cottage being near impossible to mortgage with the access problems caused by the ford... I swallowed hard. 'Sorry,' I whispered.

'*You're* sorry?' He wrapped me to his chest. 'Christ, I'm the one who's sorry, Jo,' he said thickly. 'You don't know how sorry. But everything – everything's too far down the road now. If only you'd said all this before...'

In for a penny, in for a pound. 'I'm saying it now?'

Maybe he didn't hear, because the lift doors had pinged apart and a trio of immaculately suited Japanese were bowing courteously round us. The moment was lost. Mike released me, muttering that this wasn't the time or place. I didn't argue. Sarah would have snorted that I'd made enough of a fool of myself already, but I couldn't give a stuff. Hadn't I always told her that her dad would come back to me? Yeah, well, my own faith might have wobbled these past six months, but not any longer. He'd given himself away just now. *If only you'd said all this before...* Those words had been dredged up from the very core of his soul. Inside, deep inside, even if he couldn't totally admit it to himself, Mike wanted to be back with me. I knew it, sure as eggs is eggs. So I didn't care if he was glancing guiltily over his shoulder, growling that he probably ought to go and show his face at that bloody meeting. He touched my cheek. 'Will you forgive me?'

'Oh, love,' I whispered, and was lifting my tearful face for his kiss, when I was yanked away. Dora, scenting escape, had surged into the lift.

'Everything'll work out,' he called as the doors slid shut. And he held out both hands with fingers crossed. 'Trust me. You'll realize one day soon that–'

But I never found out what I'd realize, because I was plunging earthwards.

Eileen Muxworthy, whose world-perspective was robustly Yorkshire-centric – New York, on her map, being some bastard offshoot of our venerable county town – had condescended to visit London just the once, and did not intend to repeat the experience. What she really couldn't be doing with, she'd told me, was the feeling you were breathing in other folks' dirty leavings. Standing in the bustling street that warm October afternoon, staring up at the mirrored tower of Optimax through a soupy haze of exhaust fumes, canteen fat and the disinfectant with which a boiler-suited man was swilling an entrance nearby, I knew what she meant.

'It stinks,' I whispered. 'It really, truly *stinks*.'

But I wasn't talking about the air. I was talking about what was going on in that glittering citadel. I could not believe the humiliations being inflicted on my husband. Forty-nine, rising fifty, with his company snitched from under his nose, forced to answer to that toothy little squirt. And he knew they'd suckered him – course he did, however hard the poor sap tried to kid himself otherwise. He might look full of pep and spout all that twaddle about things not being as bad as they seemed and good times lurking round the corner, but that was only because he was a congenital idiot, with the words 'something will turn up' printed through his DNA like Blackpool through the proverbial rock.

Except...

Except, actually, he'd struck lucky yet again. Something *had* turned up.

Me.

PART THREE

'I have always believed that when a man takes it into his head to accomplish some project and pursues it to the exclusion of anything else, he must succeed in it despite all difficulties...'

Giacomo Casanova, *History of My Life*

10

'Lord Bidcombe, of course.' The receptionist behind this comfortably antique mahogany desk was herself comfortably antique, with silver coiffure, pink twinset, a double string of creamy pearls on her prominent bosom and gold half-moons at the end of her nose. 'A friend of your uncle's, Paddy dear,' she announced into her telephone.

This description of me, I admit, made me shuffle my toes in the Persian rug, but it was too late for second thoughts. It had been astonishingly easy to track down P.E.F. McGinty and Partners. They were listed in Yellow Pages like any old window cleaner, if you please, under 'S' – that's 'S' for Security Services, not Spooks. Fate was obviously guiding me because I'd roared west to Mayfair with barely a red light, and found a parking spot within minutes which was both convenient and shady enough not to barbecue my dog. True, I'd quailed for a fringe-fluffing, skirt-straightening few seconds outside the splendid pillared portico, but by the time it was occurring to me that an establishment like this might charge fees as grand as its premises, I was already inside.

'First door on the right at the top of the stairs, Mrs Patterson,' said the lady to me now – 'lady' being the only possible description for one with those glassy vowels – and she resumed her study of the *Daily Telegraph* crossword.

I would flog my jewellery, I told myself as I marched up the stairs, my car, my house, *anything*. I was fired with my mission. All these months I'd been moping around up North, waiting for my husband to tire of his floozy and trot home. And just look at the mess he'd got himself into. Top right of the stairs was a tall, mahogany-panelled door, propped open behind some kind of – cabin trunk? Curious. But I wasn't here to query the fixtures and fittings. I was on the warpath and this Paddy McGinty, I sincerely trusted, would be joining me. I stiffened my spine, sidestepped the trunk, and walked in.

This was not so much an office as what might have been a private anteroom in a gentleman's club. The panelled walls were hung with venerably foxed watercolours; jam-coloured oriental rugs were scattered across glowing parquet; a long-case clock the size of Big Ben ticked sonorously in one corner, and deep casement windows were hung in a heavy-duty tapestry which, to my experienced eye, had cost not a penny less than a hundred quid a metre. In front of the window stood a hefty Victorian merchant's desk, buffed until the blond wood shone through the treacly stain and exuding the comfortable certainties of trade and empire from every gleaming angle. After the bleak, black slabs of Optimax, I found this juggernaut of a desk reassuring; all the more so because it was piled high with clutter which, even at first glance, included a telescope, a one-eared teddy bear and an opened magnum of champagne amid mountains of books and papers. It was a desk to make one feel at home. What I could not see, however, was its occupant.

'Gotcha, you little fiend,' exclaimed a muffled baritone voice. Startled, I realized that the mound of navy serge protruding from behind a large cardboard box was actually a masculine bottom. This disappeared as its owner righted himself, tossed what appeared to be a dog's collar on to the cluttered desk, and plunged round, hand out-thrust.

'My dear Mrs Patterson,' he cried, 'how perfectly *inspired* of you to turn up now, exactly in my hour of need.'

I found my hand gripped by a warm, comfortably solid fist which I noticed was generously blotched with black. He noticed, too.

'Ever known an ink bottle that *doesn't* bloody leak?' He scowled at his piebald mitt. 'If you ask me, that pot's been mouldering away at the back of the drawer since the Blitz. I trust I haven't shared the contents with you – no, seems to be dry my end. I say, do take a seat, if you can unearth one. Care for a spot of fizz?'

He was as rumpled as his office. The jacket of his suit dangled from a standard lamp in the corner and his waistcoat flapped unbuttoned around his bulky frame over trousers adorned with dust, fragments of newsprint and a streamer of fluffy sticky-tape. A blue shirt was rolled up to the elbows with collar unbuttoned, while the knot of a tie, striped to signify allegiance to some school, regiment or other manly tribe, had travelled halfway round his neck. He was tall as well as broad and could have been any age between thirty and fifty. A thick shock of rusty brown hair stuck up in question marks, and he had dark eyes over a surprisingly curvy mouth, with tortoiseshell-framed glasses which threatened to slide off his snub nose as he leaned forward to scoop up an empty glass.

'Paddy McGinty, by the way,' he murmured, groping for the magnum which he held up to the light for a minute and tutted, before filling the glass and handing it to me.

'No, really...' I began.

'Oh, do. Can't leave a chap to drink alone.' So saying, he tipped the remainder of the magnum into his own glass and took a long, reviving draught. 'Tell all, then. How is the dear old buzzard?' I gulped. But before I could attempt to explain the embarrassingly remote nature of my connection with his uncle, he'd begun prodding round his desk. 'No, look, don't say another word until you've seen this, because he's absolutely going to love it. You know what Bernard's like about gadgets.' He had retrieved and now proffered the dog collar, which I noticed had a shiny metal button plugged alongside the buckle. 'Take it away, then.'

'I'm sorry?'

'Out into the hall, anywhere, far as you like. Down to Aunt Dolly in reception, if you want, or hide in an office upstairs. Don't let me know where you're going though.'

It was occurring to me that Paddy McGinty might be ... drunk?

126

'As your average skunk,' he breezily concurred, as though he'd read my thoughts, 'but don't let that worry you. I'm several bottles short of dissolving in a heap at your feet. Well, go on then.'

So I found myself, with a champagne flute in one hand and a dog's collar in the other, bemusedly ascending the grandly curved staircase of P.E.F. McGinty and Partners, wondering what sort of madhouse I'd wandered into. Three floors up, under a pigeon-encrusted, domed skylight, I arrived amidst an assortment of cleaning equipment. Here, the stairs stopped and so perforce did I. I took a swig of my fizz and considered P.E.F. McGinty himself. I don't know what I'd expected a corporate spook to be like, but it certainly wasn't this. He was charming, to be sure – the effusive welcome, the glass of bubbly – but then he thought I was bosom buddies with his uncle.

'Aha,' echoed a voice far below – was no one else employed in this palatial joint? 'I detect that, like the lark, we have ascended.' Something was issuing electronic bleeps. I soon found out what, because when Paddy McGinty's tousled head appeared up the stairs, he was brandishing a small black box, rather like a Walkman, with a spiky aerial protruding from one corner. The bleeps were growing more piercing by the minute. 'Total success,' he cried, thrusting it towards me. There was a tiny screen, with a cross of red illuminated dots, and almost dead centre a single brighter pinpoint, flashing in time with the beeps. 'The closer we home in, the louder the bleeps get, and – *voilà!*' He whisked the dog collar out of my fingers. 'You are located and banged to rights, madam.'

I couldn't help laughing. 'What *is* this?'

'McGinty's patented mad-dog locater.' He tapped down the aerial and stuffed box and collar into his trouser pocket. 'Pressie for Uncle Bernard. I had a tame boffin run it up for me by way of a parting shot. I bought the collar, he slipped a little anti-kidnap bug in by the buckle and–'

'A *what?*'

'Gizmo you plant on snatch-risk execs,' he said, as though this were as commonplace as a spare toothbrush. 'Suddenly occurred to me, you see, that a tool like this is exactly what Bernard needs for that crazy springer of his. Total brainwave, for all I modestly say so myself. You've run across Jasper, I dare say?'

'Jasper?' I began uneasily.

'Sweet animal, but definitely one pheasant short of a brace in the brain department, forever dashing off after some entrancing scent or beguiling bitch and forgetting his way home. With this little toy round his neck, however, his roving days will be over. Didn't I say Bernard would love it? And I'd been wondering how to get it to him, along with idiot-proof operating instructions, when in you toddle like the answer to a prayer.'

'But–'

'Just remember, stick to words of one syllable and shout. He's quite obedient, shouldn't take you more than ten minutes to train him up to

128

field level. Bernard, that is, not the dog. But what am I doing, pinning you up here among the dustpans when your glass is dry? With luck, there'll be fresh supplies in Accounts which, by a happy chance, we pass on the way down. Unlikely to have polished off their bottle, such depressingly sober souls, the number crunchers.' He stepped back with a flourish, sending a mop clattering out of its steel bucket. 'After you, Mrs Patterson, or may I call you–?'

'Jo,' I said distractedly, walked down three steps and stopped short. 'Look, Mr McGinty ... sorry, should that be Major McGinty?'

'Oh, Paddy, please, aeons since I hung up m'boots. Peter, if you want to be strictly accurate, but with my surname, there was precious little chance anyone was ever going to call me that.' He hesitated an instant. 'At least, hardly anyone. You were saying?'

'Major – *Paddy* – I think I'm here under, well, under false pretences.'

'Really? How exciting.' He was ushering me downwards, and since he seemed only too likely to trip over his trailing shoelace, I fell into step beside him. 'You're an undercover VAT inspector, perhaps? But no, too pretty for that, surely, if I may be forgiven such prehistoric sexism.'

'I'm not a friend of Lord Bidcombe, as such,' I confessed. 'I suppose we're neighbours of a sort. I live on the edge of the Stowham estate, anyway, at Beck Holme.'

This stopped him in his tracks. 'Glory, do you indeed?'

I raised my chin. 'Temporarily. And not for

much longer, I trust.'

'Well, quite. Heavenly little house, but a tad restrictive. Still getting regularly cut off by the eponymous beck?'

'From time to time,' I agreed, startled to find someone so intimately acquainted with my dwelling at this distance from home.

He shook his head. 'Perfect if one is after renouncing the world and all its vanities, but a bit of a bugger when it comes to getting your dustbin emptied.'

'Difficult to mortgage, too, as I've just been reminded,' I said ruefully, because a fleeting view through open double doors of a magnificently appointed conference room had prompted me to wonder afresh about the likely scale of Major McGinty's charges. 'However, that's beside the point.'

He dodged into the doorway opposite, and emerged with another magnum, perhaps a quarter full. 'Which is?'

'I overheard your uncle talking about your line of work. Investigation. And I think – hope – you might be able to help me.'

He was already halfway down the final flight of stairs, but this, halted him. 'Oh lumme, this is my fault, for not telling Bernard.' His face, as he turned to look up at me, was a comical picture of remorse. 'I'm so sorry. Damn silly, and I wouldn't dream of burdening you with the whys and wherefores, but the truth is relations between me and the ancient relly have been rather arm's length of late. But I really should have told him.'

'Told him what?' I said

'I've retired,' he said, and waved the magnum. 'Behold the dregs of my leaving festivities. I'm quitting, selling out, doing a jolly old bunk. You see before you an ex-spook.'

I was disappointed – wickedly disappointed, for all Paddy was quick to assure me, as we re-entered his shambolic office, that the firm of McGinty would be marching on as ever with his partners. I *liked* this man, this overgrown, jokey schoolboy, with his Just William tie and ink-blotted paws; I'd liked him on sight. And I had instinctively felt, on no rational basis at all, not just that he was the man to help me, but that I could trust him absolutely.

Of course, so much else made sense now. His office was a tip because he was packing up. The building was like the *Marie Celeste* because, with the exception of twin-setted Aunt Dolly on the desk – Lady Dorothea Fullerton and apparently the godmother of one of his partners who had good-naturedly volunteered to man the phones for the afternoon – the entire staff had decamped to a restaurant in Soho.

'Bad form to sneak out of one's own leaving thrash, I know,' he said, 'but I'd sooner go with a whimper than a bang. And there's no point my summoning one of the other chaps to meet you, because they'll be swinging from the chandeliers by now. However, if you can bring yourself to spill the beans to my humble and only relatively inebriated self, I promise to co-opt the best man on to the job as soon as a cold dawn and even chillier sobriety sets in.'

131

I didn't want the best man, I wanted this one, drunk or not. 'Just half a glass,' I said disconsolately, as he wafted the bottle towards me.

'Whoops.' In leaning forward, he'd knocked a heavy silver photograph frame to the floor with an ominous crack. Planting his glass on the desk, he knelt down and began gathering up the pieces with wincing care. 'Sorry, do go on. I'm all ears.'

I supposed there was nothing to be lost by telling him the story. I took a fortifying slug of champagne. 'It's my husband's company.'

'Your husband's?' he cut in politely, dropping a jagged glass triangle into the bin.

'Half mine,' I said swiftly, 'so I've every right to involve someone like you if I want. I suppose I should explain that Mike and I are, um, slightly estranged.'

His face turned up. 'I say, forgive me, but you do realize divorce isn't our line of country? Jolly though the idea is of lurking in the lobby of a seedy Brighton hotel in a false moustache and grubby mac, I fear not for us.'

'I know *that*.'

'Actually, d'you suppose people still go in for that sort of caper, *in flagrante* pics and so on? Smile, say "sleaze" and Bob's your divorce lawyer?' He sighed. 'Probably not, because I was reading somewhere you can practically get divorced over the internet nowadays. What a world we live in, eh?'

'There's no question of our divorcing,' I snapped, caught on the quick. Did scepticism inspire his sudden grimace? But it had gone in a flicker.

'I applaud you. Red herring, anyway. Your company.'

'We've been conned,' I stated defiantly. 'My husband's company has been stolen from under his nose.'

'I say, what fun.' He was engaged in blowing glass shards off the silver frame, and I glimpsed a photograph of two bonny children with a pretty, dark-haired woman. The wife and family I supposed, although he didn't wear a wedding band. Don't ask me why I'd clocked this, I just had. His only adornment was a scuffed signet ring on the little finger of his large and solid hand. He glanced round apologetically. 'At least, I do beg your pardon. Not fun at all for your husband – totally ghastly, I've no doubt, but I have to say blatant piracy on the high seas of commerce isn't frightfully common.' At which, under my bemused gaze, he tossed the frame – an exquisitely embossed antique number – into the wastepaper basket, and tucked the photograph carefully away into a briefcase lying open nearby. 'And who are the villains? I do so love a good villain.'

Just for a moment, my conviction that McGinty was the man for the job wavered. 'An organization called Optimax?' I offered. 'Big company, but I suppose there's no particular reason for you to have heard of them.'

'US-owned, leisure publishing marketing group? Shares went up twenty pence yesterday, following an investment in some Eastern European printing concern.'

My eyes widened. 'Blimey, you don't work for

them, do you?'

'Never so much as exchanged a nod with their tea lady, best of my recollection. Brain like a hoover, that's my trouble. Sucks up endless bags of totally useless information.' He extracted a sparkling sliver of glass from the knee of his trousers. 'Correct me if I'm wrong, but didn't they take over NVT after a rather bloody fight?'

It occurred to me that when Lord Bidcombe had described his nephew as ferociously brainy, he hadn't been kidding. 'If you say so. But they took over our company last month after no fight at all, and that's what has brought me–' I broke off. 'Why are you shaking your head?'

'Quite right, foolish thing to do in my condition.' He opened and shut his eyes a couple of times. 'Makes the room spin rather sickeningly. I'd better get up from the floor while I'm still capable of so doing and take a drop more to steady the tum. I always feel champagne's such a medicinal tipple, don't you? Alka-Seltzer for the moneyed classes.'

'If you're as drunk as you say,' I commented, with some asperity, 'you're remarkably articulate.'

'Words always the last thing to go with me. Tragic, really. Nothing sadder than a chap who can't even get incoherently drunk any longer, try as he jolly well might. Tidge more in that glass? Well, if you're sure.' He lowered his not inconsiderable bulk on to the only patch of a curlicued chaise longue not stacked with books, shoved the tortoiseshell specs back up his nose and blinked owlishly at me. 'Where were we?'

'Optimax,' I said, tempted as I was to be

sidetracked into asking why a well-brought-up boy like him should *wish* to get incoherently drunk.

'Indeed, Optimax,' he sighed. 'You know, much as I hate to be the pourer of cold water – truly, no one happier than I to believe the buggers guilty until proven triple innocent – in this case, I fear not. Truly, really, absolutely not. The firm of Optimax is a by-word for virtue, squeakier clean than a duck in a Jacuzzi, ethics coming out of their corporate ears, famous for having had policies on everything from sexual harassment to ozone-friendly coffee beans when the rest of the world still thought political correctness was how you folded the napkins at a Tory party banquet.'

'But–'

'I agree they're positively *loathsome* they're so goody-goody. You know, I sometimes think the descendants of those hymn-singing Puritans we so wisely shipped off in the *Mayflower* all those centuries ago are being flown back on Concorde by way of revenge on the part of our transatlantic cousins. With exactly the same zeal their great-whatever-grandparents bible-bashed the poor bloody Red Indians into missionary schools, they now round up our grubby, gin-soaked, smoky old native companies and bludgeon us into low-cholesterol, decaffeinated, sparkling-mineral-water virtue. And, what's most galling of all, vastly increased profitability. I say,' he added, 'that was rather a fine purple passage, don't you think?'

'Dazzling, but–'

'One's almost tempted to dash off a short monograph: "The Nouveau Puritans". Bound in

135

vellum, perhaps, for a small but discerning circulation? Sorry – sorry. What I'm trying to say, in short, is that I'd be amazed if you could pin so much as the improper use of a second-class stamp on the gents of Optimax.'

'Our company,' I said fiercely, 'was worth four million pounds not so very long ago. And, yes, we got into trouble with our bank, but–'

'Four million?' he cut in incredulously.

'*Exactly*,' I said, glad to have impressed him at last. 'And they've gone and snapped us up for nothing but our debts. *Nothing*,' I repeated, because he was gaping at me rather as though he'd forgotten how to close his mouth. 'So what do you make of that?'

He shut his mouth and took to studying the bubbles rising in his glass. His expression was oddly sad. 'My dear Mrs Patterson,' he said at length. 'I promise I'm not claiming for one second that skulduggery can't lurk in the most splendiferous temples of Mammon–'

'Yes, yes,' I said impatiently, but he silenced me with a gently upraised hand.

'But for an organization like Optimax to jeopardize their good name, their integrity, by defrauding a company such as your husband's of, um, four million... Lord, how can I put this?'

'Try straight.'

'It's chicken feed.'

'I'm sorry?'

'Peanuts, petty cash, small change. Lord love you, ma'am,' he wailed, 'I shouldn't think four million would so much as cover their potted plant budget.'

11

A honey-gold moon hung plump over the hilltop. The still air, etched with a promise of frost, was spiced with woodsmoke and the rotted leaf tang of autumn, while an owl's cry quivered somewhere out in the velvety, diamond-chipped blackness. As I'd been reminded recently, you don't get skies like this over a city, this vast black silence. There, you're cocooned in an orange glow, a-buzz with your millions of fellow bees in the metropolitan hive. Here, as Paddy had so unexpectedly mused, you can stand alone and feel you're gazing straight up into the fathomless infinities of heaven.

Just now, though, I was wondering where under that fathomless sky Paddy McGinty might be hiding himself. He'd rarely been out of my thoughts since I left his office a week ago. Even as I drove home, I'd been replaying our encounter, thinking of all the clever things I should have said to him. In real life, the more I'd recounted of my experiences at Optimax, the more stubbornly he had insisted I was misreading them.

'Oh my dear, we've all encountered his type,' he groaned as I described shifty, shuffling Hank. 'Not a humorous bone in their executive-gym-toned bodies and not an ounce of anything so interesting as vice. In general, that is,' he added, but only out of courtesy. I could see he didn't believe a word I was saying, and told him as much.

The brown eyes twinkled endearingly behind the specs. 'Well, you must allow this is all pretty far-fetched. How, pray, how did these brigands persuade your husband to part with his firm? Was it a knife to the jugular, or did they whip out a Beretta along with their iniquitous contract?'

'No need to be facetious. Do you always talk like this?'

'Only when drunk. Spot of imaginative blackmail, maybe? Go on, tell me there's a wicked *femme fatale* for us to *chercher*...' He suddenly grimaced. 'I do beg your pardon, have I been tactless? You mentioned you and your man were estranged...'

'There is another woman, as it happens,' I said, 'but it's nothing to do with her. My husband signed that contract because the only thing he knows about money is how to spend the stuff.' But flitting across my mind even then was the recollection that he'd been forcefully encouraged into this deal by Gaynor. And that she was no financial innocent.

'More seriously,' Paddy resumed, 'can I ask why, out of all the events firms in all the world, Optimax should choose to jackboot into yours?'

This rather took me aback. 'Why not?'

'And even supposing they have pulled off a sharp deal,' he continued, gently but remorselessly, 'that deal is done. To take them on, you'd need a shoal of legal sharks costing more than the putative value of your firm, and to what end?'

I gulped. 'Maybe I don't want to take on

Optimax, as such...'

'So what do you want?'

To this, at least, I had the answer. 'I want to rescue my husband,' I declared. 'He's got himself into the worst trouble of his life, and he needs me to get him out of it.'

Y'all join in the chorus now: 'Stand by your man...'

Far from applauding, Paddy seemed almost to shudder. 'God save us all,' he breathed, and not jokingly either, but with what struck me as such disgust, I sprang up from my chair, snapping that I was sorry to have wasted his time. At once, he leaned forward and grasped my hand. 'Heavens, I'm so sorry. Of course you haven't wasted my time.'

I was not entirely mollified. 'You think I'm wasting my own, at any rate.'

'But I haven't enjoyed myself so much in ages, truly. It's all so deliciously Raymond Chandlerish, don't you think?' He affected a clenched-teeth Californian drawl. 'Scene: downtown Mayfair, dregs of the afternoon, and you don't know if it's you or the office is dead. Enter glamorous blonde with mysterious tale. "You gotta help me," she wails, "de Optimax mob's giving me a problem wid my old man..."'

'You're crazy,' I snorted, but anyone who describes me as a glamorous blonde can't be all bad.

'Harmless, though, on the whole. I mean, prove me wrong, please. No one more delighted than I to eat my words, my hat, lunch at Gavroche, anything you like. I say, surely you're not going?

There's still a drop more fizz.'

'Afraid I'm driving.' I was surprised nevertheless at the promptness with which he withdrew the bottle, and I gathered up my bag. 'It's a long way to Stowham.'

'Isn't it just?' he agreed. 'Another world altogether.' And it was while seeing me out that he'd waxed unexpectedly poetic about the skies over North Yorkshire – the sky I was staring up at now in such frustration, as I shivered and whistled for Dora. Because, although I'd parted from Paddy McGinty on the most cordial terms, I'd been conducting a one-sided argument with him ever since. He'd challenged me to prove him wrong, and I would have given a great deal, tonight, to lead him into my kitchen and lay before him the fruits of my past ten days' researches.

Where do I start then? More to the point, perhaps, where *did* I start?

With Gaynor Steele. This had not sprung from mere wifely prejudice. I won't deny I loathed the woman, but at the very least I'd have expected her to take good care of Mike's interests. She, however, had pushed him into this deal – had been pushing him for months, according to what he'd told me, before he eventually agreed to sign up. And even if she'd got her sums wrong about the offer – which wasn't exactly likely with a smart cookie like her – anyone who knew Mike at all, let alone a woman sharing his bed, must surely have realized he would be suicidally miserable in an organization like Optimax.

Conversely, though, I felt I could fairly claim that Gaynor herself had taken to the place like a pig to you-know-what. Whose entry into the room had been so enthusiastically received by Hank? Who had beamed sycophantically at his corporate blather? Whose sodding meeting was it anyway? And while these reflections might not impress Paddy McGinty, they were more than enough to set me digging. I'd had a busy week.

'The little hussy barely showed her nose at Ron's retirement do,' had sniffed Mike's former secretary, Sissy, who shared his mother's conviction that no woman could ever be good enough for their golden boy, me included. Gil swore she preserved his toenail clippings in a matchbox under her pillow. Since she thought even less of Mike's mistress than she did of his wife, however, she was one of the first people I'd found a pretext to phone. 'Gone in ten minutes and didn't so much as nod my way, of course, but she said something to Ron about having to work round the clock because she was taking the biggest gamble of her precious career. Make what you will of that.'

'Oh, I will,' I breathed, wishing Paddy McGinty were by my side. I'd give him his wicked *femmes fatales*. 'By the way, Sissy, have you got Tom Reilly's number?'

'In Canada?'

This wasn't the only time I was to discover how comprehensively I'd lost touch. So many of the old contacts had moved on, or even passed on. But I persevered, praying my phone bill wasn't imminent, because although I'd forced myself to finish Megan Brighouse's curtains – for which Eileen had paid on the nail and in cash, bless her – the money was melting faster than ice-cream in a sauna. And while a much more lucrative commission for a customer in Wykesea awaited my attention, in the form of several acres of a truly hideous violet velour, I fear a film of dust was gathering on my sewing machine while I subsisted on a diet of toast and eggs. I was like Dora on a hot scent. Nothing could deflect me.

'You don't want to hear about Gaynor, I know,' remarked another of my informants innocently, 'but I'll give her one thing, she works like stink. Mike had her running everything by the end, you know?'

I'd have liked Paddy to hear that, too. Given the mess our firm had got into.

'I'll never know why Mike left you for her, *never*,' declared Penny, a.k.a the Piranha, not at all innocently, 'I mean, looks aren't everything, are they?'

Ah yes, the Piranha. I hadn't actually been after her. I'd wanted a word with her husband, an amiable enough sound mixer, and would have rung off once I'd learned he was on a job in Bristol, but Penny had smelled blood. 'And it must be so awful for you,' she continued, with lip-smacking relish, 'actually having to be grateful to the woman.'

This startled me into asking why – and she told me.

That was the breakthrough. Never mind that Penny is no one's idea of a reliable witness – of course she isn't, she's a razor-fanged monster – I

142

was soon tracking down what the likes of Paddy would doubtless call corroboratory evidence.

'Sure, Gaynor used to work for Optimax,' confirmed a bemused graphic artist I must have met all of once. 'Maxi PR. With them a couple of years, I think.'

'And they really rated her,' recalled an account exec, with audible envy. 'Offered a very juicy package to try and stop her coming to you.'

Which answered Paddy's query as to why, out of all the events organizing firms in all the world Optimax had picked on ours: they had a valued ex-colleague on the inside. But there was more, much more.

'You bet your sweet life it was Gaynor brought Optimax on board, Gawd bless her,' confirmed Jerry the jolly caterer. 'And I'm sorry if I'm trampling on your corns here, sweetie, with the scene between her and your randy old man, but I gotta tell you I was seriously grateful to the lady. Sent her a case of Bolly, in fact, because if TBE'd gone belly up, our firm might well have followed, the amount we were owed.'

If I'd had the dosh, I might have sent Jerry a case of champagne, or at the very least opened a bottle myself. I could hardly believe it – and couldn't wait to tell Paddy. Selling to Optimax had been Gaynor's idea, start to finish. And to put the icing on the cake, I learned the next day – almost by chance – that Mike had even allowed her to negotiate the terms of the deal.

'Well, he made out he was too busy to go to the meetings, but if you ask me, he reckoned he hadn't enough fingers,' laughed Sam, our

143

information technology whiz-kid, whom I'd rung on quite another tack. 'Don't get me wrong, Mike's a genius in his way and a helluva nice bloke, but he needs a calculator to work out ten per cent of a hundred. And still gets the wrong answer. No, you want a sharp operator like Gaynor at the table with those hard-nosed bastards.'

And there I'd been three weeks back, tearfully wondering what a sharp operator like Gaynor Steele saw in my husband. Never had it crossed my mind that she might not have been after the pleasure of his company so much as his company, full stop. OK, maybe I couldn't prove that yet, but I certainly felt I had enough evidence to convince Paddy I'd been wasting neither his time nor my own.

'Mr McGinty? I'm sorry, he's no longer with us,' declared a flat female voice, which was definitely not that of Lady Dorothea Fullerton.

'I knew he was leaving,' I said. 'I just wondered if you might have a phone number, or a home address so I could write to him?'

Yes, I realize this was a daft question to ask the receptionist at a firm of security consultants. Also that it wasn't the brightest of ploys to claim friendship with your uncle again, because it goes without saying she frostily suggested I apply to Lord Bidcombe. You might say the same yourself,

'But I'm unnerved by the idea of a butler answering the phone?' I mused, chewing my pen.

but you mentioned that you hadn't yet told your uncle you'd left the firm. Anyway, I'm trusting they'll forward this letter to you, and that you'll forgive me for wanting to flaunt my detective work under your sceptical nose.

Don't get me wrong. I'm well aware I have yet to unearth anything my husband hasn't known all along. Obviously he realizes Gaynor used to work for Optimax, and the whole world seems to know she masterminded the takeover. Remarks at a party about taking gambles don't amount to much. I do believe, though, that Mike suspects he's been had, but is reluctant to face up to it, for the obvious reasons.

I broke off again, because I could hear a throaty car engine coming down the hill.

Of course, I could just wait for the affair to burn itself out, or perhaps even for Gaynor to ditch him, now she's milked him dry, but I don't want to. I've been sitting around up here just waiting and doing nothing for far too long. I want to open his eyes to the truth. To which end I have, as we investigators say, another line of enquiry to pursue. And even as I write, a friend is arriving to help me...

'Yeah, not a bad set-up,' pronounced Jimmy. That bespectacled, Harry Potterish face, frowning earnestly at the assorted jumble of Ben's computer, stirred the soppiest memories in my breast of the days when my son had himself been just such a pink-cheeked cherub. Little boys have such adorable necks, don't they? Fragile as flower stems. Young Jimmy, though, was plugging

145

up the bits with a confidence and speed which startled me, even if Aidan – with a scowl which entirely failed to conceal his pride – had told me the lad was a demon for computers. Within seconds, seemingly, the screen had flickered into life. Jimmy shoved his glasses back up his nose. 'What now, then?'

I gathered my wits. 'Just want to see what's inside, really. I'm afraid I'm not very clever at this sort of thing.'

That was why I'd got on to Sam, our firm's IT consultant, after realizing in a glorious flash of inspiration that I had in my possession – albeit in a sadly disconnected heap beside Ben's bed – not just one of our old office computers, but the best and most recently purchased of them. Ben had made that very clear, when still trying to persuade me to drive down and collect the thing. And since Mike is almost as technologically illiterate as I am with any machine that doesn't play tunes, I believed I had a fairish idea who might have nobbled the new iMac for her personal use...

'"Casanova is a rover,"' I heard Jimmy reciting in puzzled tones, '"screws from Istanbul to Dover..."'

'Hallelujah,' I breathed. Sam'd been right about no one bothering to wipe the hard disk, and we had Gaynor's machine here, because that could only be a lyric to the doomed musical she'd knocked off before she took to knocking off the composer instead. Didn't strike me *Lover* had been a grievous loss to the English stage.

'"Tits and bums and..."' My young friend

looked round sternly. 'This is rude.'

Feeling as though I'd been caught downloading porn, I hastily said we weren't interested in that, and settled down to investigate the other files. Fate was with me still. After ten minutes, in a folder helpfully labelled Optimax, we found it. A copy of an e-mail from Gaynor M. Steele to Henry R. Spiller.

Re our discussions yesterday. Yes, given your views, I accept you can't put our informal agreement in writing. But Mick's got no choice, so let's move. I know you'll keep your side, and I look forward to receiving the contracts a.s.a.p.

Yours, Gaynor

I cheered as, under Jimmy's supervision, I managed to print off a copy for Paddy all by myself.

So why, later tonight, was I scowling up at the velvety skies? Well, when I was refuelling my junior computer boffin with pizza and chips, he had unexpectedly observed: 'You know Paddy, don't you?'

Since I was at that moment anticipating the look on his face as he read the damning e-mail, I nearly burned myself on the baking tray. 'I, um, called to see him in London, yes. How'd you know about that?'

'Got any more chips?' Jimmy ignored the knife and fork I'd been so foolish as to lay out and took a mammoth bite from a triangle of the pizza. 'He told Grandad.'

147

My pulses quickened. 'Paddy isn't at the castle, is he?'

'Nah,' he retorted, in the same tone he'd used when I'd asked an asinine question about the workings of the computer. 'He doesn't come here any more, not since he fell out with Mr Jack.'

I knew it would be immoral to pump this innocent babe, but ever since my return from London I'd been trying to recall the odd bits of gossip people had let slip about Paddy. Eileen Muxworthy had definitely talked as though the future of Jimmy's grandad as Head Keeper – the future of the whole Stowham estate in fact – might rest with him. And I'd long wished I'd picked her up when she'd made that glancing reference to the bloody stupid things he and his cousin Jack had done. So I'm afraid I now stifled my scruples and grinned confidingly at Jimmy.

'Any idea what they quarrelled about, Paddy and, um, Mr Jack?'

'Grandad says it's none of my business,' responded the boy, which rather put me in my place. And when Aidan arrived to collect this apple of his eye – pretending to cuff him, and grumbling that I shouldn't have been so soft as to feed the greedy little tyke – I was careful to avoid sounding nosy. I just mentioned that I'd been hoping to get in touch with Major McGinty again.

'About that damn fool gadget of his?' he retorted. 'He said he'd forgot to give it you, and I said a good thing too. All that dog needs is a kick up the backside.'

I laughed. I'd actually forgotten the mad-dog

locater, and marvelled afresh at the infectious lunacy which had induced a sensible middle-aged woman like me to play hide and seek. 'No,' I said. 'Just, oh, something I wanted to ask him.' Then I cunningly continued, in the hopes I might prompt him to offer an address or phone number himself: 'But I dare say his old firm will forward a letter on to his home.'

'Very like,' he responded, 'but I wouldn't break your neck getting it in t'post. He were in Scotland when he rang us, and he didn't seem clear where he planned on going next, but it weren't back to London.' Aidan rolled his eyes. 'And if there's one thing for sure, it'll not be here, neither. Daft buggers.'

12

So heaven knows when you'll get this letter. I can't help wishing you hadn't chosen just now to fall off the map, because, to be honest, I was rather hoping for some advice as to how I should proceed from here. You didn't seem impressed when I told you that my aim was to rescue my poor husvNS

'Understatement of the year,' I muttered to myself as I fumbled for the delete button. Now I had the technology, I'd ditched pen and paper and rewritten my letter on the computer. Rewritten it several times. I'd like to say this was because of all the new discoveries I had made,

149

but it wasn't. I may have spent three more days trawling through the computer and printing out any file that looked remotely relevant – while the pile of violet velour stared at me accusingly – but it seemed Jimmy and I had stumbled on the only nugget of gold at the outset. And while the e-mail certainly confirmed Gaynor had a verbal agreement of some sort with Hank, I was equally sure she could spin an explanation to satisfy Mike. After all, the silly sap had believed everything else she'd told him. Eileen Muxworthy was right. God shouldn't have planted men's brains in their trousers.

husband, so perhaps I can be more specific. All I actually want is for him to come home, which he must if I can prove his girlfriend's sold him down the river. There's no question she engineered the takeover. Nor, to my mind, that the terms of the deal were grossly unfair to us. And since a clever businesswoman like her must have known that, the only possible explanation is that she was being paid by Optimax to deliver our firm to them – paid handsomely, too, I imagine. But I realize I need hard evidence – something that, unlike the e-mail, she can't possibly wriggle out of. I may even have it already, because I've also retrieved from the computer scads of accounts and balance sheets and so forth. The only trouble is they're about as meaningful to me as Sanskrit. So I'd be enormously grateful if you, with all your experience in company fraud, could give me a few hints just to point me in the right direction. I do hope you won't feel I'm imposing on our very slight acquaintance, and I suppose there's no tearing hurry, but...

But there was. Because within hours of my posting the letter, Gil Rydall phoned.

'The doctors think it might have been a stroke, but only a mild one,' he told me, and I could almost hear the crunch of chewed moustache. 'Still, she's back home, talking about her runner at Sandown tomorrow, so fingers crossed. I've got to keep an ear open, in case she wakes up again. Anyway, what can I do for you, love?'

'Sorry?'

'You left a message, oh, beginning of last week?'

I had? God, yes, of course I had. Gil was the first person I'd rung to check Gaynor's connection with Optimax, and I couldn't even remember the excuse I'd burbled on to his answering machine.

'You went down to town to see Mike?' he prompted. 'I'm sorry I haven't rung before, but you know what it's like on hospital patrol.'

'Mike – yes.' How much could I tell him? He and Gaynor went back a long way. 'At Optimax.'

'Bit different from our own dear old slum, eh? So cool it hurts. Not that I've seen beyond reception, but that was enough.' Gil snorted. 'You know the building won an award? I was reading the other day what they'd spent just on commissioning a sculpture – and thinking I still couldn't believe Mike had gone to them for nothing.'

That decided me. I was desperate to talk to someone knowledgeable, and no one knew more about our firm than Gil. So I rapidly explained that, while I didn't want to compromise him, he'd have to swear to keep all this to himself if I told him about – well, about how I was hoping to get Mike back. The first minor shock was his asking if I'd *want* Mike back. He must have sensed my reaction because he apologized at once, mumbling that all relationships hit bad patches and it'd obviously been silly of him to imagine that just because, in recent years, Mike and I hadn't seemed exactly... He caught himself up.

'Oh, forget it. And you know I can keep my mouth shut. Besides,' he added, with a tinge of sourness, 'there's not much chance of doing anything else, seeing that Gaynor seems to have forgotten I exist.'

He listened without interruption as I outlined my suspicions, which was encouraging. Then told me that, while he could see my point, I was wrong. Wrong, wrong, wrong. Sorry and all that, and he was as shocked as me about our firm going down the plughole, but this wasn't the answer. He even began arguing Optimax wouldn't play dirty until I told him I'd scream if I heard any more about their corporate morals. 'OK then,' he sighed, 'you're making me say this, but neither would Gaynor. I can't blame you for thinking the worst about her, but she wouldn't. No way. If nothing else, you can't seriously believe she'd set out to bankrupt the man she – well, you know.'

'The man she loves?' I jeered.

'I was going to say,' he responded, with quiet dignity, 'the man she wants to father her children.'

Aidan had to pull me up.

'Steady on, lass,' he roared, as we beat our way up a thickly wooded hillside. 'You're meant to be giving them trees a tap, not felling t'buggers.'

I moderated my savagery after that, and did my best to keep up with the line. The state I was in, I'd have cried off today's shoot if I hadn't been down to the last few coins in my purse. This was the first pheasant day of the season, so instead of wading across heather uplands, we were plunging through jungle in the valleys, as noisily as possible. I couldn't contribute much to the raucous shouts echoing round the trees, though, because my throat was still raw from last night's weeping.

'*Children?*' I'd gasped.

'Biological clock, isn't it? She told me, oh, two years back, she was sick of being messed about by rich sugar daddies, that she wanted the Real McCoy. And she always used to go on about what a great dad Mike was, so soft about his kids–'

'Has he had it done, then?' I interrupted hoarsely.

'What?' said Gil, evidently unaware of the havoc he was wreaking my end of the phone, which was unlike him. But he was distracted by worry about his mother, even now asking me to hold on a tic, because he thought he'd heard a shout from upstairs...

'The vasectomy,' I managed to utter, when he returned, 'has he had it reversed?'

Waiting for his reply nearly killed me. 'Search

153

me, Jo. You know I haven't seen either of them since they shacked up. Anyway, I didn't realize he'd had the snip.'

'More like a knot, because I remember he was very keen to be reassured they could unknot it again, if – if–' Before my feelings got the better of me, Mrs Rydall let out a wail even I heard and, after hasty farewells, I was free to fling myself across the sofa and howl my heart out. Don't ask me why it affected me so deeply, it just did. Glossy, hard-edged, razor-brained Gaynor wanted babies? *My husband's babies?* I realized now that adultery was neither here nor there. She could have his body and welcome. But that she should be plotting to hatch a cuckoo half-brother or-sister to Sarah and Ben, to create a new Patterson family was – well, it was beyond bearing.

Even this morning, black jealousy made me feel capable of murder, never mind of bashing a few tree trunks. I tried to tell myself Gil was wrong, but to no avail. The clincher, in the tear-sodden reaches of the night, had been recalling Gaynor's filthy scowl after Mike's seemingly innocuous quip about dogs being as tying as kids. Besides, at that age, a woman like her, it was only too plausible. You can't open a magazine these days without reading about some career woman's desperate quest to breed.

'Keep up on the left,' bellowed a male voice, and I hurried forward. That is to say, I hoisted myself over a fallen tree trunk, narrowly avoided tumbling into the pond I'd failed to discern glinting under its splayed roots, and instead plummeted shoulder first into a holly thicket.

Moreover, rain had begun to lace the chill air, and I'd left my anorak in the trailer. Ever feel this isn't your day?

I was in turmoil. At first, last night, I'd thought I must have got everything wrong. As Gil had said, the idea of a woman setting out to fleece the father of her kids was crazy. Presumably she wanted to marry him, then. I'd found myself thinking about divorce, and dividing up our assets. I honestly hadn't considered the financial side of divorce before, so stubbornly had I believed we'd never come to that. But I didn't need to think about it to know Mike would act generously. There wasn't a mean bone in his body. Before the Optimax takeover, though, I'd owned half the company. So he'd have had to buy me out. Which would have cost him ... two million pounds?

That was when the idea of Gaynor striking under-the-counter deals with her old friends at Optimax began to seem not quite so far-fetched after all. Was it possible she saw it not as stealing Mike's firm off him, but as simply rescuing his assets from the clutches of his ex-wife? Because once they were married, he'd get the benefit of the riches Optimax had slipped her way, even if he didn't know how she'd earned them... I thwacked a tree trunk so hard, my stick nearly broke.

Eileen had warned me earlier, in the stable-yard, that the first pheasant day can be heavy going. She wasn't kidding. The undergrowth hadn't died back, there were lakes of mud as thick and sticky as plum pudding, and I kept losing my dog in the trees.

One small consolation last night had come from looking up vasectomy reversals on the internet. I'd learned that it takes at least three months for the reproductive machinery to return to working order. Even then, as I read with grim satisfaction, the fertility prospects weren't great for a man of Mike's age, eighteen years after the original op. But Gaynor would have assessed the odds too...

'Keep your dog in tight. T'birds are thick as flies down this edge,' called Aidan. 'And get a move on.'

Get a move on – that was exactly what I had to do. Mike at least didn't want an immediate divorce; he'd said so. To me. Even if he'd then implied that was only because he was too busy to fit it in. Too busy doing what? Please God not with finding time for a little visit to hospital. I'd got to act before it was too late, because if she managed to get herself pregnant...

'Dora? *Heel!*'

I needed help, and I needed it now. To hell with waiting for Paddy McGinty to wander home and find my letter. Wherever he was, a man like him must carry a mobile phone. I'd collar Lord Bidcombe this very day and ask for his number.

'Off at his regimental dinner, in London,' replied Aidan, when I asked why I hadn't spotted his lordship in the convoy of vehicles trundling back to lunch. No al fresco banquets for pheasant shooters. They, so I gathered, are entertained to stonking great casseroles and puds in front of roaring log fires in the castle. We were munching our usual sandwiches in a draughty barn at the back of the stable-yard. 'Back tomorrow, supposedly.' He squinted at me. 'What's got thee looking so down in t'mouth? Disappointed our fancy pants hasn't showed up?'

'Sorry?'

'We'll not be seeing him for a bit now,' contributed Eileen, informing those around her that he was rehearsing down South. I realized they must be talking about Ricky Marvell. But I was in no mood for banter, so I slumped on a straw bale and opened my lunch box. Egg sandwiches. And the bread was stale. So bad was my financial plight, I couldn't afford so much as a sliced loaf until I got my pay packet today. I'd have to finish – dammit, *start* – those violet curtains soon, or I'd starve.

Brooding on my troubles, I barely listened to the conversation round me about the Bunburies, whose day this was. The Admiral was talking about Hugh Hough-Hartley, who'd apparently missed every bird we'd sent his way, telling some story about him and a gun belonging to Jack Bidcombe. I gave up on my leathery egg butty, and ambled out of the barn to offer it to Dora. Even she eyed it pretty sniffily before taking it from my fingers. The drizzle was thickening. I'd just begun to unpick a Byzantine strand of bramble from her tail, cursing the clumsiness of my chilled and wet fingers – cursing everything, in fact – when a long, low, shiny bottle-green motor car nosed under the stone arch into the stable-yard. Don't ask me what make. It was open-topped, anyway, in spite of the weather, and vaguely vintage-looking – you know the kind of thing, running boards and a spare tyre with flashy chrome spikes strapped to the boot. Far more to the point, though, was that behind the wheel of this Mr Toad-mobile, larger than life in checked cap, gaily knotted scarf and driving gloves, was seated…

'Paddy?'

'Why, Mrs Patterson,' he shouted back, braking abruptly and shoving his glasses back up his nose. 'What good fortune. Aidan did mention he'd press-ganged you into service, so this saves me a trip to Beck Holme. By the look of the weather, I fear it might have been a long damp trek from the footbridge.'

I was probably staring at him like an idiot. 'You got my letter?'

'Have you written to me? How delightful, but I've been away. No, fact is, I've had a little notion with regard to your problems – rather a bright one. At least, I trust you'll think so.'

Glad as I was to see him, after a fortnight of conducting one-sided arguments with the man, it was somehow disconcerting to re-encounter him in the flesh. He wasn't quite as I remembered. He seemed taller, rather older and, for all he was smiling charmingly at me, more serious of face. But then he was sober now. We had no chance to talk further, because he'd barely hauled himself out of his driving seat than he was besieged by my fellow beaters. He seemed astonished by their cries of welcome as they spilled out from the barn, shyly protesting that he hadn't intended to interrupt their hard-earned lunch, but he shook hands and clapped shoulders, cast up his eyes with a grin as someone asked if he'd dug any good tunnels lately – evidently an old joke because there was general laughter – and enquired after Eileen's newest grandson. He was clearly very much a local in these parts. Looked it too, in shabby cords and a pullover, and he seemed to know every last dog by name, never mind their owners. 'You're too kind,' he murmured. 'Really, I don't deserve this.' It struck me he wasn't referring to the proffered can of beer, nor the slice of Eileen's celebrated sausage pie, but I couldn't imagine to what else. He was doing his polite best to edge his way back towards me, though, when a shout rang out across the yard.

'Uncle Peter, amazing! *Wowee*, is that your car?'

I'd seen this boy with the guns. Seventeen or eighteen, perhaps, he was very tall, thin and black-haired, in an antique shooting suit which flapped slackly round his greyhound frame. Only when he exclaimed that it was a shame Gramps was away did I recognize him. This was Jack Bidcombe's son, the unlucky lad who'd driven his papa into the ford so soon after passing his driving test.

'As you perceive, dear boy, I'm at loose behind the wheel again.' Paddy spoke warmly enough, but seemed to hesitate momentarily before stumping forward to throw an arm round those thin shoulders. 'God, you're looking disgustingly handsome, Miles. And why are you backsliding here in the middle of term? Sick or sacked?'

As the boy laughingly protested he'd slipped

home for one day on his way back from an interview at Durham – which had been appalling, he'd made a total idiot of himself – I felt obliged to creep away. Paddy saw though, and beckoned me back.

'But you'll come out this afternoon, if they ask?' the boy said. 'They're still a gun down after that singer bloke dropped out. Want to bring the motor round to the forecourt? I'll drive if you like.' The longing behind this casual offer was comically patent.

'Do I want a crunched car? Oh God...' Paddy flinched as though he'd said something tactless, and the boy coloured too. They eyed one another uneasily.

'Did Dad know you were coming?'

Paddy cleared his throat. 'I didn't know myself, not until I saw the old familiar turning off the A1. I wanted to talk to Jo here. I could have telephoned, but...' He ran a hand through his hair and glanced at me. 'Lord, for better or worse, I suppose some homing demon prompted me to turn the wheel.'

'*Good*. I mean... Well, it's brilliant to see you again, that's all. Look, are you coming round to get something to eat?'

The awkwardness, whatever its cause, had gone. With a martyred sigh, Paddy tossed over the ignition keys. 'I shall expect a large drink in return.'

'Come on then.' He hurdled into the driver's seat without troubling to open the door.

'I want to speak to Mrs Patterson first. Jo, are you acquainted with this lout? My cousin's son –

160

my own godforsaken godson – Miles Bidcombe.'

Miles, with manners that would bring a glow to any mother's heart, was already hauling himself as upright as he could behind the steering wheel, hand outstretched.

'As a matter of interest, he was born on your premises,' added Paddy, with a glint of amusement. 'Both the beck and his mother's cervix having expanded faster than forecast.'

Miles accorded this the fleeting smile due to an old family joke, but reminded him in an undertone that the weather was closing in. 'And I've promised Aidan we'll get lunch over quick as poss, so...' He craned over to throw open the passenger door.

'I have business to discuss with Jo, you importunate oaf,' he retorted, but the car's engine was already growling as he turned to me, casting up his eyes in mock despair. 'Perhaps...?'

'Later,' I agreed happily.

13

'Who'd have thought it?' muttered Aidan. We were standing on a hillside, and I was observing the guns in the valley below climb back into their vehicles after the first drive of the afternoon. 'Reckon we'll see storms before long.'

I might have assumed he was talking about the weather, because great black boulders of cloud were indeed clumping overhead, but he, like me, was watching Paddy shove his gun ahead of him through a rear door, and then conjure a bottle and glass seemingly out of nowhere, before clambering aboard himself. I glanced round. The granite face was as impassive as ever, but I knew him better now and thought I sensed – unease? 'Are you talking about Paddy?'

Not just did he not reply, he didn't even look at me. 'Glad someone's happy, any road,' he grunted, and stumped off.

If he meant me, he was dead right. Barmy, I know, because my problems hadn't changed an iota, let alone gone away. I just had this irrational conviction that Paddy McGinty would help me solve them. Better yet, he was obviously willing to. I could hardly wait for the shoot to finish so I could find out what his great idea was. In the meantime, my spirits were undaunted by rain, terrain or viciously unprovoked attacks from low-flying hawthorn bushes. Even when I filled my right wellington with swamp after an over-confident leap across a gully, I only chuckled and squelched on. In fact, I was rather disappointed that none of my companions in the line, usually such jovial souls, seemed inclined to share my good humour. As half a dozen of us clustered under an oak tree at the end of the second drive, the mood was disconsolate, not to say grumpy.

'Shouldn't be shooting these pheasants yet,' opined Eileen, her bulky body so comprehensively encased in waterproofs she put me in mind of something out of a sci-fi movie: one of those geezers who come in to clear the streets when a deadly virus is on the loose. 'By, we've hardly had a decent frost yet.'

Assuming this was a reflection on the eating quality of the fowl, I was poised to chip in with my granny's identical wisdom on the subject of Brussels sprouts, only to be saved from exposing again my town-bred ignorance by Leonard speaking first. That he spoke at all was a rare event. More your strong, silent type was Leonard, although I'd been told he was a wow in the pulpit.

'Rightly said, Eileen, rightly said,' he declared sonorously. ''Tis no fit sport with these poor creatures, half-fledged and soft as chickens. In the old days, we'd not have driven this wood till nigh on Guy Fawkes, and they'd be flying straight up to heaven by then.'

'Needs must when the bank manager drives, I fear,' sighed the Admiral, drawing on his pipe. His name actually was Ludovic Digby-Willershawe-Jones. Honestly. You can see why people called him the Admiral. 'Guns these days want a sky black with birds, and right through the season. Bernard does his best, but one fears it's a losing battle.' He chewed the stem of his pipe for a moment, before adding thoughtfully, 'Odd that young McGinty should turn up when he's away at his reunion. And it's Paddy's old regiment, too, so he must have known. Still, I suppose he'll be staying over until tomorrow at least.'

'He'd better, the booze he's sunk,' muttered one of the musketeers as he bent over to tug teasels off his trousers. 'Bloody tragic if he wrapped *that* car round a tree.'

'That's enough,' said Eileen, with surprising sharpness.

'Has Aidan mentioned anything to you about the estate?' enquired the Admiral.

She scowled. 'I've learned more talking to barn doors than to my brother-in-law, and Meg's as bad. But he's still holding to it t'place won't go for a hotel or anything else. Says he's Mr Jack's word it's staying in t'family. For what that's worth, says I.'

'Oh, Eileen, isn't that rather harsh?'

'I've said it before, I'll say it again. Without Paddy, they'd have sold up two year back. And he's their only hope now.'

I wasn't going to let this pass, even if we were being called to line out. 'Why?' I demanded, at which they all turned to look at me, rather like that famous cartoon of the man who asked for a whisky and soda in the pump room at Bath.

'Major McGinty's – quite a wealthy man,' said the Admiral, after a moment. 'But money tends to bring its own problems, doesn't it? Shall we move?'

The snub was gentle but unmistakable. It was one of the few times I'd been made to remember I was newcomer, and in a less ebullient mood I might have felt squashed. As it was, I just felt glad to learn my friend was comfortably off – very comfortably, if he was in a position to bale out an estate like this. Perhaps there was a tinge of self-interest, too. I'd always intended to offer Paddy payment for his professional advice, even if I had sneakily believed he'd refuse, and I was sure of it now. Bashing on through the undergrowth, I wondered what his idea might be. Had he learned something about Optimax? The drive couldn't straggle to a soggy close soon enough for me and, as luck would have it, the beaters' wagon was parked on the track, close by the guns.

I galloped down the hill, heading straight for Paddy, who was sheltering under a tree with Hugh Hough-Hartley. He was squatting on the ground, with one arm wedged round the neck of Hugh's fat black Labrador.

'He's plottin',' the man was saying. 'I've known it for weeks, that's why I wanted a word with you. And just this mornin', he bowls out of his lair and tells me cool as you please he wants his gun back. This gun, you know' – he brandished the case hanging over his shoulder – 'the Purdey. Lent it to me years and years ago, after his accident.'

'So give it back to him. Hughie, this bitch is disgustingly overweight.'

'Hell's he want a gun for, all of a sudden?'

Neither had observed my approach. I realized that what Paddy was actually doing – or attempting to do – was strap a collar round the dog's jowly neck while muttering distractedly that other chaps in wheelchairs seemed to manage to shoot a bit, so why not Jack? Good for him. *Ouch* – he'd stabbed his finger on the blessed buckle.

'Bernard told you he's bein' chased by some hotel company?'

Paddy stopped struggling with the dog for an instant and shut his eyes. 'Not above fifty times. Where's your hip flask, Hughie? This is thirsty work.'

165

I coughed politely. They didn't hear.

'And Jack says over his dead body.'

'You amaze me. There, it's on. Hope I'm not throttling the beast, but it's only for a minute.' When I saw the little black box with aerial glinting silver in the grass beside him, I realized it must be the bugged collar he'd strapped on to the dog. 'You'll love this, Hughie. If only your blessed animal would hop it. Off you go then, Bella, old girl. Scoot, vamoose, on your bike...'

'But he said to me outright, Paddy, that he needed the Purdey back to...' Hugh hesitated, then lowered his voice to a thrilling whisper. 'To save Stowham.'

Poor man. He was obviously in dead earnest, but there was something so absurd about him – so like Dr Watson propounding a fatuous theory of his own to Holmes – I wasn't surprised Paddy laughed. Unfortunately, he let out such a hoot he overbalanced and rolled on to his back on the muddy ground. 'Jack's last stand?' he spluttered. 'You see him up on the battlements, taking pot shots at the would-be purchasers?'

The kindly, doggy face grew pinker. 'Don't be ridiculous.'

''Fyou don't want to give it back, think up some excuse,' said Paddy, heaving himself up on one elbow. 'Tell him – oh, tell him it needs servicing, dodgy safety catch or something. This dog won't move for me, Hughie.'

'Um, excuse me?' I piped up.

'Get the beast to shift, can't you?'

'Will you stop playing bloody silly games with my dog and listen? I asked if you were going to be

166

here for Jack's birthday bash.'

Paddy, still on the soggy ground, looked up blinking. 'What birthday bash?' he began, but at that instant he saw me. 'Why, hello there,' he cried – and hiccuped. 'Met my old chum, Hughie? Hughie's a spoilsport. I want to show him my dogtracker, but–'

'Oh for God's sake, man, grow up.' And with that, poor, frustrated Hugh Hough-Hartley ripped the collar off his panting dog, stuffed it into his gun case and stomped away, with the merest nod in my direction.

Paddy watched him go without moving. 'Don't – don't think too badly of him,' he sighed. 'Awfully good fellow in real life. Just a tad off colour today. Not at all a Bunbury, under the meanin' of the act. I say, how kind.' I was holding out a hand and, not without difficulty, hauled him to his feet. 'I came up with the name, you know, Oscar Wilde, all that. Lit'rary erudition's all mine. But then, racing page of the *Mirror*'s more your Bunbury's idea of literature.' Craning round to study the plastering of mud on his trousers he nearly capsized again.

'Good lunch?' I enquired satirically.

'First class,' he replied, without a blink. 'I'm told the food was excellent, too.'

'Are you ever sober?'

'Not when mixing with Bunburies. Drink's the only antidote to terminal boredom.'

'I thought you said you were a member.'

'God forbid,' he cried, so loudly one of his fellow shooters twenty yards away turned

167

enquiringly, and he pulled a face, lowering his voice. 'Naughty boys club. Dib-dib-dib, pass the port and don't tell the good lady wife what you lost at Newmarket. Founded at my cousin's stag night.' Suddenly he sounded sad. 'By my cousin, naturally.'

But I wasn't interested in the Bunburies. 'You said you'd had an idea?'

For a moment, I wasn't sure the question had registered, but then he focused on me again and smiled. 'Gosh, yes, abs'lutely. I stopped shooting after the first drive. Just like you to know that. Shouldn't mix firearms and firewater, eh? Though I'm not *really* drunk.' He took a few deep breaths, blinked and sighed. 'Not yet, anyway. I say, this ravishing creature yours?'

'You're incorrigible,' I grunted as Dora cavorted around his caressing hand with the rapture of a girl who has at last found her perfect pair of wellingtons. I was talking to the dog as it happened, but he thought otherwise.

'Strain of returning to the ancestral home,' he protested. 'Dare say the prodigal needed a few stiffies before he tucked into the fatted calf, too. Oh, don't beetle your brows at me like a Methodist great-aunt. What else's a chap to do but drink when he's jacked in the day job at forty-six?' But somehow this didn't sound like a joke, even when he added, with evident pleasure at stumbling upon the phrase, that he was entering the age of insobriety.

'Why did you jack it in, then?' I said, with a touch of impatience.

He shrugged. 'Oh, one begins wondering what

it's all for, really. Whether one mightn't just as well moulder quietly into the landscape. Least one's blood and bones would provide a handy touch of fertilizer.' His specs nearly jumped off his nose as he suddenly broke into a sergeant-major snarl. '"Ambition, McGinty, you snivelling little toe-rag?" "Sir, please sir, to become a compost heap."'

I laughed, but was rather disappointed. Had my friend – because I did think of him as that – simply succumbed to the same middle-aged malaise as my husband? What is it with forty-something men? Why can't they just accept their lot in life and get on with it? 'Your idea,' I reminded him.

'My idea,' he said. And, taking off his specs, he rubbed the rain-spattered lenses against his sleeve for a moment. 'Look, I don't want to be rude, but – well, I got the impression money might be on the tightish side for you.'

'Strangularly,' I agreed without hesitation, because the Oxfam-trawling, bill-juggling early years of marriage had blunted any sensitivity about confessing to poverty. And now I was once again reduced to totting up the small change in the bottom of my handbag, the intervening spell of designer labels and trust-funds-for-the-kids felt like some briefly glimpsed mirage. 'Although,' I added hastily, 'I could have found the means to pay for your services...'

With an air of acute embarrassment, he waved me to silence. 'Beck Holme,' he said, planting the glasses back on his nose.

'Sorry?'

'I wondered, that is to say it crossed my mind, whether you might perhaps consider selling the old place to me.' He coughed apologetically. 'I can offer cash, so no problems with mortgages or any of that sort of nonsense.'

This wasn't at all the sort of idea I'd been hoping for, and it rather knocked the wind out of me. 'But I don't want to sell,' I said stupidly. 'If nothing else, I live there. I'd have nowhere to go until – well, until I can patch my marriage up.'

'Exactly,' he cried, with the air of one slapping down his trump card. 'Because I wouldn't want to take immediate possession. Too complicated to explain, but I couldn't live up here, not as things stand at present. So it would suit me perfectly if a responsible soul like yourself were to remain *in situ,* making sure the roof wasn't caving in, or the pipes exploding or killer beetle invading.'

'You want it just as an investment?' I squeaked, rather offended by the notion of my beloved haven being reduced to the merest counter on a Monopoly board.

'No. Well, I suppose it would be that too, but...' He glanced at me sheepishly. 'Would you laugh if I said for sentimental reasons?'

'No,' I said. 'I mean, no, I wouldn't laugh, but no, anyway.'

'Sorry, I should have made clear there would be no question of rent,' he said earnestly, 'for your continuing to live there.'

'But that's barmy.'

'I mean it. Enough for me to know the old place was being cared for.'

For an instant, I admit it, I wavered. I was imagining a quarter of a million quid cascading into my shivering bank account – along with a seemingly open invitation to remain in residence?

'For as long as you like,' he confirmed, reading my thoughts. And the brown eyes behind those tortoiseshell specs were warm with concern. 'Although naturally one trusts you and Mr Patterson will soon have resolved your, um, difficulties. But that's neither here nor there. Two months, two years, makes no odds. I'd just like to know that I owned a little patch up here. Stowham's meant a great deal to me, over the years.'

'I–'

'Whoops, we're being mustered for the retreat,' he said, as car doors began to slam and his name was called. 'Besides, you need to mull it over, of course you do. This afternoon's given me a chance to confirm my tottings-up with one or two people, though, check the current state of the market, what have you. So, just to give you an idea' – and the delicacy with which he paused here was truly exquisite – 'does a hundred and fifty thou sound acceptable? Lord, Miles, yes, I'm coming, I'm *coming*.'

14

My mouth was gaping so wide I felt a raindrop splash on my tongue. I actually began to laugh, which he misunderstood because he shot me a grin over his shoulder as he loped away.

A hundred and fifty thousand – a paltry, absurd *hundred and fifty?* Sure, the property market's well known to be a morality-free zone where even the most upright citizens might try to swing a crafty deal, and if I challenged him perhaps he'd laugh the offer away as a mere opening gambit. But a hundred and fifty, barely half what Beck Holme was worth – did he think I was an idiot?

It must have been a mistake, I decided, as I hauled myself up into the wagon. A man like him, a man I'd instantly felt I could trust – a wealthy man, too, by all accounts – he wouldn't stoop to such a mean game, would he? I'd have put it down to a Londoner's ignorance of the local market if he weren't clearly as native to these parts as Aidan Brighouse. Besides, he said himself he'd taken local advice. And he knew I'd been ditched by my husband, that I was short of funds, vulnerable... As we jolted off, a clod of earth spun up from the tractor tyre, hurtled with uncanny accuracy through the trailer window and smacked me over the eye. It felt symbolic.

That extraordinary offer of rent-free accommodation almost began to look like a cynical sweetener to hustle me into selling. A hundred grand profit would cover a lot of rent... But no. I couldn't and wouldn't believe Paddy McGinty had set out deliberately to cheat me. Soon as we got back to the castle I'd find him. Give him the chance to explain.

Even with the under-keeper's neck-or-nothing tractor driving, we were well behind the guns. With the rain gathering force and everyone anxious to get home, Aidan was waiting in the stable-yard, brown envelopes in hand, as we rattled to a halt on the cobbles. I brushed past him though, chucked dog and stick into my car, and stalked off under the mossy crenellated archway to one side of the building. I'd never ventured round to the front of the castle before, although I'd viewed it often enough from the nearby hills. From a distance it looked as prettily turreted as a child's toy, with a handsome avenue of chestnuts marching down from its intricately wrought gates. Close up, it proved to be less pretty. Even the ornately kitsch Victorian wings, tacked on to a grimly arrow-slitted medieval core, had an unkempt air, with clouded windows and splintered paintwork. It was also intimidatingly vast. Nevertheless, bedraggled as I was, I'd have marched straight up that towering flight of steps to bash on the lion-flanked front door if I hadn't spotted him out here. Several of the shooters were milling around, shedding boots and waterproofs, and Paddy was crouching beside his car door. There was a bottle and brimming glass balanced on the bonnet. I wasn't surprised he swayed as he tugged off a wellington.

I'd taken barely a dozen steps towards him, however, when a curious vehicle came thumping up behind me. Looked like a golf buggy crossed with one of those farmers' go-kart things, and was shifting at a gravel-spraying lick. I actually had to hop aside as it cut across my path and swerved to a halt beside Hugh Hough-Hartley.

'Got the gun, Hugo?' enquired the driver.

I knew who he was, of course. That chariot was no golf buggy, but a Formula One invalid carriage. Hunched over its controls, gaunt-cheeked and beaky-nosed, with a thick thatch of iron-grey hair, Jack Bidcombe put me in mind of a sour-tempered eagle. I wouldn't have cared to be in Hugh Hough-Hartley's boots, as he protested, with no conviction whatsoever, that he rather felt he ought to let a gunsmith take a look at it first, safety catch seemed a bit dicky, what? I marched on to Paddy, who was bent double, lacing his second foot into a brogue.

'The offer you made me,' I began, without preamble, 'you were joking, obviously.'

Couldn't give him a fairer opening than that. I even smiled at him. Why not? I was expecting him to laugh and disclaim, or better yet, to furrow his brow and confess to having plucked a figure from the air, or even admit he was too drunk to talk sense. Almost any excuse would have served, so keen was I to exonerate him.

'Absolutely serious, I assure you,' he said. 'And don't think this was some whim conceived driving down the A1, I've given it a lot of thought.'

'I'm afraid a hundred and fifty thousand strikes me, frankly, as a ridiculous price.'

'Nonsense,' he retorted, with a grin as innocent as daylight. 'Bang on the button, take my word for it. Care to come in for a drink and negotiate?'

'Oh hell, Paddy, you tell him...' wailed Hugh.

'Thank you, no,' I snapped. 'As a matter of fact–' I stopped because Paddy wasn't listening. I can't easily describe what was passing through his face. I recall an art teacher once telling us that if you mixed all the brilliant colours in the world equally, you'd end up with black. Well, so it was with him. Myriad different emotions seemed to flash across his features and then, suddenly, there was nothing. An absolute, impenetrable blankness.

'What the fuck are you doing here?' I'd heard the hiss of the vehicle swirling up behind me before Jack Bidcombe spoke.

'Hello, coz. Glad you haven't lost your old world charm.' Paddy spoke calmly enough, but he was deathly pale and breathing too fast.

'Just go. I mean it, Paddy.'

Hugh Hough-Hartley, trotting up in pursuit with Miles beside him, flushed dully. 'I say, old friend, steady on.'

'And you can piss off too, Hugo.'

'Why, Mr Paddy,' exclaimed a reedy voice, and I saw that the pin-striped butler was picking a careful path across the wet gravel in his glassily polished black shoes. 'Well, this *is* a nice surprise. How are you, sir?'

Paddy reached for the butler's hand and clasped it, but his gaze remained locked to that of his cousin.

'Your bags in the boot, Uncle Peter?' asked

175

Miles, avoiding his father's eye.

'Leave the bloody bags where they are. Paddy's going.'

The miserable uncertainty in the boy's face as he looked from one to the other wrung my heart. Only the butler seemed bizarrely unaffected.

'Now then, Mr Jack,' he tutted, with the smile of one humouring a fractious child, 'of course your cousin's staying, nasty wet night like this.' He half turned, and lowered his voice confidingly. 'We've been careful to keep your old room well aired, sir, because you know the moment you let the damp take a hold in an old building like this, *well...*' Hoisting a gun case over his shoulder and a bag under his arm, he trotted away.

No one spoke immediately. There was a spark of lightning over towards the moor, followed by a long, purposeful grumble of thunder.

'Um, Paddy,' I said determinedly. 'When you've got a minute?' Hugh Hough-Hartley was the only one who seemed even to hear, and he just blinked at me perplexedly.

'It's over,' said Jack, quietly. 'For better or worse, Stowham's coming to me and mine. Go away, make your own life and get the hell out of ours.'

'But he wants to help,' protested his son. 'Don't you, Uncle Peter? Mummy explained it all to me–'

'*Quiet*,' roared his father, so loudly a covey of rooks exploded from the nearest chestnut, shrieking. 'We've had enough help from him to last a lifetime. Isn't that so, Paddy? You want to

176

tell my son exactly how you *helped* this family?'

Even if I weren't still smarting from his supposed offer of help to me, there was no mistaking the guilt in Paddy's face. Miles saw it too. 'Uncle Peter?' He looked round, his voice rising. 'What's going on? I'm not a child any more, why won't anyone *tell* me?'

I felt so sorry for the lad, I nearly wrapped my own arm round him. I didn't know what was going on either, but they shouldn't be inflicting it on him. Paddy started forward and for a moment I hoped – assumed – he was coming over to Miles. Not a bit of it. He opened his car door, threw himself in. And under my disbelieving gaze, and the tearful eyes of his godson, he gunned the engine into life, shot backwards in a crazily tight arc which sent the whisky bottle and glass smashing off the bonnet to the gravel, then roared away through the gates as though all the demons in hell were pursuing him.

'May I have my gun now, Hugo?' said Jack Bidcombe calmly. But I noticed a quiver in one of those gaunt cheeks, and his hands – as he lifted the gun case from the shoulder of his hapless friend – were not steady. He laid it carefully across his lap, however, and sped away without another word.

'Damn,' said Hugh Hough-Hartley. 'Damn, damn, *damn*.' Somehow he managed to invest the curse with the potency it enjoyed in Victorian melodrama, when it couldn't even be spelled out on the polite page. Sighing, he stumped off to the castle.

Poor Miles remained, staring down the avenue of trees, shoulders heaving. And what almost undid me completely was that, when he realized I was behind him, he made a heroic effort to swallow his tears and stammered an apology for his uncle's hasty departure. 'You, um, wanted to talk to him, didn't you?'

At that moment, I wanted to shoot him, even more so when the boy noticed the shattered bottle at his feet, flinched and wondered aloud if Paddy had been drinking much.

'Like a fish,' I snorted, but then was sorry, because he looked horrified. I could almost see the visions of mangled vehicles and bodies galloping across his eyes.

'I'm sure he'll come to no harm,' I amended swiftly. 'Nothing but sheep up that road for miles, is there?'

He managed a wan smile. I moved towards him – but stopped. There was nothing a stranger like me could do to comfort the poor kid. Nothing more I could do here, full stop. So I trudged off back to the stable-yard, only too vexedly aware now that my right boot was squelching with mud.

My mood wasn't improved by the discovery that Aidan had left. So much for the pay packet I'd been counting on to feed me tonight. I could have followed him to Keeper's Lodge, but it lay in the opposite direction. Wet, tired and cross, I decided I'd make do with baked beans again and collect my money in the morning. I slumped into my car, and with headlights full on and wipers a-sweep, I set off through the storm for home.

Considering I live barely a couple of miles from Stowham Castle, it's an exasperatingly long way round by car. There'd been a lane, once upon a time, connecting my cottage into the estate, but a stretch of it had vanished in a landslip, oh, some time in the 1950s I think. You could still discern traces of it up the valley. Maybe the castle had suffered financial problems even then, because the damaged road had never been rebuilt, which doubtless explained why the only access to my abode lay across the beck. And that beck, I realized resignedly as I peered between the labouring windscreen wipers, would already be flexing its watery muscles in such a deluge.

Fortunately, given the rain, the gathering gloom and a one-track, grass-crowned thoroughfare across Stowham High Moor more suited to tractors than frippery suburban runabouts like mine, I wasn't driving fast. I saw the sheep and stamped on the brake in plenty of time. The animal lay slap bang in the middle of the road, with one bony leg crooked upwards at the kind of angle which suggested it wasn't just taking a nap. Tempted though I was to steer past, conscience impelled me to yank up the handbrake, climb out into the rain and check the poor beast really was dead.

It was – very. Had fallen foul of another motorist to judge by the ugly gash in its shoulder. Only as I turned back to my car, however, did I see the wheels protruding from a gully at the roadside – the gleaming, green hindquarters of a vehicle which had come to grief in the ditch, with a chrome-spoked wheel strapped to the boot.

Paddy's car. And I'd actually said to Miles he was unlikely to come to harm, that there were nothing but sheep on this road... 'God Almighty,' I muttered, running across and slithering down the muddy embankment.

The driver's door was open, and he lay half in, half out of his seat, with one arm dangling free and his head lolling slackly against the steering wheel. I grabbed his hand. 'Paddy?'

To my relief, the shoulders stirred, and a bloodied face tilted towards me, spectacles splayed over the forehead. An eye squinted open. 'Hello. What – you doing here?'

'Hush,' I commanded, heart hammering in my chest. Phone, I needed a phone. And of course I hadn't wasted precious money on frivolities like a new card for my own. 'You got a mobile? Oh, keep still, can't you?'

But he continued to heave himself upright in his seat, taking great rasping gulps of air. Stifling a moan, he knocked his glasses back to the bridge of his nose. They were still crooked. 'I'm – not dead.'

'More than can be said for the poor bloody sheep.' I sniffed the air. Petrol?

'No, I mean I'm not dead' – he actually seemed to be trying to laugh, although only wheezy grunts were emerging – 'and, you know something? Thass fine. By me.'

Concussed? In shock as well as drunk? Rain was lashing across the moortop at us with the ferocity of a fire hose. 'Have you a telephone in your car?' I asked again, enunciating every syllable.

He touched a wary hand to his cheek, then stared at his gory fingers. 'Nose,' he muttered. 'Must've bashed the steering wheel.' He turned towards me. 'Didn't hit the sheep, though. Just lying there – middle of the road. Braked too fast, skidded.'

'Yes, yes,' I said impatiently because, in truth, I'd already realized he must have swerved off the road well short of the dead animal. 'But the point is—'

'Not me, yer honour.'

'Will you shut up about the bloody sheep and tell me if you've got a phone so I can call an ambulance?'

'No.'

'Come on, someone like you must carry a phone?'

He was shaking his head, although it clearly cost him an effort to do so. 'No amb'lances, 'swhat I meant. *Please.*'

'Don't be ridiculous. You're bleeding – injured.'

He had already hauled one leg out of the door, and with a heave which scared the wits out of me, propelled his whole body after it, only to slump face down in the muddy bank, gasping. 'Be OK. But, drunk too much. Over the limit.'

'I want to get medical help, you fool, not the police.'

'That your car?' And to my horror, he blundered to his feet. I had to grab him to stop him toppling headlong, and nearly crumpled under the weight. 'So – sorry, perishin' nuisance,' he wheezed, anchoring an arm round my neck and lurching doggedly onwards. 'But if you could

181

just give me a lift somewhere – anywhere – I'd be most awf'ly grateful.'

Since we were already parallel with my rear bumper, and there was little to be gained except pneumonia by leaving him to capsize on the tarmac, I flung open the passenger door, shooed Dora into the back and supported him the best I could as he subsided, with a stifled groan, into the seat. He flopped back, eyes closed, sweat standing out on his forehead, fighting for breath. But that didn't mean I'd given in. Shouting that I'd go and secure his own car, I scrambled down the bank again. Sure enough, tucked into the pocket between the seats, was what I'd hoped to find. I couldn't actually get the door to close properly, but I pulled out the ignition key. The stink of fuel was powerful now, but in this rain, with the engine off, I hoped there was no risk of fire.

'Don't,' he whispered. He hadn't even opened his eyes as I slid into the driver's seat beside him, so he couldn't have seen I was holding his mobile. 'Please. Just got my licence back after nine months. This time they'll lock me up and throw away the key.'

'Damn and blast,' I hissed. 'No signal.'

'You may think I deserve it. P'raps I do, but–'

'Have to try at the top of this rise.' I dropped the phone into my lap, started the engine, and cautiously manoeuvred between the sad carcass of the sheep and a treacherous scatter of boulders lining the ditch.

'I don't usually drive when I'm drunk. Truly.'

'That's your affair. The point is, you've had an accident.'

182

'Only me hurt. And – I'm fine.'

'Like hell.' I jerked to a halt on the crest of the hill and eyed him as I pulled up the handbrake. 'What are you suggesting then? That I run you back to the castle?'

'God, no,' he burst out, which surprised me because I'd expected him to jump at the offer. 'Anywhere but.'

'Dump you in the middle of Wykesea? With blood all over your face, and not so much as a raincoat? Have you any money even?'

He attempted to reach round to his trouser pocket, but the movement was clearly agonizing and he let his hand drop again. 'I'll – I'll manage something. Really, you mustn't worry. You've already been too kind.'

'You could die. Here, now, in my car. And it would be my fault.'

'Want me to sign a disclaimer?' He tried to smile, but even that was beyond him. There was a liver-coloured bruise blossoming across his cheekbone under the caked blood. At least he appeared to be in his right mind – in so far as he could be said to have one.

'Shut up and conserve your strength,' I growled, groping in the glove compartment and thrusting a handful of tissues at him. I chewed my lip for a moment. The sky ahead of us was suddenly ripped across with a blinding zig-zag of lightning.

'Oh, on your own stupid head be it,' I growled, then tapped a number into the phone, clamped it to my ear and held my breath. 'Sarah? Sarah love, thank the Lord you're there. Look, I don't know quite how to explain this...'

15

'OK, this is the deal,' I said as I tossed aside his phone and restarted the car. 'I take you back to Beck Holme, where my daughter's bringing a tame doctor to check you over. But if he says you need a hospital, you'll be into an ambulance so fast you won't know what's hit you. And it's non-negotiable, so don't even think of arguing.'

'Sorry,' he said thickly through the wad of tissues he was clutching to his nose. 'Fearful bother.'

'Just don't die on me,' I muttered, 'and start praying we can get across the ford, because you're in no condition to make it on foot.'

It was still passable, although we sliced through with a wake like a powerboat. If Sarah's friend summoned an ambulance, there'd be a long wet walk with the stretcher. I could understand how, faced with that prospect, young Miles's mother ended up giving birth in the cottage. Had the family lived here, I wondered? But this was no time to enquire into my passenger's family history. Except, perhaps, for one small detail.

Before I posed that ticklish question, I scurried round to unlock and throw wide all necessary doors, and supported him as gently as I could into the sitting room. It was clear every halting step was hellish, but he didn't emit a squeak. Just clamped his lower lip between his teeth while keeping the other Britishly stiff. I flung the mounds of violet fabric off the sofa – reflecting, with a spurt of irritation, that I was now unlikely to be plunging the scissors into them tonight – and piled up cushions to support him before steeling myself to make the necessary enquiry. I felt obliged to repeat myself, with some urgency, until I realized the wheezy hacking noise emerging from him was laughter.

'Next of kin?' he gasped.

'It isn't funny. Have you a wife, parent – a child even, in case I need to, you know, contact someone?'

'Pass.'

'What's that supposed to mean?'

'No offspring, no siblings, parents dead.' There was a spark of mischief in his eyes – well, in the eye that wasn't swollen like a cricket ball. 'Might have an address for the wife, but she's unlikely to thank you unless she thinks she figures in the will. Divorced,' he added. 'Centuries ago.'

'Of course, there's your uncle.'

'Hesitate to state the obvious, but I am still alive.'

'Don't be a fool, I was going to phone the castle anyway. They must be worrying already.'

The faint smile vanished. 'Bernard's away.'

'I was thinking of poor Miles – oh, for Pete's sake, can't you stay put?' He had lurched toward me, only to crumple back with a hiss of pain.

'Sorry – sorry.' It was a moment before he gathered the breath to continue. 'Jo, I beg you, don't say anything to alarm them. If Seddons feels obliged to contact Bernard, tells him I've been in a car smash...' His face twisted. 'He's an old man, he's had enough to bear; Miles, too. God, that poor boy. I should never have run away from him like that.'

He sounded so remorseful, I was persuaded to tell a concerned Mr Seddons only that Major McGinty had met with a small mishap, and that he was taking refuge with me for the night. Oh, the car was a bit dented but he was fine, I said airily, averting my eyes from the bloodied face staring up at me from the sofa, he was just bruised and shaken...

I slammed the phone down. 'Bloody well hope I'm right.'

'Thank you. I'm most enormously grateful.'

'Piffle.' But I didn't speak unkindly. In fact I enquired almost solicitously whether he'd be all right alone for ten minutes while I shunted my car back to the far side of the ford. 'Or I could end up marooned for days,' I added. 'As you obviously know.'

'Maddening, that beck, isn't it?' he agreed, with a face of total innocence. 'Knocks such a wicked slice off the value of the property, too.'

'Drop dead,' I grunted as I slammed out into the rain.

It began to seem, however, that he was in no imminent danger of doing so.

'I'm Sarah Patterson,' my daughter informed him in a low, efficient voice so like a doctor in a soap opera I had to suppress a giggle, 'and this is my colleague, Dr Johnson.'

'As in dictionary?' enquired the patient.

186

As in qualified all of four months ago, but the earnest-faced young man with an adenoidal voice and sweaty T-shirt seemed to know his way round an injured body, and Sarah had assured me this Simon was the shining star of Accident and Emergency. She'd hauled him out of a squash tournament and delivered him to my door within an hour and a half of my phone call. Thank God for bossy daughters.

'I've been drinking,' said the patient helpfully as a bright white light was shone into his bleary eye.

'Bashed his knee – probably only twisted it, might have a cracked rib or two, multiple bruising, doesn't appear to be concussed,' Sarah informed me in the doorway. 'Simon and I will get him into bed between us when he's done. Silly to risk the stairs when there's a loo down here, so shall we put him in Ben's cave?'

She followed me into her brother's ground-floor room, more to supervise than actually to help with the bed-making. Sarah's always had a lofty contempt for housewifely trivia. 'My beautiful daughter' is how Mike refers to her, how he's always referred to her, with his usual cheery indifference to reality, as if, by saying it often and confidently enough, he could metamorphose her into Miss World. Of course, Sarah is incomparably beautiful in my maternal eyes, too, only I do realize that this is not quite how the rest of the world may see her. Short, rounded, pert-nosed and frizzy-haired, she doesn't give a fig about her appearance, never has, and would infinitely have preferred her doting dad to admire her exam results than her new frock. There's nothing of the strident feminist about her, mark you – all that stuff is prehistoric, yawn, yawn. If God had intended her to burn her bra, she said, He shouldn't have endowed her with 36 D tits. I don't think it's ever crossed her mind that being born female could prove any impediment to the career she was mapping out at twelve when, instead of experimenting with my mascara, she was dissecting frogs. The only mystery to me is that she's never been short of boyfriends. I think she was just eighteen when she informed me that, having weighed up the documented health risks, she was, nevertheless, opting for the pill. In addition to barrier contraception where appropriate, naturally. She kindly added that she didn't want me worrying she might make the same disastrous error I had.

'That disastrous error,' I'd retorted, stung, 'was *you*.'

'Natch,' she agreed. 'But don't tell me your life wouldn't have been a bloody sight better if you'd waited ten years for me to roll along.'

'If we'd waited ten years – or even ten months,' I said, with the satisfaction of one producing the clincher, 'you probably wouldn't *ever* have rolled along, because I doubt your father and I would still have been together.'

'Quite,' she said.

And I can't tell you the number of times I've heard her exercise just such clinically smug detachment on her boyfriends. Because, while her drop-dead gorgeous younger brother had

188

never produced a single female for family approval, our door- and phone-bells had trilled night and day for years with gangly adolescents languishing for love of my unappreciative daughter. I'd spotted the symptoms in the young doctor tonight at a glance.

'Bit of a pillock, socially,' she confided now as she strolled over to the converted aquarium to peer around for a glimpse of Ben's pet snake, 'but he has hidden talents, if you know what I mean. Good at the job, too. If he says your friend's OK, you needn't worry.'

'No friend of mine,' I retorted, shaking a pillow into a slip and bashing it into fluffiness. 'All his own fault. Lucky he isn't dead, driving a car as drunk as he was.'

I expected Sarah to concur wholeheartedly. Many a time and oft had I heard her lecture her papa on the perils of alcohol, and as for his precious cigarettes...

'He was still on Lord Thingummy's land, wasn't he?' she protested. 'Not that that would've stopped the fuzz from clobbering him, as he said, but he never intended driving much further. Never meant to drive at all. He's very mortified about the whole business.'

'How would you know?' I said indignantly, but then I'd missed the low-voiced medical conversations round the sofa as I ransacked my naked cupboards to rustle up coffee and sardines on stale toast for the flying doctor squad.

Besides, this was as nothing to my indignation half an hour later. The patient, swabbed, patched, strapped up and doped, had been eased into

Ben's bed. Sarah and her swain had gathered up their coats and boots and he was reminding me to give Paddy plenty of fluids, because he was likely to be dehydrated as a result of alcohol consumption.

'Permanent condition,' I snapped. 'I've never seen him sober.'

Sarah leaned towards me, her face alight with mischief. 'But he's one seriously sexy specimen, isn't he? I mean, for a guy his age. Good on you, Mother.'

'What?' I squawked, glancing round. But Simon had loped away to retrieve his bag. 'You surely don't imagine that he and I – I mean, *me?* With *him?*'

'Why not? Like they say, a guy's sexiest organ is his brain.' She let out the filthiest drain-gurgle chuckle. 'But there's nothing wrong with the other one, either. Maybe I'll drop a word in Dad's ear. No harm in rattling his cage.'

At any other time, I'd have been marvelling yet again at my daughter's unabashed frankness about sex. I swear I was twenty-three and a parent myself before I uttered the word 'penis' to my mother, and then only with reference to a rash on my infant son's private parts. 'In case you've forgotten, I'm still married to your father,' I hissed, before turning to Simon, who was cataloguing the symptoms I should be watching for.

After they'd gone – and I waited in the doorway for ten minutes to make sure I heard their car cough into life on the far side of the beck – I thankfully shut the door on the tempest and returned to Ben's room. The new occupant was lying stiffly down the middle of the bed, eyes closed, quilt rising and falling gently. Seriously *sexy?* Even when we'd first met, when I wouldn't deny I'd liked Paddy McGinty very much, I'd only thought how funny he was, how engagingly eccentric, how transparently, endearingly *honest...*

'Am I hallucinating?' a faint voice enquired from the pillow. 'Pink rats one might expect, but – is that a snake?'

I turned to the corner, where a light glowed in the glass tank. Sarah must have switched it on. Barry, the American corn snake, was whipping his sinuous body this way and that against the glass, tongue a-flicker.

'It's a snake,' I confirmed. Which made two of them in the room.

Naturally, I couldn't maintain my frigid indignation all night, although Sarah's misplaced jests helped. Like it or not, the man was in my care, and although young Simon had assured me there was no need for a permanent vigil, the symptoms he'd reeled off as possible causes for concern seemed alarmingly comprehensive: vomiting, confusion, dilated pupils, pin-point pupils, double vision, blurred vision, bad head-ache... Any of these, I gathered, might indicate the wisdom of a swift transfer to hospital.

'After whisky, claret, port and bloody sloe-gin, what do you think?' grunted the invalid, when I asked whether his head ached.

And it was all very well to talk about pupil-size. I'd no clue what size a normal pupil was supposed to be. I ended up studying my own in a mirror and concluded his didn't look so very different. He certainly wasn't throwing up, and politely assured me he could see only one of me at the last count. Yes, of course his vision was blurred: his specs were on the bedside chair. And indeed, he knew what day of the week it was, the name of the prime minister, could recite his army number if required – and wasn't it high time, he added wearily, that I found my own bed? But I curled into Ben's beanbag at the foot of his, with two sweaters, thick socks and Dora. I'd have done the same for anyone in his condition, but I can't deny there was a sneaky intent, at the back of my mind, that my Florence Nightingale ministrations would leave him feeling rotten with guilt for his less than generous behaviour towards me. By the dim glow of the snake-tank, I brooded alternately over my troubles and the Home Medical Encyclopaedia while he slept.

It wasn't restful sleep. Every so often he would try to turn over, then groan before subsiding on to his back again. On the odd occasions he was quiet for too long, I felt obliged to tiptoe across and assure myself he was still breathing – honestly, it was like being a first-time mother again, listening to Sarah in her cot – only for a stertorous exhalation to rumble into my ear. But he didn't just snore, he also moaned and talked. Mostly it was incoherent babble. He seemed to be fretting about a cat, but there was a point when he thrashed and cried out and nearly heaved himself upright, before realizing I was gripping him by the shoulders.

'Don't tell Jack,' he mumbled, 'don't tell Jack – I wasn't driving.'

'What?' I said, and his eyes flipped open, wide with panic. Only to focus on me and then slowly droop shut again.

'Oh, Jo,' he grunted. 'Sorry.'

At least he knew who I was, and since he was already three parts asleep, I diagnosed this as a bad dream rather than an undetected skull fracture and settled back into my beanbag. I was speculating about possible causes of the animosity between him and his cousin Jack – had he tried to buy Stowham Castle for a song just as he had my cottage? – when I must have fallen asleep myself.

He was gone. That was almost the first thing I realized as I awoke with a cruelly stiff neck and frozen toes in the grey half-light of a room which was not my own. The bed was empty; the quilt tossed back.

'Paddy?' Dora promptly came skittering through the open doorway, and I heard a halting, heavy tread in the passage, accompanied by a puzzling, ear-grating screech of wood on wood. Paddy lurched in, clutching the high-backed chair from beside the bed, which he appeared to have adopted as a walking frame. He was dressed, too, in bloodied shirt and torn trousers, and a whiff of my lemon soap percolated across.

'Oh, God,' he croaked, 'this makes me feel awful.'

'Serves you right for getting up,' I responded, scrambling to my feet to support him. He looked awful, too. His face was dark with bruises, and he was holding on to the chair for dear life.

'I meant about you. Camping out at my bedside. You must be exhausted.'

'Don't give it a thought,' I replied, trusting he was giving it plenty as I thrust an arm round him. 'Back to bed?'

'I was hoping I could use your phone, actually,' he gasped. 'I know, from long experience, mobiles don't work down here, and I should be arranging to get out of your way. I've caused you a fearful amount of trouble.'

'Kitchen, then,' I said, steering him in that direction. 'Although I don't know what arrangements you had in mind, short of a chum in a helicopter.'

'I'm sorry?'

I waited until we'd squeezed along the hall and I'd deposited him in a chair by the kitchen table. 'No way you can make it to the footbridge, is there? And I doubt anything can cross the ford by now.'

'I was thinking perhaps one of the Home Farm tractors?'

I peered out of the window, where the rain was sluicing horizontally. 'Four foot high and rising, on past performance,' I said, rather smug at being able to flaunt my local knowledge. 'Not even a tractor would risk it.'

'Oh, Lord.'

'Sorry you offered to buy the place?' Well, I couldn't resist it.

He looked down at his hands with every appearance of discomfiture.

194

'Not,' I cordially continued by way of a prompt, 'that I ever had the least intention of accepting your generous offer.'

'I suppose that's as well,' he said quietly. 'Obviously, you've realized my bright idea was a tad ill thought out.'

Which, as apologies go, didn't go nearly far enough for me.

16

I had to lead the repair truck over the moor to the battered car. Paddy was profusely apologetic, but it was easier than trying to explain where, precisely, the vehicle had tumbled off that unnumbered track of a road. Then, when I reached Keeper's Lodge to collect my pay packet, Aidan was out. I'd expected that. What I'd forgotten was that this was Megan's day in the hospice shop. Onwards, then, to Wykesea, where the cash machine not only declined to disgorge a piffling ten quid, it also confiscated my card, flashing a rude message about having a word with the management. So, with fifty-four pence in my purse, and not so much as a drop of milk in the fridge, I had no choice, did I?

Nevertheless, I stomped the rain-blasted length of Fishergate twice while I psyched myself up. The dangling balls weren't so much gold as dingy mustard. In fact, the whole street looked as seedy as I felt. Even in sunshine, Wykesea isn't the prettiest of towns, although it has its picturesque nooks by the harbourside. In an affluent rural county, though, it's an outpost of semi-urban depression. The presence of a pawnbroker says everything. You wouldn't find an establishment like this in the cutesy stone-and-cobble market towns inland, where I used to go and buy organic veg and fancy charcuterie once upon a more prosperous time. Flogging my watch – what was I coming to? But I'd already earmarked this expensive timepiece as sacrificial victim, probably because I'd never much liked it. After an altercation over the wisdom or otherwise (definitely otherwise) of co-producing a touring farce, Mike had added to the losses thus incurred by treating me to this glitzy peace offering. I'd worn it all these years only because I knew it had been chosen by a thirteen-year-old Ben, presumably on the basis that it was the kind of flashy wrist-candy favoured by the blonde, bronzed and bosomy wives of his footballing heroes. However, bracing myself with those newspaper stories you read in recessions about duchesses pluckily popping their tiaras, I snapped it off my wrist and marched under the balls.

Expecting a den of darkly Dickensian depravity, complete with Fagin, I found what looked much like a downmarket video-rental joint. It was glaringly strip-lit, with a scuffed vinyl floor and walls plastered with posters advertising the latest blockbuster movies, alongside racks of tapes. There was also, however, a glass-fronted, floor-to-ceiling cabinet in which were imprisoned a sad assortment of microwaves, golf clubs, ghetto-blasters and other household goods which must have proved, so to speak, beyond redemption. The only other unusual feature of the place was a scuffed grey safe the size of a telephone kiosk behind the counter. Fagin, seated in front of it with a mug of coffee and a copy of the *Sun*, was actually a white-bearded Father Christmas lookalike, in shirt-sleeves, braces and outsize red-spotted bowtie.

'Top of the marning to ye,' he carolled in an Oirish accent as authentic as Monet's gilt-framed water lilies hanging behind his head, price £9.99. 'What can I be doing you for then, darlin'?'

The transaction was swift and clinical, but humiliating nevertheless, not least because of Santa's knowing smile when I stammered that I would be redeeming my watch within the week. You could tell he'd heard that tale before. I hurried out, tucking the ticket into my purse along with a dozen ten-pound notes. It was a fraction of what Mike must have paid for the watch, but that's what the man had offered and I couldn't have borne to haggle. I emerged into the rain lusting for revenge, and my target was ready to hand. Without Paddy, I wouldn't have had to do this. I'd have collected my pay from Aidan yesterday, which would have tided me over until I'd made up the violet curtains. The curtains which – again because of him – I hadn't so much as started. I contemplated allowing the pawn ticket to flutter from my purse as I clumped the shopping on to the table. Let him know the measures to which I'd been driven, just to put

197

milk in his coffee. But then, as I turned up North Quay towards the little supermarket, I had a better idea.

Estate agencies are among the few businesses which seem to thrive in Wykesea, and the premises of Messrs Smith, Robertson and Orrie sparkled brightly through the sodden buffets of wind. A chequerboard of colourful snapshots filled the window, and within the shop, I had no doubt, there would be glossy leaflets to match. I was going to take a selected handful of these home to present to my guest. A few ideas, I would innocently suggest, if he were thinking of purchasing a property in the area. I'd make sure the prices were clearly marked. And if that didn't force him to up his game in the apology stakes, nothing would.

I could see my smile reflected in the window as I scanned the assorted ads in search of cottages comparable to my own. I also saw that smile droop. I pressed my nose to the glass, squinting at the caption under one dinky picture after another, sure I was misreading. The next minute, I was bashing through the door into the shop.

'Surely,' murmured Paddy, 'a natural misunderstanding?'

He was sitting where I'd left him, on a hard chair in my dark and chilly kitchen with the dog coiled round his ankles. As I'd staggered in, awash with carrier bags and remorse, the silly sod had even tried to apologize for not washing up his tea mug. He was grey-faced, quaking with cold and wedged against the chair back with a rigidity which betrayed acute discomfort. I have never felt more mortified.

'Misunderstanding?' I cried, stuffing bottles and packages into the fridge, dodging across to clang the kettle on to the Aga with one hand while groping down the side for newspaper and matches with the other. *'Misunderstanding?* Look, ten minutes and I'll have a fire lit in the sitting room. Hop it, Dora. Coffee or tea and, oh God, when did you last eat? I couldn't offer you so much as a slice of toast this morning. Look, will you stop laughing?'

'Quite right,' he grunted. 'Hurts like hell. Um, coffee would be marvellous, if it isn't too much trouble.'

'Coming up. I am *so* sorry, Paddy.'

'Why?'

I grabbed the newly purchased pack of fresh-ground Kenyan and tippled it into the cafetière with reckless abundance. 'Don't pretend to be stupid. I told you, I thought you were trying to rip me off on the house price. Fleece me.' I was determined to make a clean breast of it. 'Cheat me out of a hundred grand and more.'

'How dastardly. Should have equipped myself with swirling cloak and moustache.'

'Can you never be serious?'

'Inbred. Congenital facetiousness.'

'I've been so *rude* to you.'

'As long as it wasn't on account of my jokes. You can't hit me, I'm sitting down, injured and wearing glasses.' He grinned one-sidedly up at me. The raw bruise across his cheek mingling with his unshaven stubble reminded me horribly

199

of newspaper pictures of torture victims. 'Sweet of you to be so contrite, but unnecessary. Half the world tries to pull a fast one trading properties.'

'Someone pulled a bloody fast one on my husband, that's for sure,' I responded grimly. The helpful estate agent had nearly fallen off her chair when I told her we'd paid a quarter of a million. She actually knew Beck Holme because she walked her dog up this way, as I told Paddy while unpacking my various carrier bags. On quitting Messrs Smith, Robertson and Orrie, I'd ransacked half the shops in Wykesea for penitential offerings.

'Your poor chap doesn't seem to have much luck with money, does he?' he agreed.

'He shelled out exactly *twice* what she reckoned this house is worth,' I wailed, ripping open a packet of chocolate digestives. 'Honestly, first the company goes for nothing, now it turns out he's thrown away half his mother's legacy. I cannot believe it.' Except, of course, I *could* believe it. Even if I too had taken for granted that this most desirable of detached residences with chunk of National Park attached was a snip at the price – heaven's sake, you'd be lucky to buy a bus shelter in Wimbledon for less – I, at least, would have had the wit to make a few local enquiries before whipping out my chequebook. But not my impetuous husband. 'Biscuit? Danish pastry? Lunch in about, oh, three-quarters of an hour.'

'Jo, actually, there's something I wanted to say to you, if you could spare a moment.'

'Milk? *Milk*.' I attacked the carton and a jet of

semi-skimmed pinged ceilingwards. And who was the seller who had taken such shameless advantage of Mike's Home Counties innocence? Gaynor's former lover, that's who, Ricky Marvell. I wasn't saying she'd actually pocketed a commission on the deal but I wouldn't have put anything past her. Anyway, she was responsible for introducing Mike to the randy, wrinkled rocker. I plonked down a pastry-laden plate. 'Help yourself.'

'You're spoiling me.'

'Least I can do.' I planted myself in a chair opposite his. 'The very least. You didn't just offer me a fair price, it was over the odds, heftily over the odds, as you obviously knew. On top of which–'

'Jo, last night you fished my disgustingly drunken body from my wrecked car, trundled me back here–'

'–you actually invited me to stay on.'

'You had me patched up, played guardian angel as I snored–'

'*Rent free*. Not that I'd have accepted, at least I hope I wouldn't, and I truly didn't want to believe you were the type to rip anyone off, but–'

'God's sake, can I speak?' he roared, so loudly the dog leapt to her feet, the window-panes rattled and I stared at him round-mouthed.

He smiled sweetly. 'Thank you so much. Actually, that's what I wanted to say. Thank you, Jo. I can hardly find the words to express my gratitude.'

He did, though. Find the words, I mean. Drunk

or sober, Paddy McGinty was not a man to run short of a word or two thousand. I was told I might have saved his life. No, he didn't wish to be melodramatic either, but who was to say that another car would have trundled past before the shades of night closed in? And while fading hypothermically away clutching an out-of-range mobile might have served him right, the idea of Bernard – or Miles – being told that his alcohol-stinking corpse had been found smashed into a ditch on the estate didn't bear thinking about. No, I wasn't to interrupt, he hadn't finished. Because, setting aside his worthless life, what I had saved, with no shadow of doubt at all, was his driving licence.

He hesitated for a moment, before asking whether he had mentioned that his licence had only recently been restored? Reaching for the sugar bowl, I nodded, and he sighed. 'I thought so. Nine months. But they might have chucked me in prison this time, reoffending within a couple of weeks.' He studied his signet ring for a moment, turning it this way and that, then continued quietly: 'I didn't merit that ban. I'm not weaseling out, and I won't bore you with the whys and wherefores, I'd just hate you to think I made a habit of terrorizing the highways when drunk. I don't. Yesterday, though...' He grimaced. 'Yesterday, you'd every right to hand me over to the law, or at least dump me at the castle, and Stowham would almost have been worse than police custody last night. Family relations are – a touch strained, at present.'

'You don't say,' I murmured, thrusting down

the plunger in the cafetière.

He grinned, but after I'd poured the coffee, his hand closed over mine, and he said earnestly: 'I am hugely in your debt.'

'Rot. Drink your coffee, and I'll go and light a fire.'

'I mean it,' he insisted, releasing my hand. 'I don't know how I can possibly repay your kindness.'

I did.

I didn't tell him how at once, though. Give the poor bloke a chance. Frozen, unfed and no doubt cruelly hungover as well as battered, he wasn't going anywhere in a hurry. I could wait for an appropriate moment to draw his attention to my improvised filing cabinet under the kitchen table – now expanded to two cardboard boxes, with the company records I'd printed off the computer. After lunch, maybe.

He turned out to be a perfect guest: appreciative, clever and funny. Mind, as we chatted about this, that and the inconsequential other over Chablis and smoked salmon butties, it occurred to me he was the first guest I'd *ever* entertained at Beck Holme, other than the kids, or Gil dropping by for a cup of tea. And I couldn't remember the last time I'd shared a bottle of wine at lunchtime, either, let alone in such good company as this. We'd just taken our glasses through to the fire when the telephone trilled.

'Hello? Yup, sure.' I returned to the sitting room and passed it over. 'Your uncle.'

From several feet away, I heard his lordship's demand for an explanation of this nonsense about Jack ordering him off the premises yesterday. He need scarcely have bothered with the phone. If I'd opened the window, we'd probably have heard that fruity bellow over the hill.

'Unfortunate that Jack saw me,' began Paddy, only to be silenced by another outburst, although I didn't catch the actual words this time. I would have retired tactfully to the kitchen if he hadn't gestured me back, with some urgency. '...truly, dear old ancestor, ingenious notion, and I dare say Ted Muxworthy's quad probably could make it over the hill to here, but the prospect of bouncing cross country in my present state...' He rolled his eyes towards me. 'No, no, I promise, merely a little bruised, all limbs present and correct, but I think I'd be advised to stay put for the time being. That's if Mrs Patterson can endure it?'

Nothing could suit me better than for this tame spook to haunt my house, but I was nevertheless startled to hear my smiling offer to collect his bags from the castle interpreted as Mrs Patterson's downright insistence he remain at Beck Holme. Seemed I wouldn't take no for an answer. Paddy winked confidingly at me while fluently explaining into the telephone that he and I were the oldest of old chums. 'Met in town, ages ago...Yes – well, *yes*, I suppose you could say that... Hello, Bernard?' He lowered the receiver. 'Bloody dog's after the peacocks again. I say, sorry about laying it on so thick just now, but I couldn't bear the dear old sausage to think I'm avoiding him.'

I put my head on one side. 'Do I gather you are?' When he didn't deny it, I remembered what the Admiral had said. 'You knew he was going to be away at his reunion when you came up here yesterday, didn't you?'

He hung his head like a guilty schoolboy. 'Look, I'm devoted to my uncle, truly. Like a second father – more of a father than my own, in some ways, and I'd hate to hurt his feelings. I fully intended seeing him today when he got back, but just for a couple of hours. Enough to sort out the necessary, then skedaddle before he could start browbeating me.'

'About what?' I said.

So charmingly did he respond that he wouldn't dream of returning my kindness by boring me with his family squabbles that I didn't realize I'd been snubbed until he'd gone on to say that, if I truly didn't mind collecting his kit from the castle, I could give Bernard his present while I was there. 'That's if I can find the thing.' He was delving into his trouser pocket. 'Lord knows, it imprinted itself painfully enough on my flesh yesterday afternoon.' He produced the little black tracker with a grunt of triumph, and resumed digging. 'Collar must be in here somewhere.'

'No, don't you remember?' I cut in. 'Your friend Hugh took it off his dog.' I paused to think, not very coherently because the wine had gone to my weary head. 'Actually it's probably at the castle by now, because I'm pretty sure he stuck it in his gun case.'

'Dear me, really?' Paddy had reclamped the phone to his ear, and was addressing his uncle, not me. 'Still, I dare say he'll toddle home when he's hungry.' He wiggled his brows enquiringly towards me as he went on to declare that, with luck, Bernard would soon have the means to curtail Jasper's wanderings.

'Hugh returned the gun to your cousin,' I hissed.

He didn't miss a beat. 'In fact, before Jo sets out on her mission of mercy, would you mind awfully slipping into the gun room just to see if there's such a thing as a black leather dog collar in the bag for Jack's old Purdey? Otherwise, I'll have to ring Hughie–' He broke off, frowning. 'Oh? Oh, really. Well, not to worry, I dare say we can sort something out. Yes, Jo will be over later. Goodbye – goodbye, old chap.'

The phone line was dead, but he continued to stare at the receiver in his hand.

'Paddy?'

'Odd,' he said. 'Bernard seems to think Jack's sent the Purdey off for repairs. Something about a dicky safety catch.'

17

'You cannot seriously be suggesting I prowl your uncle's stately corridors with a bug detector bleeping in my hand?'

'But it's a brilliant wheeze. Chance in a million, the dog collar being stuffed into the case like that.'

'No way.'

'Magnum of champagne?'

'I beg your pardon?'

'When all else fails, I never hesitate to resort to bribery. And you're going to the castle anyway...'

'Dream on, sunshine.' A yawn uncurled my whole body. After a hard day in the field yesterday and scant sleep in a beanbag last night, a couple of glasses of wine had done for me. I'd just decided to have a little snooze before digging out all the papers and telling my grateful guest exactly how I hoped he was going to repay my hospitality when, blow me down, here he was asking me for yet another small favour.

He grinned. 'Dinner for two? In Paris. In fact, make a weekend of it, honeymoon suite at the Georges V with the man of your choice.'

'Since the man of my choice is shacked up with his floozy,' I retorted, plumping up a cushion, 'that's a very tactless offer. And the answer's still no.'

Trivial little thing, he'd said. Just wanted me to

check that his cousin's prized Purdey wasn't in fact still kicking round the castle, given that gun repairs were expensive, Jack was careless, and Paddy frankly found it hard to believe in a faulty safety catch he'd invented himself. No, he couldn't just *ask*. Jack had specifically told Bernard he'd sent it away to be serviced.

'And if he hasn't, so what?' I said, tiring of the joke – because joke I thought it was. Another excuse to try out his gadget. I felt more than sufficiently at ease with my guest to curl up in my corner of the sofa. Is there anything more deliciously decadent than dozing off, mid-afternoon, with a storm battering outside the window and a fire crackling at your feet? A good fire, too – I'd been as profligate with my logs as my ground coffee. 'Sorry, probably rude, but I'm whacked. 'Scuse me if I snore.'

'Guns have to be locked away,' he said stubbornly, staring into the flames as he twisted Dora's ears between his fingers. 'Legal requirement.'

'Yeah, yeah, and I'm sure Mr Plod's round the castle every day, checking. Anyway, whassit matter?' You know when you can feel sleep slinking over you? Like a warm tide, drifting up from your toes? I shut my eyes. 'Don't tell me. You think Hugh was right 'bout him going round shooting people.'

'No – no, of course not.'

I opened an eye. 'Once more with feeling?' When he didn't so much as smile, I felt obliged to hoist myself up on one elbow. 'Look, I saw the man's got a vile temper, but you're surely not suggesting he's a danger to anyone?'

Paddy's face was very sad. 'Only himself.'

Thus it was that I found myself in the dark and rain-lashed forecourt of the castle, huddled over the back seat of my car, rummaging through Paddy's valise. As I'd crunched to a halt on the gravel, I realized what Bertie Wooster meant about Jeeves shimmering around the place, because at once, seemingly from nowhere, the stately Mr Seddons had materialized at my window, giant umbrella in one hand and a bulky zipped bag in the other. 'Shall I put the case directly into the boot, madam? His lordship hoped you might care to join him in the library for a glass of sherry.'

Flushing, I'd stammered that Paddy wanted me to look inside his bag immediately for – for his diary, so if he could just lob it on the back seat? No, Mr Seddons mustn't wait for me, not in this weather. I'd join him inside shortly.

'Probably alarmist,' Paddy had said. 'I can't think why Hughie didn't tell me outright if that's what he feared, instead of wittering about Jack plotting.'

But I'd reluctantly had to agree that the man had been in a rare froth of anxiety not to return the gun. And tramping over the footbridge to reach my car just now had unexpectedly reminded me of the first time the ford had flooded, when I'd encountered Jack and his faithful friend down here. Jack had surely shouted at them then to let him drown – which anyone might shout in a rage. But after everything Paddy had told me, I was remembering how oddly he'd behaved, how he hadn't seemed to care about getting out of the submerged car at all...

Yet another reason for my sifting carefully through Paddy's bag now. As if this business weren't fraught with enough potential embarrassment already, the tracker was dead. Paddy said the switch was prone to flipping on in his pocket, which must have run the battery flat. He also swore he'd brought spares, and that's what I was searching for now. I glanced over my shoulder, hoping Mr Seddons wasn't observing me from the door, because I'd been warned I must on no account put the wind up him or his employer.

'We managed to keep it from Bernard in the main,' Paddy had said, 'but when Jack first realized he was going to be chair-bound, he talked often about ending it all. Very physical sort of chap, you see, forever looking for some new way of risking his neck. The kind of gambler who thinks betting on horses is pretty tame unless you're riding them yourself, preferably in the Grand National.'

I'd asked about his unhappy cousin, of course, but I was as curious about the light being shed on Paddy. He spoke of Jack with a strange detachment – fondly, exasperatedly, but there was something more. Something colouring everything, something I couldn't put my finger on. And while the cousins might be at odds now, they'd clearly been very close in the past. When dashing Jack had wearied of the army, he'd persuaded his soberer cousin to quit with him and set up in the security business. P.E.F. McGinty and Partners began as Bidcombe and McGinty. Jack's dangerous glamour had charmed clients through the doors, according to Paddy, but he'd had scant interest in running the firm.

'So much inevitably is desk-bashing, and the only sedentary activity Jack ever took to was poker. Probably because he plays for coronary-inducing stakes. One always felt he'd been born into the wrong era, really. Napoleonic times, with a decent war and the odd duel on the side, he'd have been merry as a cricket. As it was...'

As it was, he was always seeking new outlets for his restless energies. And one drunken shooting weekend at Stowham, some fool had bet him he couldn't circumnavigate the wall of the kitchen garden on a bicycle.

'Came down through the glasshouses,' said Paddy evenly. 'Did fiendish damage to his internal workings, and at first we didn't think he'd survive. But it was the injury to the spine which was the real brute. When they told us he wouldn't walk again...' The detachment slipped, and for an instant I heard such anguish, you'd think it was Paddy himself who'd been sentenced to a wheelchair. 'Well, he said life wasn't worth living, and we had the inevitable agonies over, you know, whether one had the right to lock up the pill bottles. We did, of course. Changed the locks on the gun room, too.'

By 'we' he meant himself and Jack's wife, Katharine. As I lifted a clump of socks, wondering if he'd actually packed these damned batteries at all, a leather photograph frame flopped open. On one side, there was a serious-faced bridal couple in droopy, post-war suits – his parents obviously, so that must be Lord Bidcombe's sister – but it was the facing picture which gripped me. Two children and their mother, surely the very photo which had tumbled off Paddy's desk? Squinting, I held it up to the car's dim interior light. The boy was recognizably a younger, chubbier Miles. The girl, called Daisy apparently, was a pretty miniature of her mum, that shyly smiling woman in the background, with a hand on each of their shoulders. But was that really Katharine? God, yes, of course it was. She looked so different, though, with dark curls. I doubted I would have recognized her at all, if I hadn't pressed Paddy to tell me why he and his cousin had quarrelled.

He was patently reluctant to talk about it. In fact, as I was soon to discover, he didn't tell me the whole truth, and even at the time I sensed he was prevaricating, as he joked about Jack always having been the leader of the two of them. Heir to title and castle, older, taller, richer – handsomer. 'Hughie and I used to trot along in his wake, lusting after his strings of glorious girls, wondering why they put up with his cavalier neglect instead of perceiving the warm and wonderful souls within our rather less prepossessing bodies.' His smile faded. 'And then suddenly he was as helpless as an infant, dependent on his old acolytes to chauffeur him around – dammit, even to fetch him a bottle of wine up from the cellar.'

In that instant, I identified what I'd been hearing in Paddy's voice all along: *guilt*. The bleak, self-loathing guilt I'd seen in his face as Jack confronted him yesterday. 'But surely he can't blame you?' I exclaimed. 'Even if he does resent needing your help?'

There was a telling pause. 'He may well resent needing my money.' And while what Paddy told me about plans for him to invest in the estate only confirmed the local gossip I'd heard, I sensed he was holding back. 'Effectively we would have owned Stowham jointly, in a partnership. Probably wasn't an ideal arrangement, but it seemed preferable to the estate being sold. I should say a great-uncle of mine had died,' he hurried on, as though to avoid questions. 'Absolutely the storybook miser, the old chap was, lived in a tin-roofed shack in County Clare, privy by the pigsty, trousers held up with baler twine, that sort of thing.' Paddy pulled a face. 'But he left everything to me, quite out of the blue, and it turned out to be, well, rather a lot of money.'

It was the way he said it triggered the memory. *Rather a lot of money...* Surely the selfsame words, and uttered with just the same diffidence? I saw that pretty heart-shaped face, framed in a fur hat, blushing as she said she mentioned this windfall only to explain why her husband's cousin would pay over the odds... 'Good God, *Peter*,' I cried. 'She said she was acting for Peter. That was Katharine, wasn't it?'

He stared back, looking almost as astonished as I was.

'Didn't you know?' I continued impatiently. 'She came round here the day I arrived, offering to buy Beck Holme on your behalf.'

Hair colour changes faces so startlingly, doesn't it? And I'd only ever seen Katharine in that tawny fox hat. I studied her smiling features now, recalling our jokes about husbands in the freezing wind outside my gift-wrapped cottage. I'd liked her then, and what Paddy told me only strengthened the bond of womanly sympathy. Heavens, Katharine Bidcombe used to own my house, had even given birth in it, as she would doubtless have told me if only we'd had longer together. Not that she'd ever actually lived at Beck Holme. It had been their holiday cottage, too, but when Jack's accident forced them to move back to Yorkshire, there'd been no question of their settling anywhere other than at the castle, so they'd rented it out. She was born the same year as me, with children of similar ages, too. More to the point though, she, like me, had very evidently married an overgrown schoolboy as much in need of a mother as a wife, and then had to learn to live with the consequences.

I didn't confide these reflections to Paddy, nor did I pause to wonder why he was even more painfully reticent about her than he was about her husband. The little he did disclose was enough to confirm my impression of a kindred soul. Katharine Bidcombe, clearly, had been the linchpin of that family, the money-manager, the decision-taker – the responsible adult steering a steady course as her husband ricocheted from one crazy exploit to another. No wonder I identified with her. For while Mike, thank God, had never tried cycling along ten-foot walls, his theatrical adventures had come close to ruining us more than once, and no one knew better than I how miserable it is to be forever playing killjoy, just because *someone* has to be grown-up in a marriage.

My life, though, had been a doddle compared to hers. Goes without saying all-action hero Jack wouldn't consider a desk job at the firm after his accident, and had insisted on Paddy buying him out. So not only did Katharine have to care for a disabled and depressed husband, rear teenage kids single-handed and help her ageing father-in-law run house and estate, she was also obliged to take a part-time job in publishing to pay the school fees, and whiz down to London several times a month. And was her man grateful?

Put it this way. She came home one day to find he'd flogged Beck Holme behind her back to his old poker-playing chum Ricky Marvell in order to fund a gambling trip to the States. With half a summer's holiday lets already booked. And when she objected – to this or anything else, by the sounds of it – he just snarled that she should have let him die because she'd be better off without him. I learned this when I asked why Paddy hadn't bought my cottage off the Bidcombes in the first place. 'The irresponsible pig,' I snorted. 'If I'd been her, I'd have throttled him.'

Paddy seemed rather taken aback by my vehemence, but admitted – with a faint smile – that as he recalled Kat had been goaded for once into yelling back that, yes, she bloody well would be better off without her husband, because she'd have a whacking lump of life insurance *and* her cottage. 'She was, um, rather attached to this place,' he added.

'Her and me both,' I said warmly. 'I'd so much like to see her again. When's she due back?'

'I'm sorry?'

'You said she works in town? Obviously, you wouldn't be worrying about Jack now if she were at home, so...' My words dried up as I saw the look in his face.

The batteries turned out to be in a zipped pocket on one end of the valise. I didn't bother replacing all the clothes. I'd already been out here too long and I wanted to get on with the job. If nothing else, I felt I owed it to his wife.

Katharine had died, nearly a year ago. It must have been within days of my meeting her. She was killed outright when a tree fell smack across her car in a tempest not unlike the one buffeting my own vehicle now. And if that was what people called an act of God, I'd said bitterly, it was enough to make you wonder about God.

Paddy may have breathed something about Man having played his part, but I didn't query it. I was too busy apologizing for having pelted him already with so many thoughtless questions. 'And your poor cousin,' I continued, flooded with guilt for the uncharitable thoughts I'd been harbouring about the man. 'Give me the tracker,' I said. 'Remind me how the bloody thing works...'

I now swapped the batteries, as instructed,

muttered a prayer, flipped the switch – and the little cross of red dots duly flickered into life. Jack had a flat converted to his needs in the basement of the castle, with an entrance tucked away under the great flight of steps. There was a light showing behind two of his windows. Kneeling on the back seat, I pointed the instrument at those windows. Nothing happened. There was not a bleep, nor the faintest glimmer of flashing light, but I needed to be sure. I climbed out of the car into the rain and, feeling unutterably foolish, paced towards the windows. The only flicker in the crossed line of dots came from the shaking of my hand. I was praying Jack wouldn't bowl out in his chair. What would I say: sorry, just trying to save your life? And surely, if he had the gun, the device would have detected it long since?

'You may have more success on the far side of the courtyard,' suggested a polite masculine voice behind me. An umbrella loomed over my tottering form. 'Or perhaps you'd care to use the house phone as we go inside, madam?'

Had I been less flustered, I would have relished rather more being ushered through the echoing flagged hall to take a glass of sherry with this peer of the realm. Step up from a vacuum flask of coffee in the stable-yard, that was for sure. I just hoped Seddons had believed me when, thrusting the machine deep into my bag before he could get a closer look, I'd stammered, yes, the signal was lousy here and, no thanks, I didn't need to use their phone and, yes, I'd found Mr Paddy's address book, sorry, diary – *diary*.

Coincidentally, as we entered a cavernous apartment lined with the sort of weighty calf-bound volumes which look as if they haven't been opened since the day a long-dead craftsman stamped the gold tooling on to their spines, a muscular black and white spaniel, seemingly twice the size of my pretty Dora, careered across and hurled itself at me, much to the butler's embarrassment. This was obviously the intended recipient of Paddy's collar.

'Down, Jasper,' the man snapped, and buried his hand in the animal's shaggy neck fur. 'Would you excuse me for a moment, Mrs Patterson?'

I looked around as I waited for him to return. Once my eye had got past the grandeur of the carved bookcases and the mighty sweep of curtains sixteen feet long if they were an inch, I began to see the faded, threadbare stripes in those same curtains, the tell-tale pale squares on walls where pictures no longer hung – one of them incongruously plugged with a moth-eaten stag's head – and realized that the air in here was not just chill, it smelled of damp. Clearly the castle needed a packet spending on it – of Paddy's money? Had the plan foundered on Jack's resentment? I hadn't enquired. I'd asked too many tactless questions already.

When Seddons returned, dogless, he ushered me across to the far door of this gloomy chamber and into a small anteroom, which was brightly lit and just about adequately warmed by an antiquated two-bar electric fire, in front of which Lord Bidcombe was toasting his noble bottom. Out on the moor, I'd been aware he was a tall

218

man, but in this cluttered chamber he towered over me like an amiably tweedy giant. Minus cap, he proved to have very white hair, endearingly dishevelled in the manner of a cartoon mad professor.

'Mrs Patterson,' he cried, grasping my hand in both of his. 'How very good of you to turn out on such a beastly day. And to be taking care of my nephew, too. How is the silly boy?'

We thrashed out the medical details – not without difficulty, because I had to bellow like a boxing referee just to convey that I preferred Amontillado to Tio Pepe – and I loudly repeated that, no, Paddy wasn't fretting about being away from the office, because he'd left hadn't he, *sold out?* Then realized I might have said too much.

'He's sold the firm?' barked his lordship. 'God's sake, why?'

To moulder into a compost heap? 'I'm not … entirely sure,' I faltered. Well, Paddy had said to me himself he should have told his uncle long ago. He could hardly blame me for letting the cat out of the bag. 'Sort of early retirement?'

'At his age? Bloody ridiculous. And don't think I don't know what's at the root of it. Yes, it was a terrible business for him – terrible for all of us, dammit, but that's no excuse for throwing in the towel. All this self-indulgent twaddle about guilt and blame – I've long since lost all patience with him and Jack on the subject. The ghastly thing happened, and that's all there is to be said about it.'

'Are we talking about what happened to your daughter-in-law?' I ventured.

219

'Sorry, what?'

'Katharine – the accident with the tree?' I roared.

'*Accident*,' he bellowed back triumphantly. 'Exactly. Not Paddy's fault, not for a second.'

Thus did I learn that, when Katharine Bidcombe met her sad end, Paddy had very nearly died with her. And I soon realized that this explained an awful lot more.

18

'Poor girl never liked driving in the dark, d'you see?' observed Lord Bidcombe, absent-mindedly topping up both our glasses with Tio Pepe. I don't much care for sherry at the best of times and you could have pickled onions in this brew. 'Once told me it was some hereditary whatsit, dicky night vision, wouldn't know. Point is, not surprising Paddy offered to take the wheel once they were on our land. Yes, he'd had a glass too many, and Katharine tried to talk him out of it – she was picking him up from the airport, as you probably know – but he wouldn't listen, insisted she climb into the passenger seat while he toddled off behind a hedge to' – he cleared his throat – 'answer nature's call, as it were. Outrageous, in my opinion, the magistrate taking his licence off him for that, when he hadn't driven an inch. Mark you,' he added grumpily, 'bloody stupid of Paddy to tell them he was intending to drive. He could surely have whistled up some harmless taradiddle about why she wasn't behind the wheel. Still, I suppose him being off the road for a few months was the least of it. But for Jack to blame him is absurd.'

'Jack blames Paddy?' I said wonderingly. But of course he did. Irrationally, yes, but grieving hearts aren't rational, and this explained so much, not least Paddy's reluctance to talk about the tragedy, to face his family. It explained, most of all, his guilt. I'd spoken more to myself than Lord Bidcombe, but he heard and snorted.

'Jack's a fool, but Paddy's as bad. I don't say he isn't bound to feel it, of course he does. If he hadn't insisted on stopping, on taking over the driving – ye gods, if Katharine had still been just a couple of feet across behind the wheel, she might have survived, or so they claimed, because it was a branch through the passenger side did the damage. Although why these so-called experts have to rub it in by telling you stuff like that is beyond me. But there she was, in the seat he'd been occupying not a minute before, with him fifty yards clear.' He drained his glass and slapped it down on a side table. 'Paddy feels guilty, but so do we all, dammit. My fault for not having the bloody tree felled, when I'd been warned it was splitting. Daisy's for not going to meet her uncle's flight instead of her mother – but where does thinking like that get you? Halfway to the funny farm, and it won't bring Katharine back. Splendid girl, she was, straight as a die, and wouldn't have stood for this sort of nonsense, not for a moment. I tell you frankly,

Mrs Patterson–'

'Oh, Jo, please.'

'Joan, thank you, Bernard. As I was saying, I sometimes think nothing my son does could ever surprise me, but I expected more sense from Paddy. See him as a second son, always have, and nothing could suit me better than to let him knock this place back into shape. Damned lucky he was willing to sink his money into Stowham, plenty of other chaps would have wanted to set up on their own. Did he tell you my idea was that he turn a wing into a house for himself?' He fixed an oddly intent gaze on me. 'Some reason or other, he wasn't keen, but I assure you it's perfectly practical, acres of space, all mouldering away as things stand. Place this size is a white elephant nowadays, and Jack didn't give a fig, said as much. Still, all that can wait, eh? But no sooner had we had the agreement drafted by the lawyers, which itself cost me a pretty penny I can tell you, than *this* happens. I mean, what do you think about it all?'

I gulped, caught unawares. 'I can see it might be – difficult for your son.' Having the man you hold responsible for your wife's death take over half your inheritance? I'll say. I understood now why, in Paddy's masterly understatement, family relations at Stowham Castle were a touch strained.

'But you wouldn't be opposed to the idea in principle?'

I blinked. 'I'm sorry?'

'Jack can't stop me – it's all down to Paddy. Give it a year, he said after poor Katharine went, and that year's nearly up. I've been worried about my nephew, won't deny it. However' – here he wafted the vinegar decanter towards me again, but I was quick to whip my hand over my still-brimming glass – 'perhaps I shan't need to be quite so concerned now, eh?' I realized that those bloodshot blue eyes were looking me up and down, crinkling into a smile as he jovially tilted his sherry towards me. 'Your very good health, Jane.'

Paddy and Dora were snoring in gentle duet on the sofa when I returned. She opened an eye immediately and slithered down, but he didn't stir and I remained in the doorway for a moment, studying his sleeping face. He had lush, sooty eyelashes a girl would envy, and in spite of the bruising, the grazes and the stubble round his chin, he looked very young – and rather sad. Such an unhappy tangle at the castle. But he wouldn't welcome my two penn'orth of sympathy, and I'd blundered across enough emotional minefields for one day. Besides, what his mule-brained, cloth-eared lordship had so blithely gone on to confide over the third sherry was prompting me to look at my guest with new eyes.

'Sorry I'm late,' I said loudly, 'I had a drink with your uncle.'

The outrageous lashes fluttered, Paddy stirred and smiled sleepily up at me. Yes, I thought measuringly, that was a very winning smile. So disarmingly boyish.

'Any news?' he muttered, groping for his glasses.

Plenty, as regards you, McGinty. 'The gun's gone.'

He put on his specs, frowning. 'You sound very sure.'

I *was* sure, as I briskly informed him, because as in all the best detective novels, I'd ended up by asking the butler. No, of course I hadn't alarmed him, I'd just said Paddy had wondered about borrowing it. But Mr Jack's Purdey had been collected by carrier this morning, apparently, and Seddons personally saw him hand it over. What was more, I'd then taken the opportunity to enquire how the man was bearing up, only to be told he was planning a holiday.

'*Jack?* A holiday?'

'In Spain. Seddons sounded pretty gob-smacked, too.' I chucked down my bag. 'But that's what he said.'

'Well ... good. I suppose.' He put his head on one side. 'Forgive me, but why are you eyeing me as though I've just barbecued your budgie?'

'I'm glad you asked that. Possibly because your uncle is under the impression – no, is unshakeably convinced – that you and I are, you know...'

His eyebrows shot up. 'At it?'

'That we have a long-standing relationship,' I said frostily, 'of an intimate nature.'

He grinned. 'In my state of health? Anyway, I only told him...' But here he hesitated.

'*Yes?*'

'Well ... well, I have been rather avoiding Bernard lately, and I suppose, when he asked whether you were the reason I'd been so tied up,

224

I, um, didn't entirely deny it.'

'Oh, great.'

'I didn't want to hurt his feelings,' he protested. 'Besides, I only said we were old friends.'

'*Old* being the operative word,' I snorted. 'Because I'm here to tell you that what truly warms his heart is you settling down at last with a sturdy old trout like me, instead of one of the nubile nymphettes I gather you've been in the habit of wheeling up to Stowham.'

'Rot. I may have invited the odd female friend for a weekend...'

'By the anorexic busload. And while what you do is your own affair–'

'Affairs plural, by the sound of it.'

'–*I* am a respectable married woman.'

He let out a shout of laughter. 'My, there's a fine old turn of phrase. It wears hats to church and doesn't care to gossip about the neighbours.'

'With children, as I tried to tell him, but since he only hears one word in bloody ten, all he did was pat my cheek and assure me you'd always been marvellous with Daisy and Miles, and that I'd be so much better for you than all those flighty little stick insects. I wouldn't mind,' I concluded furiously, 'but I ended up feeling ninety-two, fat as a house and ready to book in for a facelift. Oh, stop laughing.'

'No more,' he groaned. 'Do you want to answer your telephone before I rupture another rib?'

'Serves you right, you philanderer.' I strode through to the kitchen and grabbed the phone. It occurred to me, though, that the remains of the Chablis were in the fridge, so I tucked it under my chin for a moment as I reached inside. 'Sorry, who'd you say it was?' Through the open doorway I waved the bottle at Paddy, who nodded enthusiastically.

'Who the fuck do you think?' snarled an outraged voice in my ear.

'Need any help?' called Paddy.

'Blimey, *Mike*. Hang on a tic.' I stuck my head round the door again. 'Stay where you are. I'll bring it through in a moment.'

'So you *have* got someone there. You know, I didn't believe Sarah. I was dick-brained enough to think she was just trying to wind me up. How could you do it, Jo?'

I was as much astonished as indignant. 'Is this a joke? You've been living with another woman these past six months.'

'One minute you're down here, playing martyred wife for all it's worth–'

'Excuse me, I was not *playing* anything.'

'–Making me feel the biggest shit alive, the next I hear you've jumped into bed with a total stranger.'

'I've *what?*' And if he'd only given me the chance, I would have set him *very* straight about my guest, but he was shouting I'd no right to throw Gaynor back at him, because it wasn't my morality he was questioning, only my sanity. Jesus H., wouldn't I expect him to worry, after twenty years of marriage?

'Twenty-one,' I said automatically, but he didn't draw breath and, besides, I was belatedly recognizing that my husband might be jealous. *Jealous?* Chewing the carpet, by the sound of him. Blessing my daughter, I waited for him to run out of self-righteous steam before asking, politely, if he'd rung for anything in particular. It was all I could do not to laugh aloud as he mumbled some nonsense about being away from the office a lot, and that I should ring his mobile if I wanted him urgently. 'How thoughtful of you to let me know,' I cooed, 'but if you'll forgive me now, I'm rather busy.'

I carried the wine through to the sitting room and was startled to find my guest prostate across the sofa, with his eyes shut and his arms flung wide.

'Take me,' he cried, 'I'm all yours.'

'I beg your pardon?'

'Never let it be said a McGinty wasn't prepared to sacrifice his body in a noble cause. And if a spot of adultery is all that's needed to bring your husband hurtling back...'

I grinned and kicked his foot aside. 'You got the drift of the conversation, then.'

'My heart was bleeding for the poor fellow.' He winced as he hauled himself up. 'Whereas you look as smug as a dipso in a distillery, you heartless hag.'

'Shame I didn't think to fill him in on your amorous track record. He'd be halfway up the A1 by now with a sawn-off shotgun.'

Paddy rolled his eyes. 'Flattered as I am to be cast as Don Juan, do you really think I have the figure for it?'

Possibly not, although he was by no means fat, just solid. And his appearance was startlingly

227

improved by a wash, a shave and a change into unbloodied clothing. Sarah was right, as per usual, I mused while pottering around the kitchen preparing dinner, Paddy McGinty was an attractive man. I supposed I'd always been aware of it, but I really hadn't *thought* about it. Well, you don't, do you? Not when you're my age and have been married so long you can barely remember not being married. She'd evidently put the fear of God into her dad, though.

In the middle of clattering Dora's supper into her bowl, I stopped dead. Might he really come tearing up to confront my supposed lover? Excitement mingled with horror as I imagined the ensuing scene. Paddy would doubtless find it hilarious. Still, if Mike were on his way, there was nothing I could do. So I resumed pouring, and had to whistle Dora. She, at least, had clearly fallen for my guest in a big way. Normally, at this hour, she'd have been prancing hungrily round my feet.

Lord Bidcombe's chuckling disclosures, though, were giving me a certain amount of food for thought. I was sure Paddy wouldn't, you know, pounce. Not without encouragement. He was far too well mannered and, besides, I was no nymphette. But might he misread my own open-ended invitation for him to stay here in the cottage? Having dug out candles for the table, I stuffed them away in the drawer again. Instead, I kicked forward the two bulging cardboard boxes. I was not planning to murmur sweet nothings by candlelight. I had serious business in hand.

'That's why I wrote to you,' I was informing

him half an hour or so later, 'because I wanted to tell you everything I've found out about our firm.' And before he'd lifted his first forkful of crab rillette, I plunged into doing just that, even if it did feel rather disconcertingly as if I'd told him all this before. The difference was, this flesh-and-blood McGinty didn't argue. He smiled where appropriate, laughed at my description of the Piranha, and praised my tenacity. Said, as I eventually gathered up the starter plates, that if ever I fancied a career in the investigation business, he would be happy to put me in touch with the right people.

'You obviously have a talent for the job. Gosh, that duck looks heavenly.'

'But–'

'Have you lost your watch?'

I twitched. 'Watch?'

'You asked me the time just now, before you took the duck out, and you usually wear one. Gold bracelet, interlocking, cream face with four diamond chips.' He grinned. 'Judson would be proud of me. Retired policeman who does a lot of our tailing, claims one should always note wrist-watches. Suspects may change their coats and hats, but watches and shoes are pretty reliable.'

'Blimey, do you actually have people followed?' I was diverted into exclaiming. Mistake. Because, before I could get back to my own concerns, Paddy was describing the circumstances under which, yes, once in a blueish moon, they had to follow someone. He went on to recount an episode of mistaken identities at an airport when a curate was tailed back to theological college, which led to another tall tale about a misplaced listening device, a randy chief executive and some vigorously off-agenda business under the boardroom table. There was no stopping him – through the duck, the cheese and a bottle and a half of Châteauneuf du Pape. And for all his conversation was as entertaining as it was informative – did you know you could fit a video camera into the face of a travel alarm clock? – I found myself thinking about... Scheherazade, was it? After Chablis for lunch, sherry for tea, and a lot of beefy red now, literary references were proving elusive. That mythical princess, anyhow, who warded off her execution by spinning story after story to her despotic husband. Yeah, well, my sympathy for the sultan was growing fast. As I spooned out mango and raspberries for pudding, taking particular care to aim the fruit into bowls which seemed curiously to have shrunk in the wash, I realized he'd paused for breath and I grabbed my chance.

'Paddy,' I began, and had to suppress a hiccup, 'can we go back to talking seriously for a moment?'

'I'm sorry, I'm afraid I've been boring you to tears. I meant to say that you've transformed this cottage. You know this kitchen was once a cow byre?'

Interested though I might be in the history of my home, I was not going to be diverted again. 'Thing is, you turning up here, well, it's like fate, really.'

He eyed me steadily. He suddenly seemed a lot soberer than I was. 'Would you call it that?'

'I wanted all along to ask you for your advice.' I paused and had to blink, because for a moment I was seeing two of him. 'And you did say if there was anything–'

'Don't, Jo,' he interrupted.

'Whaddya mean, don't?'

'Don't ask me to do this.' He took my hand, and I'd drunk enough to forget to be alarmed – anyway, he wasn't looking at all amorous. He looked rather sweetly troubled. Both of him. 'It's a mistake.'

'How can you say that? You haven't even seen the stuff I've printed out.'

'Well, I will, of course, if you insist... I say, steady on.'

Pointing with one foot to the cardboard boxes, I'd nearly fallen off my chair. ''Sall in there, pages and pages and pages. But I s'pose you're going to tell me it'd be a waste of your valuable time.'

'Time?' he burst out. 'Dear God, I have time by the bucketload. Boundless infinities of the stuff. The rest of my miserable existence stretches ahead with not a signpost in view.'

Some sadness in his voice must have percolated through the alcoholic fog. 'You know, thassa terrible thing to say. Man's gotta do something useful with himself. Rots the soul, doing nothing.' And never mind the tangled consonants, when I clamber into the pulpit, it's a sure sign there's a technicoloured hangover over the horizon. 'Speaking of which...' I also had the drunk's dogged fixity of purpose.

'Listen, Jo,' he cut in. 'Small companies founder every day. Bad luck, bad timing, any

231

number of things, happens to the best. And the idea that your husband's um...'

'Floozy?'

'That the woman who's presently sharing his bed and his life should set out cold-bloodedly to defraud him of his firm strikes me, frankly, as ludicrous.'

'You think I haven't worked that out?' I cut in triumphantly. *'Course* I have. Wasn't just Mike's company, that's the point. I owned half of it.'

His answer was a long time emerging. 'Quite.'

I blinked at him. Blinked harder, and focused intently on his nose to unite these glum-faced McGinty twins. 'Come again?'

'It isn't exactly unknown for the assets of a small private company like yours to melt mysteriously away. When a divorce is in the offing.'

Did I see what he was driving at? Can a goldfish do differential calculus? 'Divorce isn't in the offing,' I protested indignantly. 'I mean, *she* might think so, but he's never said anything.'

'And he isn't going to? Alimony settlements can be ruinously expensive. Believe me, I've been there. I'm just looking at the old *qui bono* question really.'

My mouth fell open. 'You're saying it's not Gaynor...'

'She may well be a party to it. In fact, almost certainly.'

I scrambled to my feet and lost a shoe on the way. 'But what you're trying to make out is that – is that my *husband's* swindled me?'

'Oh, lumme,' sighed Paddy. 'I told you not to involve me.'

19

Considering everything, my head could have been worse. And while drink usually has me blinking to sweaty, skull-thumping wakefulness in the small hours, I slept late. Paddy had been up for hours. Before there was so much as a gleam behind the curtains, I'd heard the scrape of chair on floor downstairs. So had Dora, and trotted off. He could let her out, I thought, shutting my eyes again. It was noon by the time I was up, bathed and dressed. Truth was, I was in no hurry to re-encounter my guest.

I had a clear recollection of standing in one shoe, yelling that my husband might be bird-brained, delinquent, unfaithful and a lot more besides, but one thing he was not – absolutely *not* – was mean with money. Mike was extravagantly generous with funds even when we didn't have any – *particularly* when we didn't have any. I cited the time he'd won several hundred quid in a sweepstake while away at a conference and insisted on splitting his bonanza meticulously down the middle with the wife. I hadn't added that this had taken the form of buying me an Italian handbag I didn't need. In python skin – lacquered, acid-yellow, python skin. It's the thought that counts.

'I'm sorry,' Paddy had protested, several times and in several ways, all sweetly contrite. Only it'd seemed to me he was apologizing more for suggesting the vulgarly obvious than for being plum wrong. And I'd said so. Not quite in those words, perhaps. What I'd actually said was that if he implied one more time my husband had cheated me I would smash a plate over his head. And that I wouldn't dream of imposing on his good nature by troubling him with my trivial problems any longer, and he could stop smiling at me in that irritating way because I was *not* drunk. Merely tired. And, OK, emotional. At which I had gathered up my shoe, my dog and what remained of my dignity, and retired.

I had to brace myself now before re-entering the kitchen, because I knew what I was going to find. Paddy and luggage, ready for the off. Half asleep, I'd been aware of him shifting stuff around downstairs, of the faint ting of the telephone. Only as I tottered to the bathroom, though, had I caught a snatch of him talking in a low voice about help being required for the beastly trek between the footbridge and here, and realized what he'd been up to. Packing his things, obviously. Arranging a lift to escape the house of this drunken virago. Not that I took back one word. Even if Mike *had* wanted a divorce, there was no way on earth he would try to snaffle my share of our worldly wealth, no way. I was sorry Paddy was going, though. Sorry to lose his expertise, obviously, but – well, just sorry.

'Morning, Jo,' he murmured distractedly. He was seated at the kitchen table and, despite his blossoming bruises, looked undeniably hand-some in bottle-green cashmere and cords, with snazzy red brocade slippers. My gaze fixed on these, perhaps because they hardly suggested an imminent trek down a muddy lane. Then I noticed that the table was bestrewn with papers, and he was chewing a pen. He gestured towards the boxes at his feet, now half emptied. 'You said it was all in there, so I assumed you wouldn't mind my helping myself. Made free with your phone, too, I'm afraid.'

'Are you – going, then?' I said.

He looked up. 'Gosh, did you want me to?'

'Actually Casanova's a much-maligned chap,' he was observing a few hours later, not without difficulty, because he had two pins clamped between his lips.

'Well, you would say that, wouldn't you?' I responded as I rethreaded the needle of my sewing machine.

'Spare me.' Triumphantly, he skewered the last inch of seam. 'Next?'

I was glad that my husband – tormented as I trusted he was by visions of orgiastic passion – couldn't see this domestic tableau. With my watch held hostage, I'd steeled myself at last to attack the velour for my Wykesea customer (although violet is *not* the happiest of colours when you're hungover) and Paddy had sportingly asked if he could help in any way. He was boggled with balance sheets, he said.

Not nearly as boggled as I, after our conference at the kitchen table earlier. Was I closer to proving Mike had been robbed? I'd thought so when my friend immediately conceded he'd been

235

wrong. Seems a well-known alimony-dodging ruse for unscrupulous businessmen is to set up a new company in your girlfriend's name, channel all your trade that way and let the old firm go bust. Which at least explained to me how a supposedly bankrupt motor-dealing neighbour of ours in London had mysteriously continued to swan around in a Roller with his new missus, while the old one had taken a job as a school dinner lady. But I knew Mike would never pull such a trick, and not merely because the contract drawn up by Optimax's lawyers, according to Paddy, ensured he'd be hanged, drawn and strung out to dry if he dabbled so much as an independent toe in the events industry once he'd sold his firm to them.

My guest, though, was now taking scrupulous pains not to imply any criticism of Mike. I was the one who cursed the irresponsible pillock when it emerged that the managing director of TBE had barely attended a single minuted meeting in the last six months of trading. And what Paddy kept coming back to, as if I didn't know it, was that our company effectively *was* Mike. That Mike's talent, reputation and personal goodwill had constituted the firm's principal asset. He hadn't been wasting his time while I'd slept in. He'd been dredging his address book for people who knew the industry, and was now in a position to agree – *hallelujah* – that a man with Mike Patterson's track record could have found work anywhere. So, yes, he was forced to concede it was strange that he'd sold himself, seemingly so cheaply, to Optimax.

'But he *didn't* sell himself to Optimax,' I said impatiently. 'Gaynor did. There's no dispute she created the deal. And since she, more than anyone, knew exactly what Mike and the firm were worth, there's only one possible answer. Optimax were paying her. As I've said all along.'

'On the basis of one e-mail mentioning an unwritten agreement?' he sighed. 'How can you possibly prove it?'

'You tell me.' I'd smiled brightly at him. 'Bug Gaynor's phone?'

I was joking, of course, but he didn't smile back. 'Grubbing around in other people's affairs is a filthy business,' he'd said. 'Shall we take a break?'

I admit it was more fun gossiping by the fire as I chugged on with the curtains. Paddy had been making himself useful on several fronts, for while I may have disputed his calculations about our company, I was only too happy to let him check my sums before I wielded the scissors. I hate that moment, when you have to plunge your shears into the virgin fabric. It's the point of no return.

'Like life,' I remarked dreamily. There was something about my guest encouraged such fanciful flights of metaphor. 'One minute it's stretching away ahead of you, unsullied and infinite with possibility. Then you make one snip – or slip – and, *wham*, you're committed.' Whether I was thinking literally of the curtains I'd created for this very sitting room back in July (now adorning Sarah's bedroom on account of my having sliced them a foot too short), or more fancifully of that fateful week in a draughty theatre in Yarmouth during the Easter vacation of my last year at university, when not merely had I discovered I'd failed to pack my pills, but had allowed Mike to persuade me not to worry, I'm not altogether sure.

'Oh, surely one can survive false starts,' he responded. 'My life's been a series of 'em. Quit the army; wife quit me; firm's gone now and, well, it's just been one ill-judged move after another, really. But somehow one toddles on. I'm doubtless heading straight into the next catastrophe even now.' As I glanced round to query this gloomy prophecy, he asked how I'd met my husband.

'What? Oh, on the Edinburgh Festival Fringe. I was there with a university Classics Soc. production of *Antigone*. Deeply, deeply intense.'

'In the original Greek?'

'Spanish-flavoured English because we'd relocated to Latin America. We were big on General Pinochet in those days, so it was all mirrored shades and jackboots. Dire, of course, and audiences smaller than your average prayer meeting. But Mike was packing 'em in next door with a musical he'd composed.' I paused mid-seam and sighed. 'He seemed so glamorous to us spotty students. Dammit, he *was* glamorous. Drop dead handsome, and on a good day he could light up a room just by walking in. There's no middle ground with Mike. When's he working, it's heart, body and soul, and he was so passionate about that musical, he seemed to be twice as alive as anyone else.' I pulled a face. 'Anyway, I fell head over heels, and spent the next two vacs on the road with him – squalid theatrical digs, tea and a fag for breakfast, champagne with your fish and chips, and I loved it. Felt like I was a bit player in *Bohème*. Until Sarah muscled in on the act.'

'Gosh,' said Paddy. 'I didn't realize your man was a composer.'

'That show was the first and last ever saw the light of day,' I retorted, and even though I recounted as the long-standing family joke it had become Dad's enduring conviction that, in spite of twenty-odd years evidence to the contrary, he was destined to write the next socking hit British musical, Paddy still professed admiration. 'It's rather fine to trudge through life with one's vision fixed on a lofty star, don't you think?'

'If you don't mind falling flat on your face,' I retorted.

But that was how we'd got round to Casanova, who, in my friend's opinion, had suffered such an unjustly bad press over the years. Forget the womanizing, I was advised. This chap had been a philosopher, historian, linguist, charlatan, diplomat, spy – and no one who told such good jokes against himself could be all bad.

'Rake, spook and comedian,' I mused. 'Verily a man after your own heart.'

He rolled his eyes. 'I happened to be stuck in a villa one rainy summer with his memoirs, all twelve vols. Highly entertaining they were, too. And contrary to myth, he wasn't just a wham, bam and thank you merchant, he genuinely *liked* women.'

'Oh yeah?' I was holding up our mugs.

'Fell in love at the drop of a lace hankie, and was forever being ditched, poor fellow. Gosh, yes, I'd adore a spot more tea.'

'I only wish I could offer you something stronger,' I called from the kitchen, with a trace of self-consciousness, 'but the cupboard's bare after last night. I'll get out to the shops tomorrow.'

'Oh, I shouldn't worry,' he replied, rather oddly, and began telling me about the love of Signor Casanova's life, one Henriette, who had apparently abandoned the great lover.

'*Tu aussi oubliette Henriette*,' he quoted. 'She inscribed that with her diamond ring on the window-pane of the inn they were staying in when she decided to cut and run. A respectable married woman, you see' – he grinned at me – 'hitched to a stuffy aristo back in France, and while she'd had a ball with dear old Giacomo, twin souls, all that, she felt honour-bound to trot home to husband and sprogs in the end. She followed it up with the most heart-rending letter, asking him to pretend their affair had never happened. But the point is, aeons later, when Casanova was mouldering towards death in the library of some count who'd created a job for him, he was still regretting her. She was wrong about him, you see, just as everyone else has been since. He never did forget Henriette.'

He sounded so soulful, I stopped pouring tea to look round at him. 'Spoken from the heart,' I mocked. 'Where's my violin?'

The spell broke. 'On the other hand, one could

argue womanizers always sentimentalize the one who got away, and overlook the hundred-odd others. Ah, at last.'

I'd heard it, too. A businesslike rap at the kitchen door. OmyGod, *Mike?* I put down my mug very carefully, and took a deep breath. 'I'm – not expecting anyone.'

I hurried through to open the door – and was so taken aback I barely noticed a fleeting prickle of relief. Because there, under the giant umbrella, trim as a pin in black overcoat and bowler, with only the clumsy gathering of his knife-pressed trousers into gumboots marring this perfect vision of the gentleman's gentleman, stood Mr Seddons.

'Major McGinty's shopping, madam?' he said.

'The guy's *unreal*,' I breathed to Paddy when Seddons and his brawny henchman retreated down the dark and rainy path for the last time.

'A darling, isn't he?'

'I thought butlers like him only existed in the old British movies they show in the afternoons, all frightfully tea and crumpets.'

'I suspect he watches them, too, by way of polishing the act. He certainly grows more magnificently butlerish by the year. I say, shall I pop the cork on one of these?' Numbly I watched him lift out a bottle of champagne. 'Still almost human when I first knew him, and he actually started out in life as a plumber – no, truly. Before my time, of course, but one can only imagine what a wretchedly lost soul he was in the rural Yorkshire of the forties, when men were men and the sheep were nervous.'

'God Almighty,' I squawked, but this was in response to the box I'd ripped open.

'Arrived at Stowham to mend a stopcock and found his vocation. Praise be, because he's held the place together ever since, he and his sister, the formidable Miss Seddons.' He shook his head. 'It's far too much for him now, but when I mention pensions, he nearly weeps. Stowham's his home more than anybody's, really.'

Bloodied parcels of meat, tissue-wrapped breads, fancy tins and jars, beribboned chocolates... 'Paddy, what *is* all this?'

'Oh, just a few provisions. I mustn't eat you out of house and home. Reds in the other box, I trust, beyond the fruit and veg.'

'Flowers, dog bones ... what on earth, a *book*? This is crazy.'

He shrugged. 'Small token of thanks. I phoned the list to Seddons this morning, and he duly despatched Miss S., bless her heart, with the gardener to fetch and carry.'

I was gazing at the glossy hardback. 'And I've been dying to read the new le Carré.'

'Yes, well, I noticed you had the others.'

Nor was that all. I found a whopping bottle of the scent I wear, with bath oil to match. And nearly all the various delicatessen tins and jars were the sort of thing I might have chosen for myself in an extravagant mood. Even the pretty bunch of flowers, as I wonderingly observed, was full of my favourite creams and blues.

'Colours of your sitting room,' he said. 'It used to be a rather murky yellow, after Katharine had it redecorated for letting, and the painter got the shade wrong. She'd have liked this. No, I just did a little intelligent detective work this morning, that's all.'

'It's amazing,' I said, and then turned to him. 'Fabulous, like ten birthdays and Christmas rolled into one, but it's far too much. I can't possibly accept.'

'Rot. Had to do something, and I wouldn't have dreamed of offering you money.'

'I should hope not.'

'Even though you're so desperately short of the stuff.'

I looked up from the tin of oatcakes I was inspecting. 'I'm sorry?'

'Nearly forty grand overdrawn across the various joint accounts, isn't it? With sweet fiddle-all in your own personal account.'

My face was flushing. 'How could you possibly know that?'

He met my gaze steadily. 'Matter of fact I simply read your bank statements. They're all in the boxes you invited me to rummage in.'

'But that was the TBE stuff. I didn't intend you—'

'Also your credit-card bills, along with the most helpful jumble of shopping receipts. Gave me no end of clues to your tastes. Then I had a snoop round the cupboards and bookshelves, as I say. We sleuths, you know, no stopping us once we're on the trail. Mark you,' he continued, without letting me speak, 'I could have ascertained your net worth without poking my snout into that box. Contents of your bank accounts – or non-contents in your

243

case – and where the money had gone, spending on your credit cards, all that. Not to mention health and criminal records if you happen to have one, whom you're in the habit of telephoning, motoring offences. It would just have taken me rather longer and cost money. Grossly illegal, too, but would that concern you?'

I stared at him. 'What do you mean? I suppose there's nothing exactly wrong with your looking through my financial papers–'

'There damned well is,' he cut in fiercely. 'Are you telling me you don't feel invaded? That your privacy's been violated, your trust betrayed? Of course you do. The only thing I had the remotest right to read was the copy of your letter to me. In which you asked for my professional advice about pursuing your investigations...'

I began to see I'd been given an extravagantly packaged object lesson.

'If you think snooping's such an immoral trade,' I said later, as I carried our glasses of fizz back to the sitting room and helped him to the sofa, 'why'd you go in for it?'

'Read too many spy novels? Oh, because Jack persuaded me, of course. On a good day, my cousin could recruit truck drivers into a corps de ballet, and he had an enthusiastic ally in my wife, who found army social life even more miserable than army pay. I didn't much care for soldiering myself, as it happens. Rather a foolish act of teenage rebellion.'

I had to smile. 'Becoming a British Army officer? It's hardly like joining the Hell's Angels –

or even the Foreign Legion.'

'But I was destined for Oxford, to read history. Not that my father thought any too highly of that either, because he was a Cambridge man and a mathematician. I told you, my life's been a series of wrong moves. And before you ask why I stuck the spooking so long, the answer's sordid lucre. It was very profitable. I had a wife to pay for, then a divorce, then Jack to buy out and so on. Besides, one mustn't overplay the bleeding liberal conscience. By and large our work was necessary and eminently respectable. If someone's unscrupulous enough to plant bugs in their rivals' boardrooms or burn down a warehouse supposedly full of valuables – and they do – then someone else needs to sweep 'em out or find the petrol can. We did a lot of insurance work in the early days. Then you get an accounts clerk running a Porsche and a Portuguese villa on an Escort and Butlins salary. One does even have to help the odd chap not to get kidnapped, although for every exec at genuine risk, I promise there are fifty more who simply fancy the kudos of an armour-plated limo and a couple of gorillas to tote their luggage. But I'm glad to be out.' He looked along the sofa at me. 'And I wouldn't recommend anyone to take it up as a hobby.'

I scowled back. He'd been bending my ear with a sermon on ethics this past half-hour as I trotted to and fro stacking my fridge, larder and cupboards with the fruits of his detective work. Naturally I agreed that everyone had a right to privacy, blah, blah, but all I was asking for was one small infringement – small and very specific, and Paddy himself had pointed the way. When he'd confessed to reading my bank statements he'd let slip that he could have got this information, albeit illegally, through other sources. I'd leaped on it. There was my answer. If Optimax had paid Gaynor, the evidence would be in her bank records. Or not there, as I said to Paddy. In which case I would simply have to concede I'd been wrong.

'Asking questions is easy,' he declared, swirling the bubbles round his glass. 'Living with the answers is another matter. Jack said that to me, oddly enough, because he isn't what you'd call a philosophical cove. But it was after I'd discovered that Tara, my wife, was, ah, amusing herself elsewhere. I fear the green-eyed monster in me was only too ready to find out exactly where she was sinning, when and with whom. I'm ashamed to admit I may even have mentioned phone-tapping. Fortunately, Jack reined me in, pointing out not merely that I'd be better off not knowing the gory details, but that snooping on one's nearest and dearest is a betrayal almost as heinous in its way as the original infidelity. He didn't put it quite like that, I admit. Shitting on your own doorstep was his expression.'

'Gaynor isn't my nearest and dearest,' I said, cutting through the flummery.

'Dear to your husband presumably. All this is bound to touch on him, too.'

I squared my chin. 'For his own good.'

'Oh, Jo,' he sighed, and my spirits were rising faster than the bubbles in my glass because I detected signs of weakening, when all at once, with a muffled roar, he flung himself at me – truly, plunged the length of the sofa headlong into my bosom. Before I could utter so much as a squeak, however, he was struggling upright again, one arm fumbling behind him.

'The one that got away,' he gasped, extracting from the seat of his trousers a shiny if now slightly bent pin. 'So sorry. Golly, you look pale; did I startle you?'

Not half so much as I'd startled myself. Because when, for one split second, I'd thought rampant lust had suddenly got the better of Paddy McGinty's exquisite manners, I'd recognized an unmistakable answering tingle in myself.

20

But so what?

That's what I was saying to myself the following morning as I stood in front of the mirror, with my embroidered cardigan over one arm and a skimpy rib pullover draped across my chest. Paddy was an attractive man – oh, let's not mince words, a gorgeous man – and I was lonely. Only natural he'd created a little flutter in my matronly loins. In fact it would have been downright unnatural if he hadn't, because there's no balm sweeter to the bruised soul of an abandoned wife than the idea that someone might actually be misguided enough to fancy her. And even if

Paddy had been stirred by a pin in the backside rather than uncontrollable desire, he did otherwise give the most gratifying impression that – well, that he quite liked me. Which was why, OK, I'd dug out my best cardigan for consideration this morning and had even flipped on a touch of blusher and mascara.

Nothing wrong with that. Didn't mean I was planning to *do* anything. Sure, last night, as we'd talked into the early hours about everything from Karl Marx to Groucho Marx with the travails of Marks & Spencer in between – the sort of crazily zig-zagging conversation I hadn't had since student days – I might have found my thoughts straying to what it might be like to cast twenty-one years of monogamous fidelity to the winds and tumble into bed with this likeable, intelligent man. If his ribs could take it. But only in the way, when I stand on a high bridge or cliff, I can never resist wondering what it'd be like to cast myself off into space. The thrill's delicious precisely because I know my sensible feet are never going to leave terra firma. Maybe the jumper after all. It made me look thin.

And if cynical souls are shaking their wise old heads, I can only say I'm not a fool. Of course I was aware of the risk of this delightful new friendship straying off the platonic straight and narrow. God's sake, my husband and his uncle already thought we were at it like rabbits. But I can assure you I was anticipating with relish being able to tell Mike that, while I'd had rich opportunity to stray and indeed might have felt tempted, *I* knew better than to risk my marriage for a fling. Paddy and I were friends. I hoped we were on the way to becoming very good friends. But no more than that.

What I hadn't realized was that Mike and Bernard Bidcombe were by no means alone in their misapprehension – and I'm not just talking about Mr Seddons, although he had directed at me something startlingly like a wink as he'd left yesterday evening. I was belatedly piling the breakfast pots into the sink when I saw Hugh Hough-Hartley's portly form come trudging up the garden path.

'I think I've had more visitors since you arrived than in the whole of the past month,' I remarked, groping for a towel to dry my hands before I went to the door.

Paddy, rather to my surprise, recoiled and shut his eyes. 'Lord, tell him I'm out, can't you?' he said. 'In the bath, in hospital. In fact, why not just say I'm dead?'

'I thought he was a friend of yours?'

'I'm devoted to him. Unutterably. But not now.'

'Mrs Patterson?' Hugh was wearing the deerstalker again, and whisked it courteously from his head as he stamped his boots on my front-door mat with the vigour of a mating hippopotamus. 'So good to see you, splendid, splendid.' He was pumping my hand with unusual energy, too. 'When, um, they told me at the castle Paddy was holed up here, I – well, delighted, that's all. If you'll forgive my sayin'. Poor chap's been rattlin' round on the loose too long, all those... Still, couldn't be better, couldn't be better. And how is he?'

I'd left him hobbling across the kitchen with the energy of Long John Silver in sight of treasure. We found him now in the sitting room, wilting on the sofa in an attitude, I later told him, reminiscent of Violetta in the terminal stages of consumption.

'Paddy, old chap,' said our visitor. 'Just been telling Mrs Patterson here how glad I am that you and she are, you know...'

Paddy saw my face and managed to convert his laugh into a cough. Since coughing was painful with his damaged ribs, he really did look quite sickly for a moment or two, and Hugh Hough-Hartley helpfully clouting him between the shoulder blades can't have helped. 'Jove, you do seem a bit seedy,' he said. 'Still, shan't keep you long. Just wondered if I could, um, have a quiet word?' His eyes drifted in my direction.

I was halfway to the door, but the invalid cut in. 'No need for Jo to go,' he said firmly. 'We have no secrets, do we, darling?' Ignoring my glare, he squinted up at Hugh. 'If this is about Jack, and I've no doubt it is, he hasn't got the bloody gun. Sent it off to the gunsmith's.'

'What on earth for?' began Hugh. 'Oh – oh, I *see*. You mean he believed me, about the, um, safety catch? Good God. How extraordinary.'

'And why you couldn't come straight out and tell me you were frightened he was plotting to blow his head off, I can't imagine. Heaven knows, Hughie, we've talked enough about it in years past.'

'But I wasn't,' he protested. 'Thought never crossed my mind.'

Paddy stared at him. 'Then why were you in such a lather about handing it back?'

It was extraordinary to watch. The poor man's face turned red, redder – almost purple as he strangled the deerstalker into a tweedy rope between his hands. He gulped, puffed, glanced uneasily at me, then out of the window, then back at Paddy, and still seemed unable to get a word out. Until, at length, he stammered that he supposed it didn't matter now. Gun was gone. No harm done. Enough said. Except...

'God's sake, what is it, Hughie? Come on, man, spit it out.'

'Fact of the matter is,' he mumbled, rocking to and fro in his boots, 'dreadful, I know, scarcely believe I'm saying this, but – but, oh dammit, Paddy, it was you I was frightened for.'

'For me?' Paddy began, then his mouth fell open. 'Lord save us all, you surely don't mean–'

The man's voice rose to a wail. 'Well, what was I *supposed* to think?'

'I still say it was cruel to laugh at him like that,' I told my guest sternly. 'I've never been more mortified in my life. Your friend was nearly in tears.'

'Silly chump. Anyway, at least he isn't haunted by visions of my lifeless corpse being stretchered off the shooting field. Actually, did he say whether he thought Jack was planning to mistake my head for a pheasant, or just corner me in the library and pass it off as old McGinty having done the decent thing?'

'Don't go on, he knew it was absurd. Although

251

having seen your cousin in a rage,' I added roundly, 'and with everything Hugh told you, I don't blame him for worrying.'

In spite of the hour, Hugh's tale was delivered over a large glass of the malt whisky fortuitously included in Mr Seddons's deliveries, because Paddy said the poor chap looked in need of a reviver. He himself had coffee with me, surprisingly, murmuring that he'd better keep his wits about him if – if he were likely to be dodging shotgun pellets.

'Stop it,' I'd hissed, handing Hugh a water jug.

Hugh Hough-Hartley was a solicitor. So I gathered as he told Paddy that Jack had consulted him a few months ago about the law relating to money left in trust for children. Jack wanted to know whether the trust money could be spent for their future benefit on something they hadn't yet inherited. When Hugh replied he hadn't a clue what Jack was on about, he'd admitted he was referring to Miles and Daisy. If they came into some money, could their trustees use it for the restoration and preservation of Stowham, even if ownership of the estate hadn't yet passed to Miles?

Paddy had shrugged. 'So? I've no doubt Bernard will be passing what he can on to the grandchildren when Jack inherits.'

Hugh, shaking his head, lowered his voice almost to a whisper. Clearly it offended his lawyerly scruples to speak openly of such matters – probably because of my presence, come to think of it, as the supposed new woman in McGinty's life. He reminded Paddy about his own will, that they'd drawn up together not so very long ago. He was sure, he said, sounding not in the least sure, that Paddy wouldn't object to his mentioning that the beneficiaries of his, um, not insubstantial estate were–

'Daisy and Miles. No, of course I don't object.' The fiend winked at me. 'I believe I can state with total confidence Jo isn't after me for my money. Sorry, Hughie, yes. So they're my heirs, but to imagine that Jack would do me a mischief just to set his children up in comfort is absurd, as well you know.'

The man was even quicker than Paddy to ridicule his fears, and touchingly ashamed of having ever harboured them – but I could see why he had. Cousin Jack, by his halting account, had been shutting himself away in his flat since his wife's death, roaring like a wounded tiger at anyone foolish or faithful enough to approach. That day I'd seen them at the ford had been a rare occasion on which the ever-loyal Hugh had persuaded him out, and his behaviour had grown still more reclusive since. Given the depression he'd suffered since his disablement, grief over his wife, and the rift with his cousin, it seemed only too plausible the balance of his mind might have become uncertain. So when he'd suddenly demanded a shotgun with wild talk of needing it to save Stowham, yes, I sympathized with Hugh. Not so Paddy, although he wasn't mocking any longer.

'Jack may resent me,' he said tiredly, 'may even, God knows, hate my guts, but he wouldn't harm a hair on my head.'

'But why has he taken agin you like this?' burst out Hugh. 'Fellow can't seriously blame you for what happened to Katharine. Besides, I'd swear he doesn't. I've asked him straight, but–'

'Leave it, Hughie.'

'But you were always so close, so–'

'No more,' snapped Paddy. His brusqueness certainly startled me. The next moment, though, he was apologizing for his tetchiness, confessing that his injuries were making him feel pretty bloody. I almost believed him, until he went on to claim that his doctor had recommended a nap before lunch. 'So if you'll forgive me, Hughie, I might peel off back to bed for a spell.' At which the monster shot a wicked grin at me. 'Care to join me, darling?'

'Outrageous,' I snorted. 'He nearly broke a leg he scooted to that door so fast. And never mind embarrassing him rigid–'

'How else was I going to dislodge him?'

'What about *me?* With half the neighbourhood now believing we're an item?'

'What a *revoltingly* ugly expression. Item, indeed. More redolent of supermarket queues than poetic passion. Oh, I'm sorry, I'm sorry. How could I so blacken your reputation, respectable married woman that you are?'

'It isn't funny. When we're back together, and Mike comes up here with me, I can do without everyone thinking...' I stopped. 'Oh, sod it, why should I care? He's been living openly with Gaynor these past six months.' A laugh was bubbling up in spite of myself. 'And when

254

Hughie said, as we talked down by the ford, that he really mustn't delay me any longer, I'd swear he was blushing from his toes upwards.'

Furiously indignant, I had insisted on escorting our visitor back to his car. Dora needed an airing, I'd said, the rain seemed to be holding off for the moment, and I was quite sure Paddy could make his *own* way, unaided, to his *own* bed.

'Spoilsport,' he'd cried.

'You obviously make him very happy,' was the first thing Hugh said as I ushered him out of the garden gate. And he spoke with such simple gladness, I somehow couldn't find it in me to tell him this was all a joke which had got out of hand, even though that was precisely my intention when I grabbed my jacket and glared at my irrepressible friend. I decided he could sort this out. Number of women he'd got through, he presumably had plenty of experience explaining their comings and goings.

It was a soft day. The wind had dropped and although more rain was massing in ponderous blue-black clouds, there was even a faint filtering of sun. The countryside glowed with the curious intensity of colour you sometimes get from sunlight under a dark sky: the green of the tired autumnal grass was temporarily poster-paint vivid, the few remaining leaves shone copper and gold on glistening black branches and a scattering of sheep up towards the moor's edge looked brilliantly white as snowballs. 'It's a beautiful place,' I observed. I meant the area generally, but he took me to be referring to the Stowham estate.

'If only one knew what was to become of it,' he responded. 'Tell you honestly, Jo – I may call you Jo? – I realize I've made a fool of myself, and I can see Paddy don't want me to go on, but I can't understand what's in Jack's noggin. Can't read him at all. Swears blind the castle won't be sold to these hotel people or anyone else, that it's staying with the family – but I ask you, *how?*'

I shrugged uncomfortably. It was one thing to listen to Hugh's confidences in Paddy's presence and at his insistence, but I didn't feel I should let this kind and eminently honest man open his heart to me as his friend's supposed lover. I replied guardedly that the long-standing plan for Paddy to invest in the estate was widely discussed in the area. Presumably Jack had come round to the idea again.

'But he won't hear of it,' cried Hugh, stopping so sharply. I stumbled into him. 'Whole point of what I'm saying. Way he talks you'd think he'd rather see the castle dynamited than Paddy buying in. Told his father outright that if Bernard acts over his head with Paddy or these hotel people, he'll take him to court. Not a leg to stand on, mind, as I've said to both of them. But he insists he's going to set things to rights himself.'

'Maybe he's got a Gainsborough everyone's forgotten stashed under his bed,' I said, with deliberate flippancy.

He didn't smile in return. Just growled that Jack had flogged everything worth more than twopence years ago. 'Gambled a fortune away. Dammit, gambling now. Said that to me when he'd had one over the eight – several over the eight. None too sober myself, truth be told, so maybe I got the wrong end of the stick. My wife says I generally do. But it isn't just me, d'you see? Couple of chaps in the Bunburies asked him if the estate was being sold, and he told them the shooting's safe for the foreseeable. And yet his father's said to me – black and white – it's Paddy or bust.' Hughie fixed his earnest Labrador eyes on me. 'Doesn't add up, does it? D'you think he's losing his marbles?'

'Course not.' Paddy was beside the fire with my dog sprawled in wanton abandonment across his lap. He was tickling her belly with one finger. 'Jack's only mad in the sense of bad and dangerous to know. Used to be anyway. Now...' He hesitated, and I heard the edge of guilt again. 'Now just sad, I imagine. But of course he won't countenance my buying into Stowham any longer. The idea should never have been suggested in the first place.'

'You aren't going to bail your uncle out, then?' I caught myself up, still conscious of past blunders. 'Sorry. No concern of mine.'

He gave a cough of laughter. 'Not in Bernard's eyes. Oh, don't chuck that cushion, you'll disturb Dora. She isn't embarrassed about enjoying intimate relations with me – are you, my little hussy?' He yawned. 'Oh, we move to Plan B, which I've yet to spring on the ancient relly. Call it a loan – strictly hands off, as far as I'm concerned. I suppose I should be discussing it with him even now, but he knows where to find me if the bailiffs roll up. God, why did Hughie

257

have to come round fretting? It would be so nice just to pretend Stowham estate and the whole ghastly mess didn't exist. Holed up here with you, I have the most wonderful sensation I've fallen off the edge of the known universe.'

I flashed a smile over my shoulder from the sewing machine. I knew how he felt. I too should be addressing the problems besetting me in the big, tangled world beyond the flooded ford – and persuading my yawning friend here to assist me – but at this moment I lacked the energy for one and the heart for the other. Paddy, for all his jokes, was uneasy about his cousin, particularly when I felt obliged to mention that, from the gossip I'd picked up amongst the beaters, Jack's wild claims hadn't been confined to his Bunbury friends.

'He assured *Aidan* the estate was staying in the family?'

'According to Eileen.'

'I don't believe it. What'd he say exactly?'

'How should I know? Ask Eileen – ask Aidan himself.'

'That'd look terrific,' he snorted. 'Me snooping round the estate, asking the tenants what my cousin's been promising them. As if the whole situation weren't excruciating enough already, with everyone knowing we're at loggerheads.'

It was as though a bell went off in my head. In that instant, I saw my way clear. I put down my curtain and turned to face him. 'I suppose I could poke around for you,' I said with studied casualness. 'No one would wonder at my being nosy.'

'I say, would you?' His smile was so swift and brimmingly grateful, I felt a bum for continuing that there were one or two enquiries he could make on my behalf, by way of reciprocation. I didn't have to spell it out, of course. Not with Paddy.

He stared at me for what seemed like an age. I couldn't read his face, but he certainly wasn't happy. In fact, I was almost certain he was going to start lecturing me on morality again, because he murmured something he'd said before about asking questions being the easy part. All at once, though, he cast up his eyes and flopped back in his chair. 'Oh God, then, I suppose so. On your own head be it.'

A less respectable woman would have punched the air and cheered.

21

Megan Brighouse was not in the least like her sister. Where Eileen trundled through life with the robust, suck-it-all-in, spit-it-all-out efficiency of a combine harvester, Megan was smaller, thinner, frailer – and not nearly so loquacious.

I'd called at Keeper's Lodge on the pretext of collecting my pay packet, still due from the day Paddy had arrived, only to find myself being invited to admire her new curtains. I had to exclaim at the profligacy of Eileen's poor maligned daughter-in-law in throwing out these good-as-new hangings, although I blushed faintly when I was told how beautifully made they were, and all. Still, this gave me the opening to suggest Megan must be relieved that their tenure at Keeper's Lodge was safe after all – from what I'd heard.

'Happen,' she said, tucking her hands under her elbows.

'Very worrying for you, obviously...'

She didn't even answer, just pursed her lips, and I might have elicited little else – so much for my detective skills – if young Jimmy hadn't hurtled in, black Lab bouncing behind. As it was, thanks to Jimmy, I learned rather more than I was expecting.

'Not much gets past that boy,' I told Paddy as I stripped off my dripping coat and shook out my hair. 'Anyway, his grandad told him straight, because he was fretting he might have to give up his dog. His mum's divorced, you know, and they've only got a flat in Wykesea, so he keeps Tyson at his grandparents. Lives there himself, too, half the time. God, I'm frozen to the marrow.'

My friend's investigative efforts, I should say, had amounted to one phone call. I'd come home to find him comfortably ensconced by the fireside with Dora at his feet and a book on his lap – my new le Carré, too, the cheeky sod. As I sank into the chair opposite him, I observed that this was proving to be a rather unequal bargain.

'Your idea,' he replied. 'Anyway, much against my better judgement, I have cast my crusts on the murky waters, and you'll have your information on Ms Steele's bank account within days.' He flipped shut his book. 'Would that the answers I want were as clear cut. What can Jack be thinking of, telling Aidan his job's safe with the family?'

'Yeah, well, Megan didn't contradict Jimmy, but I don't think she's as much faith in your cousin as her husband. I reckon she's secretly afraid he's talking through his hat.'

'Unthinkable,' he said instantly. 'Jack wouldn't make promises he couldn't keep to an old retainer like Aidan. God's sake, he's been with us forty years.'

'How feudal. Your cousin demand seigniorial rights over the village virgins, too?'

I'm afraid I still felt scant sympathy for Jack Bidcombe, and had been surprised to find that Megan, for all her doubts, spoke fondly of him. And while she might be tight-lipped about the present, she seemed happy enough to let Jimmy prompt her to recall the old days, when Jack and Paddy had sat at her kitchen table eating her fruit cake, just like her grandson now – except they'd better manners, she added meaningfully. Well, Mr Paddy did, at any rate. But she only shook her head over Jack's mad pranks. Silliness, she put them down to. He was always one for doing first, thinking second – and leaving his cousin to pick up the pieces.

'That I can believe,' I'd replied, with feeling. Why else, after all, was I sitting in her kitchen now?

'Tell her about the tunnel, Nan,' said Jimmy, but turned immediately to me himself. 'You know the

261

quarry, beyond Fosse Wood, where there's all caves and that?'

'Aye, and if you've been playing round there, your grandad'll skin you alive,' cut in Megan. 'His lordship told the boys time and again the old ironstone workings were out of bounds, but of course that was as good as an invitation to a scallywag like Jack. Then one day his little terrier went charging into a shaft and got stuck.'

'But it was Paddy crawled in and rescued the puppy, wasn't it, Nan?' said Jimmy. 'With the roof all falling down round him?'

'Only because I was half Jack's size,' Paddy said, when I congratulated him on an act of heroism which had evidently entered local legend. 'Whereupon the dog scrambled straight over my prone body to fling herself back into his arms.' He gave a tiny sigh. 'Jack always did have the knack of attracting blind loyalty, however little he did to merit it.'

Was he referring to himself here, I wondered? Or to long-suffering Katharine? But such a barb was unusual. He was soon defending his cousin again, dismissing outright my suggestion that Jack might be plotting to win the money to save Stowham. Rather huffily, I pointed out he'd told Hugh it was all a gamble, and added that nothing could surprise me in a man who'd sold this very cottage to fund his gaming.

'Lord, he didn't blue the lot,' protested Paddy. 'He only did a Bunbury.'

'He did a what?' I said, and was incensed to learn that these old shooting buddies had a long and dishonourable tradition of wheeler-dealering amongst themselves to conceal their gambling expenditure from their poor bloody wives. In buying Beck Holme, it seemed, Ricky Marvell had slipped his friend a few thousand in cash along with the ostensibly modest purchase price so that Jack could sneak away to enter the World Series Poker Championships in Las Vegas. 'Yet another thing Katharine Bidcombe and I have in common,' I said wrathfully.

'I beg your pardon?'

'One way or another, we were both ripped off by that sleazeball, Ricky Marvell. I wonder if he made a pass at her, too? Although at least my husband was an innocent victim, whereas Jack–' I broke off, because Paddy was staring at me. I bridled. 'Is it so amazing someone should make a pass at me?'

The moment passed. But he sounded distracted as he explained that Jack had passed off his jaunt to the States as a visit to relatives in Long Island. Only to be caught out, after a mere handful of games, by a serious infection in his one functioning lung. Hugh, who'd reluctantly gone with him, summoned Paddy to the rescue. Bit of a nightmare, he admitted, because Jack had told a stack of lies to get health insurance.

'The man's a monster,' I exclaimed.

'He might just have repaired the Stowham fortunes, though,' countered my friend, loyal to the last. 'On form, he's a terrifyingly good poker player. You know, I'm sorry you never met my cousin in happier times. I think you would have liked him.' He shot me an oddly crooked grin. 'After all, Katharine did.'

'He seems to be in – in a rather more sanguine frame of mind of late,' said Mr Seddons carefully, in answer to my question. 'You might tell Mr Paddy I would almost say a *determinedly* sanguine frame of mind.' I was at the castle to inspect the drawing-room hangings, Paddy having suggested I could advise on the feasibility of repairs. Perhaps it wasn't the smartest cover story. Repair these things? They were so rotted I scarcely dared breathe on them. And nothing I learned inclined me to like Mr Jack any better, quite the contrary, in fact – although there was plenty to reinforce my liking for his cousin.

'Determinedly sanguine,' he mused, when I reported home again to this kind soul whose young shoulder had been regularly saturated with the tears of dashing Jack's two-timed inamorata – according to Seddons. And if the butler had confided in me because he mistook my friendly curiosity about Paddy for something warmer, well, too bad. 'What d'you suppose the old bird meant by that?'

'Seddons is worried,' I stated, 'and I'm not surprised. Look at this.' I thrust into his hands the large, glossy brochure of Halo Luxury Resorts. 'He gave it to me.'

Paddy frowned as he flipped over the pages. 'These are the people who've made an offer for the castle, aren't they?'

'Correct. Which your cousin *claims* will be accepted over his dead body. Except it turns out the Spanish holiday he's quite openly told every-one he's planning is actually at their complex near Malaga. Where, by the oddest coincidence – as you'll see if you look at page sixteen, "Special Events" – they're holding an international poker tournament next month.' I had saved the best – or worst – until last. 'And just *guess* who's at the top of the list of directors of Halo Hotels?'

'Well, I've no idea where he stands on the list of directors,' said Paddy mildly, 'but I know it was your friend Ricky Marvell who approached Bernard.'

You could say we didn't see eye to eye on either of our investigations. I thought Paddy was being deliberately – OK, possibly chivalrously – obtuse. As I saw it, Jack was a serious gambler, and there was a big poker tournament at his friend's place in Spain. It seemed only too plausible an explanation of his conduct that he was aiming to win the money to keep Stowham afloat. Maybe he was even letting Ricky stake him – on the understanding that, if he lost, he'd withdraw his opposition to the castle being sold.

But Paddy no more believed in an underhand deal between Jack and Ricky Marvell than he did in one between Gaynor Steele and Optimax. He said my methods were reminiscent of the KGB. I appointed the guilty party, then cooked up the evidence to suit. Still, we didn't argue seriously, nor for long. He sighed that Jack's plans – if any – must emerge soon enough, and I was confidently waiting for Gaynor's bank statements to turn up and prove my case. In the meantime, I have to confess I was rather more interested in pursuing my enquiries into the character and curriculum vitae of Peter Edward Ffoulkes McGinty, age 46, ed. Winchester and Sandhurst, club, MCC, interests – none that he could think of. In the unlikely event he ever qualified for an entry in *Who's Who*, he declared, he would apply himself to dreaming up impressively cerebral hobbies. So what were mine?

Over meals, lazy afternoons by the fire, games of Scrabble and even poker – because he taught me the rules one gale-buffeted evening and we gambled a fortune in banknotes borrowed from Ben's Monopoly box – we traded chunks of autobiography, and Paddy was every bit as inquisitive about my life as I was about his. I remember being taken aback, when he asked – I forget how it came up – if I'd always been faithful to my husband.

'Were you faithful to your wife?' I whipped back.

'Absolutely,' he said, as though this were the most obvious thing in the world, and added for good measure that, whatever loopy notions I may have picked up to the contrary, he was at heart a very boring, one-woman sort of chap.

'One woman after another?' I riposted. But I somehow couldn't doubt him when he told me he'd stuck by his marriage vows. Honesty shone through the man – most of the time. When we'd run out of Monopoly money, though, and I'd scribbled IOUs for a further few thousand, I exasperatedly asked how many aces he had hidden about his person. We were at the table in the sitting room, I remember, with a single lamp lighting our game so that I couldn't see the still unfinished violet curtains bundled in a corner. The fire was smouldering low in the grate, Dora was stretched across the hearthrug, and a companionable bottle of port stood between us.

He looked at me for a moment or two, then grinned. 'It's the mouse-squeak.'

'Sorry?'

'Every time you get a halfway decent hand, you squeak. Then redispose your features into a gloomy scowl.'

I scowled now. 'Whereas the expression poker-face might have been coined for your good self.'

'Ah,' he said, 'but I have long experience of lying.'

He spoke sombrely, and I was puzzled for a moment.

'In your job, you mean?'

He just smiled and raised his glass of port. 'Farewell to the covert life,' he declared. 'Never again.'

Perhaps surprisingly, given the princely cellar Paddy had supplied, we didn't drink liver-endangering quantities over the ten days he stayed in my cottage, because he did stay a full ten days in the end. That is to say, it wasn't surprising I exercised circumspection, because one of the depressing features of incipient middle age, I find, is that hangovers bite more savagely with the years. Paddy, though, didn't put away any more than I, and actually said he might revise his plan to drink himself into a premature compost heap.

'Delighted to hear it,' I responded. 'So what

will you do with your life?'

'God knows.' It was one of those unguarded moments when, for no apparent reason, my friend could look terribly sad. 'Always my failing, this lack of a guiding star. Unlike your husband, I've never passionately wanted to do anything – not in my career, at any rate.' At once, typically, he turned the question back on me. 'Why, did you explode out of university ablaze with ambition?'

'Waddled out nauseously pregnant but...' I cast my mind back. I cast my mind back a long, long way. 'Well, I certainly didn't anticipate ending up like this, with only the kids and a rocky marriage to show for twenty years' hard labour. I had my share of world-changing zeal, whatever Sarah thinks. I suppose I saw myself, oh, adventuring to the far corners of the earth but...' I pulled a rueful face. 'I guess my youthful rebellion was as boringly conventional as yours. You joined the army, I got married and had children. My mum really had to sweat to make it to Head of a, big mixed comprehensive, and she was desperate for me to have a glittering career before I got bogged down in nappies.' I sighed. 'It's only with age, isn't it, that you start realizing your poor bloody parents might have had a point?'

'But with the children off your hands now?' he said. 'You could do anything.'

'You sound like my daughter. Mike, on the other hand, says I'm one of nature's rut-dwellers. Sad, but he's probably right.'

Paddy met my eyes and smiled. 'My wife used to say much the same of me.'

And I suppose that was when we got down to the real nitty-gritty. Love, marriage, all that stuff.

Not that anyone – 'anyone' being my husband – could have taken exception to our conversation, let alone to our behaviour, which was a model of middle-aged decorum. My daughter telephoned to enquire after her patient and, on hearing he was getting about quite competently now, gave her drain-gurgle laugh and said, brill, all the better for sweeping me off to bed. Had the invalid not been sitting across the table, I would have told her pretty sharply that the only time I'd so much as ventured into Paddy's bedroom was when I'd had to feed a baby rat to her bloody brother's pet. This was a task I performed weekly with distaste and eyebrow tweezers. And far from attempting to tumble me to the mattress, this supposed Casanova had nearly tumbled over his feet in his anxiety to escape.

'I have rather a thing about snakes,' he confessed.

'Don't we all,' I growled, cursing my son afresh for lumbering me with the care and control of a four-foot and still-growing reptile, presently eyeing us with beady malevolence from its knotted coil under a shard of driftwood. 'Of course Ben didn't consult me when he saw the ad in the *Wykesea Gazette*. Just staggered home with the aquarium and a sworn oath he'd take it back to York at the end of the vac. Easter, this was. And he professed total amazement on learning university residences don't allow animals.'

'I think there was a fad for keeping corn

snakes,' said Paddy from his wary vantage point in the doorway. 'Daisy had one for a bit. Not unlike that brute, as I recollect, although I can't say it and I ever got closely acquainted.'

'Funny,' I said, depositing the soggy bundle of defrosted rodent. 'He usually gets more excited at feeding time.'

'Sex deprivation. Pity's sake, put the lid back on, will you? I know when Daisy's went off its tucker she used to fret about the beast getting lonely without a mate to curl its tail round. Sounds plausible. As a fellow sex-starved bachelor, I've every sympathy.'

I glanced round, eyebrows raised.

'From a safe distance,' he added, and vanished.

See what I mean? If our conversation strayed into a vein that could remotely be construed as flirtatious, he was the first to draw back. I was married, Paddy accepted it, and there was not the faintest shimmer of awkwardness. When we were playing poker, and I'd speculated how the strip version of the game could work – seemed to me you'd only need to up the stakes a couple of times and you'd be starkers with barely a card dealt – he responded rather prudishly that he couldn't imagine. Personally he'd always assumed strip poker was a 1960s urban myth, like car-keys-on-the-hearthrug wife-swapping orgies.

So I can assure you that there was no titillating subtext when we found ourselves agreeing that we had both married too young. Paddy claimed that when the flames of passion tamed to a smoulder – 'actually more of a pilot light' – he and his wife found all they had in common otherwise was a taste for French cinema and Italian food.

'Shouldn't have come as any shock Tara went in search of a kindreder variety of spirit,' he said cheerfully. 'Although it did, of course. I suffered fifty kinds of hell.'

'And that bust you up, her affair?'

'Yes. Oh, not at once, because we had the statutory bash at reconciliation. She said the affair was over, I manfully pledged to ask no questions, bear no grudges, that sort of thing, and we staggered on for a bit, but the rot had set in. Another lover bowled along, and this time I knew exactly who he was. Balding dwarf with a château in the Loire, a flat overlooking Central Park, and halitosis. Not that I'm biased. Anyway, the end was inevitable by then, as even I had to admit. No foundation to the marriage, you see, our lives barely touched at the edges, let alone intertwined, whereas you and your chap have had so much to keep you well knitted.'

'Thankfully,' I agreed, although for one daft moment I found myself wondering what exactly Mike and I did have in common. What had we talked about these past twenty-one years, apart from the kids and money? He'd always joked that we were the original Mr and Mrs Jack Sprat, reeling off how he liked telly, parties, cities, sun and I forget what else, when his wife would sooner curl up with her radio or book in the middle of boring, raining nowhere...

'I suppose it's a good thing we never got as far as having children,' reflected Paddy, cutting across my thoughts.

'Wouldn't you have liked to, though?' I asked. 'You're obviously very fond of Miles and – what's the girl called?'

'Daisy?'

I should have known, because their names cropped up in our conversation almost as regularly as those of Ben and Sarah. I remarked now that she looked very like her mother, from the photograph of the three of them, which was propped on Ben's chest of drawers.

'Very – but with a wicked flash of Jack. I must say I miss her enormously.'

'Seddons mentioned she's taking a gap year with family in the States?' He had also confided that Paddy had been like a second father to Jack's children after their real dad rode a bike off a wall and lost interest in trivia like his poor bloody offspring. At least, loyal Mr Seddons hadn't put it quite like that, but I'd read between the lines.

'Seemed she couldn't wait to fly away.' For all he spoke flippantly, I heard the sadness. 'Very hard for her – for both of them – losing their mother.'

'Do you think Daisy blames herself?' I ventured. 'Absurd, obviously, but Bernard said something about her not having come to pick you up from the airport that night...?'

'Nonsense. If anything Daisy blames me. Not for Kat's death as such, perhaps, but for ... well, who knows? She's certainly kept a distance since.' He managed a smile. 'Literally. I haven't even had a postcard. Still, it will do her good to spread her wings over there, and I tell myself she won't come to harm. She's inherited Katharine's common sense, even if she does have Jack's temper. Oh, we'll all come about eventually. One way or another.'

Such a sad picture. This once-close family rent apart by a stupid, meaningless accident. Jack and Paddy had been like brothers, Daisy and Miles like his own children, and the girl's venting her grief on him obviously hurt Paddy profoundly. 'You should've had children of your own,' I said. 'Heavens, what am I saying? You still can.'

'I'm a bit antique, don't you think? So embarrassing for the poor brat, having an arthriticky old codger doddering down the fathers' egg-and-spoon.'

'I'd like to think my husband feels the same,' I responded, and had no hesitation in confiding my fears about Gaynor's alleged ambition to become a mother. That was the extraordinary thing. I felt I could talk to Paddy about anything.

As I observed to him on another occasion, it seemed remarkable to me that, for all we'd been flung together by chance and could scarcely have led more different lives, we seemed to rub along like the most comfortable of old friends. 'I'm sorry about your injuries, naturally, but it's been total pleasure having you stranded here.'

Paddy smiled. 'Soap-bubble living,' he said. 'Have to pop the bubble and return to the real world one day, though.'

22

He could have done so long since. The beck might be surging along still, refuelled by sporadic showers, but after three or four days – I forget exactly now – it was obvious that Paddy, with help, could easily have made it to the footbridge. He'd soon substituted a stick for the chair he initially used as a walking frame, and I well remember his jubilation when he hauled himself up the stairs for a bath. That was long before he left. I wasn't anxious to be rid of him, of course, far from it, and he said he'd be happy to be marooned here for ever. Mind, he did add that Stowham Castle at this time of year made a Soviet gulag compare favourably with the Hilton.

'And Bernard and I are going to have to talk – with Jack.' He suppressed a shudder. 'But not quite yet. We haven't finished those delightful purple curtains yet. Tell me, are you seriously proposing to stick *all* that gold tasselly stuff on?'

Also braiding, piping and cording, on these triple-fullness drapes with giant tie-backs and swagged pelmets. Paddy said they looked like the Ruritanian army uniforms in a pre-war waltz musical – 'We'll gather lilac soldiers?'

'You should see the palace they're destined for,' I murmured, looping another yard of braid over my shoulder. I did eventually complete them in all their glory, only to fold them away on Sarah's bed. Delivery and hanging could wait until my guest had moved on. A day came when I had to abandon him, though, to go beating. I'd already cried off from one shoot, pleading a migraine, to which Adrian had drily replied that that was one way of putting it. And just in case I was in any doubt as to his meaning, expressed his sincere hope that Major McGinty was feeling better.

'Remember me fondly to Adrian,' Major McGinty said now, picking up his mug of coffee and limping away to the fire. It was a wickedly cold morning, I should say, with an east wind stripping the remaining leaves and rattling the windows with a howling vigour that made my fireside fire look even more seductive than usual. 'And Bernard, of course, if you bump into him. Better tell him – oh, that my life isn't imminently in danger, but I remain too frail to be moved.'

'Which the entire neighbourhood will interpret as a polite way of saying you're too knackered to clamber out of bed,' I retorted, gathering up stick and coat. '*My* bed.'

He blew me a kiss. I was halfway down the path before I realized I'd blown him one back. But so what? The most innocent gesture of friendship.

It was a long and wearisomely muddy day, although I picked up an order to reupholster a set of dining-room chairs which, with my watch still in hock, was welcome. Naturally, my ears were attuned to any mention of Paddy's cousin, so I hurried forward to join the group round Eileen Muxworthy as we trudged down from the second drive, because they were discussing Mr Jack's planned birthday party. The idea of this bad-tempered recluse throwing a party seemed improbable, to say the least, but I recalled Hugh Hough-Hartley having mentioned something of the sort. My wind-blasted, rain-dripping companions were talking about it because an extra shoot had now been scheduled for his house guests the following morning, which apparently meant we'd be out two days on the trot.

'Still, it's a good sign,' pronounced Leonard, to general agreement. 'Nearly a year now since the poor creature was gathered. Did I hear tell he's going off to Spain and all?'

I would have enquired if anyone knew about the poker tournament, but no sooner did I mention Ricky Marvell than Eileen grabbed my sleeve, demanding to know whether I wanted the last remaining ticket for the ladies' outing to see his show in Wakeford.

'Best seats in the house,' she told me, 'right down the front, first night and all – oh, pack it in,' she snorted at the musketeer who'd warned her not to wear her long johns if she was planning on chucking her knickers. She turned back to me. 'Fortnight tomorrow, love, coach picking us up at the pub, fifteen pounds all in, bring your own sandwiches.'

I hesitated. But Paddy must surely have felt obliged to return to the castle by then, and I still suspected there was something fishy between Jack and Ricky Marvell...

'Rot,' commented my guest, predictably enough, when I finally flopped into a chair at the kitchen table, dirty, drenched and debilitated. He bent to pull a twig out of Dora's sodden ear. 'I contrived to get your son's computer to accept a fax while you were out.'

'Uhuh?' I yawned as I wondered if my legs could muster the muscle-effort to propel me up the stairs and into the bath. 'By the by, while I remember, your cousin's having a birthday party – you remember Hughie mentioned it? Strewth, I'm pooped.'

'I thought you wouldn't want to wait for the post, so all identifying details have had to be deleted, of course.'

My tiredness fell away in that instant. 'You've got Gaynor's bank statements?' I squawked, bouncing upright in my chair. 'Why didn't you say so? *And?*'

Paddy, by contrast, slid lower in his. 'I may as well give you the bottom line,' he said unhappily. 'On the face of it, it would appear that Optimax, for some reason, are paying Ms Steele a rather larger salary than the one they're paying your husband. Oh, *please*, do you mind? I have very sensitive ears.'

It led to our only serious quarrel.

I may have shouted at him the first night we had dinner together, but I'd been drunk and he hadn't taken offence. This was different. We ate early, because I'm always ravenous after beating, but we were arguing even as I laid the table and continued throughout the meal.

What disappointed as much as annoyed me was Paddy's refusal to admit he could be wrong. I might, as I said, lack his business expertise, but I'd been inside Optimax and seen that American kid shuffling and shifting. I'd *known* he was hiding something from me, and this proved it. I was triumphant to learn Optimax was paying Gaynor Steele half as much again as my husband, and thought pretty poorly of my friend for pointing out that no large lump sums had inexplicably popped into her bank account. She might have another account, I said. In Switzerland, and I didn't care how extensive the enquiries made by his trusty colleague had been. As to her having recently remortgaged her flat – how should I know why she'd done that, or where the proceeds had gone? It had nothing to do with the case.

'And you seriously propose,' said Paddy, looking every bit as exasperated as I felt, 'that this woman would sell her lover's entire company down the river, just so she could end up being paid twenty grand a year more than him? Ridiculous.'

'It's there,' I said, pointing to the fax. 'In black and white, as you would say.'

'You're *sure* your husband's only on fortyK?'

'Don't hedge.'

'Well, it's a pretty paltry salary in this day and age, that's all I can say.'

'Maybe to the likes of you,' I snapped. 'But I wouldn't turn my nose up at it.'

And that's when the argument took a vicious twist.

'I should think you wouldn't, the straits he's left you in. What does the thoughtless bastard imagine you've been living on all this time? Air?'

I stiffened. 'That thoughtless bastard,' I hissed, 'is my husband.' But to my astonishment Paddy, who was usually so swift to apologize for a lack of tact or a clumsy word, didn't back down.

'Here you are, stitching curtains to keep body and soul together, proudly announcing tonight you might have a nice little order to restuff somebody's old chairs – does the man know what he's reduced you to?'

'It isn't his fault. Anyway, I like sewing.'

'Katharine liked books, but that didn't mean she wanted to spend her life sweating over lousy manuscripts for peanuts. But she would have done, for all Jack knew or cared.'

That stung because of the parallels I'd drawn myself between his cousin's wife and me. But for all Mike's failings, he was no Jack Bidcombe. 'What the hell's Katharine Bidcombe got to do with it?'

'She–' Paddy was actually on his feet, mouth open to shout back. But he didn't. He glowered at me for an instant, then his gaze fell. 'Nothing at all,' he said, with frigid politeness. 'Singularly stupid thing for me to say. I'm sorry.'

And he stumped out of the kitchen.

I suppose we would have made up anyway. I may have been muttering to myself and the dog as I flung the dinner pots into the sink, but at every moment I was expecting Paddy to re-emerge from the sitting room. I'd already decided to open a reconciliatory bottle of fizz. He might have overstepped the mark by attacking my husband, but there was a certain justice on his side – and we were friends, for heaven's sake. Were our situations to be reversed, I dared say I might feel pretty indignant about his errant partner, might even be tempted, like him, to offer a few home truths. As to his obstinacy over Gaynor's role in the company collapse, well, no one likes to be proved wrong. Particularly by a financial illiterate like me. I never gave a thought to how and when I'd tell Mike about his floozy's treachery. I was far more concerned about finding myself at odds with my friend. And it was with blank astonishment, even as I lifted a misted bottle of Krug out of the fridge, that I detected the crunch of Paddy's bedroom door shutting. Not merely was the time barely a quarter to nine, he surely – *surely* – couldn't be intending to retire with this nasty spat hanging unresolved between us?

There was no sound of his re-emergence, however. Until, that is, just as my wrath was frothing back to the boil – how dared he walk out on me like this? – the house was rent with such an almighty roar I actually dropped the dish I was drying.

'Paddy?' I shrieked and sent spiky shards of earthenware rattling over the flags as I galloped out of the kitchen. 'My God, are you all right?'

The scene that met my eyes as I opened the bedroom door was this. Paddy, shirtless and with trousers round his knees, lay flat on the carpet. A large towel suggested some intention of taking a bath. Beside him, intact but in a shambles of shavings and driftwood, lay my son's snake tank.

'Tripped against it while I was taking my

trousers off,' he panted, squirming back into them now while twisting his head this way and that, which must have been agony with his injured ribs on a hard floor. 'Knocked it flying.' After a last heave, he yanked his trousers into decency. 'And the bloody snake catapulted out.' He rolled on to his side and propped himself up on one elbow, wincing. 'God's sake, give me a hand. The beast's on the loose somewhere.' His face was plastered with sawdust, his naked chest dripping with water from Barry's bowl, and he looked absolutely petrified. 'Jo?' he said, still holding out his hand. He began to scowl. 'Jo, this is not funny.'

I had to grab the door handle for support. 'No? You should see yourself.'

'Listen, you hag, I'm stuck down here and any minute now that confounded reptile will be back for a bite.'

'They don't,' I wailed. 'Bite. Ben promised. Least – not poisonous.'

'Great comfort,' he roared, grabbing my hand and stumbling up on to one knee. 'Oh my God, there it is, lurking under the radiator.'

'Get out,' I spluttered. 'I'll think of something.'

He'd opened the champagne by the time I joined him. Opened it and was downing a hefty glassful as he curled his bare toes on my cold flagged floor amidst the shards of broken pot. He was still naked from the waist up, and only now did I take in fully the shocking rainbow of bruises round his midriff. The shudder that convulsed him as I appeared in the doorway, though, was

281

purely for theatrical effect.

'My hero,' I said. 'Remind me not to summon you when I'm in peril.'

'Don't mock. Have you caught the fanged fiend?'

'With an old fishing net of Ben's. Slithered inside quite tamely, actually. Probably scared stiff.' And then there was a silence, as if neither of us could think what to say next.

'Look, about earlier–' I began.

'I owe you a huge apology–' said Paddy in the same moment.

We began laughing. Then he held wide his arms, and as though it were the most natural thing in the world, I walked into them. A hug between friends, to show there were no hard feelings. A kiss – to make up. Except there was more than friendliness in the hand which locked round my waist. And somehow – I can't imagine how – instead of planting a sisterly salute of truce on Paddy's sawdust-strewn cheek, I found I was twining my own arms round his naked shoulders – so deliciously warm and solid as they were – and lifting my face to his, with my eyes closing, my mouth opening...

What I don't know is what exactly happened next. Did my conscience at last blast the whistle, or had Paddy already begun to release me? Or had both of us simply heard the noise outside? I'd certainly registered something, but was in no state to recognize it as the rattle of key in lock. Whatever, even as we froze, there echoed a voice from the hallway, a familiarly froggy voice.

'Hiya, Dora – down, you brainless mutt,

geddown. Mum? You in the kitchen?'

'Well, bless my soul,' whispered Paddy – and I wouldn't mind, but as I snatched my guilty arms away, I felt his shoulders begin to rock with laughter. 'I do believe the cavalry's arrived. With immaculate timing, too.'

Well, yes, I suppose I could see it was funny. Downright hysterical – being discovered in your kitchen two seconds out of a clinch with a half-naked stranger by your nineteen-year-old son. Ben stood on the threshold, all six feet two of him, shaggy-haired, fuzzy-chinned, knees poking out of his ripped jeans, with a kit-bag the size of a fridge hoisted on his shoulder. And, having taken in the situation in one swift glance, my sunny, sweet-natured, friend-of-all-the-world, golden baby now bristled like a terrier at a rat hole.

'Darling,' I cried, with a fairish impersonation of maternal adoration. 'What a surprise – I mean, lovely surprise. What brings you home, and at this time of night?'

'Got a lift,' he grunted, shrugging off my hug, thumping his bag to the floor and ostentatiously averting his gaze as I fumbled to secure a shirt button which had somehow burst adrift in the mêlée. 'Mate of mine was driving up to Wykesea. He dropped me on the top road.'

'Why?' I said, which perhaps wasn't the most tactful way to welcome home the apple of my eye. 'I mean, it's the middle of term.'

'Flu,' said Ben – this bright-eyed, pink-cheeked picture of health, who had just hefted half a ton of baggage down a mile of country lane in the pitch-black night without so much as getting out of breath. And he was still glowering at Paddy, who limped forward with hand courteously outstretched.

'Sorry,' I said distractedly. 'Paddy – my son, Ben. Paddy's been staying with me these past few days, had a car accident, as you can probably see. *Benjamin?*'

Under my minatory eye he stumped forward and accorded Paddy's hand the kind of shake you might give to a convicted child molester with personal hygiene problems.

'I do apologize,' said my friend. 'Had you arrived fractionally earlier, you would have found me in the most fearfully embarrassing tangle with' – my heart skipped a beat – 'your snake tank. I'm afraid I upended it on my way to take a bath, and had to summon your heroic mama to rescue me from the escaped monster.' He pulled a face. 'Feeling thoroughly humiliated then, I think I'll retire to down my miseries in a large drink and leave you and Jo to yourselves. Except...' His hesitation was exquisitely timed. 'I fear I've been hogging your bed this past week and more. If you'd like me to move my kit and decamp elsewhere...?'

The fractional lifting of the thunderclouds in my son's face was absurdly transparent. He even shot a searching glance at me, as if to satisfy himself that this poncey-accented interloper was speaking the truth. If it wouldn't have wrecked Paddy's diplomatic efforts, I could have kissed him. Which, let's face it, was exactly what I'd been about to do when Ben blundered in. And would I have stopped at a kiss?

'You'll stay exactly where you are,' I told Paddy, guilt making me more brusque than brisk. 'I'm not changing bedding at this hour. Ben can go into Sarah's room. Sorry, did you say whisky? Yes, of course, in the corner cupboard.'

If Paddy hadn't borne the bottle away with him, I might have downed a hefty tot of the hard stuff myself, and I don't even like Scotch. As it was, I poured a brimming glass of champagne instead, and waited until his footsteps had limped off down the hall before turning back to my son. 'Flu, huh?'

He did at least blush. Never had a talent for fibbing, Ben, unlike his sister who, if inclined, would do her damnedest to convince you black was white and the world triangular. 'Lot of it about,' he mumbled. 'Tutor came down with it, so I thought – well, I've been really slogging this term, OK? I reckoned I needed a few days to chill.'

'A few *days?*' I squawked.

'Don't you want to see me?' protested my son, adding virtuously that I knew how concerned he'd always been about me, living out here all on my own.

'In case it has escaped your notice,' I said tartly, 'I am not, at present, on my own.'

'Yeah, exactly.'

I stiffened. 'And what's that supposed to mean?'

'Look, I s'pose you can tell me it's none of my business, but when Dad said–' He must have seen the expression on my face because he broke off, flushing.

'*Dad*,' I said furiously. 'I might have bloody known.'

'OK, so he rang me. Wanted to talk about – about some project he's working on.'

'Tell me another.'

'He did, too. Straight up.'

'And happened to mention in passing that your mother was shacked up with a strange man, and it might be a good idea if you trotted home to play gooseberry? God Almighty, the wimp couldn't face coming up himself, so he's sent you instead?'

He didn't have to answer. Just hung his shaggy head and fondled the dog's ears and mumbled something – if you can credit this, because I couldn't – about Dad being pretty busy just now.

'I've no doubt. Busy screwing his floozy.' Which was unworthy of me. I had tried – truly I had striven every noble sinew – not to involve my children in our marital quarrels. Ben had a right to lift that face of injured innocence to me.

'Yeah, well, you know what I think of *her*.'

I did. Ben had loyally refused to speak to Gaynor since the day I'd walked out, and had even kept his dad at a pretty chilly distance.

'As it happens,' I hissed, downing a defiant gulp of fizz, 'and not that it's anyone's concern but my own, the only living creature to share my bed this past six months, never mind the last fortnight, has been the dog you and your sister were so misguided as to foist on to me.' And that was unworthy too, given that we both knew I loved

286

the four-legged mud-magnet with a passion almost equalling that for my children. 'Paddy, meanwhile, has slept alone and in your room. But I would be *deeply* obliged if you didn't tell your bloody father that. He deserves everything he suspects – and more. As for sending you here to spy on me, well, words fail me.'

On that wrathful note, draining my glass in a single swallow, I marched upstairs to shift the violet curtains and find a clean quilt cover for Sarah's bed. I was so cross I was tempted to barge into Paddy's room and fling myself at him. Give my son something worth reporting to his father.

Joke.

I think.

PART FOUR

'One of the advantages of a great sorrow is that nothing else seems painful.'

Giacomo Casanova, *History of My Life*

23

Soon after what passed for dawn the following morning, I shambled down to the kitchen in my dressing gown only to find that Paddy was ahead of me, washed, shaved and dressed. I hadn't a clue how to handle this situation anyway, and the cloud of soap, toothpaste and cologne emanating from his immaculate person towards my frowsy self didn't help.

I'd already been down here at something past three, brewing tea and assuring myself there'd only be one set of pillows in my bed upstairs now whether or not Ben had come home last night. No, I didn't believe it either. You may wonder why I even *wanted* to believe it. I liked Paddy; he seemed to like me. We were consenting adults and my unfaithful husband already believed we were having a raging affair, so why shouldn't I do just that? Even up the score with a little fling of my own? Be hanged for a well-shagged sheep instead of a prissy little lamb?

I knew it would be a mistake, though. Worse than a mistake, disastrous. What had kept me chewing the pillow most of the night was that I couldn't quite define why I felt this so strongly. I wish I could claim I was thinking of my marriage vows, but the answer was neither so pious nor so simple. Was it just bloody-minded reluctance to lose the moral high ground? When Mike finally turned up on my doorstep – which he'd have to now, once he learned about Gaynor's machinations – I'd always seen myself doing the forgiving and forgetting. There was to be nothing mutual. He'd sinned; I had planned to be saintly.

This might be a less than admirable reason for fidelity, but at least it was better than the flutter of panic I felt at the mere idea of adultery. Oh, you can mock – I would myself if this were someone else – but twenty-one years of monogamy is a long time, and while confining your rutting to the marital rut might be dull, you never have to worry about your stretch marks. Mind, it says everything for my confused state that, even while I agonized over the big moral issues, I found myself wondering if I could be sure Paddy wanted to make love to me anyway. Had I imagined that fractional withdrawal, even before my son came barging in?

Oh God, I felt bewildered, frustrated and ashamed all at once. Not to say a prize fool, after kidding myself all this time that there was no danger of sex corrupting our innocent friendship. Paddy and I *were* friends, though, and that surely was reason enough for staying out of bed, because I valued this new friendship and wanted it to endure. But if we became lovers, however fleetingly, he'd have to be chucked on the sacrificial altar alongside Gaynor. I'd made clear to Mike that his mistress had to be banished completely. I couldn't invent a new set of rules for myself...

See now why I was in a quandary? Why I could have done without my friend wafting good cheer and classy cologne round the kitchen that dank morning, as I slumped against the Aga, lank-haired, bleary-eyed, foul-breathed and fuddle-brained?

'I've mashed the tea, as they say in these parts,' he declared, wincing as he bent to fish the milk out of the fridge. 'Three bags strong, because I feel a touch in need of a restorative. I fear I rather overdid the whisky last night.'

Sexual frustration? Although just now the idea of anyone needing to damp down raging passion for me seemed far-fetched, if not actually farcical. Still, I needed to clear the air. We weren't kids playing dating games. He'd had every right to assume, just a few hours ago, that when this sensible old trout flung her arms round his neck, she'd known what she was in for. I tied my dressing gown belt more firmly. 'About last night...'

Paddy, pouring milk into the mugs, barely glanced round. 'What about it?'

'I...' I was floundering already. Why couldn't I be blasé, woman-of-the-worldly? Make-up and heels would've helped. 'Ben coming home as he did. Rather unfortunate timing.'

'Oh, I don't know. On the button, wouldn't you say?'

He wasn't making this any easier. 'But if he hadn't – not that there's anything wrong as far as you're concerned, of course, but – but you may have thought, indeed had good cause to assume, we were going to...'

'Fuck?' he offered, with a wide-eyed air so reminiscent of a maiden aunt enquiring if the vicar took one lump or two, I had to laugh. He did too, although rather warily it seemed to me. 'Seriously,' he said, 'would that have been so very terrible?' He eyed me for a moment. 'Well – yes, obviously it would. Sorry. I should have known.'

'Why?' I found myself asking, which wasn't how this dialogue was meant to go.

'You're a respectable married woman.' He delivered this now familiar phrase with a suitably ironic flourish.

'Don't joke.'

'Never been more in earnest, I assure you. Have some tea; cheer you up. Besides, what's the problem? Nothing happened. Spectacularly handsome boy, isn't he?'

'Ben?' Normally I lap up praise of my offspring, but I was thrown by the change of tack and, besides, I'd only just noticed the bag shoved casually against the wall. Paddy's leather valise, bulging, strapped and – ready to go? 'Well, of course I think so,' I said distractedly. 'Although I sometimes wonder, because he's yet to bring home a girlfriend.'

'Wary of wheeling them back to Mama?'

'Am I so fearsome? Paddy, why have you packed your things?'

'Time for me to get out from under your feet, don't you think?' To my relief, his face suddenly softened into the old smile, the smile I recognized. 'Lord, it's fiendishly tricky with children around, this sort of situation, I know only too well.'

'But Ben won't be here long. He–'

There the conversation ended, however,

because the subject of it, in the outsize T-shirt and sweat pants that served him as pyjamas when he felt the need of such refinements, slumped in, yawning and scratching his hairy navel. This was barely eight a.m., and my son, who has never been known to surface voluntarily before noon, had once again blundered into my kitchen at exactly the wrong moment. I was so exasperated, I didn't notice the flush in his cheeks, the clouding of his eyes. 'You're up early,' I commented, tight-lipped.

'Yeah, well...' His voice may have been huskier than usual, but all I registered was the note of righteous indignation. 'I think I might actually have caught this sodding flu, can you believe it?'

Ignoring Paddy's stifled laugh, I stomped forward to clamp a hand to his forehead. That's when I took in the angry flush and hazy eyes. And while his brow was burning, he was shivering pitifully. Bang went any idea of running him straight back to York. 'Couldn't sleep,' he croaked. 'Came down to get a paracetamol or something. Sorry.'

'Oh, baby,' I sighed, 'we'd better get you back to bed. Sit down and take your feet off this floor before you catch your death, while I see what's in the medicine cupboard.'

'OK to use the phone?' murmured Paddy. 'The sooner I can whistle up transport back to the castle, the sooner I'll be out of your way.'

'Transport? Lumme, only a couple of aspirin, I'll have to get to a chemist. Look, sweetheart, take these for now, and stick the thermometer in your mouth.'

'I'm sure Ben will be more comfortable in his own room.' He shot a shy smile at my son. 'Thanks for the use of it.'

'Nothing to do with me,' grunted the ungracious little sod.

'I'll run you back to the castle,' I said, abandoning any idea of persuading him to stay. With my son in a foul mood and a high fever, the three of us were unlikely to co-exist in comfort. 'I'll have to go out anyway, to get some paracetamol and stuff.'

Paddy insisted so firmly that he mustn't put me to such trouble, I could almost have believed he didn't want to get into a car with me when Ben, unwittingly, resolved the impasse. He was excelling himself at mortifying his mother just now.

'Where's your watch?' he croaked as I whisked the thermometer out of his mouth. Now, this was a boy who had been known to overlook a six-foot-tall pink giraffe in the hallway of his home – and I am speaking entirely literally. The beast was a prop from a product launch, temporarily dumped on us, and, lost in his customary dream world, Ben had squeezed past it without a glance. But then he had chosen that watch for me himself, with a touchingly evident awareness it was less a timepiece than a timely peace-offering. 'The gold one *Dad* gave you,' he added now, as reproachfully as if I'd melted down my wedding ring. 'You always wear it.'

'Broken,' I trilled. 'Matter of fact, I'll pick it up while I'm in Wykesea this morning, provided I can drop off some curtains on the way and pick up the dosh. Yes, I had to take it to, um, a jeweller's for repairs. Wonky safety catch.'

I'd added this gloss only to silence my son, but I knew it was a mistake the instant the words left my mouth. The original author of this fib was across the table.

'Wonky safety catch?' echoed Paddy. 'You know, if it really wouldn't be too much of a bore for you, perhaps I will accept your offer of a lift after all.'

'OK, yes, I pawned the bloody watch,' I said as I climbed into the car beside him. 'But it's no concern of yours.'

So much for our being cut off from the world. Not just had Ben comprehensively burst our soap bubble, I'd actually managed to drive the car across the ford and up to the house. A four-wheel-drive job could doubtless have got through days ago.

'It is, if you did it to feed me with smoked salmon and Chablis.'

'I needed cash anyway.' Humiliation lent an edge to my voice. 'You should know, you read my bank statements.'

There was an uneasy silence as I steered my rather more heavily laden vehicle back across the swirling beck. I knew what he was thinking. Our quarrel last night had been about profligate husbands, and here was I, forced to resort to pawnbrokers. I bet even Katharine Bidcombe'd never had to do that.

'Would you let me redeem it for you?' Paddy flung up a hand. 'Don't bite my head off, I didn't mean to embarrass you. I just wanted to say thank you.'

Something in his tone unsettled me. 'You sound almost valedictory,' I replied lightly. 'Thank you and goodbye?'

'Oh, I hope not,' he responded – but with not quite enough conviction for me, and then we didn't speak for several miles. Crazy. We'd never found ourselves short of words before and the only reason I'd offered to run him back to the castle was so we could talk without interruption from my importunate son. As we reached the outskirts of Wykesea, however, he suddenly asked if I knew anything about a company called Newhouse.

'Sorry, what?' I was trying to remember if Windermere Avenue was the first or second on the left after the petrol station.

'Newhouse Productions?'

'Never heard of them. Why?'

'Oh, I didn't sleep awfully well last night, and I ended up riffling around the computer. Occurred to me I might just spot something you'd missed.'

'What for? We've nailed Gaynor. Does that say Windermere Avenue?'

'Wansdyke. I rather think we've passed Windermere.' He toyed with the handle of the glove locker. 'It's as simple as that, is it? You confront your chap with his lady friend's treachery, fling wide the gate, and he trots gratefully back into the marital fold?'

'Well – yes,' I said, taken aback and not quite sure why. 'Yes, that's about the shape of it. Why else have I done all this?'

'Why indeed?' he murmured, so softly I barely heard. And the next minute, as I thudded into reverse, he began talking with what struck me as deliberate inconsequentiality about the Casanova files he'd also run across. Something had changed. I couldn't define it, but I felt as if a door had been slammed in my face. 'Bit of a hoot, actually,' he was declaring. 'I was particularly taken by the rhyming of "lecher" with "you betcha".'

'Truly authentic eighteenth-century dialogue.' I stamped on the brake. 'Look, Paddy...'

But he *was* looking – staring, transfixed – at the eight-foot-tall, dolphin-flanked, cupid-topped fountain adorning this handkerchief-sized suburban lawn. 'Glory be,' he breathed. 'Now I understand all those yards of tassels. This is Wykesea's answer to Versailles, no less.'

I chuckled appreciatively as I bundled the ornate swags over my arm, glad to be laughing with him again. I didn't know this was going to be our last shared joke, that our easy companionship had already hit the buffers. I just apologized for abandoning him while I installed the curtains. He held up his mobile phone with a grimace.

'Plenty to occupy me,' he said. 'I'm awfully afraid the real world calls.'

He was flipping the thing shut when I lowered myself into the seat beside him again, clutching a satisfactory wad of banknotes and a sheet of scribbled measurements.

'Totally bizarre,' he breathed, staring at the instrument in his hand as though wondering what it was for. 'I've just been offered a job.'

'You and me both. Bedroom curtains this time, corset pink and with more frills than a can-can dancer.' I restarted the engine. 'Yours any better?'

He gave a dry cough of laughter. 'Well, the pay's a joke, the hours unspeakable, fringe benefits seem to comprise a personal mosquito net, and I've a grim suspicion that the office lavatory – if indeed there are such refinements – will harbour snakes. Venomous ones at that.'

'Clearly an offer you can't wait to refuse.' I grinned. 'This a joke?'

Not a bit of it. It transpired that some female from an executive recruitment agency had enquired, unprompted but in all seriousness, whether he might be interested in giving a year to a charitable organization operating in the Third World. Not digging ditches, Paddy explained bemusedly, more providing management experience and training to fledgling businesses. One could, he supposed, regard it as putting something back. Even as I responded I'd no idea he was considering doing his bit for humanity, I realized I didn't much care for the idea of Paddy vanishing to some obscure corner of the planet. I understate. I *hated* the idea, and if I didn't say as much, my feelings must have shown.

'But you should be cheering me on,' he protested. 'Didn't you once read me a lecture about a chap needing honest employment, idleness rotting the soul, all that bracing Calvinist stuff?'

'I was drunk.'

'*In vino veritas?*' He shot me a sideways glance. 'You've never thought about this sort of caper yourself? Reviving your youthful zeal to save the world?'

'Are you kidding?'

There was a silence. 'I suppose I was, yes.'

I detected something off-key in the way he said this and, as I pulled up at a junction, I turned to look at him. 'How come you were talking to this headhunter in the first place?'

'Old friend, absolute poppet.' But if a mouse-squeak was my give-away, then Paddy studying his signet ring was his. Always a sign of trouble in the McGinty soul. Sure enough, when I asked what was up, he sighed that I wasn't going to like it.

'Like what? Damn, I hope this car park isn't full because the other's miles away.'

'That van's pulling out, if you're quick.' He waited until I'd manoeuvred into the space, and was twisting round to retrieve my handbag. 'Look, I'm going to have to ask you this. Did you know your husband isn't actually employed full time at Optimax?'

I glanced at him in surprise. 'I'm sorry?'

'So am I,' he responded unexpectedly. 'Bloody sorry. Oh, Jo, I warned you from the outset this wasn't a good idea.'

'What wasn't?' The idea still preoccupying me was a vision of him in a pith helmet, clambering aboard a plane to nowhere. 'No need for you to get out.'

He was already doing so though, and leaned over the roof of the car towards me. 'My grubbing around in your husband's affairs. I knew it would end in tears.'

'So, Mike's only part time? Well, smart of him to swing it, I guess, because he loathes the place, although I'm surprised they were prepared to—' Bending to lock the door, I bounced back up again. 'Oh, *shit*. Don't tell me that's why Gaynor's paid more than him?'

He looked very sad. 'If only that were all.'

I'll give him one thing: he didn't crow. Never uttered the words 'I told you so'. No, it was with the deferential detachment of an undertaker handling the recently bereaved that he broke the news. Which was that if Mike, as key asset of our company, had been prepared to give Optimax more than one day a week – *'one day?'* I gasped – on a consultancy basis, they would probably have paid rather more for the firm. They'd certainly be paying him a more realistic salary and, in Paddy's view, might have put together a package comparable to the one we'd been offered two years ago, allowing for our debts.

'But you do see,' he continued diffidently, 'that this would explain your original worry about the drop in your company's value between then and now?'

I might feel, and probably looked, as though I'd walked into a wall, but I *saw* all right. Forget Gaynor, forget Hank, I was being asked to believe that my own husband had freely and of his own volition let our company go for nothing?

As we walked down Fishergate, separated by bag-laden shoppers, harassed pram-pushers and an elderly bemedalled gent holding out his tray of poppies – Paddy smilingly halted to buy one – I was remembering what Mike had said to me about that last takeover offer, the four million pounds he freely admitted he'd turned down rather than, as he put it, rot in harness. I was also remembering, feeling slightly sick, how he'd steered me away from confronting Hank. Could he *really* have done it again? When his back was to the wall, and he'd had no choice but to sell the firm, could he still have whistled away a small fortune, just to hang on to some illusion of independence?

I stopped so sharply that Paddy, trying to pin the poppy into his lapel, cannoned into me. 'How do you know all this?' I demanded. 'The file you mentioned, Newhouse or whatever. What did it actually say?'

He stiffened, and his face was as opaque as I'd ever seen it. 'Sorry, have I misled you? It's nothing to do with any computer file.' He paused only for a second, visibly bracing himself. 'The information about your husband's, ah, terms of employment came from my friend Ailsa, the headhunter. On the phone, just now.'

Thus did I discover, scarcely able to take in what I was hearing, let alone believe it, that my friend, after learning about Gaynor's salary yesterday, had contacted this woman himself. That he had actually *asked* her to approach Mike. That, under the pretext of sounding him out for a job, he'd suggested she chat Mike up and sniff out what sort of a deal he had with Optimax...? I was *beside* myself. All my anger with my husband exploded over Paddy, for stooping to such a sleazy trick. I didn't give a damn what he'd warned me, I had never in a million years asked him to snoop round my husband, had I? Well, *had* I?

He met my glare squarely. 'You made me embark on this sordid business. Jo. I had no choice but to see it through. For your sake.'

'Oh, *really?*'

We were blocking the pavement, people were staring at us, but I didn't care. Paddy, though, lowered his voice still further. 'So you'd have preferred me to let you confront him with accusations about his girlfriend I always knew were absurd?'

'Don't make excuses.'

'Never mind leaving you to explain how you came by confidential details of the woman's salary?'

I knew I was being unreasonable, and it would have been all right if he'd got angry too. But he just sounded bleak. Bleak, cold and embarrassed. I stared at him, trying to find in that stony face some trace of my good friend. 'Paddy?'

'I'm so sorry,' he said. And looked away.

I drew myself up. 'That's the pawnbroker's,' I said stiffly. 'You can wait out here.'

He followed me in, however, without a word.

24

Something was bleeping.

I was standing in front of the counter and I'd just stuffed away my purse after settling my debt when I realized that the faint electronic pips I could hear seemed to be coming from my own handbag. I dug around for my phone, wondering who on earth could be ringing me and how the bloody thing had managed to change its ringing tone again. This noise was almost as irritating as the opening bars of the William Tell Overture, which Ben had once persuaded it to chirrup, until I threatened him with castration unless he programmed it straight back.

The jovial white-whiskered proprietor, in yellow bowtie today, had lumbered off to his huge safe after counting my money, and as he swung the mighty steel door aside, the bleeps leapt to earpiercing shrillness. Whereupon Paddy, who had seemed enwrapt in a frowning study of the orphaned golf clubs and microwaves in the glass cabinet behind me, lurched round, snatched my handbag out of my grasp, and thrust his hand inside.

'What are you doing?' I hissed. 'I've settled up.'

'Absolute duffer with the new technology, my wife,' he hooted in a voice not just unnaturally loud, but quite unlike his own. 'Aren't you, my silly old darling?'

Never mind that the unexpected 'darling' inspired me with a loopy urge to sob, I gaped at him. He'd extracted a small black object from my bag. I didn't even recognize the thing at first, although I knew it wasn't my phone. 'Hello? *Hello?* Bloody mobiles,' he snorted, strolling towards the end of the counter behind which the safe gaped as he squinted in apparent perplexity at the instrument cupped in his hand. His tracking device, of course it was, shoved into my bag so long ago in the rainy forecourt of Stowham Castle and forgotten ever since. I realized I must inadvertently have flipped a switch just now, but that hardly explained why it was bleeping its head off in here.

''Scuse us, squire,' said the proprietor firmly, blocking Paddy's view as he slammed the safe door and twirled the lock. The bleeps dropped in volume the instant the door clanged shut.

'Blighter seems to have rung off,' said Paddy, shoving the tracker into his pocket. Then he leaned towards the proprietor with the most inane grin imaginable. 'I say, old chap,' he confided, 'do forgive my askin', but I didn't happen to notice a shotgun tucked into that splendid treasure chest of yours, did I?'

Father Christmas stared at him open-mouthed. I wasn't surprised. 'Mention it only because guns are rather my thing,' he continued in this bray redolent of five centuries of intensive inbreeding. 'Ask the lady wife; drives her potty. And this strikes me as the kind of establishment where one might stumble upon a bargain, as 'twere, although naturally one's only interested in a decent piece, not some farmer's bunny-popper.'

'We don't deal in guns,' said the man dispassionately, pouring my wristwatch from its brown envelope into his cupped hand and holding it out to me. But his eyes didn't leave Paddy's. 'Need a licence for that kind of thing I shouldn't wonder. Anyway, pledged items can't be sold until the redemption period's expired. It's the law.'

'But then?' said my friend promptly, and didn't wait for an answer. He was ripping a page out of his diary and scribbling. 'Name's Newhouse,' he said. 'Peter Newhouse. Perhaps if I leave this with you, you'd care to give me a bell, at the appropriate time?' And I saw that a ten-pound note was tucked in with the piece of paper. 'Thanks most awfully, my dear sir. Come along, Jo. Toodle-jolly-old-pip.'

'Toodle-pip?' I cried as soon as we were a safe distance from the shop. 'Toodle-jolly-old-pip, Mr *Newhouse?*'

'First name came into my head.'

'And do you always pretend to be a blithering upper-class twit?'

'Pretend?' But his smile barely glimmered. 'Seemed wiser than thumping the counter and demanding to know if he'd got Jack's Purdey stashed in his safe.'

'*Has* he?'

'I saw a gun case, yes, and I can't imagine what else set the bleeper off. Cut out too, when the door shut, as you heard. Six inches of steel, bound to mask the signal. Besides, it wouldn't be the first time Jack resorted to a pawnbroker to pay for his gambling.' He made a noise of contempt. 'Gunsmith, indeed. What do you suppose he got for it – ten thousand?'

I blinked. 'Is the gun worth so much?'

'Fifty at least,' he said, with a touch of impatience. 'Heirloom, came from our grand-father. One assumes that's why he hasn't sold the thing outright. Must be trusting he'll win enough to redeem it.' Stick in hand, he began stumping down the street as though in training for the Olympics. 'Seems I owe you an apology, because I can only suppose Jack was raising the stake for that poker tournament. No one locally plays for those figures–'

'No,' I interrupted, stopping dead, because I'd been thinking about this before the pantomime in the pawnshop. 'I mean, no, it's me who owes you an apology. When you told me what you'd found out about Mike, I overreacted. I wanted to believe you were wrong, but... Anyway, I shouldn't have taken it out on you.'

He flashed me an unnervingly brilliant smile. 'Don't give it a thought. Natural reaction. I agree with you, actually, deeply sleazy trick.' He was holding himself rigidly upright. 'Chemist over there, I see. Shall I wait here while you go and stock up the medicine cupboard?'

'Are you all right? You look–'

'I'm fine.'

Which he patently wasn't, and when I re-emerged from the chemist's, with a carrier bag full of pills and syrups, he set off up the crowded street almost before I reached his side. 'Back to the car?'

'Paddy,' I began uneasily, after we'd been walking for a couple of minutes, 'what should I do now?'

'In what sense?'

'Well, to find out if your headhunter friend is right.'

We were emerging from an alley into the car park, and all at once he halted, wheeling round to face me. 'Oh, for God's sake, *ask*.'

'What? I mean, who?'

'Your husband, of course. Stop playing damn-fool guessing games, and simply ask him what's going on – if you want him back. Honesty the best policy, all that. Clichéd it may be, but it's the soundest advice I can give and, believe it or not,' he added, with another dazzling smile, 'offered in a spirit of purest altruism. I feel almost saintly, in fact.'

'What are you talking about?'

'Ignore me, stir crazy. Shock of the big wide world after being cooped up so long.'

'Paddy?' I reached out to touch his arm, and he actually jerked away. 'This isn't a joke, I'm serious.'

'Serious, yes, I'll say. Always knew this business would get serious in the end. Should have put a stop to it ages ago. No, don't interrupt, Jo, listen. Much against my better judgement, I did what you asked, stirred up the pond and found no greedy pike, just the usual murky old sludge. Now it's up to you.' He wasn't even looking at me. The tortoiseshell specs were aimed fixedly over my head, and that was before a fruity voice bellowed behind me.

'Well, bless my soul, dear boy, I thought it was you. Out and about again, eh? Splendid, splendid. And Joan, too, how are you, m'dear?' My hand was clasped between both of Bernard Bidcombe's as his beaming red-veined face nodded over mine. 'Gather from Seddons you're returning my nephew to us at last?'

'On our way to the castle now,' I confirmed, glancing sideways, willing Paddy at least to look at me.

'Yes, yes, I'm on my way home,' his uncle trumpeted, deaf as ever. 'Chariot's over here. Shall I take him off your hands and save you the detour to Stowham?'

Before I could summon the breath to roar that this wouldn't be necessary, Paddy answered for me. Excellent notion, he said, barely troubling to raise his voice. Jo wanted to return to her flu-stricken son, and if Bernard could just lend a hand with his bag...

Most galling of all, Lord Bidcombe heard and understood every last word.

Ask my husband – *ask my husband?*

'And what then, Paddy?' I demanded as I sat in my parked car, alone, with only a faint whiff of cologne to remind me of my vanished passenger. 'Because if all this is true – and I'm only too afraid it is – then the next thing I'm likely to ask for is a divorce. Pronto.'

Of course it was true. Mike may have been forced to sell out to a big organization, but he wasn't going to sell his soul, was he? Luckily, he'd had Gaynor to persuade her old friends at

Optimax not only to let him get away with a one-day-a-week consultancy, but then to conceal the arrangement from his bolshie wife and co-director. I wasn't surprised Hank Spiller, as representative of that famously ethical organization, had found it hard to look me in the eye. He knew I'd been misled. Their written contract said nothing about my husband's semi-detached status because, as Mike must have warned them, I wouldn't have signed. No way would I have agreed to him sacrificing a lifetime's financial security for us – for our children – just so he could retain, in his own words, freedom to operate

'But doing *what?*' I demanded of the empty car. Because Mike wasn't lazy. He was as hyperactive as a fizzy-drink-fuelled toddler, and about as responsible. Then a disturbing possibility occurred to me.

''Scuse me?' A bobble-hatted woman was tapping on my window, peering at me rather warily, which was understandable, given that I was sitting alone, clutching the steering wheel of my stationary car, dazedly asking myself whether my husband could be planning a new career as full-time father, caring for baby at home and maybe composing the odd tune, while ambitious Gaynor went out to earn the money... 'You coming or going?'

She might well ask. I flashed an apologetic smile, rubbed a sleeve across my eyes and turned the ignition key. That, at least, was nonsense. My husband's only acquaintance with nappies was staging a conference for Babysilk. The idea of

311

him as hands-on parent was laughable. Incredible. Totally out the question. I hoped...

Besides, if not that, what *was* he up to?

'Why do you ask?' said Sarah, sharply.

Well, my beloved and eminently sensible first-born, I've reason to suspect that, while your potty old dad's chucked most of your inheritance to the winds, he may nevertheless be ungirding his vasectomized loins to father rival heirs to the pittance that remains...

I didn't say anything of the sort, of course. I'd returned home to find Sarah perched on my kitchen table, swigging coffee. Clad in puffy anorak, quilted trousers and with a monster scarf coiled round her neck, she looked rather like a fluffy-haired Michelin Man. Just called by to pick up her walking boots, she said, because she and Simon were joining a bunch of urologists for a pub-to-pub hike near Whitby. So no, sorry, she couldn't stop for lunch, they were already late. Simon was through with Ben, hypochondriacal little toad, although he did seem to be running a temperature. Oh good, she added, not hesitating to rummage through my shopping, the paracetamol would bring it down. Cough syrup was a waste of money, but he'd probably like the taste.

My mind still whirling with Paddy's revelations, I'd interrupted the flow to ask, with studied casualness, if she knew what her dad was getting up to at the moment. It was her response that had put the fear of God into me. Sarah, my street-smart, worldly-wise, unshockable daughter suddenly couldn't meet my eyes.

'Put me on the spot there a bit, Mum.'

My heart began thumping at double speed. 'He's told you not to tell me?'

'God, what am I supposed to say?'

'It's just, well, his having a younger partner...' Having come this far, I had to go on. I swung away to pick up the kettle so she couldn't see my face. 'I wondered if he was thinking of having his vasectomy reversed. May've done it already, for all I know.'

Her squawk didn't just silence me, it nearly deafened me. 'You telling me Dad had the snip? Well, good on him. Nice to know he did the decent thing for once in his life.'

'*Sarah*...' I said, clanging down the kettle and turning back.

'Come on, Mum, he's hardly likely to confide in me about his intimate plumbing, is he? But what I can tell you is that when I asked him months back if he was thinking of embarrassing us with another litter of baby Pattersons he turned so pale I thought he was going to vomit. "Not fucking likely", were his exact words, as I recall.' She chuckled merrily, but I felt quite faint. All that needless angst? 'Anyway, much as I love him,' she swept on, 'who cares about the sad old fart now? We've got to be on the road in one minute flat, so spill the juicy beans, Ma. How's it going with hunky Paddy?'

'What's got into you, Mum?' grumbled Ben a few days later.

Good question. I wasn't admitting to myself,

313

let alone my son, what might have got into me, but it was impelling me to turn out every drawer and cupboard, strip and rewax my kitchen table, walk the legs off the dog, and somehow still left me rattling with nervous energy at midnight. The contents of Ben's backpack – half a term's accumulated laundry, naturally – were washed, mended, ironed and aired and I was even now struggling to reinsert them into his bag without ruining my labours. And this in spite of years of promising myself that I would *not* spoil my son, that I would not repeat my mother-in-law's mistake of rearing a male child who thought that the universe revolved around him and that a fast spin cycle was something performed by Torvill and Dean. To his credit – to our collective credit, given that I doted on my son as hopelessly as only a mother can – Ben had a healthily balanced ego, but a shamefully slight acquaintance with the washing machine. He was treating his flu with copious doses of oven chips, strong beer, loud music – administered through headphones, mercifully – and gore-spattered videos.

'You're even upsetting the dog,' he grunted, watching my fevered activity with half-closed eyes from his burrow on the sofa. 'Dora's acting dead weird too, in case you haven't noticed. Anyway, what're you packing my stuff for? Trying to give me a hint?'

'Halfway through term,' I responded grittily. 'And you look much better to me.'

'Is he at the castle?'

'Who?' As if I didn't know.

'Peter – Paddy, whatever he calls himself.'

314

'As it happens, his real name is Peter, although as you know full well, everyone calls him Paddy.'

'Yeah, yeah. Well, is he?'

'How should I know?' I snapped, and slammed back into the kitchen.

I'd spoken to Paddy, of course, since he was whisked away from me in the Wykesea car park, – correction, since he had whisked *himself* away from me. I had rung Stowham Castle the following day, a little self-consciously given the awkward terms on which we'd parted, but he'd been his usual charming self. Asked after my health, my son's, my dog's – and then seemed to run out of small talk. I waited a moment. I was hoping – no, *expecting* – he would suggest we get together again soon for a drink, a meal, whatever. When the silence grew unbearable, I gave up and asked how he was.

'Much better since I bribed the garage to work overtime. All being well, I'll have my car back this afternoon. Should be in town by dinnertime.'

I had a momentary sensation that the floor had given way. 'You're going?'

'I'll be back,' he responded, with reassuring swiftness. 'Have to. Sort this bloody business out with Bernard. Only ... well, the fact is, it's the anniversary of Kat's death the day after tomorrow. Seems a good idea to, ah, make myself scarce.' But the real shock was yet to come, because he went on to explain that he had a ridiculous amount to organize in London. 'Not least a painful visit to the docs for God knows how many jabs, judging by the list of dread

315

diseases I've been sent. Stoicism required in industrial quantities.'

And not just by him. I swallowed hard, then forced my voice into airy brightness. 'You're taking up this job abroad, then? I'm – surprised.'

'Not as surprised as Bernard, I dare say. Actually, appalled is nearer the mark with him. The kindest thing he's said is that I must get it from Great-uncle Seymour, who spent half his life heroically decimating Africa's wildlife, and the remainder in a lunatic asylum. I suspect it's the latter years Bernard's thinking of. Who knows? He may be right.'

'So why are you doing it?'

'I've accepted, belatedly, that I need to get away. Principally for my own sake, but other people's too. The plans are by no means set in stone yet, though.' There was a tiny pause. 'Tell me, have you cleared things up with your husband?'

'What?' I was still dazedly grappling with the prospect of my friend flying off into the blue yonder. Would he write? 'Oh – no. No, not yet. I was so angry yesterday I suppose I was frightened of saying something irreparable.' Which wasn't the whole truth – indeed it was hardly the truth at all. I'd pounced on the phone after Sarah left, only to realize that Mike, like her, would inevitably ask me about Paddy. Funny old world when you're reluctant to confess to daughter and husband you *haven't* got a lover.

'How sensible,' murmured Paddy, with a politeness which froze my soul. 'Do let me know if – well, how you get on.'

A moment or two later I was staring down at the dead telephone receiver.

'Is that it?' I said.

25

I didn't believe that *was* it, of course. Didn't suppose for one instant that my good friend was intending to vanish out of my life thus. Before ringing off, he had promised – unprompted – to get in touch when he returned, so I'd been daily expecting him to knock on the door as I darted hither and thither, like a nesting bird on amphetamines. I told myself I'd no idea what lay behind this restlessness, why I was feeling so fizzy one moment, so groundlessly wretched the next. Hormonal perhaps? Or a touch of Ben's flu?

And if my thoughts seemed to revolve an awful lot round my departed guest, that was only to be expected. There was so much here to remind me of him – not least a kitchen and larder still piled high with his largesse. I couldn't bring myself to throw out his flowers until Ben said they were stinking. I retorted that if his nose was working so well, he must be recovered. Of course I was happy to have my son at home, but I didn't mind admitting to myself that it wasn't the same as having Paddy here. Adult company, you understand, and such congenial company at that. Ben was at least leaving soon. Returning to York and his studies first thing Thursday morning when a scientist friend was picking him up on the way back from a field trip. My home would be my own again. I wondered if Paddy would be back from London by then.

It was only because he'd mentioned it that I slipped through to Ben's computer one evening to look up this Newhouse file. I found three with that title, which I'd seen before and disregarded because all they contained, in an assortment of typefaces, were letter headings for a company called Newhouse Productions, based in Notting Hill. So? Paddy could hardly suspect Mike of setting up another events firm on the side, because he'd told me himself the Optimax contract unequivocally ruled it out. I reckoned one of the graphics whiz-kids had been moonlighting some design work.

I could, of course, have asked Mike. And not just about trivia like those files, but about everything. More than once I had the phone in my hand – only to put it down again. There was nothing I could do about our company, after all: it was gone. And about our marriage? Well, I didn't want to embark on a screaming row with Ben in the house. That's what I told myself. And thanked heaven there was a shoot on Wednesday, because I could at least ask round the castle when Paddy was due back. If, of course, he hadn't telephoned by then.

My phone was ringing more often than usual, because of Ben, and I suppose I was aware that I was charging to answer it from wherever I happened to be – up a ladder, head-down in a cupboard – but it took my son to force me finally to acknowledge what was amiss with me: my gruff-voiced, wide-eyed boy whose only acknowledged passion in life was for Tottenham Hotspur. He'd answered a call first, for once, because I was ladling up for his lunch a very excellent tinned cassoulet supplied by Paddy, instead of the Heinz baked beans my philistine chick would probably have preferred. I nearly saved him from his gourmet treat, however, because I all but dropped his plate in my haste to grab the phone he wordlessly held out to me.

'Hello?' I dashed my fringe out of my eyes with one sauce-smeared hand.

'Hey-up, what's got thee so nattered?'

'Aidan?

'Fit for tomorrow?'

'Christ, Mum,' grunted Ben after I'd rung off, 'what is all this? You in love or what?'

Yes, of course I bloody was. As if I hadn't known all along.

'No, of course I'm bloody not,' I squawked at my son. As if he should have known better than to ask such a stupid question.

And as far as I was concerned, both answers were true – give or take the odd preposition. I was gloomily pondering this as, puffing like an ageing steam engine, I trudged up Blackwater Ridge in the autumnal sunshine that afternoon, with the dog trotting effortlessly beside me. Nothing like vigorous exercise to work off humiliation.

I felt humiliated, all right. As foolish as only a sturdy old trout can feel when she's forced to admit she's been behaving like a dizzy schoolgirl in the throes of a crush. All the frenzied busyness, the highs, the lows, the pouncing on the phone...

'So I'm in love with Paddy,' I said to Dora, plonking my weary bum against a wall. 'So I'm a silly cow. I wasn't fibbing to Ben, though, because being *in* love is just infatuation, and that's not the same as the real thing, is it? But we can't expect my son to get his head round grown-up distinctions like that.'

Dora was already well across this argument herself, being as she and I had often debated the nature of Real Love – with particular reference to my husband – while I'd been polishing my forgive-and-forget sermon against the day he trundled back down the hill to me. I felt no inclination to preach now. Experiencing for myself how the love bug does indeed clobber you out of the blue, exactly like the bloody measles – with a spot of dementia thrown in – I was, if you can believe it, feeling a twinge of sympathy for my adulterous husband.

'All very well my yelling at him to grow up and forget it,' I sighed, 'I do see it's not quite as easy as that. I mean, you can't just will the symptoms away, can you? Order the spots to vanish and the temperature to drop?'

Since there's nothing on earth more boring than someone maundering on about their lovelorn plight, I wasn't surprised the dog yawned and flopped at my feet, although it was unlike her to ignore an enticingly muddy ditch not five yards away. Ben was right. Dora was behaving strangely.

It was a crisp afternoon, more wintry than autumnal, with frost still glimmering on the shady sides of hedgerows and walls. The sun was bright, though, and the sky glassy blue. The sheep-studded valley below looped haphazardly towards the distant chink of sea, and immediately beneath me, pigeon-grey and pretty as a toy, lay Stowham Castle. On this crystalline day, I felt I could lean over and scoop it up. Still, that's where I would be headed tomorrow morning for the shoot, praying I might find Paddy back from town.

Oh, there was no denying the sparkle of hope in my silly little heart. But then love, *real* love, as I'd been only too ready to tell my husband, means recognizing infatuation for the gloriously intoxicating mirage it is, and turning your back on it to stick by your marriage. Would I have the strength to do that? Did Mike *deserve* it after the way he'd behaved? For better, for worse, for richer for poorer, in sickness and in health – how about in adultery, deception and fraud? However, as I shame-facedly admitted to Dora, what was exercising me even more at that moment was not which way I'd jump, but whether I was ever going to be confronted with that agonizing choice in the first place.

'Because I have to tell you, woman-to-woman, I am beginning to doubt it.' I shifted the foot she was sitting on which was knotted with cramp. She promptly redeposited herself on the other. 'We've reached the moment of truth, kiddo. I've confessed all. I'm starry-eyed and dippy-brained over Paddy bloody McGinty, yeah, yeah, yeah.

But what about him? Let's face it, no one on God's earth is too busy to pick up a telephone for six solid days – *no one* – so it strikes me we have two options. You paying attention, sweetie? OK, two options. One: he's dreaming about me night, day and all hours between, but being the decent, honourable, upstanding chap he is, he's quite rightly inhibited by me being married. Doesn't want to embarrass me by making advances I might not – I mean, couldn't, that is to say, *shouldn't* – respond to. I'd like to believe it, except... Small point, but d'you remember when he seemed to pull back, just as he was going to kiss me? You were there at the time. Course, he'd probably just heard Ben in the hall, but it was almost like he'd had second thoughts, you know? Suddenly wondered what the hell he was letting himself in for. Which brings me to the alternative scenario...'

I hauled myself off the wall. 'Option Two: I'm an idiot, and he's got more entertaining fish to fry. Skinny, young, fancy-free fish, in large shoals.' My shoulders slumped as I stumped off down the hill. 'I ought to be glad if he has, of course. Save me no end of trouble.'

'Major McGinty?' said Aidan in the stable-yard in the chill mists of the following morning. 'You tell me, bonny lass, for I've not seen him. Why, was he supposed to be coming out today?'

'Oh, not exactly,' I replied as nonchalantly as I could, only to feel my knees buckle when the Admiral said he'd been told young McGinty was in West Africa.

'Bernard sounded distraught, poor chap.'

'Nay, Paddy's not gone yet,' snorted Eileen, bustling up to me with an envelope in her hand. 'He's back here at t'castle tonight.' She lowered her voice to a foghorn whisper and winked. 'He saw my lad Harry when he were picking up his car last week. Said it were worth crashing, he'd had such a good time with you.'

And that nearly undid me completely because my soul roared skywards like a twenty-quid rocket, and I found myself thanking her with absurd effusiveness for the theatre ticket which I stuffed into my back pocket as I scuffled back to the car to find my purse. I was in no state to wonder why there were a couple of Labradors sniffing excitedly round my vehicle. Still less was I prepared, when I opened the door, for them both to try and scramble in. Fortunately they collided and I contrived to shut it again without trapping noses or paws, but they wouldn't be shooed away. I looked round for help, and the Admiral strolled across, eyebrows raised.

'Down, Nelson,' he bellowed in a voice which I have no doubt had caused many a raw midshipman to quake in his bell-bottoms, but had no discernible impact on his slavering dog. He turned to me. 'Haven't a bitch in there, by any chance?'

'You mean Dora?' My pet having seemed most uncharacteristically disinclined to hurtle out of the car the moment I braked in the stable-yard, I'd left her curled in the well until we were ready for the off.

'She wouldn't be in an interesting condition?'

323

'I beg your pardon?'

'What's this kerfuffle then?' demanded Aidan, following his own elderly cocker across, because even that stately and immaculately mannered creature had joined the canine cluster at my car door, tail flapping like a flag. The Keeper squinted through the window, then back at me. 'You never brought her out when she's on heat?'

I began to laugh. Like owner like dog? Casting up his eyes at my admission that she'd been behaving a bit peculiarly, Aidan declared that Madam here would have to stay in the car if I were planning on coming out, or she'd disrupt the whole bloody field. But – and he sighed, as if in disbelief at his own softheartedness – if I wanted to give the day a miss and tek her home, he supposed they'd manage. Good turnout this morning.

Bingo. 'I'll wait here until you go,' I said promptly, 'because I can do without a pack of lusty animals trying to join me in the driving seat.' Because I could do without a pack of sharp-eyed beaters watching me sneak off to the front of the castle, more like. Nothing like grabbing your chances. Eileen had said he was here. Instead of flushing out pheasants, I was going to try a spot of flushing out Paddy McGinty. Once the wagon had rattled away, and I was quite sure I was alone in the stable-yard, I peered into the wing mirror of my car, fluffed up my hair, bit my lips and, after a moment's indecision, flung open the passenger door.

'Come on, you sexpot,' I whispered. 'I need moral support on this job.'

I should have realized that the guns wouldn't have headed up to the woods yet. The forecourt was crowded with vehicles and wax-jacketed men, puffing on boots and passing round flasks. Luckily none of them seemed to have dogs, and I was saved the daunting march up the great flight of steps by spotting Mr Seddons as he wove a skilful path through the mêlée. He was carrying, incongruously in this sporting tableau, a flower arrangement of a size which would have filled an entire room in my house, but I managed to attract his attention through the foliage.

'Mrs Patterson,' he said, instantly diverting towards me. 'How can I help you?'

'Paddy anywhere about?'

'Oh, I'm so sorry,' he said – and indeed, between two football-sized bronze chrysanthemums his face was regretful, if harassed. 'Major McGinty isn't due until – I believe lunchtime, his lordship said. I'm afraid you find us in some confusion today. We might almost say *chaos...*' He was glancing round, lips pursed in a way which suggested his orderly sensibilities were offended by this seething maelstrom. 'A great deal to organize at sadly short notice. Would you excuse me?' And he added, as he bustled away with his floral burden, 'I'll tell Mr Paddy you were asking after him. He will be so very sorry to have missed you.'

Would he? That's what I was asking myself as I stood forlornly on the gravel, with the red-faced, bluff-voiced shooters joking and joshing by their cars. I noticed now, behind their encampment, there was a white florist's van. And a navy Transit with the logo of a catering company emblazoned in gold on the panels was nosing in through the gates. Seddons, having relinquished his flowers, imperiously gestured the driver of this vehicle round to the rear of the castle. Feeling adrift in the busy crowd, realizing these must be the preparations for Cousin Jack's birthday party, I paid no heed to Dora's sudden bark – although I should have done, because my dog virtually never barks. Lord knows how they instil this in gun dogs, but they do. Anyway, with the discreet cough of a dowager duchess who regards loud noises as a failing of the vulgar masses, Dora made a half-hearted attempt to jump up at me – then bolted. Really bolted, tail between her legs and off as though fired from a cannon. I soon realized why. Jasper, Lord Bidcombe's muscular black-and-white springer, was bounding across the gravel after her with only too evident intent.

'Dora!' I yelped, wheeling round in pursuit. Where had she scarpered? Just as I caught a glimpse of Jasper's flailing tail vanishing seemingly into the great flight of steps at the castle entrance, I heard a gruff masculine roar.

'The bitch's in here. Oh get down, you randy bastard, beat it.' Thus did I find myself venturing into the subterranean lair of Jack Bidcombe.

The first thing I saw was my pet, actually perched on his lap, head pressed into his chest, quivering like a bird. I couldn't but be amused. Seemed Dora shared my qualms about casual sex. Jasper, meanwhile, was doing his panting damnedest to clamber aboard and join her, but Jack Bidcombe was holding him off with one powerful fist buried in his ruff.

'Grab the bugger and shut him out,' he commanded. 'Don't worry, I've got her safe.'

Not without difficulty, because Jasper had three times the strength of my own pooch, I bundled his squirming body across the room and outside. When I whipped the door shut, he hurled himself against it with a thump and a howl.

'Thank you,' I said breathlessly as I returned. 'Thanks a lot. I can do without an accidental batch of puppies. Come on then, Dora.'

But to my surprise, even though the immediate peril was vanquished, my pet showed none of her usual eagerness to bounce back to my side. She was no longer quivering. No, she was cuddling up to her protector with the soupiest air of hero-worship as he murmured sweet nothings and toyed with her satiny ears. He was dressed in a rather mangy Arran pullover and balding cord trousers which fell away cruelly from his wasted legs. He still reminded me of an eagle, with that gaunt face, beaky nose and Brillo-pad sheaf of hair, but had now the marginally softened look of a parent bird delivering strips of mice to a nest-bound chick. Call me daft – I would myself in the days before I joined the ranks of dog-doters – but I found I couldn't think wholly ill of a man with whom my pet was so instantly, blatantly besotted. Well, I'm sorry, but Dora had proved a reliable judge of character in the past.

'Take a pew,' he invited, without looking up from her eyes. 'You'd better wait until my father comes in search of his demented mutt if you want to get away with this lady's virtue intact. There, my sweet, don't be frightened. We won't let big bad Jasper ravish you.'

Given that big bad Jasper was continuing to fling himself at the door like a sex-starved battering ram, I supposed he was right, although, as I looked round, it wasn't immediately apparent where I *could* sit down. This was not an unattractive sitting room, light and airy for a basement, with walls of sunny yellow and a shiny cream stone-tiled floor. For ease of manoeuvring the wheelchair, I supposed. There was a small vestibule insulating it from the castle forecourt, and through a doorway, I glimpsed a hall with a kitchen and a couple of other rooms opening off it. The place was untidy, though, and it wasn't a comfortable clutter. Newspapers seemed to have been tossed aside unread; books likewise. A big television, showing a cable sports channel by the look of it, flickered soundlessly in the corner, and a low table was crowded with bottles, clouded glasses and overflowing ashtrays. There were ashtrays everywhere, in fact, and a sour fug of old smoke in the air. I wasn't surprised to see a big shiny fire extinguisher positioned prominently beside the front door. Smoking can damage your health in more ways than the obvious.

'Have one?' enquired my host, knocking open a packet, and I saw, with a twinge of self-consciousness given the comparisons I'd drawn, that he smoked the same brand as Mike. I shook my head. Then, in the act of lighting his own, he paused and lowered the flame again, frowning at me. 'Do I know you?'

I'd found a straight-backed chair by the window which was littered only with a few torn envelopes and greetings cards that I gathered up before seating myself. Birthday cards.

'We, um, bumped into one another here after a shoot, oh, a fortnight or more ago.' Almost literally, since he'd come within an inch of running over my toe in his revved-up chair. 'I'm Jo Patterson, from Beck Holme. I know who you are, of course.' I added this with the vague discomfiture you feel on meeting someone with whose history and character you're already far better acquainted than any stranger has the right to be.

'Beck Holme, eh?' he echoed, touching the light to his fag and drawing deep. 'Lord yes, I know, you're Paddy's little friend.'

And suddenly there was something so *like* Paddy in the way he said this, I had to swallow hard. 'Yes, your cousin stayed with me for a few days. After he pranged his car.'

'Silly oaf,' responded Jack, but without malice. 'Well, how interesting.' And he put his head on one side and surveyed me. What was extraordinary was that he did this without any apology or inhibition. Just stared – as though I were a painting or a dummy in a shop window. So I stared right back.

There was undoubtedly a family likeness. He looked older than Paddy, although there was only a year or so between them, but it could be argued he was, if anything, the handsomer of the two. He had a lean-jawed, steely-eyed Heathcliffian ruggedness to set the ink flowing in the pen of many a romantic novelist. I found I had no difficulty in believing this Jack-the-lad had been a dangerous ladykiller in his prime.

'You called round inspecting the curtains or some such not so long ago, didn't you? Seddons told me,' he added, with a smile. I must say he had a very charming smile. 'Seddons is the source of all my information, and much more besides, poor mug. My eyes, ears, legs – brain. I often think he must wish me dead, but he assures me otherwise. I need only pick this up and press the button,' he gestured to the telephone – 'and at any time of day or night, assuming he is actually on the premises, he appears in nine minutes and forty-two seconds. On average.'

I had to laugh. The absurdity of the detail was so like Paddy. 'I suppose you time him?'

'Set my watch by him,' he said gravely, 'Greenwich Mean has nothing on Albert Seddons. Alarmingly perceptive, too. He doesn't seem to think you're fucking Paddy – oh, I'm sorry. No, clearly you're not, and I assure you Seddons didn't phrase it at all like that. Please don't feel obliged to stamp out. Would you care for a drink?'

26

'At this hour in the morning?' I managed to say.

'My birthday,' he said as he reached round to the low table beside him. 'Forty-seven years on this Godforsaken planet in spite of my best endeavours' – with cigarette poking between his fingers, he brandished the whisky bottle – 'to see myself off. I've only one lung worth mentioning, you know.' He sniffed a glass with a moue of distaste and groped for an alternative. 'Odds against my having survived this long must be astronomical. Shame I didn't risk a few quid at the time. You a gambler – Jo, isn't it?'

'Yes. I mean, no. Not at all.'

'How wise. Look at me. Mind, if I'd only stuck to horses, I might still be walking – bankrupt, I shouldn't wonder, but kicking as well as alive. If you can call this being alive, which I sometimes doubt. Water in your whisky? Oh, come on, you'd have been out on the field if you hadn't found the little lady was off games, wouldn't you? So regard this as the merest bracer from a hip-flask.' I found I was accepting a tumbler of Scotch and being waved in the direction of a water jug. 'Yes, my downfall is – was, and no doubt ever shall be – to prefer to bet on my misbegotten self. Your health.'

I choked on my first sip, and my head was spinning before the whisky exploded into my

331

empty stomach. The alcohol wasn't responsible for pitching me off balance, though, it was him, Cousin Jack. Never mind his rude questions, this was the man outside whose windows I'd once lurked in search of a potential suicide weapon, and here he was cheerily joking about death in every other sentence. And yet his conversation, in a bleaker, blacker way, was reminiscent of Paddy – achingly so. I was remembering my friend laughing at my kitchen table, could almost hear him joking about drinking himself into a compost heap, bribing me to use his blessed tracking device, saying I might have liked Cousin Jack...

'So what has Paddy told you?'

Oh God, and that was like Paddy too, seeming to read my thoughts. 'What about?'

He eyed me for a speculative moment – then changed the subject. There was nothing subtle about it, he simply yawned and remarked it was a shame Seddons hadn't thought to wheel me down here the other day, because I could have spared him the most tedious two hours of his life with a little man from Brewster and Ackroyd's. 'There are those who seem to find my company rather unnerving,' he observed, and watched with undisguised amusement as I flushed. 'Can't imagine why, but I can only say Cyril Higgins or Hickson or whatever he was called isn't among them. Sat and lectured me on the theory and practice of furniture stuffing for so long I began to regret letting my Purdey go. Although whether I'd have shot him or myself is a moot point. Sorry, did I say something to startle you?'

I was chancing another sip of whisky when he'd mentioned the gun and had nearly choked. 'Brewster and Ackroyd's?' I stammered. 'The, um, furnishing store?'

'I asked him here to quote for recovering a chair. That one by the far window.'

I looked round. In a room where handsome antiques mingled tastefully with a few solidly well-designed modern pieces, this was an ugly, wooden-armed easy chair of the kind that was top of the furnishing pops in about 1962, still upholstered in the puke-coloured, knobbly stretch nylon I remembered, without affection, from my childhood. The only thing I'd have been tempted to cover it with was petrol before lobbing it on a bonfire.

'It has sentimental value,' said Jack, yet again reading my thoughts with disconcerting accuracy. 'My nanny's old chair. But I'm afraid sentiment doesn't stretch to the three-hundred-odd quid he quoted. Bloody man insisted he'd have to reupholster from scratch, old foam being deadlier than anthrax-soaked nuclear waste, according to him. What on earth's the matter with you?'

'Sorry?' I made an effort. 'I mean, um, yes, he was right. Fire hazard, toxic gases, illegal, too.' Truth was, I'd suddenly felt overwhelmed by the sadness of it all: this handsome wreck of a man, knocking back whisky at nine in the morning as though it were orange juice, kippering his lungs with one fag after another, flogging the family heirlooms to fund his gambling, joking blackly about death – and yet crooning over Dora and soppy enough to preserve a memento of his old nanny. That in itself distressed me. There's something poignantly wrong about sentimentalizing your family retainer rather than your family. I might even have been moved to offer to renovate the bloody chair for him myself– maybe that's what he'd hoped – only Jasper and Lord Bidcombe erupted into the room. Fortunately, the dog was on a lead, although he was plunging about with a ferocity which made me fear for his owner's footing on the shiny floor.

'Shut the bloody animal out again, Papa,' said Jack wearily. 'Ladies present.'

He managed to do so, and returned red-faced and looking every bit as harassed as his butler. 'Running late,' he barked. 'Guns went up quarter of an hour back, but I wanted to tell you Hugh Hough-Hartley seems to think he and Hetty are staying overnight, and I now hear the Leeburns are coming, too. Dear God, Jack, how many more? Seddons is already flapping round like a fart in a colander.'

'Did I forget to mention Martin?' said Jack, drawing on his cigarette. 'No objection, surely? Chap's Deputy Lieutenant of the County. Anyway, I've laid on the caterers, I can't see why Seddons is fussing.'

'Ask him. Been bending my ear this past ten minutes about beds, flowers, seating plans, God knows what else, and...' His eye fell on me. 'Oh, hello, m'dear.'

I had a suspicion that, on this occasion, he couldn't even call to mind who I was, let alone come up with an approximation of my name, but perhaps I'd wronged him. 'In the pink, as ever,' he boomed. 'Shall we be seeing you this evening?'

'This evening?' I echoed, as though I didn't know what he was talking about, as though my heart weren't all at once threatening to batter its way through my ribcage with the desperation of the dog again chucking itself at the door panels.

'Paddy hasn't mentioned it to you?' He shook his head, tutting.

'Paddy is coming?' cut in Jack sharply.

'Absolutely. Arriving after lunch. I suppose he's had a lot on his mind, silly fool.' Suddenly he smiled – smiled quite brilliantly. 'But you should come – fact, you *must*. The very thing. Won't take no for an answer, will we, Jack?'

Jack, draining his whisky glass, frankly looked as though he couldn't give a toss, but there was no danger of my refusing. It was all I could do not to leap up and embrace Bernard Bidcombe.

'Seven-thirty for eight?' he added. 'Black tie, if it isn't too much of a bore. Still, that doesn't usually worry the ladies, does it?'

'Oh, *shit*,' hissed Ben when I told him I was trying to decide what the bloody hell to wear for a party at Stowham Castle tonight; that I was leaving in thirty-five minutes flat and he was running me there; that he would have known all this hours ago if he hadn't still been snoring his head off when I left for the hairdresser's and out when I got back – and why was he looking at me as though I'd sprouted fangs? Supper cooked by Mum was not, contrary to what he might believe, a divine right of sons. At which he rolled his eyes and slouched out, leaving me standing in the middle of my bedroom, with clothes spread across the bed, hanging from the wardrobe door and crumpled on the floor after being tried on and rejected in despair. Lord Bidcombe was wrong about black tie not worrying this lady.

Such a frenzied day I'd had, of preening, plucking and generally polishing my long-neglected person. I'd managed to book in for a manicure and facial at the hairdresser's in Wykesea, as well as the full grey-vanquishing, two-colour-streaking cut-and-blow, all at a fraction of what it used to cost back South. So I'd still felt rich enough to splash out on three pairs of luxuriously cobwebby tights – had to get three because I didn't know what colour I'd be wearing – along with a seductively packaged plum-coloured lipstick on special offer, which proved to give me an unnerving resemblance to Morticia Addams. No matter, I'd unearthed plenty of old lipsticks in less blood-curdling shades from the back of my dressing-table drawer. Probably as well Wykesea has no smart designer-frock emporia – more your polyester and pleats merchants with yellow sunblinds and half-day closing on Wednesdays – because, broke as I was, despair might have driven me to ruinous measures. Instead, I was reduced to reviewing the contents of my own wardrobe, although a late inspiration had led me to search my daughter's as well. Sure enough, stuffed away at the back in a dry-cleaner's bag hung the slinky pink sheath I'd bought her last Christmas for the medical society ball. Back then my credit card hadn't even squeaked at a price tag more suggestive of a week's holiday for two than a scant couple of metres of velvet – silk velvet admittedly, and liquid soft.

'Can't I have the black corset in Top Shop and a new gearbox?' she'd complained in the palatial changing room as I'd gazed misty-eyed at her little figure, suddenly deliciously voluptuous instead of just sweetly dumpy. Sarah might grumble the thing clung like a condom, but the bias cut only hugged the right bits and slithered over the rest with a genius I argued was worth twice the price. 'Oh come on, Mum,' she'd sighed. 'I'm more your up and at 'em dominatrix than some fluffy, flirty sex-kitten.'

Sex-kitten, exactly. And for all the frock skimmed over my own bum as flatteringly as it had over Sarah's, I was not going to this party as anybody's idea of a sex-kitten. Problem was, as I perplexedly surveyed the array of shoulder-padded jackets, mumsy prints and musty blacks, I didn't know quite what I *was* going as.

There were excellent reasons for not going at all – although Ben's dark prediction as he'd exited the room of lethal black ice on the roads tonight was not amongst them. Some men will do anything to get their home-cooked shepherd's pie. But I had asked myself if it was sensible to court temptation like this. To risk ending up even more soul-shatteringly bereft tomorrow, because an evening in the company of my departing friend would only remind me afresh what I was losing. Did I take these arguments seriously? Was I planning to wear a fertilizer sack?

I was glaring at the mirror as I held against my

337

body the dingy black shift which had seen me through many a weary clients' drinks party, when Ben shambled back, holding out the telephone. I flung away the dress to grab it in a sudden flutter of fear that the party had been called off, or that Paddy couldn't make it back from London, or...

'Jo? Shorry, Ben said you're going out, but shomething I gotta tell you.'

'Who...?' Then I recognized the voice behind the haze of alcohol and subsided, faint with relief, on to the bed. 'Oh, *Gil*, hi. Yup, 'fraid I'm in a flat spin, you OK?' I smiled into the phone. 'Other than being pissed as a newt, by the sounds of you. How's your mum?'

'Dead,' he said.

Well, I couldn't just ring off after that, even if I was still in my bra and knickers with no time to spare. At least I'd got my face on, and was back at the mirror, checking my eye-shadow, I murmured condolences. I could hear voices behind Gil. The wake was still going, apparently, although the funeral had been first thing this morning.

'Only shlot we could get down the crem.,' he informed me with a mournful hiccup. Obviously been drowning his sorrows with a vengeance, poor lamb, and Gil'd never had a head for booze. 'Vicar had a cold, and kept calling her Betty instead of Betsy. Never mind, she'd have liked the flowers. Lovely flowers.'

'Gil, I'm sorry, I should have been there.' I was reappraising a floaty gold-thread shirt. Should be silk trousers to match it somewhere. 'You know I would have been there, if I'd realized.' And I did

338

my valiant best to stifle relief that I *hadn't* known, hadn't been forced to miss this party...

'Don't be silly. 'Slong way, Eastbourne, helluva long way. But he couldn't even be bothered to come down from town. She did, though, bless her. He was too busy with his show.'

'Mike?' Gorgeous fabric, but the billows made me look seven months gone. 'What show?'

'Thass why I'm ringing. I mean, partly. But I've told her – everything, so 'sonly fair, telling you. Wouldn't, mark you, I wouldn't say a single word, if she hadn't said I could. She should've known that, her and Mike, not just left me out in the cold. She was really sweet, really 'pologetic. I mean, I know you don't like her, course you wouldn't, but iss terrible what he's done to her, terrible.' Dress in hand, I pulled a face at the phone. I'd never heard Gil this drunk – even that Christmas Mike had spiked the office punch with Polish vodka. 'Talked her into getting 'nother mortgage on her flat, poor cow, can you believe it? Jush – just hearing what she's paying a month gives me the screaming habdabs. I love Mike, course I do, we all do, but he's a selfish bastard, charges on with what he wants, never mind anybody else, and–'

'*Gil?*' I'd let him rabbit while I returned to the black shift, but this was getting ridiculous. 'What are you talking about?'

'*Casanova.*'

'Sorry?'

He let out a huge sigh. 'Putting the thing on, isn't he? At the Theatre Royal – wait for it – the Theatre Royal in bloody Wakeford. I mean, you

339

ever *been* to Wakeford? And you'll never, *never* guess in a million years who's playing Casanova...'

But with the phone tucked under my chin, I was already on my knees, scrabbling among the discarded clothes on the floor. Here were my jeans, and in the back pocket, yes, Eileen's envelope from this morning. I ripped it open, and found a ticket for Row B, Seat 15, along with a lurid orange flyer proclaiming, in fat black capitals, the world premier – yes, that's how it was spelt – of CASANOVA, a new musical by Mick Patterson and Gaynor Steele, which was to star, in letters three times the size...

'...sponsorship from the makers of Viagra, if you ask me...' Gil's voice was mumbling into my chin.

'Ricky Marvell,' I breathed. *'Ricky Marvell?'*

I started laughing. In fact I flopped back against the bed and roared. Crazy, because, even as I sat there hooting, clamping a finger to my eye to stop tears wrecking my mascara, I was realizing that this was why my idiotic, stage-struck husband had let our firm go for peanuts; that this explained how he could only spare one day a week to Optimax, so obsessed as he was with chasing – what had Paddy called it? – his guiding star? His guiding star, oh my giddy aunt. No, of course it wasn't funny, just like Gil was protesting into my ear, it was awful – heart-breaking, totally mad. But the idea that he and bloody Gaynor really *had* been collaborating on a musical... The idea, as I spluttered to Gil, that after all these years someone had actually been persuaded to stage one of Mike's masterpieces, well, maybe I'd wronged the boy, maybe this show wasn't as dire as... 'Sorry?' I gasped, dabbing the other eye, 'what'd you say?'

'*They're* putting it on,' he shouted. 'The pair of them. I told you, the poor tart's remortgaged her flat to raise 'nother sixty grand. 'Swicked of him, even if she'll only lose half what he does.'

'Mike's – put in money, too?' I gulped back the last tremor of a laugh. 'But Mike hasn't got any money.' I found myself thinking about our overdrafts, even about the company. 'Gil?' I said sharply, when he didn't respond.

'It was his legacy,' he said at last, suddenly very quiet. 'Fuck it, you ought to know. What his mum left him.'

'Rubbish. I'm sitting in the old witch's legacy at this minute. He blew the whole quarter of a million giving me...' The words were petering out even before Gil told me that my cottage had cost half that, *exactly* half... The phone slid out of my hand and dropped to the bed.

Know the first thought came into my head? That this was the yellow python handbag all over again. A windfall split conscientiously down the middle, with a splosh pressie for the wife. But I wasn't laughing now. No, I was remembering. Seeing Mike a year ago, presenting me with this cottage – all mine, my name on the deeds, him modestly insisting I deserved every penny. Fast forward to last month. Mike, outside the lifts at Optimax, as I tearfully offered to sell my beloved cottage for his sake, with him gripping my shoulders, saying again the house was mine, he wouldn't hear of it... I'll bet he wouldn't. *My* cottage. Not the best and most romantic present ever; not my stones-and-mortar evidence of his enduring love; not a beacon of hope for our marriage – not even a bloody toy to distract me from his affair. Beck Holme was...

'A con trick,' I breathed. 'Nothing but a lousy, cheap con trick. Pulling the wool over my eyes so he could scuttle off and play big-shot producer.'

And while the witless, reckless way he'd let our company go had cost us more – much, much more – I knew it was Beck Holme I couldn't forgive.

'Gil, I must go,' I said, sweeping up the phone again and cutting across whatever he was saying without compunction. 'I'm desperately sorry about your mum, and we'll talk soon, very soon. But just now I'm half dressed, late and – and, well, what you've told me has rather knocked me sideways.'

It had. After ringing off, I remained on the bed, trying to work out what this strange sensation was. I knew I was angry – murderously angry – but at this moment I didn't *feel* angry. I just knew the rage was there, locked away somewhere. Then all at once it came to me. I was feeling ... free. *Free?* I felt as though a rock the size of Gibraltar had fallen from my neck. As though I were ten pounds lighter and twenty years younger. As though I was a helium balloon whose string has finally been snipped...

Springing to my feet, I kicked aside the whole tangle of safe, sensible clothes and seized the slinky pink sheath. Sex-kitten? She-tiger, more like. A she-tiger on heat.

'Were you in on the big secret, too?' I enquired chirpily of my son as I folded myself and my slithery frock into the passenger seat beside him. I may have spent most of the past ten minutes patrolling from one mirror to another, reassuring myself that my outfit wasn't unsuitably youthful – she-tigers are one thing, mutton dressed as lamb another – but I'd also found time to do some more joined-up thinking. 'Sarah obviously is. I'm talking about Casanova, your dad's blockbuster musical, imminently to dazzle the world.'

The poor lad was just backing the car round and his foot lurched off the accelerator, stalling the engine. 'You really do know about it?'

'What do you mean, *really?*'

'Shit, Mum, I wanted to tell you, but he made me promise.'

'I'll bet.'

'No, like he said, you've never reckoned he could do it.'

I actually smiled. 'Can't deny that.'

'And he wants to show you. Surprise you.'

'Oh, I'm surprised all right,' I murmured. Between studying my assorted reflections, I'd snatched a moment to study the neon-orange flyer. Learned that this grand if misspelt world premier (very grand, in Wakeford), presented by none other than Newhouse Productions, was to be followed by a pitiful – sorry, *strictly limited* – provincial tour. An immediate West End transfer was hoped for. I was sure it was. Like I hoped I'd win the lottery. I told Ben only that I'd already, all unbeknowing, bought a ticket to the show. That I couldn't wait to see it.

'Jesus,' he breathed. 'I mean, what's the big joke?'

'Nothing,' I said brightly – because I felt bright. I felt bright, brittle and lit up with more dangerous sparkles than the Trafalgar Square Christmas tree. I hurried on to confirm our arrangements for later. If I wanted picking up I would ring him before midnight, otherwise he should get to bed, because his friend was collecting him first thing tomorrow. No late-night telly for my boy, I declared with a passable impersonation of the caring responsible mother I most certainly did not feel just now. 'Still, chances are someone will offer me a lift, with so many people. If not, I can call a taxi from Wykesea.' And the whopping lie bounced out quite naturally. I had not the remotest intention of requiring transport home from Stowham tonight, although I was hardly likely to confide this to my son. However, I couldn't but notice he said nothing. Not another word, until we were turning off the moor road down towards the castle.

'I suppose he'll be there.'

I didn't play games. 'Paddy? Yup.'

Ben heaved a long sigh. 'He phoned. This afternoon.'

I nearly went through the windscreen. '*What?* God's sake, why didn't you tell me? What did he say?'

'Nothing. What's he likely to say to me?' And

then, to my astonishment, he burst out: 'I just didn't want you to get hurt, that's all. I'm not really expecting you and Dad to get together again, I'm not a complete moron. I know it hasn't been right for ages.'

I caught my breath. *Ben* had seen this?

'God, Mum, I've been really worried about you, don't you know that?' Ben, my big, butch boy who, for all he still liked the odd sneaky cuddle with his ma, squirmed at any lovey-dovey crap on the telly and would groan aloud if one of his movie heroes was primitive enough to kiss another human being instead of civilizedly blasting out their entrails. I felt a dangerous prickle in my eyes, and groped desperately for a tissue, but before terminal damage could be done to the make-up, Ben continued passionately: 'Just not him, OK? He's not right for you.'

I lowered the tissue. 'In what sense?'

'He's a lech, Mum, total bastard. Everyone knows that.'

We'd turned into the castle gates and were pulled up by the steps, with another vehicle nosing round behind us, dipping its headlights. I was more amazed by Ben's outburst than offended. 'Where'd you get that idea?'

'I've been living up here with you, haven't I? I do get around. Do – like – talk to people.' His voice was nearly soprano with embarrassment.

'Village gossip.'

'I got it from his own family,' he roared. 'Christ, you should hear what Daisy says about her randy Uncle Peter.'

345

27

Every woman should be allowed to make one perfect entrance in her lifetime. You know what I mean. Think dewy-eyed, swirly-skirted Ginger Rogers pausing atop the curving marble stairs in a froth of marabou, while at the far end of the crowded ballroom, top-hatted, white-tied and tailed Fred Astaire catches sight of her and – *pow!* Yeah, well, indulge me while I describe my own moment of glory. And since it was exactly that, a moment – say two seconds, to be generous – the rhapsodies won't take long, so I dare say you'll forgive me for padding the scene out with a bit of preamble.

The castle, I should tell you, was looking fairy-tale glamorous that frosty night, darkness drawing a forgiving veil over the splintered woodwork and weed-sprouting gutters. Lights shone gold in the tall, mullioned windows, while six flaming torches – the real roaring McCoy – lit a magnificently theatrical path up the lion-guarded steps to the door. I could scarcely wait to get inside, but I had to ask how my son had come to be trading family gossip with Paddy's niece, or cousin, or whatever she was – and why on earth he'd never seen fit to mention his acquaintance with Daisy Bidcombe before.

'I got the snake off her, didn't I, at Easter?' I'd never heard Ben talk this way before. He was growling like a puppy with a new bone, half proud, half defensive. 'She advertised for a good home, because she was going out to the States straight after her A-levels, and – and, OK, we hung round a bit together that vac. And before you ask, I saw her in the States, too. Oh, stop squawking, that's why I didn't tell you. I knew you'd make a fuss, but she's over there and I'm here, so just forget I ever mentioned her, OK? No big deal.'

Like hell it was no big deal. There was no mistaking the symptoms: my little boy was in love. At any other time maternal curiosity would have driven me to probe mercilessly. Fortunately for him, I was too preoccupied with the affairs of my own heart. I gave his frigid shoulder a squeeze as I clambered out of the car, to show there were no hard feelings, repeated that I would call if I wanted a lift home, and if I hadn't rung before midnight–

'I'll have turned into a pumpkin,' he finished gruffly, and with a guarded smile in my direction, rather as you might smile at a loved one just about to be wheeled down for major surgery, he stretched across and yanked shut the door.

As I teetered up the steps on my spindly gold heels – silly, wispy sandals I'd bought in a sale three years ago and in which I'd wrenched my ankles and lacerated my toes only once before – I wasn't unduly perturbed by this Daisy's jaundiced view of her Uncle Peter. Kids, with the exception of my unnatural daughter, are always embarrassed by the romantic antics of their elders, aren't they? And Lord Bidcombe had told me at the outset about his nephew's stream of girlfriends. Perhaps I'd been naïve to believe Paddy's laughing claims that these were only friends, but I suppose high-scoring libertines need to be pretty smooth talkers. How many women would flop back on the mattress with a smile if it were clear they were merely being invited to add one more notch to a bedpost already bearing a close resemblance to a fretsaw? Besides which, as I boldly assured myself, even the most hardened rake can succumb in the end, when he meets his twin soul. Don't mock. Just remember, as I was, the story Paddy had so soulfully recounted about Casanova himself, and his passion-until-death for the respectable wife and mother – what was her name, Henriette? There you go. Clearly, my destiny was to play Henriette to Paddy's Giacomo.

Eased out of my wrap by a smiling Seddons, I accepted an offer from his frilly-pinnied, rosy-cheeked minion to be shown to the room set aside for ladies. Then regretted it, because the route twisted along treacherously pocked stone-flagged corridors for what seemed miles in those lethal heels, and I was like a racehorse at the starting line, quivering to let rip. Delivered to an underlit cavern, the size of a barn and twice as cold, I found two pewter-haired matrons hissing at each other's reflections between tight-stretched lips as they touched up their make-up. The profligacy of one of their husbands seemed to be incensing them. An ornately framed mirror, crazed with a spider's web of tarnish, was vast enough for me to inspect my own face alongside theirs. I tugged a comb from my bag, and hastily tucked back the toothbrush which had also clattered to the floor – yes, a toothbrush. A girl should always travel prepared.

'...three days at Cheltenham and then expected me to believe he'd paid five thousand for that clapped-out Land-Rover?' barked the woman beside me. 'Bloody Bunburies. Does he think I'm totally stupid?' She caught my startled eye on her in the mirror, flashed a chilly smile and stuffed her lipstick away.

I beamed sunnily in return and nearly laughed aloud. Lord, I really should have remembered before now that Ricky Marvell belonged to a band of brothers well used to hiding un-authorized expenditure from wives. I could have told this indignant lady that my own husband had out-Bunburied hers by a mile, out-Bunburied the entire bloody syndicate, come to that, but that tonight I, for one, was planning to take my revenge. I planned to revenge myself quite gloriously, and Mike deserved everything that was coming.

After they'd tip-tapped out in a miasma of powder and hairspray, I swiftly hoisted up my bra-free boobs – although it was wonderful the way this frock glossed over any suggestion of droop – and twisted round to scrutinize the rear view. My bum had never looked so pert. You certainly gets what you pays for. Yup, whatever happened tonight, Mike had brought it on himself. I had only ever sought out Paddy McGinty because of my husband's money troubles, and pursued that acquaintance with the aim of rescuing him. If this had led, ultimately, to my developing warmer feelings for the spook – well, was that poetic justice or what? With a final flick to my pleasingly streaky fringe, I tucked my bag under my arm and followed the scent of hairspray down the crepuscular passageway, feeling much as I had at fifteen, when the youth club heart-throb, in an absent-minded moment, had seen fit to invite me to the boys' grammar school disco.

Seddons glided across the entrance hall to meet me at the drawing-room doors, mighty oak numbers, strapped and studded ferociously enough to repel armies. I'd more than half expected to find my friend out here too, waiting to escort me in, and asked Seddons, with a twinge of anxiety, whether Paddy was indeed here.

'Mr Jack insisted,' said the butler, slightly misunderstanding my question – although, now he came to mention it, I supposed it was remarkable that Jack should wish to invite his cousin. 'I'm sure Mr Paddy will be glad to see you, madam.'

'I sincerely hope so,' I responded gaily, not troubling my pretty little head to wonder why the guy sounded so gloomy. I just threw back my shoulders and lifted my chin as he flung wide the door. So here it comes, folks. Stand by for the big entrance.

There were, I suppose, twenty-odd guests already milling around the lofty chandeliered chamber whose crimson damask hangings I'd inspected so recently. The room looked less decrepit by night, with the curtains in shadow and lights trained on the motley collection of age-blackened ancestral portraits. At least, I assumed these lantern-jawed cavaliers and piggy-eyed fat females were ancestors, because one could imagine precious little reason for enduring their dyspeptic glares otherwise. Still, I was not here to appreciate art. And as I stood on the threshold, looking around, I'd swear – *swear* – an instant's hush fell on the room. What was certain is that, at the very moment my gaze found Paddy, his likewise found me. You know, the classic eyes-meeting-across-a-crowded-room scenario? And he looked – *stunned*. In fact I do myself an injustice. He looked eye-poppingly, jaw-droppingly, heart-stoppingly gob-smacked. Sloshed half his drink over his hand. I have never felt so headily irresistible in my life. I beamed back at him with the subtlety of a lighthouse, and at once, with the barest nod of apology to a whiskery old gent in scarlet mess jacket beside him, he shouldered across towards me. I won't say the crowd melted back to let him pass, like they do in all the best movies, but almost.

'Hi, Paddy,' I said, and while I'd like to claim this emerged in a husky, *femme fatale* drawl, even I was aware I sounded more Minnie Mouse than Marilyn Monroe. Nerves. No matter, ignore the squeaky voice, I was on a roll. At that moment I could have ascended Everest, invented a cure for the common cold and danced *Swan Lake* with-out pausing for breath.

'Jo,' he gasped, and I was gratified to note his voice sounded even more strangled than mine.

'What on earth are you doing here?'

So there you have it – that's to say, you've had it.
That was my moment of glory, and it was already
over, even if I didn't quite realize it at the time.
Well, yes, it occurred to me that Paddy's
flattering impersonation of a man struck by a
thunderbolt might have *something* to do with the
fact that he obviously hadn't a clue I'd been
invited, but I was sure there'd been more to it
than that. Perhaps I also noticed that almost the
instant his hands closed on my shoulders, they
fell away again, and that his kiss landed
somewhere between my ear and the chandelier.
Never mind, it was with palpable sincerity he
murmured I was looking wonderful – even if his
voice was a tad short on the slavering lust one
might have expected in this famous womanizer.
  He looked pretty bloody wonderful himself, I
must say. I've always reckoned evening dress is a
male's ultimate weapon. Nothing sets off even
the average man better than austere black and
white, and Paddy was far from your average man.
Only too easily could I imagine squadrons of
anorexic bimbos flinging themselves at his glacé
leather toes – but not tonight. I'd conducted a
one-second survey of rival talent in the room,
and found no women present under forty-five in
age or hip measurement. The boy was all mine.
His rusty dark hair was neatly brushed, but not
so neatly as to spoil the ruffle of curls; the
bruising had all-but vanished from his face; and
his large frame was superbly packaged in a
severely plain dinner jacket which didn't shriek

that it had originated in a green-baized workroom in Savile Row and had never seen a peg in its life, but rather whispered this information with a discreet cough. A snowy pleated shirt was topped with the barest hint of black bowtie, just asymmetrical enough to show it had been knotted by hand, and naturally was unspoiled by any of the rainbow cummerbunds or witty tartan waistcoats favoured by Mike's cronies on the rare event we graced a black-tie do together.

'You look terrific,' I blurted out, before realizing this was more gushing schoolgirl than tail-lashing she-tiger. Dressing the *femme fatale* is one thing, acting it another. I was wondering how best to communicate my newly unshackled status with appropriate wit and cool when Paddy threw me by saying he gathered my husband's great musical had at last reached the stage.

'Blimey, how'd you know? I've only just found out.' But it was as good a cue as any, so before I lost my nerve I plunged on: 'And I've got to tell you, Paddy, it's changed everything for me. Realizing what Mike has actually been up to. The truth is—'

'My dear girl.' Lord Bidcombe had lumbered over to do his hostly duty, followed by a white-aproned waitress bearing a silver salver of champagne flutes. He stooped to plant an avuncular salute on my forehead. 'Delighted you could come, and at such short notice. You're looking quite lovely.' He glanced at his nephew with – or so it seemed to me – a hint of defiance. 'Isn't Jane looking lovely, Paddy?'

'*Jo*,' he snapped, with a glare at his uncle which suggested he didn't welcome this intrusion into our tête-à-tête any more than I. I ventured a conspiratorial wink. Mistake, because a glob of mascara was thereby dislodged into my eye, and I spent the next minute or more blinking manically. Did Cleopatra have this problem?

'I'm hoping she's going to talk some sense into you where I've so signally failed,' boomed his lordship. 'That right, *Jo?*' I blinked up at him, and not just because I was clearing my muddied eye. 'You don't want him to go wandering off to the back of beyond, do you? You want him here, with us, at Stowham.'

'Hardly fair to embroil Jo, is it, sir?' Paddy's tone would have put icicles on an Aga, but it didn't daunt his uncle* who pitched back that he'd embroil whom he damn well pleased, if he could make Paddy reconsider. Evidently his failure to tell his nephew he'd invited me was no oversight. I was being sprung as his last-ditch secret weapon. Absolute last ditch because I heard, with a surge of now-or-never adrenalin, that Paddy was quitting Stowham first thing tomorrow morning. And Bernard wasn't just after dissuading his nephew from going overseas, nor did he merely want to resuscitate the plan of his coming into partnership in the estate. Since the foghorn boom grew louder as he grew crosser, I doubt I was the only guest to learn that the one thing on which he and Paddy agreed was that any such scheme was now unworkable. My friend – or so I understood, as these two tall men argued over my elegantly-coiffed head – was

354

offering a loan. An enormous loan, by the sounds of it, made possible by selling his firm – with no strings and open-ended. Seemed extraordinarily generous to me, but Bernard wouldn't hear of it. Growled that if he popped his clogs, and the estate was afloat on Paddy's money when it passed to Jack – well, he was sorry to say this, but there was no knowing what follies his son might commit. No, Paddy must have security. He must *buy* the place outright. Settle here, knock it into shape. His firm was gone, exactly, so he needed something to keep him out of mischief.

'I've told you Bernard–'

So much for my sexual magnetism. Paddy seemed to have forgotten I was here. I took a swig of champagne and studied the fat lady ancestor behind Lord B. Her long-nosed, bored scowl expressed my own feelings exactly. Don't get me wrong, I was all in favour of his bright idea. The prospect of my friend moving up here was infinitely more intoxicating than this lukewarm fizz, but I agreed with Paddy, too, when he snapped, in a rare loss of self-restraint, that a party was neither the time nor place for such an argument.

'Time's running out,' roared his uncle. 'I tell you, m'boy, we're finished here without you. I'm too old and too tired. You quit tomorrow, and I'm ringing Marvell's people, see what they're offering.'

'That's blackmail, Bernard, and you know it. Take the bloody money and employ a decent agent. Better still, get Jack to do the job. He's only lost the use of his legs.' As he spoke, he glanced across the room towards the fire, and I saw, for the first time, the birthday boy himself, with a flashy pink rose in the lapel of his dinner jacket. There was a cluster of men round his wheelchair; with cigarette in one gesticulating hand and glass in the other, he threw back his head, laughing uproariously.

'Jack's had years to pull his finger out, and he's failed me, failed–' Here Bernard Bidcombe must have remembered this was his son's party after all. Lowering his voice, he swung towards me. 'See if you can convince this fool we need him here, not wandering the world in search of his perishin' soul. Come m'dear.' But this was addressed to the waitress. 'I see the Leeburns have arrived. *Martin*, my very dear fellow, and the delicious Dilly, how are you?'

I waited for him to stump away, hand outstretched, before turning to Paddy with a grin. 'Alone at last?' I whispered. And if you're wincing at this line of chat, I can't blame you. As the words left my mouth I was wishing I'd gleaned a few tips from my worldly-wise daughter. Mind, her idea of a sophisticated chat-up line is probably to ask a likely candidate if he fancies a shag. Paddy didn't seem too impressed, either. Just offered a stiff apology for his uncle having embarrassed me. The way he phrased it almost sounded as though he were apologizing for my having been invited at all, and I said so. 'Anyone'd think you didn't want to see me,' I added gaily, thrusting my glass towards a passing bottle.

'Don't awfully want to be here myself.' His

smile was strained. 'Anyway, it's hardly an ideal place for us – to talk.'

'Bernard's obviously expecting me to, though. So just for the record, I'd love you to settle up here...' Something in his face made my courage falter momentarily. 'I mean, it's always nice to have friends living nearby, isn't it?'

For an instant, I had an inkling of how Banquo must have felt when he shimmered along, dead as well as uninvited, to Macbeth's beanfeast. The Scottish King can't have looked bleaker than my friend did.

'Gosh, yes, super,' he cried. A second too late. 'And who knows, we may yet end up as neighbours, once I've exhausted this beastly wanderlust.'

'Paddy–'

'But I've been hogging you to myself in this corner far too long. The other fellows will be demanding pistols at dawn if I don't circulate you at once.' He had taken my elbow and was steering me relentlessly forward. 'Alistair Merrill-Browne, Rupert Gutteridge, have you met my charming friend, Mrs Patterson? Jo – Al, Rupe. On your best behaviour, you ruffians, because I'm leaving her in your care.'

Even then I wasn't entirely cast down. I was telling myself Paddy's look of, well, horror almost, could have been provoked by – someone behind me? A twinge from his injuries? Besides, under the outrageous flattery of Al and whatever his red-nosed and chinless chum was called, my spirits perked up faster than a wilting geranium in a cloudburst. Their conversation might consist largely of clunking gallantries and honking guffaws, but at least they'd had the sense to secure their own bottle of champers. Paddy had slipped out of the room after leaving me with them, and if he didn't make a bee-line back on returning – in fact ended up beside the scarlet mess jacket again– well, he'd obviously been trapped by an old bore, and was too well mannered to bolt. Al and red-nose – Rupert, actually, and it was all I could do not to call him Rudolph – had been joined by a couple of other men, whose names I didn't even bother to take in, although I recognized their faces from Bunbury shoots.

A Stowham Castle dinner party being on a different scale to the Wimbledon variety, there must have been at least forty guests here by now, and it did vaguely strike me they were an odd mix. I could see plenty of hearty Bunbury types, sure, but there was also a scattering of stiff-spined, elderly gents with pewter-haired wives sipping orange juice, who looked more like Bernard's friends than his son's. That the men outnumbered the women did not surprise me. To the Jack Bidcombes of this world, the word 'friend' is generally synonymous with 'chap'. Women have their place, in kitchen, nursery or bedroom, but they're not chums. Still, I can't deny it was heartening to collect around me a circle of men behaving in a manner strongly reminiscent of the Labradors who'd tried to scramble into my car after Dora this morning, even if I was aware this could only be because I'd no competition to speak of. At least, I hadn't until, beside the portly, pink-faced form of Hugh Hough-Hartley, I spotted a raven-haired creature in bottle-green velvet with a gold bodice cut so low you could, as my gran used to say, see what she'd had for breakfast. Even her sultry good looks didn't perturb me, though, because if there was one thing of which I was certain, it was that Bernard Bidcombe would have seated me next to Paddy at dinner. And the sooner we got in there, the better.

Just when I was beginning to think that my stilettoed feet couldn't take much more of this standing around, we were at last ushered through to a mighty dining hall, oak-panelled with soaring, stone-vaulted ceiling, and a bonfire roaring in a medieval fireplace probably designed for the roasting of venison. Several at a time. Seddons himself ushered me down to the foot of the gleaming table, thickly clustered with glasses and flowers, lit by silver candelabra tall as palm trees, with life-sized silver pheasants pecking round their bases. Sure enough, I'd just read Paddy's card in the place beside mine, when Seddons, in the act of pulling back my chair, halted and squinted at the card in front of me. Then turned to me, with evident perplexity.

'I do beg your pardon, Mrs Patterson. I seem to have made a mistake...'

Seddons? A *mistake?* To my chagrin, he led me inexorably back towards the head of the table, casting surreptitious glances down at each place card as he threaded through the other guests, and deposited me, at length, in the chair to the right of the birthday boy. This card was indeed inscribed with my own moniker. Well, very flattering, I dared say, to be accorded the seat of honour beside Jack Bidcombe, but this was just about as far from Paddy as you could get without climbing out of a mullioned bloody window. And if there were any doubt about this not being Lord B.'s intended placement, it was immediately quashed by his son.

'Hello, you joining me up here?' said Jack. 'Thought it was old Hetty. Oh, obviously not, she's down there with the coz.' I followed his gaze. And being helped into the chair beside his own by the ever-courteous Major McGinty was she of the raven hair, gold bodice and fathomless cleavage. 'Lucky for me,' said my host, adding gallantly that someone had done him a favour by changing the plan.

Someone. That same someone I'd noticed sneaking out of the pre-dinner drinks after discovering I was here? Of course it was Paddy who'd switched the place cards. And while I'd like to have believed he was afraid I might bend his ear on behalf of Lord Bidcombe all evening, even I wasn't that gullible. Paddy McGinty, my one-time friend, had failed to invite me to this party himself, had been palpably annoyed with his uncle for doing so, and now was deliberately avoiding me. Since I'd already drunk enough to be at risk of dissolving in a maudlin tear-puddle, it was perhaps as well that, just then, I heard a voice behind me, a voice redolent of warm molasses trickled from a spoon.

'Well, hi there...' There were about fifteen

syllables packed into those three words, and every one of them screamed sex. There was no need to turn my head to see who had thus addressed me, although naturally I did.

I saw a bronzed face, a creamy white tuxedo, and a peacock blue shirt with frills flamboyant enough for a flamenco dancer, cummerbunded into the snuggest crotch-hugging black trousers you ever saw. There was a chunky gold sovereign ring on the hand that lifted mine to his lips. Add in the candlelight, and this was surely a moment such as is fantasized about by a million menopausal housewives. I snatched the tiniest glance down the table. Paddy's head was inclined towards his neighbour, and he was smiling in the intimate, enjoying-a-private-joke way I remembered only too vividly.

It was the final straw. I composed my own features into a smile that could out-sizzle the sun in August. In the Sahara.

'Ricky Marvell,' I purred. 'Wow, what a thrill.'

28

'The thrill's all mine, baby,' he responded.

Now this might strike you as the kind of corny line to send quite the wrong sort of shiver up a girl's spine, but I can assure you that, in Ricky Marvell's treacly drawl and my state of mingled indignation and inebriation, it played just fine with this girl. As I peered along the table again, through a dancing twilight of candle flames splaying this way and that in arctic draughts, I was fiercely willing Paddy to turn his head towards me and observe the lusty leer on the face of my neighbour. No way. The tortoiseshell specs were focused firmly down his neighbour's décolletage. Well, maybe: I couldn't detect exactly where they were aiming, but it sure as hell wasn't in my direction.

'I get this amazing feeling I know you from somewhere,' confided Ricky, as he must have confided to a hundred other women. Since last Tuesday. He took up his napkin and shook it open with one fast flap, like a matador preparing for the fray. I noticed his eyes were straying downwards, and realized that icy draughts affect more than candle flames, if you happen to be braless in clinging velvet. Twenty-four hours ago, I'd have been rounding my shoulders and blushing pinker than my dress. The new me took a bracing snifter of the Sancerre Jack had ladled into my glass and arched my spine. Waitresses were trooping round with dinkily garnished plates of some fishy salad, don't ask me exactly what. Food was the last thing on my mind, even if I'd eaten nothing since my breakfast slice of toast.

'Give us a clue,' he prompted, his shoulder pressing against mine as he leaned aside to let the waitress put down his starter. 'Have our paths crossed before?'

'Sort of,' I responded brightly, and took the opportunity, as he turned to flash a grin at the girl, of whipping my place card off the table and into my handbag. Smart of me to twig that, since this man was presently employed by my husband, I might be advised not to advertise my surname.

'Sort of how?' he echoed.

Let me count the ways. I looked him in the eye, with my head on one side. Well, I was thinking, I could start by announcing that you and my husband have had a mistress in common. Also that I live in a house you once owned – and until this very evening, by the by, I sincerely believed you'd rooked us into paying double for it. Silly me. You were just helping my husband stage the musical in which you're about to star – you know, that grand world premiere in Wakeford? I wonder if you've realized yet it's destined to be the biggest turkey this side of Christmas. Anything else? Oh yes, I don't know *quite* what the connection is between the neighbour on my right here pawning his shotgun, a poker tournament at your place in Spain, and the fact you're after buying this castle, but I personally wouldn't put anything beyond a pair of Bunburies like you ...

'We met out on the moor here, on a shoot a couple of months ago,' I said demurely. 'I was picking up by the butts.'

What does he respond? As if you can't see it coming a mile off. 'You can pick me up any day,' he whispers. And I'm only too aware that if I wanted to take a truly *bloody* revenge on my husband, fate has surely delivered me the means, gift-wrapped in a tuxedo. I'm also aware he's got a lot of expensive dentistry.

By the time we finished the starters, of which I'd managed a scant couple of mouthfuls before abandoning my fork, the evening was already taking on an air of surreality. Not least when Ricky – draping a heavy arm round me – leaned across to tell Jack there was a serious card game back home in Spain soon.

'Oh, he knows *that*,' I snorted merrily and, when Jack evinced surprise, reminded him he was planning a holiday at Ricky's complex.

'Yeah?' said Ricky, sounding even more amazed.

'Oh – only an idea. Seddons had the brochure you left with my father and it seemed as good a place as any other.'

Ricky grinned. 'Checking the business out before you flog us this place?'

'Like hell,' responded Jack pleasantly, and I'd barely time to absorb that whatever he'd pawned his gun for, it clearly wasn't to play poker in Spain, when I found myself giggling as he deftly removed Ricky's wandering hand from my shoulder blade and replaced it with his own. This wasn't the me I knew, fluttering and flirting like a caged canary between two cartoon wolves – oh, definitely two, because the slavering was by no means all on Ricky's side. Jack Bidcombe might give just the teensiest impression of a man feeling honour-bound to go through the motions, lusting on auto-pilot as it were, but he was by far the more sophisticated operator. It was Jack who kept my glass topped up, Jack who caught my wrist to blow a fleck of his cigarette ash off my forearm and then smilingly touched his lips to the goose-pimples raised by his own warm breath. And it was Jack who said he believed I had what it takes to save a man's soul. Not just was this an odd sort of compliment – well, it isn't quite in the 'if I said you had a beautiful body...' category, is it? – but he said it oddly, too. He wasn't leering as Ricky had when admiring my three-quid junk-shop earrings – from close enough quarters to eat them – no, it was as though Jack had weighed me up, balanced pros against cons, and formed this as his considered verdict. Flattering, if disconcerting. I hoped he'd convey his views to his cousin, who was even now laughing gaily at one of her jokes down there. Throwing back his head, seemingly happy as a sandboy. What the hell are sandboys anyway? Still, two could play at that game.

I laid my pearly-nailed hand on Ricky's sleeve. 'So tell me about this musical you're starring in,' I cooed. 'I want to hear *all* about it.'

Food came, food went. Could have been cardboard as far as I was concerned, and Jack evidently felt the same. He was sticking rigorously to a liquid diet, and chain smoking not merely between courses but as near as dammit through them. I supposed it was his party, and he could die if he wanted to. Besides, he was by no means the only one puffing away. A blue pall of smoke soon began blurring the view of my distant one-time friend. At least, I told myself it was only the smoke fogging my vision, as I allowed Jack to top up my wine as regularly as his own. My other neighbour, by contrast, was soon covering his glass with one be-ringed hand. Ricky had a hearty appetite for the food, but drank only sparingly. He wasn't a big wine man any road, he told me, a Yorkshire burr unexpectedly seasoning his smoochy transatlantic drawl, and he'd got to be fit for the sodding dress rehearsal tomorrow. Reckoned he was lucky they'd let him off the tech tonight – technical run-through, he added for my benefit, as if I hadn't yelled the lighting cues at many a tech myself in that long-gone life when I'd been married to a producer of two-bit summer shows. Hypnotically bizarre, it was, being told about this stranger called Mick Patterson, who was throwing his whole heart and soul into the production, not to mention his every last penny...

'No, really?' I marvelled.

Poor bugger was chewing his fingernails off at every rehearsal, driving the director demented, although he was a helluva good bloke even if he was a bit ... well, it was like he couldn't keep still, or shut up for two seconds, know what Ricky meant? And it got everybody else twitching round him.

'You would not believe how clearly I can imagine it,' I declared, so tickled by the absurdities of this exchange I was caught off-guard when, picking up my left hand and looking down at my rings, he casually enquired whether I was married.

'Yes,' I said automatically, feeling blood flood upwards. 'I mean, *no*. Well, up to a point.'

Jack had overheard. 'Oh, Christ, you're not, are you?' And, to my astonishment, he let out a roar of laughter. 'How bloody ironical. How bloody, *bloody* ironical. Paddy does it again.'

I didn't bother telling him Paddy hadn't done anything as far as I was concerned, and manifestly had no wish to. I just absorbed the implication that my so-decent, so-honourable friend hadn't excluded married women from his romantic attentions. Well, look at him now, with that Hetty creature – and she, I'd since established, was indeed his friend Hugh's wife, an unlikely pairing if ever I saw one. Any lingering hope that enlightening him about my soon-to-be-divorced status would make a difference was extinguished in that instant. A grinning Ricky confided that as long as my up-to-a-point husband wasn't around tonight, that was fine by him. His old lady believed he was tucked up in the crummy hotel the producers had found for him in Wakeford, where he'd been lonely as sin these past few days, strung-up with nerves as he was ...

'Nervous, you? Surely not.' The response was mere social reflex because, for all I was doing my lash-fluttering best to look as though I was hanging on his every word, I was actually according him only about two per cent of my attention. I had at last caught Paddy staring this way, and was determined to show the bastard that *somebody* fancied me.

'Shitting breezeblocks, pardon me, if you want the God-honest truth.'

It did penetrate to whatever remnant of intelligence still functioned in my skull that Ricky Marvell, smoothy supreme, suddenly sounded in dead earnest. I could see even why. Had it ever occurred to my husband that this was a man who (as he was telling me himself) had never *acted* before, never spoken lines, never performed with other people, beyond a gyrating doo-wop-wop-ping backing group? Ricky's natural habitat was a cabaret floor with a phallic microphone, flashing lights and grannies swooning into their Bacardi and Cokes. Was it surprising he was scared witless by a proscenium arch and a script? And that was without his being the star turn in a show with rather less going for it than *Springtime for Hitler*. It would have been downright cruel to enquire whether they were rigging him out in powdered wig and knee breeches – God, what a vision – because the tiny corner of my brain which was engaged in this conversation felt quite sorry for him, almost maternally protective, which shows how drunk I was getting. But my serious attention remained focused exclusively on the real-life Casanova currently performing at the far end of this dining room. And even if, with my view impeded by smoke and people leaning across the table, I couldn't see exactly what he was up to, I could guess.

'Thanks,' I said to Jack, gulping back a hiccup. ''Nother glass would be just divine.'

Doesn't take a genius to predict the evening was destined to end in tears.

There were toasts and speeches. All to the effect that it was marvellous to welcome dear old Jack back into the land of the living. A birthday cake was borne in under such a blaze of candles I found myself wondering if medieval architects allowed for fire exits, and the cake was followed – wouldn't you just know it – by a surprise strippergram, laid on by the contingent of hooting, whistling Bunburies. The girl strutted in, clad in policewoman's uniform with truncheon suggestively a-twirl, and if, as I heard someone claim, she was toning down her act in deference to the ladies present, I boggle to think what the uncensored version was like. What was more, seated at Jack's right hand, I was close enough to see her appendix scar. I crashed into Ricky as I ducked sideways to avoid a low-flying bra.

You have to hand it to my neighbour, he didn't miss his chance. One minute I was in my own chair, albeit leaning to one side, the next I was in his lap. A lap with an unmistakable protuberance under my lower spine, which prompted me to recall, with a squeak, Gaynor Steele's tales of Ricky's hidden talents. One bronzed hand was locked like a vice round my waist, the other stroked a businesslike path up my thigh, while the hot breath in my ear was whispering that, with the hotel in Wakeford being such a dump, he'd booked himself into a seriously classy joint for tonight halfway between here and there, four-poster bed, Jacuzzi, the works; that he really needed someone to be with tonight; that we could make sweet, sweet music together; that his Jag was outside...

'Attaboy,' howled the stripper, bouncing her naked and improbably globular tits in Jack Bidcombe's glassy face. At least it stopped him clocking what was going on beside him. Somewhere down the table I saw his father's eyes popping, along with those of several of his contemporaries, while Hugh Hough-Hartley buried his nose in a handkerchief. The couple of women I could see, locked as I was into the frills of Ricky Marvell's chest, seemed to be exchanging world-weary grimaces as they reached for cigarettes and the port decanters. Whooping Bunburies, though, were scrambling round the furniture like obese spaniels to retrieve every last far-flung garment. The stately homes of England? This was more like Wykesea working men's club on a Saturday night. Only rowdier, I shouldn't wonder. Meanwhile, in intimate counterpoint to the din, a treacly voice whispered in my ear that the two of us would have a ball together; we'd travel to heaven and back.

All at once I became aware that something was throbbing against my back – no, not what you might be forgiven for imagining. This was digging into my ribcage, small and sharp-cornered, and it was vibrating insistently. Ricky evidently felt it too because his arm-lock on me relaxed and I won't say I escaped so much as slithered unexpectedly floorwards. More through luck than skill, I landed my bum safely back in my own chair, albeit with my skirt halfway to my waist. Fortunately all eyes were on the stripper as she pranced out to wild cheers, waving a spangled G-string over her head.

'Bloody mobile,' muttered Ricky, groping in his breast pocket. 'Hardly anyone's got this number – but don't worry, sweetheart, the wife isn't one of them.' He found the thing and squinted perplexedly down at the screen before surreptitiously whipping out a pair of half-moon specs and holding them in front of his eyes. 'Someone from the show,' he grunted, and chewed his lip for a moment before, with a sigh, he leaned forward to plant a kiss on my neck. 'Guess I'd better check in, see what she wants, but it won't take two tics. I'll just go outside. Stay hot, honey.' Two hands briefly clasped my shoulders, and he followed the stripper out of the room.

I was left slumped in my chair, wide-eyed and slack-jawed. If a cartoonist had drawn me at that moment, the thought bubble over my head would have contained no words, just exclamation marks, question marks and asterisks. Lots of them.

'But you haven't a drink,' said Jack Bidcombe, who should have been comatose long since, the amount he'd drunk, but still seemed to be talking in sentences. Eyes were a bit dead as he looked at me now, though. Like the windows of a house when the lights are still on but the owners are out. 'Port, brandy, or do you prefer a sticky?'

'Sticky?' I echoed stupidly, thinking of the situation I seemed to have landed in. 'You're not kidding...' Then saw he'd taken me at my word and was summoning a waitress. 'No, not f'me. Thank you. Had 'nuff. More than enough.' I was dazedly realizing how true this was.

'Nonsense,' he mocked, filling his own glass to the brim. 'This is my birthday. You're duty bound to toast my health and happiness.' Even in my state, it occurred to me that he didn't sound very happy. Didn't look it either, for all he was smiling. In fact, now I bothered to think about it, he hadn't seemed to be enjoying himself much all night, not really, just playing along. Or was I imagining things? I concentrated on him, trying to bring his features back into focus.

'*Why?*' I said.

'I'm sorry?'

'All this – this...' I wanted to ask why he was putting on this act of manic jollity, why he'd organized this party in the first place, sprung it on his unsuspecting family, but... Finding words was suddenly beyond me. Funny thing about alcohol, that. You can bob along on the tide of booze for really an awfully long time, knowing you're tiddly, but still afloat, still able to organize one syllable roughly in front of another, even if it's doggy-paddling rather than your usual sensible breaststroke, and then – woomph – it's like you've gone over Niagara Falls. And now I was drowning fast.

'Eat, drink and be merry,' he murmured, 'for we all know what happens tomorrow.'

Tomorrow, I thought, Paddy was going, and that was the end of my little pipe dream. Tomorrow, I thought, I would tell my husband this was the end of twenty-one years of marriage. And tomorrow wouldn't they just be sorry, the lousy rotten pair of them, when I woke up in a four-poster bed with adjoining Jacuzzi somewhere between here and Wakeford...

'You believe a single act can right a lifetime of wrongs?' said Jack dreamily, and I was too drunk even to wonder at his mind-reading skills.

'You mean revenge?' I croaked. Which is sweet? Is a dish best eaten cold? Is ... stinking breath in a grey dawn with Ricky Marvell's dentistry leering at me from the adjoining pillow?

'No, no,' he was saying. 'Not revenge...'

Was I stark, raving *mad?*

I like to think I rose to my feet with dignity, even if my chair unaccountably clattered to the floor behind me. I believe I contrived to frame a few words of thanks to my host, although he seemed more interested in the contents of his glass. I contemplated doing the same by his father. But Bernard Bidcombe was halfway down the room, and I decided that was several steps too far. I did not deign, however, to so much as glance towards the far end of the table where sat my friend. I hoped he bloody suffocated in her cleavage. Instead, I picked a careful path, upright and smiling, to the door which someone – Seddons, a waitress, the castle ghost? – flung open for me to quit the party. My exit may have lacked the glamorous panache of my arrival but, in that I did actually manage to remain vertical throughout, you could say it was even more of a triumph.

The cold air in the great flagged hall hit me like an avalanche. Not merely was I unable to remember where the loo was, for one panicked instant I couldn't remember where *I* was. Phone, I thought. Gotta phone Ben. Or is it too late already? I goggled at the freckles on my watch-free wrist. And just looking downwards had caused my stomach to plummet alarmingly upwards, into my throat. Suits of armour on the walls of this empty, echoing cavern oozed in and out of focus like props in a horror movie. This was a dungeon and I couldn't find the right way out – any way out. My gaze alighted on a door – the huge main doors. Get outside, that was it. Air, fresh air, do me a power of good. I'd staggered halfway across when my heel must have snagged in a crack between flagstones. Quite extraordinarily slowly, I felt myself losing my balance, dropping my bag, thrusting out my hands and gently tipping forward, unable to do a thing to save myself – until two beefy masculine arms locked round my waist.

'No!' I shrieked, squirming frantically this way and that. ''Smistake. All wrong. Lemme go.'

But the voice which whispered exasperatedly in my ear that it might be a good notion, under the circs, to keep the noise down a touch, wasn't in the least treacly.

That was when my rubber legs capsized completely. 'OmyGod, no,' I whimpered. 'Not you. Anyone – *anyone*, 'cept you.'

29

Somebody was shaking my shoulder.

'Go 'way,' I moaned, ''m 'sleep.'

The shaking didn't stop. In fact, someone was also hissing my name. Loudly and too close to my ear. I managed to screw open my eyes. Not easy because they seemed glued together. *Were* glued together, with congealed tears and mascara. I was in a four-poster bed. My God, I was in a four-poster bed I'd never seen before in my life... But there above me, framed by a looped and tasselled canopy, was the tortoiseshell-spectacled face of my friend, gazing lovingly down at me – so lovingly, I knew I must be dreaming. I blinked. Was dreaming. He was still gazing down at me, but not at all lovingly. Apologetically. Touch of irritation, possibly.

'Frightfully sorry, my old dear,' he murmured, 'but I really do want to hit the road before the household starts jumping, and I didn't suppose you'd want me just to abandon you here.'

'Where?' I croaked. 'I mean, where'm I?' But even as I spoke, memory was trickling back, pouring back, thundering back in gory, Technicolor detail. I shut my eyes again, in a pitiful attempt to escape. 'I think I want to die,' I whimpered.

'You said that last night,' agreed Paddy cheerfully, 'but it'll pass. Trust me, these things do.'

A tiny tear burned in the corner of my sticky eye. He was talking about hangovers. I wasn't.

I'll spare you the intimate details of what had passed between Major Peter Edward Ffoulkes McGinty, well-known seducer of these parts, and Mrs Josephine Patterson, trainee temptress. Suffice to say it had begun with my flinging myself out of his arms, lurching over to the towering front doors and somehow – God knows

375

how – hauling one open, before collapsing across the stone balustrade which flanked the steps outside and being helplessly, comprehensively sick. I would like to claim that Major McGinty did not witness this humiliation, but the truth is he supported my shoulders throughout. To set the seal on my misery, when I eventually stopped retching, he handed me a crisply folded white handkerchief and draped his superbly cut dinner jacket round my quaking body.

'Good show,' he murmured kindly. 'You'll feel heaps better now.'

I think that was probably when, with perfect sincerity, I told him I wanted to die. But in the meantime, if he could just, *hic*, direct me to the ladies'? No need to s'port me, I croaked, I was perffly capable of walking under my own two legs, that is, on my own steam – and, oh God, there were two women coming out of the dining room, I must go outside again, couldn't let anyone see me in this state...

'Oh, come on then, you chump,' he sighed, swiftly steering me – well, I don't know where he steered me. Off down a passageway, up a lot of stairs, tall, twisty spiral stairs that made my head spin and my legs tangle and meant he had to half carry me in the end. However, we eventually stumbled into a bathroom, that's for sure. I remember there were swirly blue flowers etched in the crazed porcelain of the handbasin. His bathroom. I worked that out because I'd recognized his green leather sponge bag. Many a time and oft had I seen that bag in my own bathroom. I think that's possibly when I started weeping, not just a few graceful sparklers, but great racking sobs, as I wailed my fathomless miseries all over his snowily pleated shirtfront.

'Poor old sausage,' he murmured, patting my shoulder, before contriving to unpeel me from his chest. 'Look, help yourself to anything in here you want. I'll be back in a trice.'

At least I'd brought a toothbrush with me, even if these weren't quite the circumstances under which I'd envisaged needing it. And although it took ferocious concentration to stop myself tumbling head first into the flowered porcelain, I nevertheless contrived to scrub my teeth. I scrubbed my teeth, my gums, my tongue – I must have used half a tube of Paddy's toothpaste. Then I splashed cold water all over my face. Then I made my big mistake: I glanced up at the mirror. I think I might actually have run screaming from the fearful hag who squinted back at me, a creature looking much as I'd expect my exhumed corpse to look after several months underground. Certainly I found myself cannoning into Paddy's large body again with a moan of anguish. And he looked pretty grim too. I mean, not ashy-faced, un-dead grim like my reflection, grim as in angry. As in gloweringly, toweringly furious. Wasn't surprising really, faced with Jo the inebriate old trout.

'Steady,' he snapped. 'You nearly made me spill it.'

'Whatizzit?'

'Water. Do you a damn sight more good than brandy and Coca Cola. God's sake, don't try and take it from me, I'll carry it. No, the stairs aren't through there... Oh, well, I suppose you can sit down for a few minutes if you must, just while you pull yourself together. Look, get this down you.'

And he stood over me, huge and blackly thunder-faced, as I glugged back water. He kept refilling my glass, what was more, curtly telling me I'd be grateful to him in the morning. Wherever I happened to wake up. And what the bloody hell did I think I was doing now?

''Sall right,' I muttered, closing my eyes and tucking my legs up to my chest. This was an old-fashioned, silky, squidgy eiderdown. Hadn't felt one like this since I was a kid. So cosy, so comforting. 'Don't worry. Jush leave me. Been enough trouble already.'

I think the last words I heard were: 'So much for cheese-and-onion sandwiches in the honeymoon suite.' Which didn't seem to make much sense and, since I was the drunk one, I assumed I'd imagined it.

I was in Paddy's bedroom. Obviously it was his room, because his valise stood by the door. There was a matching leather hanging bag draped across it now. Dinner jacket, I thought, and was dimly gratified at my own intelligence in working this out.

The curtains, long, drooping and threadbare, had been pulled back. The sky was lightening, just, with silvery streaks cracking the inky horizon outside tall, narrow stone windows. We were in one of the tower rooms, evidently. The air in here was so cold, I could see my breath rising.

Paddy had vanished off downstairs – to retrieve his coat, he'd said, and give me a chance to get up and sort myself out. Bathroom through that door, as I probably remembered. Sorry to hurry me, he'd added curtly, but he needed to be away by seven at the latest.

As an afterthought, before quitting the room, he'd unzipped his bag, yanked out a thick sweater and tossed it across the foot of the bed for me. I was dressed exactly as I had been last night, although someone seemed to have removed my shoes. I noticed them now, standing neatly side by side under a chair. There was something shockingly decadent about their spangly gold frailty in this bleak pre-dawn light, like a gin bottle on a milk float. Shivering, I hauled one leaden limb after another over the side of the bed and saw a potato-sized hole in one heel of my tights, and an obscenely wide ladder streaking up the other leg. God, how sordid this all was. As for my head – well, my head felt as though my brain had turned to a jellied football and was lolling free-range inside my skull, smashing into bone every time I moved. I also felt seasick, arthritic, feverish, hypothermic and generally within a couple of flimsy heartbeats of death.

I managed to propel myself as far as the bathroom, however, where the blue flowers etched in the handbasin triggered a fresh lurch of memory of my ghastly visage last night. Now I was careful to avoid the mirror as I scoured my mouth once again, and this time went on to wash the plastering of make-up off my face. Took a bit of doing, with mere soap and water, but I succeeded, and felt marginally the better for it. Risked the mirror. At least I now looked merely ready for interment, freshly deceased rather than three parts decomposed. I tottered back to the bedroom, tugged Paddy's huge sweater over my head, winced as I reinserted my feet into the crippling sandals and lowered myself carefully into a chair to await his return.

He hadn't been to bed. I could see that now. There was just one burrow under the covers where I had snored like a comatose newt for however long the night had lasted. The other side of the ancient, bowed couch was unruffled. No wonder he was so cross with me, if I'd deprived him of his sleep. Unless, that is, having tucked me up, he'd sneaked off to that Hetty woman? Tricky, with poor Hughie here, but nothing would surprise me now. Hetty Hough-Hartley, God what a tongue-twister, and even worse if it was short for... Henrietta? *Henrietta?* Paddy staring into space in my sitting room, talking about the love of Casanova's life – the love of *his* life? – who dutifully stuck by her boring, bourgeois husband...

He strode in wearing a waxed jacket, with black woolly wrap bundled under his arm. 'This yours? Thought it must be.'

I had to avert my face, sniffing furiously, and only then saw that a roll-top desk lay open beside one of the windows. A green-shaded brass lamp illuminated a blotting pad, with a sheaf of paper and envelopes to one side. Maybe he hadn't been creeping the corridors, after all. Looked as though he'd been writing, probably sorting stuff

out ready to quit the country. Quit the country...
I groped for my bag and a wad of tissue.

'Sorry I can't run to tea and so forth,' Paddy was saying, 'but I dare say you'll feel happier having your breakfast in comfort at home. Oh, don't pull faces like that. I find a bacon sandwich works wonders for the liver. Coming?'

I hoisted myself miserably to my feet. Took a deep breath. 'I'm sorry,' I said as I wound the wrap round my shoulders and teetered after him towards the door. 'Really, truly sorry. For everything.'

'Oh, but it's I who should be apologizing to you,' he retorted brightly, pulling the door to behind us, careful not to let it slam. 'I'm sure you'd have had much more fun last night if I hadn't so tactlessly barged in. Honeymoon suite, too, my word. He really was pushing the boat out, wasn't he?'

I was minding my high-heeled feet on the twisting stone steps, and since my sense of balance was not all it might be, I waited until we reached the foot of the spiral before asking what he thought he was talking about.

'Your friend, of course,' he retorted, striding off down the dimly lit passage without so much as a glance over his shoulder as I wobbled along in his wake. 'Although, hand on heart, I assure you that for once in my eavesdropping career it was quite by chance, when I came down to find some water for you, that I overheard him making the necessary arrangements into his mobile.'

'You mean' – I gulped, ashamed even to voice the name – 'Ricky Marvell?'

'Cheese-and-onion sandwiches featured. I thought that was a touch unworthy – smoked salmon at the least, one would think. Better still, oysters, if it isn't too much of a cliché.'

Swamped with mortification as I was after my shameless conduct last night, I didn't think Paddy need grind on quite so cruelly. 'I shouldn't have let it happen, I know,' I began, 'but–'

'Although he strikes one as the kind of chap to leave no cliché unturned. However, I dare say oysters might be tricky for even the smartest hotel to rustle up at midnight.'

'Hang on a minute,' I protested, 'he didn't book that hotel for me, you know.' We were in the entrance hall now, huge and sepulchrally shadowed, lit only by an ugly naked bulb dangling, presumably for safety reasons, above the doors. 'He'd fixed it before he came to the party last night.'

'One can only admire his optimism, then.'

'Look, Ricky may have thought... OK, he *did* invite me back to his hotel, but–'

'But you fell into my clutches instead. Only too literally.'

'I may have been disgustingly drunk,' I said stiffly, 'but when you found me here, I was about to ring my son.'

'Just to let him know that for all you were indeed heading for Wakeford, it wasn't actually to see his father?'

'*What?*' Was I mad or was he? 'I was ringing for a lift home.'

'Don't say you'd remembered at last you're a respectable married woman,' he snorted, sliding back the bolts on the door. 'No one would have guessed it last night.'

'Well, you're a *fine* one to talk,' I burst out, so loudly my words bounced round the vaulted roof and stone walls and Paddy spun back glaring, with a warning finger to his lips as he pulled open the door. I lowered my voice to a fierce whisper. 'Never mind about me, what about you and that Hetty?'

'Hell's teeth, you've torn it now. The bloody dog heard you.' And, indeed, an exuberant Jasper was hurtling across the stone flags, claws a-clatter, and had squeezed past the door and away before Paddy could shut it again. He let out a cry of exasperation. 'Another ten minutes and Seddons'll be down. He always goes into Jack around seven, and I can do without him weeping into my shoulder again, begging me not to desert the sinking ship. Let's just pray that godforsaken mongrel hasn't gone far.' He flung the door wide, chucked his bags through and then stepped back with an ironic flourish to let me pass into the dark and icy morning. 'And for your information,' he continued in a savage undertone, 'Hetty's an old girlfriend of Jack's whom I've known since schooldays. Never mind that she happens to be married to one of my oldest friends.'

'And that would stop you?' I cried, stung by his tone. 'I don't think so, lover boy. Not from what I've heard.'

He'd bent to pick up his bags, but at this he let them drop again and spun round. It was as though I'd hit him. Even in this half-light I could see the expression in his face, and it scared the wits out of me. But I saw something else, too, a snaking flicker of black and white, below in the forecourt.

'The dog,' I yelled, plunging forward and nearly plummeting headlong as my ankle gave way, but I made it down the steps upright, and wheeled back towards Jack's front door. 'Dora was here this morning, on heat.' I yelped as my vulnerable sandalled toes hit cruelly sharp gravel. 'Probably can still smell her. Come here, you little sod.'

Paddy pounded up behind me. 'At least *I'm* not married,' he snarled. 'Which is more than I can say for both you and your antique crooner.'

My head was thudding fit to bust, I'd twisted my ankle, I was cold to the marrow, with the worst hangover in my life and my hands locked round the neck of a wriggling, yapping spaniel who was clawing my shins along with Jack Bidcombe's door... I'd had *enough*.

'No,' I yelled, 'you just screw anything in a skirt – anything apart from me, that is.'

'I've been to bed with one woman and one woman only these past seven years,' he bellowed.

But I was still in full flight: 'And what's more, my marriage is over, and I wasn't going to any bloody hotel with Ricky *bloody* Marvell, but at least he wanted me, which is more than' – my voice was slowing down, the brain belatedly catching up – 'more than you do. What'd you just say?'

'Not want you?' cried Paddy. 'Not fucking *want* you?'

'*One* woman?' But I couldn't say anything more, because I was in his arms and he was kissing me. Kissing me? He was devouring me. And I was wrapping my arms, my whole body round his, as he cradled my face, kissing my eyes, my cheeks, my nose, asking was it true? Was I really leaving my husband?

I unglued myself a reluctant half-inch, gasping for breath to tell him yes, yes, it was all true, I was divorcing Mike and not least because I was madly, ludicrously, *schoolgirlishly* besotted with him, and that the only reason I'd wanted to die this morning was because he was going away – and very likely a great deal more along the same lines. But I uttered not a word. In the very instant of drawing my face away from his, I was distracted by a flicker of light in the crack between the curtains of Jack's flat. You might be pardoned for expressing amazement that an entire Millennial fireworks display could have caught my attention at that moment. It surprises me, too – but there was something unnatural about the light, the way it flared, vanished, then flashed back even more brilliantly.

'Sweetheart?' Paddy was still cupping my face in his hands, gazing down at me in seeming wonderment.

'I–' I love you. That was what, without any premeditation, I was about to say. The words had composed themselves in my head as naturally as my own name. Forget all this nonsense about infatuation not being the same as love, about grown-ups understanding these things, being in rational control of their emotions – I understood all right. I understood that I loved Paddy McGinty, heart, body and soul, simple as that, and I didn't have the least qualm about telling him so. Nevertheless...

'Thought I saw something,' I whispered, returning my gaze to his, about to resume where I'd left off, but then my nose twitched. 'Smell, what's that smell? God Almighty,' I shrieked, twisting out of his arms, 'there's a fire in there. Your cousin's flat. It's bloody well on fire.'

30

It all happened so quickly. The door was locked, but Paddy kicked it open and plunged through.

A lamp glowed in the far corner of the sitting room, barely visible through a black wall of stinking smoke, but I could see Jack. Slumped in his wheelchair in the middle of the room, still in evening dress, head lolling, mouth shockingly agape. I couldn't make out where the fire was, though, until a tongue of blue flame hissed across the seat of the chair beside him and – oh God, there was a whisky bottle overturned on the seat, a brimming ashtray, on the ugly old chair of his nanny's he'd wanted recovering... Before I could scream a warning, Paddy had grabbed the fire extinguisher by the door.

'Forget it,' I yelled, retching with the smoke. 'Fumes from that'll kill you–'

I was silenced by the crash. Paddy made no

attempt to douse the flames, just swung the heavy canister at a window, smashing out glass and frame together, then plucked up the burning chair by the front legs and hurled it through. A colony of rooks exploded in a shrieking cloud as it crashed to the gravel, brilliantly ablaze in the rush of air. He stepped back from the window, smacking a forearm where his jacket was smouldering, and dropped on one knee beside his cousin.

'Come on now, Jack.' He pressed his ear to the man's chest.

I crunched across the remains of whisky bottle and ashtray to retrieve the extinguisher, looking this way and that for flames. The smoke was melting fast in the icy draught, but you could still feel the stench reaming out your lungs. Two minutes, that's how fast it could kill you, the gas from old foam, *two minutes...* It was surely nothing short of a miracle we'd emerged from the castle when we did, that Jack was still alive – poor, drunken fool, leaving his fag to burn in a puddle of spilled Scotch, and on that chair of all places...

'Can't peg out on me now. Get you outside, eh? Climate's none too salubrious in here... Oh, to hell with this thing.' He was prodding the controls of the wheelchair. 'Battery must be flat.'

'Here, let me help.' Between us, we carried his cousin's long, limp body outside. Paddy flung his coat on the gravel. I bundled my wrap into a makeshift pillow.

'Sorry, but I have to get undesirably intimate here, coz.' Paddy pinched Jack's nostrils, covering his mouth with his own. 'Cleaned my teeth, promise.' For all the flippancy, his face was knotted with fear as he pressed his fingers into the crook of Jack's neck. With a sudden intake of breath, he locked his fists on the man's chest and gave three swift thrusts, before blowing again into his mouth. Three thrusts, blow. Three thrusts, blow. The rhythm was mesmeric, familiar from a hundred hospital dramas. I found I was praying – for Jack, yes, of course, but also for Paddy. You only had to look at him to see what this death would cost him.

I'm ashamed to say I was probably praying for myself, too. For a few seconds Paddy and I had been so extravagantly, exultantly happy, I couldn't bear that to dissolve into tragedy. Besides, Paddy had been right. I *did* like Cousin Jack. And I could scarcely take in that this frighteningly limp body was the man who only hours ago had been flirting with me, kissing my arm, urging me to eat, drink and be merry for tomorrow... I shook off my reverie with a shudder, shouted that I'd go and ring for an ambulance, and nearly tripped over Jasper who lay in the doorway of the flat, chewing my dropped handbag. Kicking the door shut to stop him following me across the glass-strewn floor, I picked a path to the phone. The receiver was already off the hook. Had Jack known what was happening, then? Rung for help because he couldn't move his chair? God, how terrible.

'That's right, *Stowham* Castle.' I tried not to curse as I had to spell it, spell my name, wait for the details to be recited back to me. I was looking ound, wincing at the horribly blackened patch of tiles where the chair had burned – lucky it was a stone floor. But in a room plentifully supplied with small tables, and squarely solid dining chairs, why did the stupid sod have to balance his drink and his overflowing ashtray on the lumpy padded seat of that old chair? Had he got a death wish or something?

'No, doesn't seem to be anything alight, even though the smell's appalling. But it's the ambulance we need – urgently.' Outside, Paddy had stopped the cardiac thumps, but his head was still locked over his cousin's. 'Thank you – thank you, yes.'

I crashed the phone down, but I didn't go outside at once. Silly detail, but somewhere at the back of my mind, I'd noticed that the newspapers and books which had been piled everywhere yesterday morning seemed to have vanished. And now I came to look, surely the furniture had been adjusted too, shoved away towards the walls? Moreover, why had Jack chosen to park himself alongside his nanny's chair in splendid isolation there, slap bang in the middle of an otherwise empty floor?

I was interrupted by a quavering howl of anguish from outside.

'Paddy?' I yelled, running out. 'My God, what is it?'

But Paddy, with pale zig-zags of sweat streaking his sooty face, was still crouched over his cousin. The wail had come from Albert Seddons, although it was Hughie I saw first, in a crimson quilted dressing gown, with his arm clasped awkwardly round a grey-faced, hunched old man I barely recognized.

'I knew it,' gasped the butler, shoulders heaving. '*Knew* he was up to one of his mad games. I said to him, whatever it is, Mr Jack, don't do it. And I was so relieved when he rang just now, as usual, because all last night I was worrying myself senseless, and even though he asked me to bring Mr Paddy down to give him a hand, I never thought–'

'Course you didn't, old chap. You found me instead, anyway.' Hugh turned his head towards me. 'What happened?'

One eye on Jack's inert form, I explained, waving towards the smouldering remains as I thanked God Paddy had managed to chuck the noxious thing outdoors before we were all gassed. 'No, his nanny's,' I added, when Seddons, squinting at the pyre, asked if it was the gardener's old chair. 'Mustard-coloured, wooden arms...'

'His *nanny?*' cut in Hugh blankly.

'It *is* – it's that dreadful old thing from the potting shed he made me bring in,' cried the butler. He looked from the smoking remains to the figure on the ground, and his face crumpled. 'Oh, Mr Jack, what have you *done?*'

'But it was an accident,' I began. 'Anyone could see how it happened. And you said he'd rung for you as usual, so...' I faltered, because I remembered Jack joking – *joking?* – about the nine minutes whatever it took the butler to get down to his flat.

'Dear heaven, no,' muttered Hugh, shutting his

eyes. 'Such a horrible, *horrible* way to do it... No, not possible. Dammit, could've burned all of us in our beds.'

'But he'd cleared away all his papers,' I heard myself saying, 'rearranged the furniture...' I even began to wonder about that spanking new fire extinguisher, left prominently by the door – but then Seddons started forward with a cry, and I saw that Paddy had ceased the respirations, was holding his cousin, with tears shining on his sooty cheeks.

'*No...*' breathed Hugh.

'Oh, love,' I whispered.

But he was shaking his head, smiling. 'Breathing under his own steam.' He pressed a forearm to his filthy, sweaty forehead. 'Pulse whacking away like a steam hammer, too. Can't kill the bugger so easily.' All at once, he leaned forward intently. 'What was that, coz? You back with us again?'

Jack's body heaved with a violent storm of coughing, but when it subsided, his eyes opened and focused blearily on Paddy. '*Fuck,*' he croaked, which even surprised a tearful hiccup of laughter out of Seddons.

'Hush,' murmured his cousin, 'don't try to talk.'

Jack shook his head fiercely, labouring with every breath. 'Accident,' he rasped. 'If I peg out, tell 'em – *accident.*'

'Of course it was an accident, old friend,' said his cousin calmly.

And of course, as we all knew for certain then, it had been nothing of the kind.

The man was superb. Extrarordinary. Just like I'd always said, unreal.

'Am I right in remembering Madam doesn't take sugar in tea?'

No longer the frail, hunched figure of a minute ago, this was Seddons again, epitome of dignified imperturbability, even if he was clad – now I came to notice such irrelevancies – in cardigan and flannel trousers rather than the customary black coat and pinstripes.

'What?' I said stupidly, before feeling duty-bound to aspire to his standards of conduct. 'I mean, yes. Thank you. Tea would be, um, most welcome.'

'I shall ask my sister to add a tot of brandy, if that is acceptable. I myself, meanwhile, will locate blankets and pillows for Mr Jack, although we must trust the ambulance will arrive shortly.'

'Take Mrs Patterson inside with you,' called Paddy. 'Bloody freezing out here and she's next to nothing on.'

He knew I wouldn't go, of course. I squatted on the bottom step, arms wrapped round my knees while he sat on the ground with Jack supported across his lap. I felt dizzy with gratitude, drunk with happiness and helpless with love all at once. Hughie, who'd stumped over to the gates to scan the horizon for ambulances, returned just as Paddy looked up from his cousin and smiled across at me. His friend, blushing as crimson as his dressing gown, averted his eyes and asked if, um, if Jack really was all right.

'Not dead.' It was Jack who'd unexpectedly

grunted this, although he hadn't opened his eyes. 'Not yet.'

'Despite your best endeavours,' said Paddy evenly.

'Come, come,' expostulated Hugh. 'Can't believe old Jacko really meant... I mean, pity's sake, whole place could've gone up in smoke.'

'Oh, he did his utmost to prevent that,' said my friend. 'Didn't you, old chap? Tell me, was my role just to stop Seddons attempting any heroics and summon the fire brigade, or were you expecting me to square the insurers, as well? Although you could hardly have laid things out more clearly for them, short of pinning a storyboard to the wall. I've been doing my sums, too. I calculate you had three lawyers, two JPs, a retired Brigadier and the Deputy Lieutenant of the County to testify you were chirpy as a canary on the night in question, any verdict other than accident inconceivable. Astonishingly dim of me not to smell a rat, really, with that bizarre assembly of guests.' He glanced round. 'Is that a siren?'

Jack's eyes had opened, but he said nothing, although I'd swear a ghost of amusement flickered in his eyes when a profoundly shocked Hughie stuttered that Paddy surely couldn't be implyin' this had been, you know, an insurance scam? Since neither of the cousins answered, he demanded indignantly to know how on earth Jack could have got life insurance in his state of health.

'Had it for years,' said Paddy. 'Kat made him take it out when Daisy was born.'

Jack stared defiantly at him a moment longer, then his eyes fell. 'Better odds than bookies,' he wheezed. 'Worth enough to – tide this place over.'

'Oh God, coz...' There was a crack in Paddy's voice now as he brushed the hair away from his cousin's forehead. 'Haven't you pulled enough mad pranks in your life?'

'Look, I'm–' His voice splintered into painfully hacking coughs again as the ambulance with lights flashing and siren shrieking erupted through the gates and swirled to a halt a few yards away. A green boiler-suited paramedic scrambled out and came racing across the gravel.

Jack grabbed a handful of Paddy's sweater and hoisted himself up a few inches. 'Look, just in case–'

The paramedic dropped to one knee beside them. 'Best not to talk, chum.' He craned round. 'What's his name?' He didn't seem perturbed by the invalid growling at him to piss off.

'Listen, Paddy, I'm sorry. Want to tell you–'

'Hush, old friend. There's nothing for you to be sorry about.' Paddy spoke so quietly, I barely caught his words, and even then didn't understand, because as another ambulance man bustled up with stretcher and oxygen cylinder, he seemed to be telling Jack that it was for *him* to apologize. He was insisting, in a rapid undertone, that he knew he could never make amends, that he couldn't even honestly say he was sorry for what he'd done, but that he regretted betraying Jack, bitterly regretted it, and could never have forgiven himself if Jack had died like this, after–

'Balls,' roared the man hoarsely, veins standing out on his forehead as he shoved aside the proffered oxygen mask and fought for breath. 'I meant sorry for – for not topping myself years back. Should've done. For both your sakes.'

Paddy was going to the hospital with his cousin. Of course I could drive myself home, I said, if he trusted me with his newly repaired motor. We were sorting out these mundane practicalities – luggage, car keys, the whereabouts of my well-chewed handbag – as though nothing remarkable had happened, as though our entire world wasn't spinning on a giddy pivot of bliss. While they loaded Jack's stretcher into the ambulance, I sipped my tea and Paddy rustled through his wallet. He would, he said, get a taxi back to Beck Holme from the hospital, as soon as he felt he could leave Jack. Not that he doubted the idiot would pull through, but...

'You and he have things to talk about,' I offered. And it wasn't a question.

Paddy's smile flickered gratefully. 'Hard to put a time on it.'

'Whenever,' I said.

'Whenever,' he echoed.

We just stood there like fools, gazing at one another in wondering silence, while yellow-wellied firemen stomped hither and thither round us. When there was everything to say, it seemed there was nothing to be said at all. Paddy touched my arm lightly by way of farewell, turned to climb into the ambulance, then halted, clapping a hand to his head and wheeling back towards me.

'Lord, I'd better give you this.' From the pocket of his charred jacket, he extracted an envelope inscribed with my name. 'Spent most of last night writing the thing. Long overdue, although...' He shrugged. 'Well, much of it seems to have been overtaken by events.' His smile glimmered brilliantly again. 'I hope so, at any rate. But you should have it, nevertheless.'

I had a fairish idea what the letter might tell me, but I caught his arm. There was a question I had to ask. '*One* woman?' I whispered. 'These past seven years?'

He smiled wryly. 'She was married, too.'

Of course she was.

31

In the low-slung driving seat of Paddy's car, I ripped open the envelope and shuffled through seven – no, eight – sheets filled with handwriting, a comfortably square script in broad-nibbed black ink. I actually read the signature first. *Your good friend, Paddy McGinty.* My good friend. Flipping backwards, I knew the name I was looking for, knew I would find it across page after page, and of course I did – *Katharine.* Katharine this, Katharine that. Often just Kat. With a faint smile, I remembered Paddy's delirious mumblings after his car crash, when I'd supposed he was worrying about a pet moggy.

'Oh my good friend,' I murmured, and peered at the clock on the dashboard, wondering how much time I had to get home and boot my son out of bed. I'd need to change, first. There were shocks a-plenty coming Ben's way about his mother, and it seemed kinder not to let him find her tottering around in laddered tights and a party frock at eight-thirty in the morning. Even so, I couldn't turn the ignition key. I had to go back to the beginning of the letter and read a bit – just a bit.

My dear Jo,
I don't know how to begin. Absurd, because I've had masses of practice. I must have begun at least six letters to you this past week, and not got past the first fence on any. Habit of secrecy, you see. It's so ingrained that spilling the beans becomes like tearing out one's own toenails. Doesn't help that you're lying ten feet away, curled into my bed like a drunken dormouse. The temptation to shake you out of your stupor to ask what the hell you thought you were doing tonight is well nigh overwhelming. But I'm putting pen to paper to explain my own behaviour, not question yours. I have to, because there was a moment this evening, when you looked so hurt after making some pifflingly innocent remark about our being friends and neighbours, it seemed the only decent course for me was to withdraw to the library and shoot myself. How should you realize that the notion of living across the hill from you, sharing the odd companionable G & T, would be for me the most exquisite torture imaginable? As it was, after concluding I was unlikely to survive even the starter

without flinging myself at your spangled toes or blubbing into your shoulder, I adjusted the seating for dinner – and look what happened. One might say your flitting off with Mr Marvell would have been no more than I deserved, but I can't quite bring myself to believe you'd have fallen into his arms sober.

Lord, you're probably cringing already. As far as you're concerned, I'm just your good friend. But I fear the plain, sad truth is I want – wanted – to be much more than that. I think I've known from the moment you marched into the office and found me playing with spy toys. I acquit myself of folly then, I was drunk. Refreshing to cite blood-alcohol levels in one's defence, eh? And when I offered to buy Beck Holme, I can claim real enough sentimental motives in mitigation, even if at some unacknowledged level, I was probably looking for a ploy to come and see you. By the time I was staying in your cottage, though, the excuses ran out. I knew exactly what I wanted, knew I couldn't have it, and that I was making the situation infinitely worse for myself with every day that passed. God knows what would have happened if your son hadn't come home – although, naturally, I know what I wanted to happen. I'd like to think I might have resisted the temptation to embarrass us both – such a respectable married woman as you are, Mrs Patterson – but I doubt it. And I sensed, if you'll forgive such an outrageously sweeping assumption, that your loneliness and liking for me might just have led you to do something you'd regret. Still, we were saved from ourselves, and when I say that, you may be surprised to hear I mean myself as much as you. Perhaps even more than you.

The point, if you haven't already guessed, is that for

many years I was the shadowy third party in someone else's marriage, and if there's one thing I know for sure, it's that I could not, under any circumstances, bear to find myself in that position again...

And now I understood – I understood so much. I carefully folded the letter away and set off for home. Over the moor I was driving east, into a vast morning sky, navy clouds split by bands of gold, shifting and brightening with every second that passed, as a brilliantly white sun surged aloft. I felt I was driving into the rest of my life.

I was to read and reread Paddy's letter throughout the day. Covertly behind a cereal packet, as my cloudy-eyed son shovelled down breakfast. As I walked a restive Dora a token few yards up the lane – not so far that the house was ever out of view, because who could tell when Paddy would return? I studied it, careful not to smudge the ink, in the bath. I even sneaked the odd glance while sitting at my dressing table, repairing my hungover face with a dab of make-up. Not last night's multi-layered warpaint, just first aid for the mature skin. My hair didn't look nearly as ravaged as I deserved. In fact, once I'd pulled on clean jeans and dug out my best sweater – cream cashmere and comfortingly soft as a kitten's belly – I could have looked a damn sight worse. I didn't suppose Paddy would give a hoot, but I felt a sense of occasion. Since this was shaping up to be the happiest day of my life, a certain effort seemed to be called for. But the glow in the face beaming dizzily back at me out of the mirror didn't come from a pot, and was worth a week at a health farm, a facelift and a bucketload of Botox all rolled into one. May not last, may put you through hell on the way, but there's nothing like love to take years off a girl.

Still, this is to jump ahead. At a quarter to nine, temporarily packaged in a tracksuit, I was yanking the duvet off my sleeping son and being informed, in stentorian if sleep-fogged tones, that I must have got home *very* late last night.

'Uhuh,' I said. 'Only just fallen through the door, in fact. That was because I fought off the advances of an ageing rock idol while dodging low-flying garments from a stripper; got disgustingly drunk; threw up over the stately parapets; passed out cold in a strange four-poster – alone – and was temporarily delayed in the early hours by fire, police and ambulance, after saving Stowham Castle from burning to the ground. Whereupon I drove home at reckless speed in a hi-jacked sports car, resolving to change my entire life forthwith...' I fell silent for an instant as I realized, dazedly, I was speaking nothing less than the truth here. The days of sheltering in a rut had gone. I'd left the rut behind the day I moved up here, and I was never going back. I had, as my husband himself had once so memorably put it, seen over the horizon. And how. I smiled. 'Other than that, pretty average sort of party.'

'Very funny,' grunted Ben, his suspicious scowl lifting.

Which all goes to show that, when dealing with children, honesty is *always* the best policy.

400

'Breakfast in ten minutes,' I said.

...you must be wondering how such decent, upstanding chaps as Katharine and I could dream of embarking on an affair under the circs. No easy answer, I fear, because neither of us looked for excuses. It wasn't an act of revenge, for sure, although Jack could have been forgiven for thinking otherwise, had he known about us – which he didn't, thank heaven, not while Katharine was alive.

I hate to rake up sordid and long-dead history, but I suppose I'll have to explain that my wife, Tara's, first extra-marital peccadillo was with none other than the handsome coz. I didn't know this at the time, of course, although if I'd hadn't been so busy stamping and ranting I might have wondered at Jack's unusual good sense in urging me not to snoop out the sordid details, but to let sleeping wives lie. Or lying wives sleep, as he cheerfully put it. Anyway, by the time I did learn the truth, my marriage was long dissolved and I'd come to accept had probably been destined for disaster from the start. But it was Katharine who told me the identity of Tara's grand passion, after she turned up an old love letter from my ex-wife to her husband – and she was devastated. Not, one has to admit, that this was Jack's first extra-marital adventure – well, you've met him: the fidelity gene's generally missing from the DNA of men like Jack. I once read an article about Alpha Male lions, feeling duty-bound to cover every female for miles. Reminded me quite uncannily of my cousin. Still, that's neither here nor there. Katharine may have suspected there were other women and managed to forgive or pretend – but for him to betray me? His cousin, partner, oldest friend? The blackest irony was that I actually persuaded her to say nothing, and forgive him for the sake of her children. As I told her – and I can still remember saying this – a fling like that would have meant nothing to Jack. He would never willingly jeopardize his marriage, he was just a spoiled child, he did truly love Katharine.

Do you know, to my astonishment, I'm actually finding it the most enormous relief to write all this? After so many years of guarding every word and memorizing a running inventory of lies, telling the simple truth is blessedly cathartic. Bore for you to read, I'm afraid, but – for friendship's sake – bear with me. Where was I? Oh yes, the letter. Our relationship didn't actually begin then. We'd always been close, however, and after that I suppose we just grew closer. And while there's no denying that the knowledge of our respective partners' infidelity made it that much easier for us to cross the line, the guilt was still excruciating. However, there was no question of our letting the sordid triangle continue for long. Kat and I recognized almost from the outset that we wanted to be together for good, so it was simply a matter of waiting for the right moment to break the news. But Jack's mother was terminally ill, then Daisy was changing schools – there seemed to be all manner of excellent reasons for delay, as I suspect there usually are in situations like this. Then, of course, before we'd finally steeled ourselves to do the dreadful deed, you know what happened. Jack decided to bet on his aerial cycling skills...

Hunched at one end of the kitchen table, I caught my breath as I tried to imagine myself in

Katharine's situation. I glanced at Ben, but he was spooning up cereal, seemingly engrossed in his motorcycle magazine, so I read on. No, of course the poor woman hadn't felt able to abandon her husband then, particularly as he seemed at first unlikely even to survive for very long. He'd suffered one complication or infection after another, endured interminable operations. And when it became clear he was going to live?

...perhaps the most distressing thing for Katharine, although she was an entirely rational creature, was that she felt in part responsible. She'd always been the restraining influence on her husband, and for all he kicked and cavilled, Jack seemed to need her firm hand on the reins. It was as though, subconsciously, he depended on her to step in and save him from himself. Forgive me, but from certain remarks you've let slip, I think perhaps you understand this rather well. Katharine used to say it was like having three children, only two of whom were ever likely to grow up. And with the family and a huge mortgage in town, you can see why she insisted on substantial life insurance once Jack left the relative security of the army.

However, after she and I came together, she found she no longer cared what follies he was committing, and left him to his own devices. Of course she couldn't possibly have predicted what happened – which would doubtless have happened even if she'd been at Stowham with her husband that night. But she wasn't. She was in London, in my bed, and her sense of guilt, along with Jack's pitifully increased need of her now, and her children – well, I'm sure you can

403

understand why she felt unable to quit immediately. So we postponed it, waiting for the day she felt she could break away. But as Jack's health improved, his depression darkened and the suicide threats began. Whether he would have harmed himself if she'd left, I don't know, but that's what hung over her. I suppose we hoped something would happen to end the impasse – God knows what, because even at my most wretched I could never wish for Jack's death. Anyway, miracles weren't forthcoming, months stretched into years and somehow we just blundered murkily on...

As I read about the subterfuges to which they had been reduced, I could feel Paddy's shame in every line. Small wonder he'd talked to me with distaste about his long experience of lying. Their lives, he said, had been a soul-corroding tapestry of deceit. Even Katharine's job in London was a sham, a means not just of spending time with Paddy, but of his subsidizing the upbringing of her children by paying her a larger salary than even a publishing house could have afforded – which was also why he couldn't quit his own profession. And the parade of girlfriends he shipped up to Stowham at weekends was for the benefit of Jack and his father. 'Window dressing' as my friend Gil said of the ladies he'd occasionally felt obliged to wheel home for tea with Mum. At the castle itself, Paddy said he and Katharine had always observed the proprieties. But when Beck Holme wasn't occupied by a holiday tenant, or in the weekend change-over between lets...

I looked round the kitchen with new eyes. My

God. This had been their haven – no wonder she'd wanted to buy it back. Jealous? Of course I wasn't jealous. I'd spent half my life with another man, and I was fiercely glad she and Paddy had found some kind of consolation. What must it have been like for my friend, though, coming back here with me that first night? Perhaps he'd been too groggy to care. Besides, as he'd observed later, the place looked very different now...

'Uh, Mum?' piped up Ben, unusually tentatively.

'In a minute. Have you gathered up your stuff from the bathroom yet? No, well go and do it.'

...once Jack sold Beck Holme, though, life became more complicated. I won't insult your intelligence by telling you why we were parked in that secluded lay-by on the night Kat died, but it wasn't to enable me to take over the wheel, still less to answer a call of nature. Both of which stories I somehow dredged out of a grief-frozen brain while I sat holding the hand I could just reach, waiting for the police. She was dead – died instantly, blessedly, can't have known anything about it. The truly unbearable thing in the days and weeks that followed was that I wasn't allowed to grieve, although on the night itself – God, the awful unreality of it all – one of the firemen cutting open the car handed me Kat's dog. Poor little Floss had been on her lap and was done for. But at least, because I was holding this dying animal, I could weep buckets, and such is the crazy English attitude to dogs, no one wondered at it. I think perhaps I'd have gone mad otherwise. Jasper is Floss's pup, incidentally, which is why Bernard tolerates the fiend, for Katharine's sake.

405

What was cruel in the long term, though, was having to face the idea that Kat was killed by our own obsessive precautions. She never wore scent when she was with me, but I, nevertheless, was walking around outside so that the wind could blast away any possible traces. And she'd climbed into the passenger seat where there was a light over the mirror to repair her make-up. She was meticulous that night because Daisy was at home, and they'd had a confrontation just before she set out. Totally out of the blue, Daisy had demanded to know whether she was in love with me, and Kat, perhaps because she'd been caught unawares, perhaps because she was sick of all the shoddy pretences, found she couldn't tell an outright lie. But she wouldn't compromise me, so she fudged it somehow, and thought she'd convinced Daisy that it was just a passing infatuation, all on her own side. She obviously underrated her daughter's intelligence, because Daisy has made clear ever since that she doesn't want anything to do with me. I can't blame her any more than I blame Jack, who was evidently not as gullible as his father or the police about my explanations for pulling up in that lay-by. No fool, my cousin.

I doubt he'll ever forgive me – why should he? – but I'd like to think that one day I'll be able to explain to Daisy…

'Ben?' I yelled, 'Come back here. I want a word with you. *Now.*'

32

'OK, OK, cool it, Mum,' said Ben, advancing no more than one wary pace into the kitchen. 'I'm sorry. It was stupid of me. Juvenile and stupid.'

'What was?'

He stared at me. 'Well, like, what's the fuss about?'

'Your friend Daisy,' I said firmly. 'No, don't clam up on me, I don't want to pry, truly, but you've got to tell me why she's so screwed up about her Uncle Paddy.'

'Peter,' he said slowly. 'She always calls him Uncle Peter.' A flush crept into his cheeks. 'For why?'

'Because I've a feeling she might have misread certain things. Look, cards on the table. I know she asked her mother about – well, about her feelings for Paddy.'

He eyed me, chewing his lip, patently debating whether he could share the precious secrets of his heart with his antique parent. 'It was really awful for Daze,' he offered at length. 'God, I mean *now* I really understand how she must've felt. I said to her last night, when I was telling her about you and him, I–'

'Last night?' I yelped, looking round, half expecting the girl to materialize from the sitting room.

'On the phone, Mother,' he squawked, soprano

407

with embarrassment.

'You've been ringing the States? And talking about *me?*'

'Well, it's the same all over again, isn't it?' he retorted. 'I mean, when Daze first told me, ages ago, about how her mother'd been completely obsessed with this guy, I didn't get it. You know, so what? It wasn't like she blamed her mum, just felt sorry for her, with her dad being how he is. But her Uncle Peter obviously knew and didn't give a toss–'

'*What?*'

'Oh, come on. OK, OK, so Daisy's mother was pretty old and that, but it was the way he kept bringing all his girlfriends up to their house – you know, like he was flaunting them? Daze reckoned it must've been crucifying her. That's why she had a go, told her she should stop being a wimp and tell the bastard to piss off from Stowham. Only that was the last thing she ever said to her before she died, a huge row, with her mum in tears and everything – so, sure, she was mad at him, because it was all his fault.' Ben heaved a sigh and eyed me defiantly. 'She did actually say last night she thinks she might've overreacted, but I told her she'd every right. I mean, look what he's done to you.'

I shut my eyes for a moment. Children, I thought, who'd have 'em? And Daisy wasn't even Paddy's daughter.

'She's got it wrong,' was all I said to Ben. 'Don't ask me how, she'll have to sort it out herself with her uncle.' I heard a sound and leaned towards the window. 'Looks like your

408

friend's here.' I bobbed forward to kiss him. Much though I doted on his every golden hair, I couldn't wait to be rid of my son at this moment. I wanted a house with only me in it for Paddy to come back to.

'That it?' he squeaked, sounding both startled and curiously relieved. 'OK, fine. Guess I'll be seeing you in Wakeford, then.'

'Wakeford? Oh, you mean the show. Well, maybe, eh?' In his dreams. But it wasn't the time to open that can of worms with my son.

I should have been suspicious, of course, when he enveloped me in a crushingly warm hug. But he'd roared off up the hill and I was rereading the concluding pages of Paddy's letter before I finally found out just what my beloved child had been up to.

I'd skipped over this section during my first hasty scan, because it was largely to do with Jack. Paddy explained that any idea of his coming up to live at Stowham was unthinkable, as I could obviously appreciate, still more so Bernard's loopy if well-meaning scheme of his buying the estate outright. He'd already appropriated Jack's wife – was he now to assume his birthright, too? He could only hope his uncle would accept the loan, and that Jack might be persuaded to take over the running of the place.

Because he does seem anxious to give the impression he's re-entering the world, with talk of holidays and that ghastly jamboree tonight. He organized it himself, you know, keeping the household quite in the dark about the scale of the thing until the eleventh hour – but at least he's paying for it, according to a bemused Bernard. I hadn't the heart to tell him Grandpapa's Purdey probably footed the bills, because I can't imagine where else the money came from. Why, though? Much as I'd like to believe the coz is finding a purpose in life again, something smells wrong. Hetty and I were talking about it tonight, and she agrees with her husband. She thinks Jack's plotting, too, and she knows him as well as any of us. Something illegal, immoral or just plain crackpot, she said – or very likely all three, knowing Jack. One's heart rather sinks...

I shivered at the prescience, then read on.

And I can't imagine why he was insistent I should grace the event, because he still doesn't speak to me. I doubt I'd have agreed, actually, if I hadn't telephoned you and got the impression from Ben it was tonight you were off to Wakeford

'What?' I squeaked.

to see your husband's musical. Obviously when you turned up at the castle I realized I must have slightly misunderstood him, but not – sadly – you, when you told me that finding out about the show had changed everything for you.

The letter dropped from my hands.
'Well, strike me dead,' I said, 'the little bastard.' And stomped up to my bath.

In the hours that followed, though, it was the last

page of his letter that I returned to, foggy-eyed. The part where he said he couldn't regret the ten days he'd spent with me; that, for the first time since Katharine died, he'd felt happy – truly happy. It had begun to seem there was a point to life outside a bottle, might even be a point to Paddy McGinty himself.

So the idea of actually helping you to patch up your marriage was pretty appalling. And even while I never doubted that the answer to your company's misfortunes lay with your husband, I didn't want to be the one who told you so. It's well known that the messenger is rarely forgiven for the bad news. There's a part of me, then, that's almost glad this was no common-or-garden alimony-dodging scam, and that Mr Patterson has just – at long last – been getting his show on the road. At the very least, one has to take one's hat off to the chap for sustained effort. I did half wonder if something of the sort was afoot when I stumbled across those Newhouse Productions files – you know, with the Italian for 'new' and 'house' being nova *and* casa, *etc. I forgot to ask if you'd made the connection.*

None the less, it's unfortunate – concludes your correspondent with positively heroic self-restraint – that the resolving of the great Optimax mystery may also prove to be the resolving of your marital problems. I can't bring myself to ask outright if you think you and he will get back together, still less can I ask you to leave him for my sake. I was painfully vulnerable when I met you, and I dare say I'm being foolish to build so much on a friendship. Well, of course I am. But, somehow, in you, I felt as though I'd met

411

more than a friend, I'd found a twin soul.

And that's why, crazily, in the face of all the excellent evidence to the contrary, I can't help cherishing a tiny thread of hope that you might yet decide against your marriage. Might even want to give me a try. But I have to leave that to you. What this tedious scrawl must have made clear is why I couldn't bear any messy compromises, our embarking on an affair, while you made your choice. Don't think I'm being prissily moral – I'm afraid I wouldn't give a stuff about cuckolding your husband – this is pure selfishness. I spent seven years in that shadowy half-life of hope, lies and guilt, and it damn near destroyed what I laughingly call my soul. I couldn't go through it again.

So, I'm off to pastures new – actually more of a desert, although I'm reliably assured that snakes, at least, are scarce. It will be good, not to say novel, to find myself doing something genuinely useful. And one hundred per cent legal. And even, one might say, moral.

Thank you once again for everything.

Just my luck to fall for another respectable married woman.

I'm re-reading this for the fiftieth time, and it's still filling my throat with tears, when – at long, long last – I think I detect the growl of a car coming down the hill. I've lost track of time, but it must be mid-afternoon, because the wintry sun is melting down towards the horizon. Stifling a twinge of worry that he's late because the news from the hospital is bad, I toss aside his letter, run to the front door and fling it wide.

And I'm beaming and waving because, sure enough, a car is nosing down the hill between the faded banks of brambles, the drifts of coppery leaves... Only now I blink, frown, and have to shield my eyes against the sun that is casting its warm forgiving rays over me because I don't believe this – *won't* believe this – tell myself this can't be happening. My dream coming true? But it's the old dream, the wrong dream – jeepers creepers, this dream's now my worst imaginable nightmare. With a sick plunge in the stomach, I've recognized the all-too-familiar car, the dent in the right wing where I fell foul of a supermarket trolley. And the bloody vehicle does indeed jerk to a halt with a squeal indicating that the dodgy brake-pad still needs attention.

I'm even prettied-up in make-up, with newly streaked hair, plucked eyebrows, painted fingernails – every last planned detail is present and correct. But this isn't the gracious smile of a domestic goddess stretching my lips, it's a frozen rictus of horror, as my husband throws open the driver's door and falls out – yes, he does, he flops sideways, even more bonelessly than I'd envisaged. And, boy oh boy, doesn't he look older? Never mind the lines knotting his forehead, there are bruised bags under his red-rimmed eyes; that ridiculously cropped hair is one hundred per cent dingy grey now and there are shining streaks of tears on his cheeks ... *tears?*

'Oh, my love,' he gasps. 'Oh Jo, I've fucked everything. What am I going to do?'

The domestic goddess doesn't hold out her conveniently manicured hands. She flings them up with a wail of anguish. Which he doesn't understand, and anyway, it's too late. He's wrapped his arms round her, and he's sobbing his desolate, humiliated and altogether repentant heart into her fluffy white shoulder.

Cue music, applause – curtains?

PART FIVE

'Once we are parted by fate, my best and only friend, never enquire after me, and, should chance throw you in my way, do not appear to know me...'

Letter to the author from 'Henriette', Giacomo Casanova, *History of My Life*

33

There's a full house, at any rate. Barely an empty seat that I can see in this dingy, underlit auditorium with its balding velvet, tarnished gilt and peeling flock wallpaper. What a dump. Mind, it doesn't help that a cheaply varnished, bleakly square wooden frame has been fitted over the Edwardian proscenium arch by some 1960s barbarian. The result reminds me of nothing so much as a canteen dining hatch. I've never before set foot in the Grand Theatre, Wakeford, but I feel I have. It's every other neglected, one-step-from-the-bulldozers local theatre I've ever found myself in, chasing Mike's dreams. Not that any of his long-ago summer shows compared in scale to this. There's an eleven-piece band in the pit. I've counted them, and, while the cast list in the programme may not be of *Les Mis* length, I know enough about Equity rates to estimate the production should bankrupt him within a fortnight. Maybe a bit longer if they manage any more houses as full as this. I suppose Ricky Marvell will pull in a few fans – why, after all, are my party here? Not because they're interested in the grand world première of a new musical by Patterson and Steele, that's for sure.

I didn't take my paid-for seat on the coach, I drove myself here, but I am nevertheless sitting with the ladies of Stowham. I haven't mentioned to them that there's a chair standing empty for me somewhere up in one of those gilt-edged boxes, and I'm doing my utmost not to look in that direction. Sarah and Ben will be there, with whoever they've dragged along to support them. Half their respective universities very like, because their dad was apparently dishing out free tickets like confetti. I prefer not to speculate what fraction of tonight's audience might actually have paid for their seats. Sarah spotted me across the crowded foyer as we arrived, and I gave her a swift wave, just so she could report I'd turned up to do my wifely duty, but I'm avoiding my family, have been avoiding them assiduously all week. Avoiding the whole world, to be honest. I wish I could have avoided myself. I've been bloody awful company.

There's comfort now, though, in being surrounded by these commonsensical Yorkshire voices, with Eileen clucking over me, telling me I'm still looking peaky, and shoving the box of Black Magic my way. She and her sister Megan are giddy as a couple of schoolgirls tonight, not least because the Brighouses' future, along with that of the estate, is now secure. But the whole party is twittering with excitement like a pen full of pheasant poults – and there's a good rural metaphor for you. I haven't the heart to tell them they're about to see a turkey. I'm so glad to be sitting with them, though. It's bad enough to suffer this with people who don't realize the author of the disaster is still named in your diary as your next of kin. It would be well nigh unbearable amongst loved ones sharing your agonies of embarrassment. However, as the band stops tuning and twiddling, and the house lights begin to dim, I suddenly realize that, even away from my kids, I can't do it. I simply cannot bear to witness this fiasco. It'd be like watching a motorway pile-up for light entertainment. I spring up, muttering an excuse to Eileen about my flu. This isn't wholly untrue. I've been laid low all week with a milder dose of Ben's malady, although it was as nothing to my other afflictions. Blundering into knees and handbags with whispered apologies, I reach the aisle just as the band strikes up. I recognize the tune, and wince. Not that it's bad. Mike could always spin a pretty melody. But he never did twig that there's a lot more to a musical than a string of pretty tunes...

Five minutes later, I'm hunched over something calling itself a cappuccino in the greasiest of greasy spoon cafés across the rain-lashed street. It's the kind of plastic-plant, Formica table and tinfoil-ashtray joint you always find across the road from rundown theatres, much patronized before curtain-up by sweaty stagehands wolfing back the statutory barrowloads of cholesterol. It's called the Ritzy, would you believe, with a flashing lime-green and sugar-pink neon sign in the steamy window spelling this out. I feel I've been transported into a 1960s French movie. Paddy would appreciate the atmospheric scene setting – oh, God, *Paddy* – rainy night, seedy café, wail of piped music, lone woman moodily stirring her coffee. I should be smoking. *Merde*, if there were a packet of Gauloises to hand, I *would* be smoking. I can't even weep any more. I'm wept-out, worn-out and washed-up and if God felt inclined to strike me down now, I wouldn't argue.

Ten minutes must have passed before I realize I've been stirring salt into my coffee. I don't even take sugar. Mike always used to. Seems he doesn't any more.

I did, in the end, give him a mug of coffee, although I wouldn't even allow him to set foot across the threshold at first. I blocked the doorway while he bawled his eyes out, and I scanned the hill for another car. I was praying now that Paddy wouldn't arrive, that he'd be delayed long enough for me to get rid of my husband. Agitated as I was, though, I couldn't find it in me to order this sobbing wreck straight back into his car. The state he was in, he'd probably crash before he reached the ford.

Gaynor had dumped him. That was the first thing I learned. They were through, finished, caput. She'd phoned him from Gil's yesterday lunchtime, from the funeral party no less, and given him the big heave-ho. 'Don't say anything,' mumbled Mike, not that I was going to. He gulped. ''Sall right. Had to happen sooner or later, I guess, but...'

But that wasn't all. By mid-afternoon, Ms Steele was back at Optimax, negotiating to take over his job and have him sacked. Bang went not just the monthly pittance they were currently paying him, he said, but all the bonuses, share options, profits incentives...

'The *what?*' I'd said, moved for the first time to

utter actual words instead of ill-concealed hisses of impatience.

Mike lifted a tear-stained face to me. 'Strewth, you didn't really think I'd have gone to those bastards for nothing? I just had a six-month time-lag built into the deal. Got them to suspend the full package until I could see how the show worked out. If it took off, fine, I'd go and they'd have the firm outright. Thing is, though...' He broke off to blow his nose on the tissue I'd dredged from my sleeve for him. 'The totally fucking ironical thing is that it was Gaynor hammered out the deal. I never wanted to stage another sales conference in my life. I'd have called in the receivers and let the firm sink. She was the one running round, brown-nosing Hank Spiller, because she kept on and on at me to cover my bets. Told me I had to have a fallback if the worst happened and the musical bombed. Which it won't, of course,' he added hastily, although there was a telltale quaver in his voice as he admitted that it had been comforting to know there was a big salary, company car, share options, all that, waiting for him at Optimax just in case, by some totally impossible fluke... 'But, like they say, a verbal agreement's not worth the paper it's written on,' he finished bitterly. 'So now I'm out on my ear, with three months' pay and not a leg to stand on. Sure, sure, you should always get things in writing but–' Here, though, he caught himself up.

'But you couldn't, because I'd have found out.' I spoke flatly enough – the company was the last thing on my mind at that moment – but he

421

whipped back.

'Just *don't*, OK? Not now. I was going to tell you, course I was, everything. Soon as the show was up and away, only now – Christ, as if Gaynor sticking the knife in wasn't enough, Ricky's done a runner, can you believe it? And where's the fucking show without him?'

'Ricky's vanished?' I said, because this did rather startle me. 'Are you sure?'

He was sure. They'd let the star off the tech to go to some party or other; he'd driven away late afternoon yesterday, and that was it. Hadn't been back to his hotel, hadn't rung – nothing. With a dress rehearsal, final costume fittings, and an extra band call for his big first act number, and did I know what Musician's Union rates were now? He'd been getting edgy, sure, but the guy was brilliant, Jo, totally amazing–

'I was at that party,' I interrupted, cutting short the eulogies. My husband evidently still operated on the principle that ugly ducklings need only be described loudly and often enough as swans for them to start pirouetting to Tchaikovsky. 'Here, at Stowham Castle. He, um, did actually mention to me he'd booked himself into a hotel. Somewhere between here and Wakeford.'

His head flipped up. 'You get the name?'

As I shook my own head, I saw a vehicle coming down the hill with – yes, a white sign on top, a taxi. Too late now to shovel Mike back into his car. 'Get inside the house,' I hissed.

'What?'

Desperation is the mother of invention. 'Ring the theatre. I'm sure he'll have turned up by now, but you'll have to use my phone, mobiles don't work down here. Help yourself to a drink – no, not a drink,' I amended with a flutter of panic, 'you'll be driving. With you in a minute, but I've got to see someone. About a car.'

At least Mike did go inside and, what was more, he stayed there.

'Another coffee, love?'

The proprietress of the Ritzy is a strapping redhead, no younger than me, I would have thought, but clad in an eye-catching fuchsia leather mini-skirt over fishnets and platform-stacked trainers. Kind face, though. She leans over my shoulder 'Haven't hardly touched that one, by the looks of it.'

'I, um, accidentally put salt in.'

'Have another on t'house. Pardon me for saying, but you look like you could do with it.' Plonking a fresh cup in front of me, she gives my shoulder a squeeze. 'Cheer up, cherub, it might never happen.'

I could have told her it already has.

'He's all right.' Those were Paddy's first beaming words as he climbed out of the taxi. Then froze, with his wallet open in his hand. 'Jo, darling, what's the matter?' His gaze flickered to the strange car parked behind his own outside my gate. He paid off the taxi-driver, however, and let him accelerate away, before turning to me with a quizzical smile which didn't quite hide the wariness. 'Can I guess? I'd cheerfully chop off the odd arm or leg to be told I'm wrong – but, no.

Your face confirms it.'

'He just arrived. I couldn't turn him away, he was in tears, almost hysterical.'

Paddy thrust up a hand to silence me, but it was as though he was warding off a blow. 'No need to explain. I'm sure you and he have a great deal to talk about.'

'No, we bloody well don't,' I began, but he wouldn't let me continue, stating with devastating politeness that my marriage was none of his business. And the next minute I was being told that perhaps, after all, it might be sensible if he returned to London today, as per his original plans. He had commitments, loose ends, appointments with everyone from his dentist to his great-aunt, all of which had to be fitted in somehow if he was to take up the new job on time.

I caught my breath. 'You're still intending to go abroad?'

'I – don't know. Most of today, I've been assuming it rather depended on you.' He smiled, but as though at a poignantly sweet memory. 'Whether you might be up for sharing a mosquito net, that sort of thing. Because if you'd prefer not, although I might feel a bit of a heel, I'd pull straight out offering grovelling apologies and a hefty donation. Personally, I've become rather keen on the idea. Even found time to have a word with HQ today, while Bernard was with Jack, and if you thought you'd be up to a spot of English conversation coaching, they'd fall on your neck.' The rapid flow of words was dizzying. 'However, no point worrying our heads over that when you have so much to sort out here, is there? Crazy gamble, anyway. We might find we're screamingly incompatible within days, but I can only say I'd be prepared to chance it. No, hush. We can talk another time. After all, we've either nothing to talk about – or we've got everything and for ever, haven't we?' At last he caught himself up, with a rueful cough of laughter. 'Gosh, what a magnificently purple turn of phrase. Everything and for ever.' There was a crack in his voice. 'I do hope it's true.'

I started towards him and caught his arm, swiftly glancing back towards the kitchen window to check Mike wasn't looking. And felt Paddy recoil. My hand fell away as I realized what I'd done.

He smiled sadly. 'Poisonous, isn't it? Believe me, I've spent years looking over my shoulder.' Then he gently took his car keys from me. I couldn't bear him to leave like this, though, and plunged into asking about Jack. Much of what he said washed past me, but I gathered his doctors were happy, his children coming home to see him, and his father cock-a-hoop because the original scheme of joint ownership was to be revived, with Paddy as sleeping partner, and Jack assuming management of the estate.

'Stowham was almost the least of what the coz and I talked about though,' said Paddy diffidently. 'That's why I've been so long. It was – slightly shattering, actually. I'll, um, fill you in at another time...' He didn't add 'perhaps', but the word hovered in the air, unspoken. As did far too much else when he finally insisted on climbing into his car.

'I want to come with you,' I said passionately. 'I want to come now, this minute.'

'*But...?*' he said, raising his eyebrows. 'No – no, that's unfair. And you know I want nothing more in my whole life. Would you promise me one thing, though?'

'Anything.'

He smiled faintly. 'Could you bear to keep a distance until, well, until you've decided. Truly decided for good and all.'

'But surely you know–'

'Perhaps I should have said, until you're free. Sounds hopelessly melodramatic, I'm sorry, but I don't think I could bear your phoning me just to say – well, to say anything really, except that you'd left your husband. I've learned there's a world of difference between wanting to quit and actually doing it.' He pulled a face. 'Still, I've bored you with all that already. The castle will always know where I can be found.'

I had decided, of course. There was not the faintest shimmer of doubt in my mind what I was going to do. Goodbye Rutsville, hello big wide world. So why am I sitting here now, in this crummy café with an illuminated, larger-than-life-size photograph of Ricky Marvell leering at me from across the rainy street? Actually, the rain's freezing to sleet. There are spatters of tiny white crystals clinging to the window.

After I'd watched Paddy's car melt over the hill, I strode straight back into the house, along the hall to the kitchen. Mike was at the table with his back to me, fag in hand, phone jammed to his ear.

'No, honestly, you did right, I had to know... Christ, it's not your fault, mate. Sure, we'll hack it... The French routine, shit, what now?'

For a moment, I stood in the doorway watching him. Extraordinary. It was like looking at a stranger. I could see what had attracted me in this handsome, vibrant man, for all he was at this moment cursing fluently into the phone, bouncing in his chair with exasperation. I even found myself smiling nostalgically as he clicked his fingers, singing the tune for some dance routine – stamp, shuffle, stamp, *kick*, double-back, *splits*. And I felt – nothing. Not even anger, let alone anything warmer. You can't hate, unless you love. And whatever it was Mike and I had shared – passion, kids, creating the company together – all that was long gone. For years, we'd been living on parallel tracks, with lives that barely touched. *That* was why I'd been so frightened of Paddy and me becoming lovers, of course it was. Deep down, I must have known it would blast apart the lifeless shell of my marriage for good and all. So I had no qualms about telling Mike we were through. It was – well, just a matter of stating the obvious. He'd understand. Why had he gone off with Gaynor, after all? I only wished the bloody woman hadn't chosen now to ditch him, never mind whipping his job. I waited patiently for him to finish his call. He didn't turn round immediately. In fact as soon as he disconnected it was as though all the finger-clicking, fast-talking energy was switched off in that instant, because he crumpled over the table like a discarded puppet.

'Mike?'

'He's back.' He didn't turn his head. 'Walked through the stage door half an hour ago.'

'Ricky? Good, I told you he would. Listen, Mike, this won't take long, but–'

He cut across as though I hadn't spoken. 'Know who wheeled him in? Gaynor. She found him last night.'

That did rather take my breath away. 'Gaynor?'

'Phoned him at his party, met him at his hotel. Outskirts of York, apparently.'

I couldn't help it, I began to laugh. I mean, there I'd been, clasped to the bosom of the great lover, actually feeling the throb of his mobile – as my husband's mistress summoned him?

'Yeah, seems everyone thinks it's a hoot.' Mike lurched round towards me, and I registered that his face was whey-pale, jaw clenched rigid. 'They've only just got back because she thought she better let him sleep in, to be fit for the dress. Being as they spent all of last night shafting one another senseless. At least that's what she's told the company – the whole company. Most fantastic sex she's had for years.'

'Oh,' I whispered. 'I mean – oh, God.'

'Ricky's left a bottle of Scotch for me at the stage door, apparently. A bottle of fucking Scotch.'

'But – why?' I said feebly. 'I mean, why's she turned on you like this?'

'Why the fuck do you think?' he burst out. 'You trying to tell me it isn't what you've been working

428

towards all along? To get me out of her claws?'

I opened my mouth to protest – but I couldn't. Of course I'd never in my barmiest dreams envisaged anything like this, but hadn't detaching Mike from Gaynor been precisely my intention when I'd first walked into Paddy McGinty's office? Hadn't I said I wanted to show my husband what a ruthless monster his girlfriend was, and bring him scuttling penitently back to me?

'All your fault I got in so deep with her in the first place,' he added savagely, because my husband has never been slow to take advantage when he senses he's wrong-footed me.

I gasped. 'I shoved you into bed with her, did I?'

'If you'd ever believed in me, listened to me–'

'Oh, for God's sake, Mike.'

His face was crumpling. 'I was a lost soul, Jo. Going nowhere, desperate. She – well, she had faith in me.'

I gripped the chairback. 'I don't want to hear this.'

'So I shouldn't have let it turn into an affair. Course I shouldn't, what can I say? But I knew it couldn't last, not with her wanting kids. And if you hadn't ploughed in, making me choose – you did, you gave me a straight choice, you or her. What was I supposed to do? I didn't want to lose you, but she and I, it was something again–'

'Don't,' I gasped. 'You don't have to tell me what it's like being in love.'

'I'm talking about the fucking *show*. We were committed, up to our necks. She'd even borrowed money against her flat, but you said if I finished with her that had to be it. No contact, nothing. It was hell, Jo, I was being ripped apart.' He groped for another cigarette with shaking fingers. The strain showed in every knotted sinew of his neck. 'And now all this. The whole show's riding on that guy, and she knows it. I can't take it. It's just too much.'

'Amazing the old crotch-wiggler's still going, isn't it?' comments my friendly waitress, nodding at Ricky's picture across the road. She perches one buttock on the corner of a nearby table and sips her coffee. 'Most blokes his age can just about manage a trip down the bowling green once a week. You reckon he can still do it?'

With Gaynor in a honeymoon suite? There's a whole company across the road can testify to his performance. I've wondered since how long it took the great lover to decide to dump the chance of luring me back to his hotel in favour of Gaynor's guaranteed offer to present herself there. Ten seconds? I'm tempted to tell my waitress I have it on reliable authority he keeps up his strength in the four-poster with cheese-and-onion sandwiches. But maybe she isn't talking about sex. Maybe she's talking about his performance in the show opposite – and that's a very different matter.

I didn't tell my husband what I thought of Ricky's prospects, naturally. And nor, in the end, had I told him we were through. Look, I *couldn't*. Not that afternoon, when he was such a knotted, twitching, chain-smoking bag of misery. I told myself, instead, that Paddy would understand the slight delay. And Mike that he should go.

'I mean, get back to your theatre,' I amended, when his eyes widened as though I'd spat at him. At least he didn't argue. Nor did he seem to notice that I flinched when he hugged me, and stifled a shudder when he confided that he felt a million times better just for seeing me, that he hadn't realized how much he'd missed me. Truth was, he was nothing without me. I'd been right all along. Real love was what we'd had all along, rock solid, built on the family, on everything we'd shared over the years...

'Just *go*,' I shrieked.

'Jo?'

'I'll call you.'

But of course it was Paddy I rushed inside to call, the moment I'd shut the front door, because I was desperate to reassure him that, even if I hadn't actually demanded a divorce yet, this was only a temporary delay. It wasn't remembering that I didn't know his mobile number which had stopped me. It was remembering what I'd promised him.

That was the first time I put my head down on the kitchen table and wept. It certainly wasn't the last.

34

'Well, I hate to chuck you out, pet,' says the waitress as she drapes a checked tea-towel across the counter, 'but I've got to shut up and get home. Practically bloody snowing out there now and all.'

'Don't worry,' I respond with a wan smile. A Siberian blizzard couldn't make me feel any bleaker. 'The curtain'll be down for the interval any minute, and I'll have to show my face.' I winced. 'I'm supposed to be going to a private drinks party, in some room behind the Dress Circle.'

'Very nice, too. Oh, give over looking so glum – a free drink's a free drink, innit? Bloke in here earlier on from t'evening paper said it were the première tonight, that right?'

That was right. It followed a week of previews, an interminable week for me, in which I had spoken neither to my husband, nor to Paddy. And yet throughout, I never doubted what I was going to do. The only problem was finding the right moment. Not easy when Mike was grappling with a succession of disasters, according to reports from my children. Sticky set changes, ill-fitting costumes, sprained ankles, sore throats – nothing catastrophic, but enough to keep him on sixty fags a day and high-dose Valium, tutted Sarah.

But she didn't know what he was going through on the personal front. The last thing I wanted was to sympathize with my husband, but you'd have to be an out-and-out monster not to feel for the poor bugger. I could hardly believe Gaynor's savagery, let alone guess what inspired it. Was it just because she blamed him for entangling her in this expensive fiasco? But to humiliate him publicly by sleeping with the star of the show, on whom his every hope was pinned? Mike couldn't risk a crossed word with Ricky Marvell, let alone a punch on the nose. In his shoes, I might have been gulping tranquilizers, too. I think it was when I heard about the malfunctioning trap door – no bones broken, just a threatened walk-out by the dancers – I finally admitted to myself that I wasn't going to be able to confront my husband until the show opened. So I'm letting him get through tonight, the grand première.

Only problem is, Paddy will be gone. He's flying at some unspeakable hour from Heathrow tomorrow morning. Not that it matters, as I keep telling myself. The world's a village these days, phones work everywhere. Even so, as I open the door of the Ritzy into the street, flinching as the sleet-spiked wind slashes into my face, I can hardly bear to think of him sitting, at this moment, in the bar of an airport hotel, drinking himself into a desolate stupor. That, at least, is what Jack Bidcombe grimly predicts he'll be doing. He's probably right. He knows Paddy better than anyone.

Cousin Jack turned up at my cottage without warning at noon today, in a Range Rover driven by an amiable young man not just the size of an orang-utan, but with the carroty hair to match, who effortlessly swung his passenger down into a natty collapsible wheelchair.

'Meet Dafydd,' said Jack, and the orang-utan extended a hand the size of a dinner plate, grinning as his employer caustically commented that he'd actually asked for a blonde Swedish masseuse by way of personal assistant, but that Dafydd could at least talk intelligently about rugby. 'The first employee of new, improved Stowham Estates,' he said. 'You presumably know the coz and I are in partnership again?'

He was pale, even gaunter and wheezed alarmingly as his burly assistant settled him in my kitchen, but there was a new animation about him. I told him he was looking better.

'Bloody hope so, considering I was three parts dead and blind drunk the last time you saw me,' he retorted, testily refusing my offer of refreshment. 'I loathe tea, and much as I'd give what remains of my soul for a whisky, I'm under oath. Stingy half-bott of wine a night, three meals a day, disgusting nicotine gum and I'm cross-eyed with accounts, but I haven't come to flaunt my halo,' he continued, without drawing breath, 'I'm here to talk about Paddy.'

I jumped. 'Is he all right?'

'Don't be bloody silly. Listen, you want him don't you? Yes, just look at you. Good, well go to him, then. Last chance tonight.'

'That's ridiculous.'

'Why?'

I stiffened. 'Is it any of your business? Anyway

434

– there are complications, with my husband. You wouldn't understand.'

'Not *understand*?' he roared, so loudly Dora rocketed out of the sitting room, barking. 'Jesus Christ, I lived with those sorts of complications for seven fucking years – all my married life, in fact, if you want to throw my own affairs back at me. And it's very much my business. It was because of me Paddy never got Katharine, and that damn near wrecked the poor bastard's life. Don't you dare make the same mistake my wife did.'

I won't say we argued. I hardly got a word in as he harangued me.

I soon realized why Paddy had been so shattered by talking to his cousin at the hospital. Jack knew everything about him and Katharine, and always had done, right from the start. 'I had them tailed back to a hotel. Anyway, they were lousy liars, the pair of them, although Paddy's improved with time.' Jack had done nothing though, because of what he called his own wing-ding with Paddy's silly tart of a wife. 'Perhaps I felt it was tit for tat. I could hardly play the wronged husband, at any rate. So I just waited to see which way they'd jump. I'd have said it was about evens whether Kat went or stayed. Wrong, apparently. The coz tells me it was a dead cert from the outset she'd leave me for him.' He gestured down towards his chair, with a bitter smile. 'But then I ended up in here, and the odds changed dramatically.'

'Pity's sake,' I protested. 'How can you talk

435

about it like this?'

'I'm a betting man. I couldn't see Katharine deserting this poor cripple, still less Paddy trying to persuade her to. If he'd been in my position, of course, he'd have done the honourable thing, insisted she trot off and find happiness elsewhere. I can almost hear him saying it. But I...' Here he paused, and his mouth twisted into an ugly sneer. 'I couldn't – or wouldn't. Even though, every minute of every bloody day, I knew I should. Topping myself was the other option, and I certainly talked about that. My God, didn't I just talk about it. Truth is, I lacked the guts. Paddy's the brave one. I may have risked my neck in hot blood, but only because I don't think first.'

'Surely–' I began.

But he wouldn't let me speak. Hoarsely swept on, telling the story of losing his puppy up the shaft in the quarry, of seeing the roof crumbling. 'And I was in a blue funk, but not Paddy. He stood there, added it all up, and crawled in. If he wanted to end it all, he'd–'

I started forward. 'Don't even say it.'

'He's not the suicidal type,' snapped Jack, beginning to cough, 'thank Christ. For all he's as wretched as any man could be, poor bastard. Whereas I – whereas I, if the chance to do myself a mischief had just presented itself, on impulse–' He was overtaken by coughing. As I bustled away to get him a glass of water, I found myself thinking back to the first time I'd clapped eyes on Jack Bidcombe, down at the ford. He'd tried to open his car door into the roaring floodwater – had that been the impulse of a black moment?

436

But he was wronging himself. The one thing he surely didn't lack was courage. He'd planned every detail of his seeming accident at the castle a week ago, and sat there waiting to die a choking horrible death...

'Had to,' he muttered, when I told him this as I handed him the glass. 'Only way I could think of to raise some money for my poor bloody heirs. Anyway, I made sure I was brainlessly drunk first. God, I wish there were whisky in this – no, not really. Christ's sake, don't let me see the bottle.'

But of course he hadn't done it for his children's sake – he'd done it for his cousin. Paddy had to be made to escape, he told me flatly, forced away to find a new life out of Katharine's shadow. He wasn't going to let the poor bastard chain himself to Stowham, support Daisy and Miles, he'd given too much already. 'And if I'd only swallowed a few lousy pills years ago,' he said bitterly, 'Katharine wouldn't have ended up smashed under a tree trunk, and Paddy wouldn't be eating his heart out now, and pickling his liver. God knows, if I hadn't sold this little love nest of theirs in a fit of pique she'd still be alive, wouldn't she?' He leaned forward intently. 'Why d'you think I couldn't face Paddy after she died? Because I couldn't bear seeing his grief, knowing that for all these years I'd deliberately blocked his chances of having a normal, happy life.' He grasped my hand. 'But you – *you*, thank God – can put it right now.'

'You think I don't want to be with Paddy?' I retorted. 'Want it more than anything? Anyway, we will end up together, it's just–'

'Fuck the justs and the buts.'

'Jack, I appreciate you mean well, but I haven't the time to argue this now.' Hadn't the courage, more like. 'I've – I've got to run my dog over to Aidan's, I'm away overnight.'

'Give her to me. Pleasure. Long as you like, preferably the next twelve months, although I suppose you probably can't just hop on the plane with him.'

And when I tried to protest, he simply talked across me.

'My cousin's a good man. He deserves a better deal than he's had. The only reason Kat didn't leave me for him was because I was stupid enough to break my back.' He had hold of both my hands now; he wouldn't let me escape. 'But your husband hasn't fucked his life as I did. He'll survive you going – people do, marriages bust up every day. Go to Paddy.'

Those words are ringing in my head as I trudge across the bleak, sleet-laced street and nudge open the door of the theatre. The foyer, hushed and deserted, looks even dingier without crowds to hide the stained, burn-pocked carpet, the scuffs and scars in the crimson paintwork. As I sidle in, two gum-chewing girls, with trays of ice-creams slung round their necks, bash bum-first through a side door and plonk themselves on adjoining radiators, which can't be good for their wares, but at least suggests the interval is nigh. One of them catches sight of me.

'Can't sneak in without a ticket tonight, love.

438

Full house.'

'I've got a ticket,' I respond. 'I, um, had to go out during the first half. Needed some fresh air.'

She pulls a face. 'Not surprised, with that load of old crap.'

At which her mate chips in. 'You seen it then?'

'Are you kidding, Ricky Marvell? I'd sooner watch my toenails grow. I mean, my gran wets her knickers over him.' At which, belatedly, she seems to recall my aged and respectable presence, and mutters an apology. But they're still sniggering.

And that's when I finally hit rock bottom. That silly child forces me to face the truth I've been dodging all week. This show, dimly thudding through the wall, is – as she so succinctly puts it – a load of old crap. Well, did anyone apart from my husband expect otherwise? But that's his dream in there, the summit of his life's ambitions. Chasing that lofty star he's lost his business, his money, his wife – even his mistress along the way. And when it all crashes to earth? Jack Bidcombe was wrong: my situation is cruelly parallel to Katharine's. Her husband was broken in body. Mine will be broken in just about every other way – emotionally, financially, creatively, professionally – and although I never thought I'd have such fears about Mike, I've been wondering if you can overdose on Valium...

'Hiya, Ma. God, you look shagged.'

'Sarah!' She's startled me. 'On your own?'

'Nipped out during the last chorus because there's only one working lav in this dump, and I'm busting for a pee from all the champers I pushed back before by way of anaesthetic.' She chortles richly. 'Pretty painless so far, though, isn't it? Mind, Dad always said I was tone deaf, and after all that pink fizz, I should think a chainsaw'd sound like Mozart. Bloody good thing I volunteered Simon to drive. Anyway, see you in a minute for a top-up dose, when I can uncross my legs. Been murder laughing, the last twenty minutes.' Halfway across the foyer, she turns and raises her voice. 'And you can tell me what all this rubbish is about Paddy going abroad.'

How has she got wind of that? I'll have to tell her something, because I'm staying in her flat tonight. Mike may think I'm accompanying him back to his hotel after the first-night party, but there are limits to wifely altruism, and sharing a bed is way, way beyond them.

Will my daughter give me hell, like Jack Bidcombe, or will concern for Mike win out? Because for all her jokes, Sarah adores her dad, always has, and she's been worried silly about him this past week. Ben too. With all his failings, Mike's a loving and much-loved father. The father of my children, and – I've let him down.

There, I've said it. And no, I'm not crazy. I know he's been unfaithful, lied, cheated – all the rest. But he didn't *want* to. All the poor sap ever wanted was to see his show mounted, and if I'd shown a shred of faith, if I'd let him squander his mum's money on his heart's desire openly instead of resorting to the ridiculous stratagems which have cost him his company, he wouldn't be facing total ruin now. Sure, the musical would still be sinking without trace, our marriage would still be a lifeless husk, but he'd have work, money – something to live for. As it is, all he's got left is us, his family. He needs us. He needs – me.

'Hey-up,' murmurs one of the gum-chewing girls, hoisting herself off the radiator. 'Stand by for the charge of the Zimmer brigade. Bet you we shift some choc ices tonight.'

I straighten up, too. Twiddle my fingers through my hair, bite my lips, practise smiling. I don't need a mirror to tell me it's the kind of quavering grimace you might expect to see on Death Row. Three stout ladies are first through the doors, handbags already agape as they plunge purposefully towards the ice-cream tray.

'*Well*,' snorts one of them. 'What d'you make of that, then?'

I don't wait for the answer. I'm heading for the stairs up to the Circle Bar, where anaesthetic awaits in the Priestley Room, wondering if I can leave my car here and cadge a lift back to Sarah's with Simon. The condemned woman deserves several drinks. I *will* go to Paddy, of course I will – when I can. When I've pieced Mike and his shattered life back together again. I can't do anything about the great dream, but I can sort out his finances, remortgage the house, pay off the overdrafts, bolster him up enough to get him back into some kind of sensible paid employment. I don't dare to imagine how long this will take, I just tell myself Paddy will wait – won't he? I don't care what I promised him, I'm going to write and explain, reassure him I will be coming. I just hope some other woman doesn't prowl by and snap him up first, lovable and vulnerable as he is. There could be a red-taloned predator circling him even now in that lonely hotel bar...

This must be the Priestley Room, and it's chock-a-block. Gil's is the first face I recognize, that mournful, droopy-moustached visage staring into his glass. But half a dozen paces beyond, there's a much more familiar figure. Mike. In a trendy cream linen suit, buttoned high to his neck like a chef's tunic, and already crumpled to hell. He has a bottle in one hand, fag in the other, and a glassy, cross-eyed grin which suggests he's also been taking plenty of hooch to numb the pain. I try and blend into the wallpaper, but he's watching the door.

'Well, Jo?' he bellows, and I'm hearing the defiant roar of an ageing, baffle-weary lion at bay. 'Who's going to say I told you so?'

35

Gil is singing under his breath as I sidle up behind him. '"And if too much slap and tickle gives you clap, you know your prick'll..."'

'Spare me.'

'"Rise to fight another..." Jo, love, there you are.' He looks even gloomier than usual. 'What a fucking mess, huh?'

'Wouldn't know. Is there a drink going?'

Mike has been ambushed on his way to me by

a short woman with a long cigarette-holder. This room is already packed tighter than a tube train in rush hour, and bottles of Veuve Cliquot rosé are being passed hand-to-hand over the chattering heads as if it were lemonade. How much is this reception costing? With a cast party still to come? I begin to wonder whether remortgaging the family home will be enough to bale out Newhouse Productions.

'It isn't Gaynor's fault,' says Gil, without preamble, and I think he's talking about the show – pray, who else penned the deathless couplet he's just been reprising? – but he plunges on to declare that Mike's talking his usual bullshit if he claims Gaynor got him sacked from Optimax. 'They've been after his scalp for weeks,' he says, rolling his eyes. 'Only thing he ever did in that office was photocopy band parts and shove out his own press releases.'

This may be true, but I'm in no mood to hear any defence of Gaynor Steele. Never mind Optimax, I snap back at Gil, what about her and Ricky Marvell?

'Yeah, well, she was mad. But you've got to admit she'd a right. Every right.' He tugs his moustache, clearing his throat. 'Look, Jo, she wants a word with you, OK?'

And to my horror she's gliding up behind him, an elegant streak of slashed-thigh black velvet. In this crush, I can't retreat. I'm penned into a corner with *her*, author of nine-tenths of my miseries as well as tonight's turkey. At which moment, setting the seal on my miseries, Mike ploughs up from the opposite direction to wrap a crumpled arm round my shoulders, and press a squelchy, smoky kiss on my cheek. Then he sees who's standing next to me. Even in my own desolation, I feel a pang for him. The worst night of his life, and he's confronted with stony-faced wife and vengeful ex-mistress side by side? So when his response is to grin even more inanely and make to plant an equally fond smacker on Gaynor's cheek, I realize how very drunk he must be. She shrinks away. Frankly, I know how she feels.

'See that bloke in the dark shirt?' hisses Gil, grabbing Mike by the elbow. 'He's been looking for you. No, not him, little geezer with... Oh, come on, I'll show you.'

So now there's only her and I. Typically, she finds her voice first.

'I owe you, Jo,' she says.

And, typically, I'm thrown off balance at once. 'Sorry?'

'I told Gil I wanted to thank you.' She hesitates a moment, then takes a slug of wine. 'Perhaps I should be apologizing, too, but it seems a bit late for all that. And I can hardly expect you to believe me if I say I took Mick at his word about your marriage being washed up.' She gave a brittle burst of laughter. 'Tough cookie like me, falling for that old line? But I kind of thought you'd had enough, too. He says you're having him back, by the way. Are you?'

No! Yes? Temporarily...? I find I can't answer at all.

'Do him a power of good to be booted out into the real world for a bit, if you ask me. Mind, he'd find another Mummy-substitute to warm his rut soon enough.'

'Rut? *Mick?*'

She casts up her eyes. 'Come on, honey, it must've crossed your mind, too? You've never imagined Mick at nine years old, the precocious boy genius playing with his toy theatres while his mother clapped and cooked and coddled, and thought to yourself, this bastard's not moved on in forty years? Still, that's not the point now.' She downs another gulp of wine. 'I just wanted to say thanks – thanks for putting me out of my misery with, you know, the tip-off. Gil passed it on at his ma's funeral. Another few months of thermometers and dip-sticks and rescheduling my entire working life round the red stars in my diary, with all this mayhem on top' – she waves a hand – 'and I might just have tipped over the edge. Bloody lucky I found the time to go down to Eastbourne.'

I'm several steps behind in this extraordinary conversation. I'm still grappling with the notion of Mike – in his cosy rut? 'Um, thermometer? Why, have you been ill?'

'Ovulation days,' she retorts impatiently. 'But then you wouldn't know, would you? You got the breeding business over and done with when you were still in your gym slip, bursting with bonny fecundity.' She smiles faintly. 'Funny, I used to sneer at women who got themselves pregnant before they'd done anything with their lives, but these days I wonder. I'd be having more fun now if I were packing the brats off to college and could concentrate on my life instead of on my bloody ovaries. Speaking of brats, your gorgeous son's waving at you. Glowering at me as if I were Myra Hindley, of course. Shall I make myself scarce, now I've said my piece? Which is, well, sorry – and thanks.'

I'm aware my mouth is sagging, but I gather my wits in time to grab her arm, then peer round. A scarlet-faced Ben is indeed towering over the crowd, with a dark-haired girl beside him. 'Not now,' I mouth across the ear-splitting din. Public executions were always riotous parties, too, one gathers. 'I'll see you later.' I spin back to Gaynor, bending close so that I don't broadcast my words to the room. 'Are you saying,' I hiss, 'that Mike never told you he'd had–' I lower my voice further. 'That he wasn't able to give you a child?'

'That he'd had a vasectomy?' Gaynor does not lower her voice. The pink spots atop each of her elegantly sculpted cheekbones betoken anger, not embarrassment. And her smile is cynical. 'Come on, Jo, you know your husband. I'm sure he'd have got round to letting me know one day, but the poor lamb had so much else on his mind. And I can quite see the longer he left it, the harder it became.' A steely edge enters her voice. 'What I find a *teensy* bit difficult to forgive is the way he went along with my carefully scheduled attempts in the middle of every month, did his manly duty by me every single red-star day.' And for all she's still smiling, her eyes are a mite over-shiny. 'So sweet when it came to comforting me, too, at the end of the month. Every fucking month. Because, you know, at my age there aren't so many eggs left, and you do tend to get a bit desperate.'

'He...?' There aren't merely red spots on my cheeks, my whole face is flaming. 'The *bastard*,' I cry, no longer caring who hears. 'How *could* he?'

'He never did like breaking bad news, did he?' She shrugs, pulling a face. 'I mean, if the idiot had only let me know the trouble he was having with some of our clients, I might have saved the firm from folding. Not that I've done badly out of the takeover in the end, but I seriously did not want to go back to Optimax.' She rolls her eyes. 'Well, you've visited our grand and glorious HQ, you can imagine. Bit like joining the Mormons, working for the Optimax boys, you know? You trot into the sodding office at dawn, reeking with mints to hide the hangover, practically singing the company song. Still, who knows, I may not have to stick it much longer.' She grins. 'Why're you looking so pole-axed?'

'Gaynor,' I say breathlessly. 'I have *wronged* you. I – I don't even know where to begin.'

'Bollocks, I'm fine. The show's on the road and last Wednesday night, for your information, was a triple red-star day in the diary.' She chuckles and leans close to my ear. 'Just tell me one thing, darling, because I've been *dying* to know. That party I yanked Casanova out of at Stowham Castle, by way of teaching your husband a long-overdue lesson. You weren't there, too, by any chance, wearing a very sexy pink dress?' When she sees my expression, she hoots. 'Ricky told me he felt bad about abandoning a lovely lady at the table, and when he said he only knew her name was Jo, I couldn't help wondering, with you living up the road. What a joke, eh? Sorry to steal him, but my need was greater, and you never know your luck.' She pats her ironing-board tummy. 'Plenty of lead in Ricky's pencil, that's for sure, because even the ferocious Mavis could never have got a scalpel near his precious manhood.'

Gil reappears tutting, telling Gaynor she should be giving up drink.

'For a putative eight-day pregnancy? On your bike, honey. You can boss me around when we're installed.' Turning back to me, she's just explaining that she and Gil are thinking of buying a house together in town when her eyes narrow. She darts forward to peer over my shoulder. 'Who's that talking to Lover Boy?'

'Stone? Harry Stone?' says Gil vaguely.

Her eyes widen. 'You cannot mean *Larry?*' Her voice tightens to a squeak. 'Glory frigging Hallelujah, it is, too. Laurence Stone, and Mick's talking to him. Well, not without me, he's not.' She cruises away through the press of bodies like a shark through a seal pool.

'Laurence Stone,' murmurs Gil as we watch her close in on my husband and a rotund, shaven-headed man in a funereal black suit. 'Well I never.'

'She's *smiling* at him,' I exclaim in total disbelief. 'Beaming as if she thinks the sun shines out of his–'

'It does. It surely, surely does. Laurence Stone, my God.'

'Not him, you fool, *Mike*. Look, she's actually put her arm round his waist. And he's hugging her back. I mean, after what he's done to her? What she's done to him?' A crazy hope comes to

448

me. 'You don't think it was just – just a lovers' tiff?'

'Only one love in our boy's life,' breathes Gil, not taking his eyes off the trio opposite as he chews his moustache for dear life.

My heart contracts. 'God, Gil, don't say that, please...'

'His show. Jesus H., he's laughing. *Is* he laughing?'

'Drunk,' I say dazedly. 'Thought so, soon as I saw him.'

'Mr Stone, I'm talking about.' And there's a gleam I don't think I've ever seen in those bloodhound eyes. 'You reckon I should go and get my new fedora from the cloakroom?'

'What for?'

He casts up his eyes. 'So I can eat it?'

'Absolute disgrace, when you consider what they're charging for tickets,' snorts the stately iron-permed dame beyond Eileen Muxworthy, whose name I can't immediately recall, as I squeeze back to my seat. 'One is tempted to demand a refund.'

I won't claim this august critique of the evening's entertainment makes my heart sink, because it couldn't get much lower. Much as I'd have liked to, I can't believe what Gil has just been telling me. No, of course he hadn't meant the show when he said what a fucking mess it all was. He'd been talking about the very public bust-up between Mike and Gaynor. The show, well, really wasn't at all bad. And in Gil-speak, believe me, that equals a paean of unqualified superlatives from anyone else. Tunes catchy, lyrics clever, while as for the great Ricky himself...

At that point the bell trilled for the second half. I drained my glass in one, reflecting that this classy pink fizz was probably the only sensible investment my husband's made in recent times. Talk about rose-tinted glasses. I didn't ask Gil how much he'd put away, just observed it was a shame that journalists have such notoriously hard heads – if he was right, that is, and the unlikely looking duo by the window really were the theatre critics of the *Daily Telegraph* and the *Independent* respectively. As for the great Laurence Stone – yes, I'd heard of him, naturally, and maybe he had put on more socking hit West End shows than I'd had hot dinners, but he was probably just being polite.

'He's a bastard,' breathed Gil, shaking his head as though to assure himself he was actually awake. 'Famous for it.'

So maybe my hopes did twitch up a centimetre, until Eileen's iron-permed neighbour pronounced judgement just now. Audrey, that's what she's called. Vicar's wife, too. And while she may not be anyone's idea of a theatre buff, she, unlike Gilbert Rydall, isn't the loyal and well-oiled friend of the authors. Moreover, the entire party of Stowham ladies is nodding and clucking their disgruntled agreement. I am *so* glad I didn't bump into the kids during the interval and have to see their misery. I wasn't avoiding them deliberately, I was just attempting to nip to the loo before the lights went down, until I saw that the queue stretched from here to the far side of the pantomime season.

'I reckon they could be prosecuted for it,' pronounces Eileen, which gives me a start. I've always known the show would be dire, but I didn't expect it to be indecent. With the vicar's wife two seats along. Please let it not occur to anyone my name's Patterson. 'Only two cubicles working in this whole blooming great theatre? And them that cramped you'd get hammered by the RSPCA if you tried keeping a hen in there.' There are more murmurs of sisterly solidarity.

I gulp. 'Are you – just now – were you and Audrey complaining about the ladies'?'

'You tried spending a penny? I tell you I'm going to write and give them a piece of my mind.'

The house lights have faded, and the hush is as sudden as it's absolute. Anyone else could be fooled into imagining this is a hush of breathless anticipation, but I plough on. 'Not the show?' I whisper hoarsely.

'*What?*' roars Eileen, fortunately in the same split second as the drummer thumps a fast four and the band are away. 'Bloody great night, love. Can't remember when I've laughed so much.'

Of course, that can be taken two ways. There's laughter – and there's laughter. Funny ha-ha and funny excruciating. At first I fear it's obviously the latter sort. For here's Ricky, looking every inch the raddled, frazzled has-been he is, clutching a mike the size of an Italian waiter's pepper grinder, with antique hips gamely a-wiggle. At least they haven't tarted him up in wig and tights. The plot has evidently been updated because he looks just like Ricky Marvell, only more so. White hipster flares cling tighter round his bulging crotch than you'd think possible without strangling that treacly baritone into soprano candy-floss; a spangled scarlet shirt is slashed down to his hairy navel; and a gold medallion the size of a digestive biscuit nestles in his chest hair. He's a joke. He's your caricature club crooner. And only slowly – very, *very* slowly – does it dawn on me that this might actually be the point.

Ricky isn't acting. Ricky's playing himself – but bigger. An ageing rock idol at the beginning of the twenty-first century, he's still bashing out hits from the 70S, except these days he's strutting his stuff in a seedy holiday resort on the Costa del Grot instead of the London Palladium. He's called Jacky Casanova, incidentally, and is recounting his life history to a fresh-faced lad who's after winning the club talent contest or some such. But our Ricky's not so much a predatory playboy as a priapic plaything for all these lusty, gutsy ladies who aren't backward in coming forward and singing their appreciation of his, ahem, biggest asset. This, I realize, is a Casanova for our own egalitarian times.

And while I've never been totally clear what post-modern irony is, I've a suspicion I might be reading about it in the *Daily Tel* and the *Indy* tomorrow. Maybe, with the likes of Tom Jones and Tony Bennett getting back into the charts, Ricky's renaissance is also nigh. Besides, not merely is he playing the script for laughs, with exactly the right self-mocking cool, I have to admit the man has a charisma all of his own. In fact he packs a sexual charge that could ignite a nunnery. He's ... amazing. I need only tell you that, for one aberrant second, I actually find myself regretting Gaynor knew the number of his mobile, and you'll get some idea of the impact he's having on the audience round me.

He rocks, croons, struts, clowns. He's doing a Chevalierish number at this moment about all things French. As in kissing, letters – and polish – which is rip-roaringly vulgar and you should see what he does with a French loaf, but Audrey, the vicar's wife, is mopping her cheeks.

'She is *incredible*,' I say to myself as the auditorium erupts into screams for encores. And I'm not talking about Mrs Vicar, still less about the dark-haired female who's just appeared – ping! – in a moody spotlight, I'm talking about Gaynor Steele. These lyrics are fantastic. I'm craning round to see if I can spot her in the audience, when Casanova whispers 'Henriette', which yanks my attention back to the stage and the luminous, smiling creature who's walked into our Ricky's arms. Of course, I know now why Paddy told her story so eloquently. He loved and lost one respectable married woman, and probably thinks he's fast losing another now as he sits in his lonely airport hotel. But for the first time, ever since he drove away from my gate, I'm not swamped in helpless misery just at the thought of him. No, I'm saying disbelievingly to myself that if this show really is as good as it seems, if – against all the laws of nature and probability – this turkey might actually fly, and my husband is not going to end up bereft, bankrupt and bewildered...

'But ze poor fool will steell be lost without me,' she's saying. She's French, you understand. ''E *needs* me.'

'Need ain't love, babe,' retorts Casanova, stroking her face, 'not like you and I know love.'

'Too right, Cas,' I breathe. 'Too *bloody* right.' Mike may need me – but that ain't love, just like the man said. And they get into this witty, touching duet about the bliss of the chaise longue versus the deep, deep boredom of the marital bed. The message is so close to home, not to say near the knuckle, I could singalonga Henriette when she laughs at herself for mothering her 'usband and smothering 'er kids. Brilliant, quite brilliant.

Commercial break. I do realize there's nothing more irritating than someone ranting on about how marvellous a show is – guaranteed to make me, for one, feel I'd rather see Chekhov performed in Swahili – but since it's crossed my mind that my children stand to benefit from the box office success of *Casanova*, I feel duty bound to recommend it to you. Wholeheartedly. Book now.

Still, there's no danger of my boring you with the plot, because I'm too preoccupied with the fast-shifting course of my own life to pay much attention. In fact, I half rise to go and phone Paddy *now*, this very instant, before he flies away, to assure him all will now be well. Thank God Jack insisted on giving me the name of his hotel...

454

It isn't the buzz of indignation from the row behind which cows me back into my seat, though, it's the memory of my promise. Not until I'm free. OK, so I'll have to have a word with Mike before I phone. Which I will. Soon as the curtain's down.

'Darling!' I will trill, kiss, kiss. 'Million congratulations on a fantastic show; trillion apologies for twenty-one years' lack of faith; I freely admit you're a genius, I'm an idiot – and by the way, can I have a divorce?'

Perhaps not at the first-night party. So – tomorrow?

'Wow, fab reviews, you must be over the moon – mind awfully if I leave you?'

Next week – next month? How do I do it? How *can* I spoil everything for him now and ruin his hour of glory? Will the kids think I'm just being spiteful?'

'"I'm a mother and a wife,"' Henriette's singing, alone now on a darkened stage, in her single moody spotlight. '"I don't own my own life..."'

There's a trumpeting snort to my left. Stout, sturdy Eileen is wet-eyed with a hankie clamped to her nose

'I love my kids, they love their dad.
Can I live without you? Am I going mad?'

Henriette's in a seedy motel room, case packed. There are stifled snivels all round me as she sings her sad little heart out. But this talk of kids has prompted me, at last, to seek out my own. No

455

worries about looking them in the eye now, and there they are, in a box barely four rows away from me. Sarah is tugging at her ear as she's done since she was a toddler when she's trying not to cry; Ben is clutching the friend next to him, bless his soppy heart, while Henriette warbles on about love being unselfish, unfair, costing more than she can bear. As my poor Paddy knows, I think, so selflessly as he devoted himself all those years to...

'*Katharine?*' I yelp, and have to convert the cry to a cough before I get lynched. God Almighty, am I going crackers? Because I am seeing Katharine Bidcombe. I *am*. I'd know that pretty heart-shaped face anywhere. She's up there in that box with my own son's arm clamped round her and what's more I could almost swear she's staring straight back at me. *You've loved before, you'll love again.* Daisy, of course, it has to be; Daisy Bidcombe summoned back from the States. But while everyone round her is shiny-eyed and twitchy-nosed as Henriette renounces her lover for her husband, she looks – well, pretty pissed off. And when our heroine inevitably gets to scrawling with her diamond ring on the motel window, just as Paddy told me she did – *You will also forget Henriette* – I see Daisy's lips move.

Can she *really* be muttering 'silly cow'?

The silly cow, meanwhile, launches into singing farewell, farewell and, one more time, farewell. In fact, the scene having blossomed into full violin-sobbing, timp-rolling grand opera in which, as is well known, even the simplest message takes at least five choruses, she's probably still wailing her farewells, with not a dry eye in the house, as I slam myself into my car.

Me, I just whispered a hasty toodle-pip to a startled Eileen and told her to warn Jack Bidcombe that Doggynutz make Dora fart.

The Beginning

OK, so the time has finally come for you to renounce any right to describe yourself as a respectable married woman. You've left your husband, as you keep reminding yourself – although is it really necessary to sing at the top of your frankly rather tuneless voice while doing so? Married you are no longer, in any meaningful sense, even if a lawyer might not see it quite that way. But did you really intend to dump your respectability along with your married status? And so very comprehensively, too.

Because there's no denying that between the hours of ten p.m. and one-thirty a.m. on the night in question, you're roaring down the public highway with your foot glued to the accelerator, a dodgy blood-alcohol level and so little of the care and attention due to these filthy driving conditions, you'd be unlikely to notice a fleet of flying saucers landing on the M1, unless they happened to block your carriageway.

There's also the small matter of your purchasing fuel for your severely overtaxed little vehicle (which is simultaneously under-taxed, incidentally, as you notice that its licence to be on the road expired at the end of last month) with a cheque drawn on an account you know full well to have been frozen by the bank, owing to a deficit of several thousand pounds. You forget exactly how many thousand, but you can almost hear the *boing* of that little slip of paper you've just signed your name to bouncing as you skip back to the car. But, hell, what are a few motoring offences in the great scale of things? You've barely embarked on your real crime spree yet.

It begins to gather momentum when you coolly assume a false identity.

'That's right, McGinty. Mrs Peter Edward Ffoulkes McGinty. Lord, did my silly husband forget to tell you I was joining him here tonight?'

And having flexed your felonious muscles you feel quite up to a little dabble in fraud. 'If there's a surcharge for double occupancy, just stick it on his credit card. He hasn't settled up yet, has he? Ah, a bar bill. A substantial bar bill? Well, there's a surprise. Thanks, I'll take the key.'

Now, does trespass constitute an actual crime, or is it merely a civil offence? You're trying to remember this as, with a stifled giggle, you let yourself into room 403. Wait a minute, though. Weren't you once told it's only an offence if you actually commit some *damage* in the course of your trespassing? Well, we'll soon be seeing to that, won't we? First, you flick on the lights, blink, and then prowl silently as any cat burglar across the carpet to inspect the occupant of the bed.

'Comatose, wouldn't you just know it?' you murmur fondly. 'But not for long, my poppet.'

You always knew this horrible purple lipstick would come in handy one day, and it certainly isn't to do your remarkable impersonation of Morticia Addams. In fact, considering you're barely recovered from flu, you've spent most of the past week in a puddle of tears, and you've just driven for three and a half solid hours through fog and sleet, a life of crime must suit you, because you're not looking at all bad in this usefully enormous hotel mirror. It's slap bang opposite the bed, too. Couldn't be better. You grin to yourself as you set about committing this carefully premeditated act of wanton vandalism. Shocking really, because lipstick, as a housewife like you knows, is a bugger to shift off glass. Particularly when plastered on in letters a foot high. Your efforts consume nearly the whole tube – and you chuck the greasy stub into the bin with a flourish.

For now, at last, you can get down to the serious stuff. Motoring offences, false names, vandalism, they're only for beginners. Probably wouldn't earn you more than a fine, maybe a spot of community service. But what you have in mind now must surely be worth several years in clink. And does that deter you? Does a fox stop to admire the dandelions round the chicken coop? Work of a minute to whip off your every stitch of clothing and clamber into bed. Sleeping princesses are famously woken with a kiss. Sleeping drunken ex-spooks you feel require stronger measures, particularly with flight check-in time a mere three hours away.

'My word,' you breathe on lifting your head to view your handiwork. 'My *word*. Eat your heart out, Ricky Marvell.'

By the time the victim of this act of gross indecency opens his eyes, the perpetrator is bestride him.

'My God, I've died,' he croaks. 'Died and gone to heaven.'

'Heaven's the word,' you agree wholeheartedly, clasping his flailing hands to your naked breasts. 'Oh, gorblimey, heaven and a half.'

'What – what you doing?'

'That a dumb question, or what?'

His head's shifted marginally on the pillow; he seems to be peering round your heaving shoulder. Golly, yes. You nearly forgot your graffiti. Since his specs are nowhere to be seen, you were quite right not to go piddling around with spidery diamond rings.

'"You can't go"' – the pace is picking up and he's having difficulty breathing, never mind reading – '"without Jo?"'

'Correct. Rhymes, too. Notice that?'

'"You can't go without Jo?"'

'I'm coming with you,' you confirm, then let out a squealing whoop of triumph. 'In *every* sense...'

'You know – I never thought–'

'Oh, yes – *yes!*'

'God, oh, wow, oh...' So sweet the way he manages to keep on talking, your friend, such stamina, on and on and on. 'No, I never thought – OmyGod I love you, sweetheart, you know that – but I never thought, we'd end like–'

'*End?*' you shriek, at the very pinnacle of pleasure and at a decibel level which probably adds waking the occupants of an entire hotel to your catalogue of misdemeanours, 'who's talking about ends, you pillock?' Whereupon, with a last,

461

jubilant, collision-of-the-stars convulsion you collapse on to his chest, flaked, fucked and happy – so very, very happy.

'This is no ending, my dearest friend,' you whisper, and twine your hand in his. 'This is just the beginning.'

The publishers hope that this book has given you enjoyable reading. Large Print Books are especially designed to be as easy to see and hold as possible. If you wish a complete list of our books please ask at your local library or write directly to:

Magna Large Print Books
Magna House, Long Preston,
Skipton, North Yorkshire.
BD23 4ND

This Large Print Book for the partially sighted, who cannot read normal print, is published under the auspices of

THE ULVERSCROFT FOUNDATION